P9-DJL-867

ROSEMARY ROGERS

A DANGEROUS MAN

AVON BOOKS ◆ NEW YORK

AVON BOOKS, INC.
1350 Avenue of the Americas
New York, New York 10019

Copyright © 1996 by Rosemary Rogers
Front cover art by Liz Kenyon
Inside front cover art by Victor Gadino
Published by arrangement with the author
Visit our website at http://www.AvonBooks.com
Library of Congress Catalog Card Number: 96-96437
ISBN: 0-380-78604-4

First Avon Books Printing: November 1996

AVON TRADEMARK REG. U.S. PAT. OFF. AND IN OTHER COUNTRIES, MARCA REGISTRADA, HECHO EN U.S.A.

Printed in the U.S.A.

WCD 10 9 8 7 6 5 4 3

Part
One

Prologue

Boston
September 1845

It was always exhilarating on the waterfront, but Victoria Maria Ryan had never visited this section in all her years in Boston. Her first glimpse of the bustling wharves and long rows of red-brick warehouses had been six years ago, as a frightened, awed ten-year-old sent from her home in California to stay with her aunt and uncle. That arrival remained a vivid memory, but the awe had altered to a keen appreciation.

She thought it must be the sense of adventure in the autumn air, the excitement generated by the tumultuous clamor of so many people, wagons, and carriages rushing to and fro that made it all so exotic. And, of course, the lure of faraway places inherent in wondrous cargo being unloaded from the holds of ships just back from ports such as India and China: silks, spices, precious metals dug from Burmese mountainsides . . .

Even the foreign smells—some foul enough to cause several of her companions to cover their noses with their scarves—were exciting, she thought, laughing a little at their

3

disgusted comments. Not even her favorite cousin was immune to *that*, and made his displeasure known by irritably tugging his thick wool scarf up over his nose and mouth, cutting her a frowning glance from beneath his brows as he did so, pointedly, to remind her that he thought this entire expedition was ridiculous and far too outrageous even for her.

But, of course, Sean had already forcibly expressed *his* thoughts about coming down to the Boston waterfront with Reverend Gideon—privately so as not to betray her plan to Uncle Seamus and Aunt Katherine, but quite bluntly for all of that. Even while Sean objected, shouting as he did when he knew it was a futile effort, she had known that he would agree to chaperon her, as he always did.

Now Tory shivered and tucked her hand deeper into the crook of her older cousin's arm and elbow when she felt his muscles tense. Sean was still unhappy and she knew it, but, really, nothing could possibly happen with so *many* of them down here, an entire group under the supervision and protection of Reverend Peter Gideon.

Her gaze drifted toward the tall, blond minister striding at the head of their group, his visage one of spiritual determination and intensity that reminded her of the saints of her Catholic childhood. Now, of course, she worshipped as a Protestant—as Papa had been before he converted for her mother's sake—and admired Peter Gideon with all the pent-up adulation of a sixteen-year-old girl.

Sean was not as admiring of the reverend, his voice an angry mutter: "It defies logic to imagine why you think it will do any good to come down here preaching temperance to sailors and stevedores. We're all likely to end up at the bottom of the harbor. Or impressed into some foreign navy."

"I doubt any of that will happen. There are too many of us." Tory slid her gaze around their group. Most of them were Peter Gideon's followers or parishioners. A few—like Sean—were grudging attendants sent to chaperon female family members. It was apparent that she was not the *only* admirer of the good Reverend Gideon.

Her eyes moved to Peter Gideon again. He was easily singled out in any group. With his tall, golden intensity and booming rhetoric, he had quickly gained an extensive congregation in Boston.

"Look at them, the dregs of humanity . . ." Peter Gideon's disapproving words could barely be heard above the tumult of delivery wagons, shouts, and the high-pitched creaks of ship moorings. Immigrants crowded the wharves in teeming knots of excitement, most of them poorly clad, or garbed in only serviceable garments.

Bending down so that his blond head was next to hers, Sean whispered in Tory's ear, "Does your precious Saint Peter disapprove of poverty, too?"

Her gloved hand dug hard into his arm, though with all the folds of coat and shirt, it was doubtful the grip was as hard as she wanted. "Don't be so cruel."

"Ah, little cousin, I could never be cruel to *you*," Sean said with a grudging sigh. Then, with resignation: "As you well know. You've been leading me by the nose since you were twelve."

"Eleven. And you don't mind at all, so don't pretend you do."

Her triumphant smile would have melted the heart of a stone statue, and she pushed daintily at an errant curl of hair that strayed from beneath the brim of her bonnet, dimpling prettily at him. Hints of the mature beauty she would become were evident in her heart-shaped face, framed by clouds of dark auburn hair that was usually neatly confined but now curled rebelliously over her shoulders, making her look like a wayward gypsy. Even her eyes—slanted upward at the corners and gleaming with a rich violet luster—were exotic, dominating her face beneath delicately arched brows.

Reaching out, Sean tugged at one of her curls. "Vixen."

"Only when I *want* to be." Tory gave her cousin an admonishing stare, but it was obvious her reproof was ignored. Sean grinned, pursed his lips, and whistled a strain from a popular tavern song. Really. There were times he was *insufferable*, and if she had known a way to get out of the house without him as her chaperon, she would have done it without a qualm.

"Don't be insulting," she settled for saying. "And if you're unhappy accompanying us, just go back home."

"And miss all the excitement?" Sean's blue eyes danced with mischief. He straightened, and under the guise of tucking her hair beneath the confines of her prim bonnet, murmured wickedly, "Not a chance. I might miss seeing your Saint Peter tossed out of a tavern on his pompous ass if I leave."

"Don't be vulgar." She jerked irritably at the trailing end of her bonnet sash, yanked it from his fingers, and glared at him. "And you're speaking ill of a wonderful man whose intentions are noble and pure, not that *you* would understand such commendable sentiments."

Sean's mocking smile was evidence enough of his opinion, and Tory turned her head with deliberate silence. She tied her bonnet sash firmly under her chin. No point bandying words with him. Her cousin loved nothing better than to belabor an issue long past exhaustion. On other occasions, she might have enjoyed a vigorous discussion. Not now. Not when the debate was about Peter Gideon and she was anxious that nothing go wrong.

Peter must notice her as more than just one of his followers. Hadn't she done all in her power to bring herself to his notice during the past four months? Yes, for all the *good* it had done her! Infuriatingly, he still treated her with the same polite indifference he did the other young women who flocked to his sermons or attended all his lectures on the necessity of temperance in modern society. Still, there were moments when she'd seen him look at her differently, with a gleam of interest in his beautiful eyes that wasn't there for the others. It kept her in turmoil, that veiled interest that she was *certain* was not her imagination.

Too bad, really, that Peter Gideon did not look at her as her cousin did at times; she had seen Sean staring at her when he thought she wasn't looking, a rather puzzled expression on his face, seeming almost unhappy. He was noticing, of course, that she was growing up. And she was. The childish awkwardness was disappearing, and womanly curves were beneath the gowns she wore now, at last! Sean had noticed— but he was only her cousin, and she did so want Peter to see her, *really* see her—as a woman, not a child.

"Stop gawking at him." Sean nudged her rudely, and Tory flushed with embarrassment and indignation.

"I wasn't gawking."

"No use denying it. I can tell the difference. It's the saliva on your chin that gives you away every time."

Before she could form a scathing response, Peter called a halt in front of the tavern he'd chosen for their first demonstration. It looked rougher than she'd imagined, even in this area abounding with crude seamen and stevedores. Men lounged in front of the shabby wood front, and the door hung crookedly open. Noise and laughter drifted out on currents of tobacco smoke.

"I don't like this," Sean muttered uneasily. His hand tightened on her arm, and he pulled her back a step.

Tory pulled free before he could stop her, and pushed her way through the others to be at Peter's side. He looked down at her, smiling faintly in that ethereal way he had, and her breath caught. Only for her did he spare a rare smile. Oh, then she hadn't imagined his interest . . .

Afternoon light glinted in his pale hair as Reverend Gideon smiled down at her, and his voice was soft instead of his usual thunderous tone. "Miss Ryan, would you care to accompany me inside?"

"Of course." Ignoring Sean's inarticulate protest, she promptly moved forward to precede Peter inside the tavern.

It was dark and smoky. Her eyes stung, and she blinked rapidly to adjust her vision to the dim gloom. Much of the noise and laughter had stopped when she entered, and now there was an expectant hush. A chair scraped across the wooden floor with a loud noise, breaking the silence, and Peter smiled serenely when they stared at him suspiciously.

After a few moments, he began to speak, his voice rising in the familiar harangue of rhetoric that she knew and admired, and she had the sighing thought that he was so very inspiring, *surely* these men would repent their wicked ways and listen to his heartfelt words of wisdom.

Oh, Peter . . . *Saint Peter,* her irrepressible cousin called him, with no repentance at all even when she pointed out everything that Peter had managed to accomplish. But that was Sean. No reverence for anything, particularly a man he likened to being stuffed with horsehair and pride—an opinion that was significantly singular, and not at all shared by anyone else of her acquaintance. Especially the young ladies of Boston, who flocked to his church and his causes with a fervor that bordered on hysteria at times.

Tory thought Sean had come along today only to irritate Peter. Or her. She wasn't certain which action Sean deemed more enjoyable.

Some of the men in the tavern began to mutter, and when Sean reached out for her with grim determination in his eyes, she quickly avoided his grasp, stepping away from him in a lithe glide. Somehow, she *had* to make Peter notice her, and convincing one of these rough men to give up his whiskey would be quite a decent method.

She looked around the gloomy tavern for a likely prospect. One man leaned against the counter, ignoring them all, not even glancing around when Peter stood on a chair and held up his Bible to extol the virtues of repentance, to plead for the surrender of their whiskey and their souls.

Tory made her way toward the dark man at the bar, determination in the swing of her skirts and the set of her jaw. "Sir," she said loudly, and reached out to take his glass, "the Lord would like for you to give up strong drink and adhere to His words."

"Don't try it, lady."

Nick Kincade's palm slammed down to cover his whiskey glass. The intruding female hand hovered over his, long fingers quivering but not touching him. He'd heard her come up beside him, a muslin-skirted shadow that he'd managed quite handily to ignore—until she reached for his whiskey. At his snarl, her head jerked up in a shimmy of hat feathers and ugly

lace trimming, and she made a small breathy sound like
"Oh!"

Though the wide brim of her hat shadowed her face, the
dingy gas lamps in the tavern's common room shed enough
light for him to see that she was very young. He frowned.
She was with the Quakers, no doubt, who were busily annoying all the other patrons. He'd hoped he was safe, standing
alone in the shadows at the far end of the bar. Apparently,
he'd misjudged their zeal.

Snatches of a hymn mingled with the oaths and snarls of
longshoremen and sailors, and above it rose the ringing tones
of a temperance lecture. Nick spared them only the briefest
of glances. He'd seen the group enter the tavern's front doors,
and he'd known immediately why they were there. Temperance zealots. Usually religious fanatics as well. These were
better dressed than most, upon second glance. Though drab,
their garments were of good quality, and here and there he
spotted a flash of gold watch fob or jeweled cravat pin. Fools.
In this part of Boston, it bordered on stupidity to flaunt afflu-
ence. He would have been glad to ignore them, but it seemed
that was not to be. Especially not with this girl's foolish attempt to reach for his drink. She'd intended to pour it on the
floor, no doubt, as he'd observed happening across the common room.

The man on the bench grew louder. Light glittered in his
pale hair as he held up a Bible. His voice seemed to fill the
smoky tavern, its deep resonance as powerful among sinners
as if in the pristine halls of Boston's Methodist churches.
"Brethren, put down your cups of wickedness and drink from
the fountain of life," he intoned. "It is said in the Good
Book, 'For the drunkard and the glutton shall come to poverty, and drowsiness shall clothe a man with rags . . . ' "

Guffaws and irritated mutters greeted these warnings, but
only spurred the preacher to greater lengths. His voice soared
higher, words falling among the patrons like stones. Some
men milled about uneasily, while a few made their way to
the tavern door. It slammed heavily behind them. Few seemed

willing to drink under the watchful eyes of the drably garbed intruders.

A beefy hand slapped loudly against the bar, and the tavern keeper glared at the blond orator. "Git outa me tavern, Reverend. Ye're scarin' away me customers, ye are, w'en I'm only tryin' ta earn a decent livin' in this town . . ."

The reverend gazed at the tavern keeper with rich compassion. His tone was soft, as if he were speaking to an errant child. "The Bible says, 'Take away the dross from the silver, and there shall come forth a vessel for the finer,' my brother. The Good Book promises salvation to him who seeks it, but it will not be found at the bottom of an empty cup."

Nick had heard enough. He swore softly and impatiently, then lifted his glass and drained the last of his whiskey. When he turned away from the bar, the girl stumbled back a step, blinking at the sharp spray of lamplight that slanted across her face. He paused, looking down at her.

Her ridiculous hat framed unexpected features. He had a brief, eerie impression of a Caravaggio painting peering at him from beneath an impossible collage of ugly feathers and lace. Large, startled eyes caught his attention, looking for all the world like polished amethysts beneath thick black lashes. His gaze traveled over a straight, delicate nose and a small, determined chin with a hint of a cleft, to her mouth. Jesus, her mouth. A woman's mouth in a girl's face, the upper lip shorter than the tumble of her sumptuous lower lip, full, sultry, and tempting. It was a sensual mouth, a mouth made for kissing a man, not spouting high-flown words of temperance at him. Behind the fiery eyes lurked a smoldering energy that should be devoted to pursuits of pleasure, not to annoying men.

That pleasing image was quickly dispelled.

She seemed to gather herself up, and her chin jutted up at him pugnaciously. "Only fools ignore words of warning," she said calmly. Her fingers curled into gloved fists against her breast, a prayerful attitude if a bit defiant.

His brow lifted with faint amusement. So the Quaker had backbone as well as audacity. Not that she was the only one.

Dull-garbed drabs ranged like scrawny, quarrelsome crows along the long line of the dingy bar that stretched across an entire wall of the waterfront tavern. They were making enough racket to wake the dead. Deafening hymns were interspersed with warnings about the "devil's brew" being imbibed in hell's kitchen. It was only a matter of time before a brawl erupted, and he had a pretty good notion of who would come out the winners in any contest of brute strength. Ordinarily, he wouldn't have bothered with a warning, reasoning that any person with common sense would be aware of the danger inherent in accosting drunken sailors on their own turf, but there was something about the earnest face gazing up at him, as if expecting either a lightning bolt to strike him or salvation to overwhelm him, that was rather captivating.

"You are in the wrong part of town, little lady. Go home before you get hurt. All hell is about to break loose, in case you haven't noticed."

She blinked, a flicker of long black lashes. Something like disappointment passed over her features, and her lush mouth pursed in a knot of displeasure. Rather cautiously, she looked around them. Angry voices were being raised, and across the smoky tavern, a furious sailor was pounding his fist atop a table. It had to be obvious to her that trouble was brewing, yet to his grim astonishment, she shook her head and looked back up at him with a determined smile.

Lashes lowered over her eyes, then lifted again, almost as if she were flirting with him. "An obviously well-bred gentleman such as you would never allow harm to come to a lady," she said primly. "Especially not one who seeks only to lend you comfort."

Amused by her new tactic, Nick leaned against the bar and studied her for a moment. Silly chit. Did she think he would melt into vows of abstinence just because she batted her admittedly pretty lashes at him? Perhaps it was time he broadened her education. If he did a thorough job of intimidating her, she might have the good sense to flee the tavern before another man with less altruistic motives took it upon himself to educate her in ways she could never dream existed.

He straightened slowly and reached out a hand. Softly, he murmured, "Whoever said I was a gentleman, my sweet?" His thumb drew along the soft line of her jaw, dipping into the slight cleft of her chin in a leisurely glide before gripping her firmly between his thumb and fingers. He heard the swift intake of her breath, saw her eyes widen with shock and realization as he lifted her face to his. Then his mouth covered her lips and smothered her faint protests of alarm.

He'd been right. Her mouth was definitely made for kissing. Soft, sweet, and—despite her protests—yielding. He was tempted to give her a thorough lesson in provoking a strange man, but he wasn't really in the mood to be so benevolent. Not with someone shouting outrage at him from across the room. Rather reluctantly, he released the girl's mouth and chin and took a step back, half-turning.

Fury emanated from the man approaching at a rapid rate, and Nick had barely enough time to brace himself before the hurtling body slammed into him. Well-accustomed to tavern brawling, he turned slightly to absorb the brunt of the blow on his upper arm and shoulder, then retaliated by shoving his adversary backward in a quick, hard thrust. It sent him stumbling to the floor, and Nick followed quickly, jerking him up by his shirtfront, a fist ready. At the last moment, he paused, slightly surprised by the youthful face glaring up at him in defiance.

"Go ahead. Hit me. A man who would take advantage of a young girl like that would do anything."

Opening his fist, Nick released the youth so suddenly that he fell back onto the filthy floor with a resounding smack. "I don't fight children. What the hell are you doing down here in a tavern?"

The youth had rolled to his knees and was staring up at him warily, his hands doubled as if expecting combat. "I came to protect my cousin—the girl you just violated."

Nick's mouth curled into a faint smile of derision. "Violation takes a bit longer, with any luck. And if you wanted to protect her, you should have kept her at home." He gestured toward the door. "Leave now, before this gets out of hand."

Sullenly, the young man lurched to his feet, still wary. "I will, if she would only listen." His glance slid sideways to the girl, and his brows lowered. "See, Tory? We'd best leave before things get too rough—"

It was too late. A man's voice raised in an angry oath, followed by a loud crack. *Damn!* The tavern erupted into violence, and Nick had a brief glimpse of the tall, blond preacher being knocked from his bench into the seething knot of rough-clad seamen around him. Screams and shouts replaced hymns.

Nick reacted instinctively, years of riding the Texas plains and dodging outlaw bullets and Indian arrows having honed his senses to a sharp edge. He scooped up the girl, grabbing her by one arm, heedless of her bonnet or cry of alarm, and headed for the back of the tavern. She struggled furiously against him, and he swore when one of her flailing hands caught him across the face. He grabbed her wrist with one hand, fingers digging into the tendons until she gasped with pain.

"Cooperate, or I'll leave you here, and you can damn well take your chances!"

He tightened his hands on her arms, angry now as he jerked her along with him, back into the dark, fetid recesses of the hallway behind the main tavern room. He'd used the back door on occasion, and found it now by feel more than by sight, half-hidden in the gloom by a stack of wooden crates.

"What are you . . . Oh, where are you taking me?" The girl's furious struggles had melted into half-sobs, punctuated with an occasional threat that her family would see him punished if he harmed her in any way. "My uncle is an important man . . . You'll hang if you dare to touch me . . . So help me . . . If you attempt me harm . . . Oh, where is Sean? Help! Someone help me!"

Tightening his arm around her, across her middle just under the slight swell of her breasts, he choked off her incoherent protests and threats with only a slight squeeze. Silly brat.

When he swung the door open, he slung the girl outside into the alley; her hat was tilted over her face in a tattered mess of net and muslin, and her scarf had come unraveled, trailing behind her like a wilted banner. He released her abruptly.

If he'd thought she would appreciate his efforts, he was mistaken. She flung herself at him like a wildcat, clawing and spitting and hissing, until he was forced to grab her again, using sheer muscle to hold her until she finally quieted, her breath coming in harsh gasps for air. He gave her a slight shake, irritated.

"Will you just be still a minute? I have never known such an ungrateful brat. I suppose you'd rather I'd left you in there? Not that most of the patrons would have complained, but your cousin might have been a bit put out. And I assure you, little wildcat, that no one would have bothered to ask your permission for anything they chose to do to you."

"You . . . you . . . blackhearted *villain!*"

Nick laughed. "You're right, of course, but you have very little to base that opinion on. You should at least know me better before you offer such estimations as to my character."

Dark hair with streaks of copper fire in its thick length tumbled over her face and in her eyes, and she pushed at it angrily, glaring up at him through the mess of her hair and bonnet. "I would not waste my *time* trying to know you better . . . You've bruised my wrist, and dragged me out—I don't even know where my cousin is and if he's all right—" Her eyes widened, deep purple jewels in a peach-tinted face that went pale as she stared up at him with trembling lips. "*Sean*—I must go back inside and find him! Oh, what if he's hurt or—"

Nick put up a hand, shaking his head. "You would only cause a riot if you went back inside. Your dress is torn. And if you don't mind me saying, what's underneath would be an open invitation to any man in there."

She glanced down, gasped, and put a hand over the bodice of her gown, where a large rip revealed smooth, creamy skin beneath the ugly material. Quite enticing, he thought, amused when her head jerked up again and she glared at him.

"You could have told me!"

"And miss such a pleasing sight? I'm not that gallant. No, don't bother trying to hit me. We both know where that will lead. If you ignore my warning I'll kiss you again, and though *you* may not know where that will lead, I certainly do." He smiled slightly when she colored and took a step back, still holding together the torn edges of her bodice. The bare skin that peeped between her fingers would have been quite tempting on an older female, but on this young girl who couldn't be more than fifteen or sixteen, it was only a promise of things to come. "I'll find your cousin for you. Wait here. Unless you have a penchant for sailors."

Pivoting on his heel, he stalked back into the tavern, but in the confusion of the melee, it was hard to see, and it didn't help that he could barely remember what her cousin looked like. In any case, it soon became apparent that the youth was gone. When he returned to the alley, the girl was gone as well, and he shook his head in disgust. So much for altruism. He should know better. No good deed went unpunished.

Oh, she was safe, having finally drummed up enough courage to leave her hiding place in the alley behind the tavern; fortunately, she had run straight into her cousin, who was frantically searching for her in the crowded street out front. Police had been called, and blue uniforms and shrill whistles filled the air, with billy clubs being wielded handily atop the heads of the brawlers.

Sean got her out of the way as quickly as possible. The tavern was a shambles, and when Sean handed her up into a hired hack, she caught a glimpse of the interior through the front door that had broken completely off its hinges. Tables and chairs were fit only for kindling, and men with bloody, broken heads groaned on the floor or even sagged against the wooden front of the tavern.

Reverend Gideon sat on a stone curb, cradling his arm against his body, looking dazed, but Sean would not allow her to go to him, holding fast to her arm. "You are staying with me, so don't even think about it. Hasn't there been enough trouble?''

He was right, and she flinched at his hard tone and unspoken accusation. It was her fault they were here, and she had no excuse.

Sean didn't wait for the others, but gave a terse command for the driver to go on, and the hack lurched forward, wheels rumbling noisily over the cobblestones of the wharf. When the hack neared the townhouse on Beacon Hill, Tory was still shaking. She'd hidden behind a half-empty rain barrel at the mouth of the alley for what seemed like hours, and then had seen her . . . rescuer? captor? . . . step out into the alley again. He frightened her so, though she would never have admitted it to him. And strangely, it was the kiss that frightened her more than the rough handling, or even the furious brawl raging inside the tavern. She had never been kissed—oh, except for a few brushes of lips against her own, usually by an immature youth with damp, shaking hands. This had been entirely different; hard, intimidating—dangerous.

Exciting.

"Are you all right?" Sean put a hand over hers to still its trembling, and she nodded, looking up at him, her voice a hoarse whisper.

"Yes. Yes, I will be fine. It was just so—frightening."

Sean's mouth tightened into a taut slash, and his eyes were a hard, winter blue. "I alerted the authorities, and the police are looking for him now. I hope they find him."

"Police? Looking for—but Sean, he did not really *do* anything. I mean—he saved me, in an odd kind of way—oh no, you cannot have him arrested when all he did was try to help me!"

"Look here, he dragged you out of the tavern, didn't he? Screaming and fighting—God, I can still see it, and me not able to do a blasted thing because of some foul sailor hitting me . . .''

Sean drew in a ragged breath, and Tory bit her lip. Bruises traced his battered face in shades of blue and purple, and she felt so guilty. It was all *her* fault, of course, for not listening to him when he told her it was dangerous to go down there, even with a large group. Reverend Gideon was nursing a broken arm, and two of the women with their group had been roughly handled, with torn garments and rude jeers. God, Sean was right when he said she never listened to anyone but did just what she wanted to do. She should have listened, should have known—

"But we are all right now, Sean, and you know that the man did not harm me."

"Yes, *now* we know. But not then. I thought he'd taken you. And anyway, a man who frequents those kinds of places can only be one kind of man, Tory, so whatever the police do to him, he deserves." Sean's eyes darkened. "Arrogant bastard."

The next day, as she lay on the stuffed sofa in the downstairs parlor, she heard her Uncle Seamus tell Sean that the man had been arrested by the authorities; he'd been put aboard a Texas-bound ship, and good riddance, by God, for he'd better never show his face in Boston again.

Tory closed her eyes, shuddering. Thank God. He was gone, and she would never have to see him again. Why, she couldn't even recall the color of his eyes, only that they had stared at her—brown, she thought, a very light brown, almost a yellow-brown, like the eyes of a wolf. How odd that she couldn't quite remember what he looked like, only that he'd made her think of a lithe, dangerous animal, a predator, dark and lean and hungry.

And exciting, whispered that tiny voice in the back of her mind, the contradictory, willful little reminder that she hadn't really minded his kiss at all. But she would never tell anyone that, and soon she would forget all about it. Yes, she would. It wouldn't even be an unpleasant memory.

One

It had come by the morning post, a neat square envelope to accompany a large parcel, delivered to the elegant brick townhouse and addressed to Seamus Ryan. He'd not opened it immediately, recognizing his brother's penmanship and uncertain, as always, what news this letter would bring. Patrick could usually be depended on to surprise or disturb him with only a few lines of ink, and it had been no different this time.

After reluctantly opening the envelope, he went to find his wife, Katherine. She was in the parlor, where sunlight streamed through lace-covered windows and made shifting patterns on the carpet.

"A letter from Patrick." Seamus showed the missive to his wife where she sat at her writing desk in front of the parlor window.

Katherine looked up, pen poised in mid-air over a dissertation on women's rights that she was composing for her next lecture; diffused sunlight through window glass and lace made a halo of her pale hair. "He's not asking for Victoria to come home, is he?"

Shaking his head, Seamus smiled at her. "Not with all the unrest out there in California right now. War with Mexico is imminent, and Monterey is in the thick of it. No, Patrick is on business in New Orleans and he writes that his current business venture will earn him ten times the income he made as a sea captain if I wish to invest. His agent will be in Boston next month, and he hopes that I will be interested enough to entrust a rather large sum of money to him, an investment that he assures me will return huge profits within a very short length of time."

"And will you invest?"

Seamus hesitated, frowning, then slowly shook his head. "No, Patrick and I never seem to agree on business matters. It's best I pursue my own interests and leave him to his." Tapping a long envelope against his palm, he added, "He has also enclosed a letter for Tory, as usual."

Katherine frowned slightly, and her delicate fingers tightened around her black lacquer pen. Concern was evident on her lovely face, a pressing worry that Patrick would demand his daughter's return to California. It was a valid concern, for the original purpose of her extended stay with them had been an education in society as well as more intellectual pursuits, a goal that Katherine had accomplished admirably. Victoria was well-versed in many attributes and could conduct herself properly in any social setting, as well as converse in French and comprehend Latin. Not a mean accomplishment, Seamus thought proudly, for any woman in this day and time, when females were not required to be educated. At least Patrick had the foresight to know that women's roles in society were changing.

Katherine laid down her pen and sighed. "I always worry that the next letter will be the one saying she must return home to him. She's been with us so long, I think of her as one of ours now."

Seamus moved to the window and rested a hand on his wife's shoulder. "I, too, think of Tory as our daughter. But it's only natural, I suppose, as she's been with us since she was not quite ten. And now—now, she's a young lady. Seventeen, almost eighteen. Almost grown . . .''

Almost. But not quite. There was still the youthful exuberance that worked its way through the thin veneer of Tory's carefully polished manners at times, popping out just when it seemed as if she had grown past the stage to allow it.

"I don't think Patrick meant for her to stay quite this long." Seamus reflected upon his younger brother, who never really could be trusted to remember his daughter. "But I know she writes him that she's happy here with her friends and her studies."

"Odd, don't you think," Katherine said tartly, "that he takes business trips, yet never comes back to Boston, not even to see his daughter? He always sends his business agent, but never comes himself. A rather lackadaisical father at best, in my opinion, though of course, because he's your brother, I've not voiced that sentiment to anyone else."

Seamus rocked back on his heels, staring out the window. His brother's reluctance to visit Boston was still a mystery. Surely Patrick couldn't still be pining after Portia Wicker, not after all this time. That disappointment had been so long ago, when he was still only a captain of an American merchant ship. Afterward, he'd seemed to make it a point not to return to Boston, and they heard nothing from him for years. Then Patrick wrote that he had married the daughter of a Spanish alcalde in California and had two children, a boy and a girl.

Victoria was the older child by a few years; sweet, willful, and exotically lovely. He smiled, thinking of how Tory had looked in her first ball gown last spring, standing on the landing of the staircase and hesitating with uncharacteristic shyness, as if afraid her newfound maturity and composure might dissolve.

It had been Sean, only two years older than Tory, who'd broken the spell woven by her appearance on the stairs, looking up at his cousin and quoting, " 'She walks in beauty like the night/Of cloudless climes and starry skies;/And all that's best of dark and bright/Meet in her aspect and her eyes . . . ' ''

The quotation had earned Sean one of Tory's sweetest smiles, and she'd glided down the remaining steps to take his outstretched hand like a queen, allowing him to escort her to the waiting carriage. Her dark hair was piled atop her head in a fiery cloud, the burnished curls glinting with copper lights, framing a small, heart-shaped face. If one only glanced at her, the impression was of sweetness, but a closer inspection revealed a stubbornly rounded chin with a hint of a cleft in the middle, and above that, full lips that could change with mercurial swiftness from a charming smile to turbulent wrath. But it was her eyes that commanded instant attention, huge and thickly fringed with long, dark lashes over a startling shade of purple.

"Like spring violets," Katherine had once said admiringly of her niece's eyes.

"Like storm clouds on the open sea," Sean had countered, half in exasperation, half in admiration.

There were times, Seamus mused, that his oldest son and heir seemed more than half in love with Tory, but of course that was impossible. She was his cousin, for all that she seemed so different and exotic, probably like her mother, whom none of them had ever met. The distant Paloma was as much a mystery to his family in Boston as Patrick's refusal to come home. At least he'd had the good sense to send Tory to them, to see to her education and proper training. Even if there had been schools for young ladies in Monterey, Paloma was ill, an invalid, much too frail to ensure her daughter's proper upbringing. Tory herself said little enough about her mother, as if she was just a shadow in the California household.

"Where is Tory?" he asked his wife now. "I'll take her his letter."

"In the garden with the girls. They're reading Wordsworth aloud and drinking tea. A masquerade, I fear, to hide their usual plotting. This time it's the theater that lures them." Katherine took up her pen again, amusement curving her lips. "After seeing her performance last year at Tremont Theatre, Victoria developed a great admiration for Charlotte Cushman, and now fancies herself as the world's next great actress. It is not, of course, as lofty an ambition as a dedication to women's rights, but Victoria is young yet, and must explore many avenues before she matures enough to decide what is truly important.''

Seamus had no intention of discussing with his wife the inherent rights of women versus the inherited rights of men—having met that particular brick wall one too many times to consider it safe—and just smiled as he went out into the garden. Tory, Maura, and Megan sat on quilts beneath the twisted branches of a white-flowering apple tree. Teacups were scattered on small trays atop the grass, with remnants of lemon cake left on plates. Tulips and jonquils nodded in the warm afternoon sunshine. To him, the girls were the loveliest flowers in the garden, the bright heads of copper, blond, and dark auburn hair an enchanting contrast. It was a pleasant scene, evoking images of sweet femininity and gracious womanhood.

That image was rather quickly dispelled at his daughter's greeting, however, leaving Seamus Ryan a bit nonplussed.

"Papa," Maura said, looking up to see him, her face dimpled and pretty, "come and tell us what you think. Tory has been reading to us from a book published last year by Margaret Fuller. It's entitled *Women in the Nineteenth Century*, and is all about women's rights. Miss Fuller is a friend of Mama's, you know. You believe in women's rights, don't you, Papa?"

Taken aback by her ingenuous question, he rumpled Maura's bright red hair with an affectionate hand and sat down on a garden bench. "Of course. How could I not believe, with your mother so staunch a supporter?" It was, in his opinion, the most politic reply he could give in a household of four strong-willed females. Sean, he feared, had not yet learned the art of dissembling, and there had been more than one spirited discussion with his sisters and cousin that had sent the outnumbered youth running to him for solace.

Glancing at Tory, he saw that she was gazing at him with a faint smile as if she suspected he had other views, and he smiled back at her. "So you've taken to reading seditious literature, have you, poppet?"

"Yes, Uncle Seamus. It's very enlightening. Aunt Katherine used to attend Miss Fuller's discussions when she was still in Boston, and I went with her once to a conversational class at Elizabeth Peabody's home. Now Miss Fuller is in New York at the invitation of Horace Greeley, where she is a literary critic for his paper, the *New York Tribune*. She's a most admirable woman."

Seamus said, rather musingly, "You could do much worse, I suppose."

"I'm not certain I could do any better." Tory studied her uncle. "Miss Fuller is quite bright. A prodigy, I think, for she began Latin at six, and was reading Ovid at eight years of age. She speaks Greek, French, Italian, and German, and is very conversant in English literature."

Her uncle looked faintly bewildered at this recitation, and she smiled. It was obvious he had no idea what to say, and was known to flee to his study behind closed doors at the first hint of any ripples in the calm pool of his household. She leaned forward, her mane of hair obscuring the pages of the book in her lap. "If you promise to take us to the theater this Thursday, I promise not to tell you any more about Margaret Fuller. Is it a bargain?"

Laughing softly, Seamus leaned forward to lightly tap her chin. "Sly baggage. Of course I shall take you to the theater, if you like. And why not? I've the most beautiful daughters in all of Boston, and there's not a one in the city can hold a candle to any of you."

Everything sounded so much more lyrical in Uncle Seamus's rich brogue, the way he rolled his letters, and she was suddenly reminded of her father. Papa spoke like that, with the same Irish lilt to his words, a lingering reminder of his heritage. She didn't think of her father as often as she used to, for after all, she'd left California when she wasn't even ten, and now she was almost a grown woman. It wasn't that she didn't love Papa, for she did, but it all seemed so long ago that there were times she barely remembered the home where she'd been born.

Mama was a vague, dreamy image that she had trouble recalling in detail most of the time. After the birth of Diego, Mama did not get up again, but stayed in her room. *An invalid,* Tía Benita had said, *her health destroyed by the birth of a child the doctors had warned her against having . . .*

It had been left to Tía Benita to tend the infant, and Diego had grown into a sturdy, if rather annoying, boy. Tory thought of him often as she'd last seen him, a solemn child of eight years, with the thick black hair of his mother and the vivid blue eyes of his father. Diego's was a world of male pursuits, a blending of his heritages in a society that saved its most rigid strictures for the females. She'd not forgotten how strict life in California could be, where women were expected to be obedient and submissive, not to speak out about things like equality. Thanks heavens for Aunt Katherine, who understood something of the longing in her niece's heart, and who was a proponent of liberation for women, and took her daughters and niece to frequent lectures and discussions.

Just recently, they had gone with Aunt Katherine to visit Mrs. Elizabeth Cady Stanton, who would soon be moving to Seneca Falls in New York. Her husband was an attorney and well-known abolitionist, Henry Brewster Stanton. On a visit to London the summer after their marriage, Elizabeth had met Mrs. Lucretia Mott. When the ladies were refused admission to the world antislavery convention because of their sex, they vowed to organize a women's rights convention in the United States. It had not yet been organized, but Mrs. Stanton shared freely her views on woman's suffrage with those who would listen, among them Katherine Ryan and her niece and daughters. There were times Tory felt most fervently that the wrongs being done to so many women must be righted quickly, and vowed that she would help bring it about.

It was possible, if only Papa didn't insist that she return to California and allowed her to stay in Boston, where there were so many worthwhile causes. Why, perhaps she could assist in organizing the women's rights convention if she stayed . . . and, of course, there was always the theater that she so loved, and soirees and balls and teas—so much to do, so many interesting diversions in Boston, where life was much more sophisticated. Of course, she would *never* mention to Papa certain activities, like the time she had accompanied Reverend Gideon to the Boston waterfront. She shuddered to remember it, how they had so narrowly escaped disaster, and that *dangerous* man—she'd tried to invoke his image a few times, but the entire affair had been such a blur of horror and fear that she'd retained only a vague recollection of a tall, dark man with wicked eyes and a sardonic drawl.

Well, all that was behind her now. Her days of temperance reform were conducted more discreetly, especially as Reverend Gideon had curtailed his forays into such dangerous dens of iniquity. Still, it was best not to mention such things to Papa, not even her recent surge of interest in the rights of women and slaves.

Papa would be horrified if he knew, but she did not think it to her best advantage to write him of her pastimes. He might *insist* she return to California, when she was happy here, with her cousins and her stimulating pursuits. And after all, she had Sean to watch over her, as long as she did not attempt to push him *too* far with her escapades. Only on occasion did he protest, and after the debacle at the waterfront, she was more disposed to listen to him now.

Sean had always been her most ardent defender. He had been the one to comfort her when, at her first ball, she had overheard herself being discussed and dissected, her life and character assessed in idle gossip that still made her flinch when she thought of it.

"Mrs. Ryan's niece is too *wild* to be considered quite proper, don't you think? All that dark hair in unruly masses— like a *gypsy*," Mrs. Fitzhugh had said in a loud whisper to her companion.

Mrs. Quincy had agreed, nodding wisely. "Oh yes, much too wild, and I would not be a bit surprised to learn that her mother is one of those wild Indians that roam about only *half-clothed*—scandalous pagans, they are."

"Well, she may *pretend* to be *quality*—and I must admit her carriage is beyond reproach due to Katherine Ryan's impeccable standards of excellence—*but* mark my words, blood will tell. It always does."

"*Always,* Lavinia. If not for the fact that Katherine is a New York Van Pelt, and *very* well-connected, Seamus Ryan would never have done as well as he has. He would be like his brother, I suppose, who was always too much of a rogue for my taste, sailing off as he did to wed one of those California girls . . ."

"Only after that dreadful scandal, if you'll recall. Winston Wicker refused to allow a mere ship's captain—an *immigrant*—to wed his only daughter. Why, it simply isn't *done*, though, of course, now I understand he has accumulated a very decent fortune, enough to send that wild daughter of his to the *best* schools—humph! Foolish, if you ask me. A waste of good money, like dressing a savage in silks."

Standing behind a tall potted palm, Tory had curled her gloved hands into such tight fists they'd begun to ache, but she'd not betrayed her presence. Not even when Sean had found her still behind the glossy green leaves of the plant, and known immediately that something was wrong, swearing under his breath about the vicious old harpies, had she let anyone see how hurt she was by their gossip.

It was untrue, all of it! Oh, perhaps Papa had been something of an adventurer, and it was true her mother was Spanish, but she was definitely not Indian or only half-clothed . . . Her skin was the pale cream of a Spanish *criolla*, not dark and dusky. And Uncle Seamus might have wed a New York beauty of *good blood,* but he worked hard and was successful, first with shipping, and now with railroads. Everyone said trains were the wave of the future, and it was certain that Seamus Ryan would be Boston's next millionaire.

"I forgot," Uncle Seamus was saying, distracting her as he held out a letter, "this came for you today. Your father is in New Orleans, and is sending a box of laces and material for new gowns before he goes to Texas."

Maura and Megan gave squeals of delight, for Patrick Ryan

always sent more than enough for the three girls—bolts and bolts of the best cloth, and lace trimmings, and feathers and furs—even pearl buttons, gloves, and silk stockings. And in the last parcel from him had been four pairs of the new vulcanized rubber garters that were all the rage, as well as yards and yards of elastic in cotton and silk, in colors of black, white, and tea-rose.

"Texas?" Tory took the letter almost reluctantly. "Why would he go there when all that fighting is close by?"

"Fighting, poppet?"

She looked up at her uncle, frowning slightly. "Yes. It's in all the papers, how an American army moved into disputed territory close to the Rio Grande, and is daring the Mexicans to take it back. War will soon be declared, for Mexico has no intentions of giving up Texas or New Mexico, or even California."

Seamus smiled wryly. "You're very well-informed, I see. But don't let it worry you. You're safe here in Boston."

It wasn't that at all. Her safety didn't concern her.

Will Papa send for me when the war ends? she wondered. She had been in Boston so long now, when it was supposed to have been only for a short time. Papa's last few letters had hinted that he wanted her home again now that she was older and well-versed in her studies, as he'd intended.

But I don't want to go back, Tory thought rebelliously. Why should I? Alta California was vastly different from Boston. Marriages were still arranged there—a feudal custom in her opinion—and she would never wed a man who did not view her as an equal. It would work against the grain of everything she believed in, and she could not bear the thought of it.

So she scanned the letter almost fearfully, but Papa contented himself with wishing her well, reminding her to be always courteous and meek, and not to let her temper get the best of her. He ended his letter with fondest wishes, saying that soon they would be together again for he missed her very much. She felt almost guilty for hoping she did not have to go home.

"I'm sure that Patrick is being very careful," Uncle Seamus was saying, "and that he's staying far away from where the war is being fought."

Tory looked up from the letter and smiled. "I'm sure he is."

Two

Palo Alto, Mexico
May 8, 1846

A cannonball lobbed through the air, making a loud, peculiar whistling noise. Nick Kincade recognized the sound immediately. Still kneeling, he looked up, squinting against the bright glare of the noon sun. Heat waves blurred the air, and smoke lay in a thick, choking haze over the vast, level plain. The combined smells of blood, dust, and gunpowder filled his nose. He quickened his efforts at slicing through a leather strap binding the dispatch pouch to a dead Mexican courier. His fingers were burned, but he didn't remember how it happened. The strap came loose finally, and he gave it a hard tug and got to his feet in a sort of rolling run.

He was just in time.

The cannonball dropped from the sky, bouncing several times in an erratic path, then plowed a trough indiscriminately over the ground and the dead courier. Dry chunks of sparse yellow and brown prairie grass spewed upward. Burning powder smelled of hot sulfur, and sunlight glinted from the ball's copper surface. The Mexicans still had not figured out that copper cannonballs were too slow and clumsy to be effective ammunition. They were fatal only by accident, unlike the Mexican soldiers, who were adept at hand-to-hand combat, and could use their Spanish-made bayonets with lethal efficiency. Given a choice, he'd take his chances with their cannon any day.

And it looked like he was about to face that choice.

American gun crews were swiftly wheeling their light cannon into position on the stretch of open, level ground, and began firing. Despite an unimpressive bark, these mobile field pieces sent vicious loads of grapeshot screaming across the battlefield. Scores of enemies went down in waves as they advanced. And Nick was caught between two armies.

Another wave of grape screamed overhead, and he threw himself to the ground behind a silvery-blue clump of needle-tipped agave. He rolled to his side and brought his rifle into firing position. A sharp-spined agave leaf jabbed him in the thigh. There wasn't enough cover here to hide a jackrabbit. Swearing, he pulled his legs up under him and studied the barren terrain. Two hundred yards ahead, chaparral edged the flat prairie, providing the only decent cover within sight. Once in the thick brush, he could make his way to the American lines. It was his only chance. If he made it, they might recognize him as one of their scouts before shooting him. Maybe.

As the battle escalated, the two lines drew closer, pinning him between them. He swore softly. It would be sheer suicide to attempt to make his way to the American line with the Mexicans so close. He'd have to risk a run across open ground to the chaparral, work his way up from there in full view of Mexican troops. Hardly an easy task . . . Then a flash of light caught his eye and he turned, squinting against the bright glare. Sunlight glinted from bayonets, swords, and uniform buttons. A Mexican brigade of cavalrymen formed a line to charge the Americans' right flank. A diversion—just what he needed.

It began quickly, with shouted orders and a barrage of gunfire. Nick seized the opportunity and ran, zigzagging across the field littered with bodies and smoldering earth. His boots pounded against the dry, dusty ground, adding choking clouds to the already hazy air, but he didn't dare stop or even slow down. Two hundred yards was a long way when bullets flew so indiscriminately.

He wasn't even halfway when he heard a heavy, humming whistle overhead, signifying an American cannonball, more lethal and accurate than the Mexican ones. He sprinted for a shallow trench a few feet ahead, lined with rocks that were charred black, vivid against the ocher color of the prairie. Cursing, he reached the ditch and slid into it in a shower of dirt and pebbles, almost landing atop a burly corpse sprawled in the depression. Startled, he jerked back, and realized that the "corpse" was still alive.

Blue eyes dark with pain looked up from a soot-streaked, bloodied face. A thatch of red hair was matted with dark blood. A weak grin wavered. "And it's glad I am . . . to see you, lad," he said in a thick Irish brogue. "Would you be after . . . mindin' a wee bit of water . . . to ease a dyin' man?"

The cannonball landed several yards away, exploding in a hot barrage of rocks, dirt, and flying metal, and Nick ducked instinctively, his body covering the man beneath him. When the lethal shower ended, he sat up, dusting himself off as he eyed his companion.

"What the hell are you doing out here?" He uncorked his canteen and handed it to him. "It's no place for a civilian to be right now."

"And I could be . . . sayin' the same thing . . . to y'lad . . ." Bloody hands gripped the canteen tightly. "But it's a blessing you're here . . ."

Nick shrugged. "That could change at any minute. It's a little early to tell, but it looks like our boys are destroying the Mexican cavalry. Arista's only option if that happens is to shift his attack to the left, and in that case, we'll be run over by infantry. We have to get out of here now."

Groaning, the man shook his head. "I'm hurt too . . . bad. Leave me. Save yourself. Just give me a pistol . . . before you go. I'd rather . . . shoot myself than let the enemy . . ."

Nick looked down; bright red blood stained the lower right of the man's white linen shirt. But he didn't intend to leave a wounded civilian for the frustrated Mexicans to find, either.

"Yeah, well I ain't leaving my pistol behind. Sorry. Looks like you'll have to go with me. Take another couple of swigs of water. As soon as the shooting slows down, we'll give it a try." Nick checked the chambers of his rifle, then the cylinders of his Colts. All loaded and ready. He looked back at the Irishman.

Relief lit the man's eyes, and he managed another grin. "You're a good lad, you . . . are. A good . . . lad."

"There are more than a few folks who'd argue that point with you," Nick said dryly, and looked back toward the battlefield. American cannon had changed position to meet the new threat, and storms of grape were blasting huge holes in the line of running Mexican infantry. Muzzle blasts flashed red against thick smoke. Shifting streamers of acrid smoke drifted above the battlefield, and a tiny yellow and orange line snaked slowly over the dry prairie grass with greedy, licking tongues of flame. Fire . . .

Nick swore softly. "Get ready. The muzzle blasts have started a wildfire. When the smoke gets thick enough, we'll use it for cover to make it to that chaparral. Think you can do it?"

"I think I've . . . no choice. By the way . . . my name is Patrick Ryan, in case—just in case."

Nick turned to look at him. Ryan was terrified, and obviously aware of his mortal danger. Nick flicked a slight smile that was meant to be encouraging.

"Kincade. Don't give up just yet. I've been through worse than this." It was true, but it was going to take more than a little smoke and dumb luck to get them unscathed through a tight spot between two armies. Damn the luck. He'd followed the courier all the way from Mexican General Arista's field quarters just to get his hands on these dispatches; it was his job to get them to General Taylor. Even if he had to walk through hell to do so.

Ten days earlier, General Taylor had taken three thousand men from Fort Brown and marched to nearby Point Isabel for supplies, leaving behind only five hundred men to hold the garrison. The dust hadn't settled behind him before Arista moved his army ten miles north to Palo Alto, straddled the road from Point Isabel, and began bombarding the fort with fire.

Information had been intercepted by Captain Samuel Walker of the Texas Rangers that the Mexicans were making their way across the river and intended to sever Taylor's lines and isolate him when he came to the fort's rescue. Walker had set out to warn Taylor, but been caught by fifteen hundred Mexican cavalry. In the ensuing fight, Walker was reported killed, but made it back to camp and asked for six more volunteers. Though he generally rode with Jack Hays, Nick was familiar with the area and volunteered. He considered the risks preferable to the boredom of waiting.

This time, Walker succeeded. After warning the general, Walker headed back to Fort Brown to assure the besieged that help was on the way, while Nick circled around on a reconnaissance mission. By his estimate, there were close to four thousand Mexican soldiers massed to attack. Grim odds.

"You didn't say how you got caught out here," Nick said to Ryan after a minute, glancing down at him.

Ryan shrugged sheepishly, then grimaced at the pain. "Stupidity."

"Yeah, there's a lot of that going around lately. Mind telling me just how you managed it, though? I find I'm rather curious to come upon a civilian out here instead of back at the fort or in town."

"It's simple enough . . . I was in Point Isabel when the Mexicans began bombarding Fort Brown . . . We heard the cannons, of course. I wanted to watch the battle from a . . . safe distance. My horse . . . spooked and threw me . . . and the next thing I know . . . I'm wounded, and left for dead by marching troops . . . until you . . . came along."

Nick eyed him cynically. It was implausible enough to be the truth, he guessed, but damn unlikely.

The western wind finally began to pick up, and the fire burned brighter. Choking clouds of smoke billowed upward—and into the faces of the advancing Mexican army. The infantry began to pull back under the press of smoke, but the greedy flames drew closer and closer. There was only a narrow band of possibility between two dangers: Within minutes either the fire or the Mexicans would be on top of them.

Nick stepped up to the edge of the trench. American cannon sent incessant barrages toward the enemy. The smoke made things worse, and frustrated curses and shouts mingled with the screams of dying men and horses. Everywhere he looked there was carnage. He thought of a painting he had seen once in Italy, by Botticelli, depicting a scene from Dante's *Inferno*. It had made very little impression on him then.

But that had been six years before, when he was only nineteen, and hadn't seen much of the world. Since then, he'd seen enough to give him a better appreciation of Dante's visions of hell.

Another cannonball exploded nearby and he ducked. "All right, Ryan," he said when the deluge stopped. "Let's go."

Ryan didn't move, and when Nick glanced back at him, he was staring at the battlefield with the sudden blank look of animal fear on his face. "I don't think . . . I can make it . . ."

"Damn you, get up!" There wasn't time to argue. Nick hefted Ryan upward with an arm across his chest and up under his arms, and clambered to the ridge of the shallow trench. Tangled heaps of Mexican cavalry lay scattered about the field, and the constant battery of the American field pieces barked withering grapeshot indiscriminately. Tiny flames licked around his boots, hot and searing. Ryan was a heavy weight, slung half over his back. All around him, cannon exploded. The blasts were deafening, pelting him with hot bits of ball and dirt. He stumbled and went to one knee in the dirt, almost losing his burden. Somehow, he managed to stand again, and tighten his grip. Ryan gave a grunt of pain. The screams of the dying were high and piercing, a constant sound above the cannon fire and crackle of flames.

The fire took off, with the rising wind pushing it across the dry prairie grass. Nick kept to the fringes just beyond the blaze. At any minute, he fully expected the flying artillery to blast them into oblivion. The smoke was thick, too thick to

see more than a foot ahead of him, and he depended on blind
luck and intuition to get him to safety.

Not for the first time in his life, it worked.

He stumbled into the American lines instead of the chaparral as he'd expected, and was stopped by a sentry.

"Halt—who goes?" the soldier demanded, peering at them
through the deepening shadows of dusk.

"Lieutenant Kincade." Between the weight of the Irishman
and the choking smoke, he was surprised he could say that
much, but apparently the soldier wasn't easily convinced.

Stepping forward, he used the tip of his bayonet to hold
Nick back. A hellish light from the prairie fire illuminated
everything in stark shades of red and black, leaving the soldier's face in shadow. "You ain't in uniform and I don't
know any Kincade. You look Mex to me."

Nick looked up. The corporal was scared, most likely, with
a bad case of battle nerves. He let Patrick Ryan slide slowly
to the ground, and straightened. "I ride with Colonel Hays.
Texas Rangers. He'll know me."

"Yeah?" The soldier hesitated, but kept the bayonet at the
ready. "I don't know no Colonel Hays, neither."

"Get Hays up here—"

"Naw, I don't think so." The tip of the bayonet moved
forward, pushing sharply against Nick's belly above his belt
buckle. "Put yer hands out to yer side . . . away from yer gun.
And gimme that pouch around yer neck."

"It's a courier pouch, Corporal. You know the rules."

"All I know is, you ain't goin' no farther till I see what's
in that there pouch."

The bayonet punctuated every few words with a sharp jab
against Nick's belt buckle. His temper rose. He gauged his
moment, and knocked the bayonet away from his belly with
a rapid swipe of his arm.

The corporal yelped, bristling into aggression, but something in Nick's eyes made him hesitate and bluster. "Hey!
I'd prob'ly get a medal for shootin' you, so you'd better
watch what yer doing—"

Tired, irritable, and impatient with a confrontation that

looked to drag on a while, Nick took a short step backward, as if retreating. When the corporal jabbed at him with the bayonet again, Nick half-turned, lifting his left foot in a short, hard kick to the belly that sent the man sprawling on the charred ground. By the time he recovered, Nick was kneeling over him, his drawn knife at the corporal's throat. Reflected firelight glinted along the wicked, curved edge of the blade, and above it, staring down dispassionately, Nick smiled.

"Now send somebody to look for Hays. And while you're at it, get an orderly for this wounded man."

Dismay was reflected on the corporal's face, tinged with humiliation that he had been so easily defeated, but he nodded once, shortly, and swallowed hard. "Yeah. Yeah, I will."

"Good." Nick rose in a lithe motion, but didn't put his knife back in the sheath. He held it loosely in one hand, so there was no misunderstanding how fast he could use it again if he chose.

The corporal got clumsily to his feet and barked an order over his shoulder, then looked back at Nick, cautiously. Two uniformed men came running through the smoke and gloom, eyes sizing up Nick and the wounded Irishman.

"Fetch Colonel Hays," the corporal said, sullenly, "and an orderly."

By the time John Coffee Hays and an orderly arrived, it was dark. Campfires dotted the ground at intervals, and both sides had broken off the fight for the night. The thick smoke of battle and prairie fire still hung in the air, and an occasional shot was fired, harmless and defiant.

Hays identified Nick, much to the corporal's chagrin. "This is one of my Rangers, Corporal. Can't you tell a Texian when you see one? Look at him—those are the new Colt revolvers stuck in his belt, regular issue to Rangers, but not Mexican soldiers."

Though not a large man, in fact, rather slender and only five-eight, Jack Hays nevertheless had a commanding presence that made him seem huge. With black hair and eyes and a high, noble forehead, he portrayed an air of authority and character. None of his men would think of questioning his judgment or his leadership abilities.

Clearly impatient, Jack Hays jerked a thumb in Nick's direction. "Hell, he's wearing a damn arsenal, Corporal. You're lucky you aren't sporting too many holes to hold your water."

The corporal—humiliated and intimidated—muttered a reply, but his eyes were thin and hot with rage when he looked at Nick. "Yessir, Colonel." Resentment laced the corporal's tone, and his expression was belligerent. "I didn't look at him that close."

"You should have. It would have saved me some trouble." Hays shook his head. "Common sense might have helped. Dismissed, Corporal."

Hays turned to look at Nick. Shrugging, Nick held out the leather pouch. "Took this off a dead courier."

Lifting his brows slightly, Hays took the pouch. The leather was charred in places and stained with blood, the buckle crusted with mud. "Good work, Kincade."

Neither man bothered to mention the high risks Nick had taken to get the dispatches through to their destination. It was part of the job, and expected. Nick had been riding with Hays since San Antonio, fighting Mexicans, Comanche, and Apache with equal ferocity and grim determination. Though they were rumored to be undisciplined, the character of the work performed by the Texas Rangers made formal discipline impossible. Officers weren't appointed, they were proven, tempered like steel in the fire of battle and command. Hays was one of the best, and earned the respect of his men.

Hays nodded toward Patrick Ryan. "Where'd you find him?"

"In the middle of the battle." Nick frowned. "Says he got himself there by accident."

"Hell of an accident." Hays studied the wounded man, then knelt on the ground beside him. He asked a few questions and received the same replies Nick had gotten, and, after a moment, nodded and stood up. Taking Nick aside, he said, "Sounds dumb enough to be true. Check it out."

Nick grinned. Trust was not one of the required qualifications of a Ranger.

The orderlies arrived to retrieve Ryan and put him on a litter. Weak now, and gasping for every breath, Ryan waved away the orderlies and clutched at Nick's arm, pulling him down to the litter with a surprisingly strong grip. "Must say . . . something . . . first."

"Save your strength, Ryan. I'll visit you in the surgeon's tent when you're feeling better—"

"No. Might not . . . feel like it." Ryan's fingers tightened on Nick's sleeve. "If I don't make it . . . must . . . send word to m'family. Please . . . promise me you'll . . . send word . . ."

"I'll be certain they get word what happened to you."

"No, not that . . . something . . . else." Wheezing now, Ryan fumbled at the front of his coat and drew from his breast pocket a small packet. It was damp, a little blood-smeared, and tied with string. He shoved it into Nick's hand, mumbling, "For m'daughter . . . Victoria."

Nick looked down at the small package. It was wrapped in oiled paper, thick and slightly bulky. He hefted it, frowning. "What's in here?"

Grimacing, Ryan clung to Nick's arm, his fingers digging tenaciously into the buckskin sleeve. "A little cash . . . from business deal . . . and some papers. Hold . . . until I'm . . . dead or . . . ask for it back."

"I'll make sure it's safe. Go on with the orderlies now, and you can give it to your family yourself."

He stood up and motioned for Ryan to be taken away, then gave the packet into the safekeeping of Colonel Hays. He didn't really expect Patrick Ryan to survive the night, much less the war, and he wasn't too sure about his own chances.

The battle moved from Palo Alto Prairie to Resaca de la Palma the next morning, and was fierce. When it ended, the Mexicans had been defeated, leaving many dead and wounded behind in their frantic retreat: Infantry abandoned artillery and wagons, the cavalry lost most of their horses, and even the ammunition had been rendered useless. Mexican troops suffered from lack of food and water and their own compatriots' greed, as some stole army supplies and resold them to the troops at very high prices. Of General Arista's original five thousand men, fewer than three thousand remained fit for duty by the time the army reached Linares. It seemed that the Alamo had taught the Mexicans little about American rifles and resolution.

And the American army grew to some sixty-six hundred men.

After the Americans removed the threat to Fort Brown, Nick stopped by the field hospital to visit Patrick Ryan. He'd been moved to a hospital barracks, and was doing better than he had a right to expect, the surgeon said wryly, shaking his head.

"Couldn't get the bullet out, but he's a tough old bird. Never can tell about these cases. A visit would cheer him up. He's asked about you anyway, Kincade."

Nick felt a little uncomfortable in the barracks lined with cots and wounded men. He wasn't much on bedside manners or small talk, and spent the first few minutes standing beside Ryan's cot shifting from one foot to the other, wishing the hell he was someplace else.

Ryan didn't seem to notice, and greeted him gladly. He managed a weak grin. "Guess it's not my time yet, huh Kincade?"

"Looks that way." Nick held out the packet Ryan had given him, not bothering to mention that Colonel Hays had already taken the liberty of going through Ryan's papers. "Here's your money. You'll find it's all there."

"I have no doubts as to that." Ryan looked at him thoughtfully. He lay the packet on the thin blanket spread over him. "Any man who'd stop in the heat of battle to rescue a stranger could hardly be a thief."

Nick shrugged. "I wouldn't depend on that too much, Mr. Ryan. There are a lot of dishonest men ducking bullets these days."

"Aye, but not many of them risk their own lives for a stranger." Ryan shifted slightly, grimacing. "The surgeon informs me that I'll most likely live, though not without pain and some lack of mobility. Alas, it seems that I won't be able to return home as quickly as I'd hoped, though if not for you—''

"Where's home?" Unwilling to dwell on expressions of gratitude, Nick deliberately changed the subject.

Patrick Ryan's voice grew stronger. "California. I have a hacienda there, and acres of cattle and vineyards—it's beautiful. Buena Vista, I call it. I'd welcome you there if ever you're in Monterey, Mr. Kincade."

"I'll keep that in mind." Nick listened politely, if a little impatiently, while Ryan talked of his home, his son, and his beautiful daughter.

"Victoria is in Boston now, attending school and living with my brother. But soon she'll return, once all this is over and the sticky question of governments is settled."

"I get the idea that you've no particular wish for California to be part of the United States, Mr. Ryan."

Looking rather startled, Ryan said slowly, "Of course, I confess to a certain amount of concern about my California holdings. When I married, I became as one of my wife's family, a *Californio*. That's how it's done out there, you see. I changed my religion from Protestant to Catholic to please my new inlaws, and even changed my name. In some circles, I am known as Don Patricio Ryan y Montoya—taking on my wife's maiden name. Of necessity, my loyalties became as my wife's. But now that Monterey is in American hands, I shall yield to the inevitable. After all, I've no reason not to want to be part of the United States as long as my land titles are recognized."

Nick didn't respond. Hays had already mentioned—casually assuming Nick would take it from there—that Ryan was suspected of being in Point Isabel to sell weapons to the Mexican military. Nothing that could be proved, but if more evidence could be found, it would certainly keep the Mexicans from getting their hands on modern, effective munitions. It was a more likely explanation for Ryan's presence on the battlefield than ignorance, Hays had said dryly, and Nick had to agree.

But now Patrick Ryan was rambling on about his daughter and the man to whom he intended to marry her, a *criollo* with adjoining lands to Buena Vista, a true gentleman who had vast Spanish land grants and was an ardent patriot.

"Won't that be like crawling in bed with the enemy?" Nick drawled, and watched Ryan's face flood with color.

"Not at all," he replied stiffly. "Don Luis is no fool. He'll gladly submit to American rule. Most Californios are more sympathetic to Americans than the harsh Mexican government, as you should know. Rebellion has been brewing for some time. Don Luis and his son were behind the recent overthrow of Micheltorena, the Mexican governor, and supported the appointment of Pío Pico, who is a Californio. Even a prominent man like Mariano Vallejo is in favor of American annexation, and enthusiastically advocates such a measure."

"Sort of a moot point now, wouldn't you say?"

For a moment, Patrick Ryan studied him silently, as if reassessing him. Then he smiled faintly. "Perhaps I misjudged you, Mr. Kincade. But only in certain matters. Your courage cannot be mistaken, and I find myself still at a loss how to properly show my gratitude for saving my life as you did."

"Don't. I would have done the same for anyone."

"Yes, and that is precisely what impresses me about you." Ryan looked down at the packet atop his blanket, then up at Nick again. "I should like very much for you to accept a small gift, if—"

Nick straightened. "No. I don't need gifts, Mr. Ryan."

"Then promise you will visit me at Buena Vista one day. It would be the least I can do to show my gratitude."

"If I'm ever in California again, I'll keep it in mind." He was ready to leave. Damn Hays and his obtuse suggestions. Why the hell didn't he just show up at Ryan's bedside and demand some answers instead of this roundabout way of conducting matters? It would be a lot quicker, if not as subtle.

"Do that, Mr. Kincade. I have plenty of land for men who are willing to work and perhaps start their own enterprise, if you've an interest in ranching as a profitable business."

"I might," Nick said, but knew he wouldn't. He was no

rancher. He had decided that at a young age, when it was obvious his father wanted him to stay on their sprawling East Texas ranch and raise beef and grandchildren. It had held no interest for him. It still didn't. Reckless, his father had called him, too wild to take any responsibility, and Nick supposed he was right. But the thought of spending his days as his father did, worrying over feed prices and cattle values, and how to get them to market, held no appeal for him.

After a final, decisive argument, he'd left home and, for a few years, made his own way in the world. His last visit to the ranch had been pleasant, but strangely uncomfortable. It had been a long time since he'd been back. Since then he'd been a lot of places, seen a lot of things, and had no regrets, even if he ended up a casualty of war. He liked the idea of making a difference, of living on the edge and not knowing if each minute was going to be his last. There was an exhilaration in cheating death, in walking away when all the odds were against it. It was a lot more exciting life than paperwork and market prices.

But now he'd heard all he wanted to hear of Mr. Ryan for the moment, and made his excuses to leave. He'd be back. They both knew he would, and why.

When it came time to leave Fort Brown a few weeks later, Nick had no regrets in leaving behind the cat-and-mouse game with Patrick Ryan. The old man was wily, and if he knew they suspected him of selling guns to the enemy, he never let on. Neither did he betray himself in any way.

On his last day in Fort Brown, Nick stopped by the infirmary to tell him he was leaving. ''We're heading out in the morning, Mr. Ryan.''

''That's what I hear. Arista lost over two thousand men before he reached Linares. Looks like he's finished for now.''

''Maybe, but not for good. They haven't quit. I know better. This is just a lull before it starts again.''

It was a grim prophecy.

Three

When Hays's Rangers left Matamoros in August, their reputations preceded them across Mexico. Entire villages emptied in panic upon news of their approach; not only did each Ranger carry an arsenal of weapons, but he rarely took prisoners. Nick Kincade didn't find it very surprising in light of what he'd seen in their march across the countryside. It wasn't just Americans who killed Mexicans, but their own troops.

Defeat after defeat swamped the Mexican army, until finally Mexico City fell the next September, 1847. In seventeen months of war, more than twenty-five thousand Mexicans had died in combat, while only five thousand Americans lost their lives.

The treaty of peace was signed on February 2, 1848, in the palace at Guadalupe-Hidalgo, four miles north of Mexico City. The terms were that the United States would keep what it had already taken, and Mexico would recognize the Rio Grande as its border with Texas. In exchange for fifteen million dollars, Mexico ceded one third of its territory—New Mexico and California.

It wasn't long after the treaty was signed that the American occupation army began to return home, leaving Mexico to the Mexicans. General Taylor—faced with the uneasy prospect of a thousand idle Texas Rangers raising hell—thanked them and bade them all go home as well.

Nick Kincade left Fort Brown and crossed the dirty, shallow ribbon of the Rio Grande into Matamoros, headed for the small adobe hut he'd been sharing with a sweet young señorita named Gisela.

She greeted him at the door, as she had for the past few months, wearing a thin cotton camisa and bright patterned skirt, smiling happily. Not bothering to close the door behind him, he pulled her into his embrace, hungry for her suddenly, and uncertain how he was going to say goodbye. He had to leave; he'd overstayed his assignment as it was, and the others were already back in Texas. Matamoros was on the Mexican side of the Rio Grande, a border town now, with Texas only a thin slash of muddy water away. But he hadn't been able to leave Gisela yet. He knew that she'd come to depend on him for more than just a few pesos here and there. He was her security, a defense against reprisals from not only American soldiers, but her own people. Mexico had been horribly defeated and stripped of American possessions, and hatred for their northern neighbor still smoldered beneath the thin veneer of civility toward the conquerors—and toward those who befriended them. Nick intended to take Gisela with him, as far as Galveston, anyway, where he knew a Mexican-American family who would be glad to take her in and care for her.

This was the closest he'd come to domesticity, and he had to admit that he'd grown very fond of Gisela. She was eager to please, passionate in bed, and a great cook.

"Tonight, *amante*," she whispered in his ear, "I have something very special for you."

With a sultry gleam in her dark eyes, she took his hand and led him to the table, where steam rose from clay pots and dishes. The table was small, salvaged from a scrap heap, and he'd mended its broken leg for her. She had managed to make the hut inviting, with handwoven rugs covering the floor and hanging on the walls, and flowers planted in fat gourds and cracked dishes. Even broken window shutters had been used, fashioning a screen around the straw-stuffed pallet where they slept at night.

Making a grand flourish, she proudly showed him each dish—beans and rice and steamed squash, and a huge strip of beefsteak that she had grilled with peppers and onions. Their normal fare consisted of tortillas and beans, and maybe a little rice and peppers, but rarely meat, and never beef.

"Where'd you get the money to pay for all this, Gisela?" he couldn't help asking in surprise. "Hell, you do damn good with what I give you, but I know you're no magician . . ."

Shrugging, she tossed back a strand of gleaming black hair, her voice light. "I traded for it. You said you missed the beef from your papa's ranch, *sí*? You did say that, *amante*?"

"Yes, I said that, but I didn't mean you had to get it for me. Ah, chica, I never meant for you to think I expected it."

"Then . . ." Her large eyes registered hurt and dismay as she stared at him. "Then you are not pleased?"

"Pleased? Of course I'm pleased, but you shouldn't have done it. Not for one night, for one meal. We could have done something else with the money you must have spent on this. Finding a cow in Matamoros now is like finding gold. Christ, chica, don't cry. I like it, I do. I just can't believe you went to so much trouble for me like this . . ."

Taking her in his arms, he kissed away her tears, soothed her with assurances that he was happy she'd cooked such a wonderful meal for him, and he would savor every bite, but only if she ate with him . . . She was so thin, like a rail, and he knew she held back on her own meals to be sure he had enough.

"I'm never very hungry," she whispered against his throat, where her tears wet the skin and the collar of his shirt, "and I only want to make you happy, *amante* . . ."

"You make me happy, *amada mía*, you do," he said in a sort of groan as she began to unbutton his shirt. He turned her face up to his, a finger beneath her chin, and kissed her, long and sweet, tasting the salt of her tears on his mouth. "Don't cry, little one," he whispered, folding her into his embrace and pressing his palm against the back of her head to hold her face next to his heart, "you make me happy."

And after they'd eaten—feeding each other the choicest tidbits—he lifted Gisela into his arms and carried her across the gay striped rugs to the little mattress behind the wooden shutters, and undressed her slowly, kissing every portion of her body he uncovered. God, she was sweet, and passionate in bed, wild and uninhibited, and if she was a bit too clinging, her sweetness made up for it.

When the night shadows were long, and moonlight threaded through the small open window above their bed and the candle was low, Nick stirred enough to look down at her. She was half-asleep, damp from their lovemaking, the rough wool blanket a wad at their feet. He lifted a strand of her hair in his palm and let it slide free. His gaze drifted over the small room, over the neatly arranged table and benches, the rugs on the wall, and to the small chest where Gisela kept only her most precious belongings. He frowned. Her lace shawl was gone from its usual place of honor atop the chest, the shawl that she wore over her head to Mass every Sunday and on feast days. She cherished that shawl, one of the few things she'd salvaged from her former home. It came to him then, what she must have traded for the beef, and he felt suddenly emotionally deficient. Gisela's unselfish act of love only emphasized his own lack, and it was painfully obvious.

He drew a finger along the curve of her cheekbone to her mouth, and traced the outline of her lips. She stirred beneath his caress, and her eyes opened slowly, blinking a little.

"I forgot," he said gruffly. "I brought you a present, chica."

She caught his hand, gazing up at him with wide eyes. "A present? For me, Nicholas?"

He liked the way she said his name in Spanish, the silky accents sounding much more elegant to his ear than the short American version. He grinned. "Sí. For you, greedy one. A box. In my pants pocket."

Squealing with delight, Gisela scrambled up from the bed and fumbled in the dark for his pants. She found them and dug the small wooden box from his pocket. It lay in her palm, a rich golden wood not quite as dark as her skin, a peace offering and farewell gift, and he wondered if she'd realize his intent when she saw it.

"Open it," he said roughly, almost ashamed at the regret he felt. He'd known when he first saw her it was for only a little while, and he'd warned her of it then. She'd known, too, or said she did, but somehow he knew she would not remember those words now, only the fact that he was leaving her.

"Nicholas," she breathed with a little catch in her voice as she lifted a thin gold chain from the box. An intricately carved gold cross hung from the chain, and a tiny ebony chip glinted in the center of the crosspiece. Candlelight flickered over it, and the piece of jet winked in the dim light. "It's the most beautiful . . . You remembered. You remembered how on my feast day I said I had always wanted a holy cross to wear around my neck, to keep me safe because I was so alone—" Her eyes widened, and she looked up at him with her mouth a round O of shock and pain. "But now I am not alone . . . you are with me, are you not, *amante*? Nicholas . . . ?"

She threw herself into his arms and began to sob. Her naked breasts were against his bare skin, rubbing against him with each shuddering breath. Yes, she knew. She knew that he'd given her the cross to keep her safe because he would no longer be there to do it himself.

When he left the next morning, he kissed her tenderly and promised to return after noon. Her eyes were still slightly swollen from her tears, but there were no recriminations in them now, just a drenched sorrow that he found hard to bear.

She caught his hand, holding tight. The gold chain and cross hung around her neck, gleaming soft on the muted gold of the bare skin between her round, firm breasts. Her throat worked soundlessly.

"Pack our clothes, chica." He kissed her and eased his hand free of her clinging grip. "I'll be back soon for you, so be ready."

He turned, once, to look back, and she was framed in the open doorway, the white adobe walls stark around her, her hand lifted to the chain around her throat and a scared smile on her mouth. The sun went behind a cloud, casting a shadow, and she looked up, shivering. She took a step forward, bare feet puffing up tiny clouds of dust, but he only waved, determined not to indulge her fears. It would be fine. He'd take her to stay with Jose and Manuela Lopez in Galveston, and she would be happy there.

Nick was almost to the border crossing when he saw a lanky, blond-haired American leaning against the wall of a cantina. In this part of Matamoros, cantinas were outnumbered only by whorehouses, and he figured that the American was doing business in one of the establishments. But there was a strange intensity that bothered him enough to make him give the man a second look. Instinct more than recognition told Nick he'd tangled with him in the past, but he didn't remember where or how.

"Hey, Texas," the blond American drawled when Nick was almost past him, "didn't I see you at the marketplace the other day?"

"Maybe." Nick paused, his eyes narrowing slightly. He didn't like the looks of the man, or of the dark, stocky hombre with him who took up the thread of conversation, stepping close to block his path.

"Yeah, you were. Saw you with a little Mexican chili pepper. Oooee, she's a purty one. All dark eyes and hair . . . You gone and got some hot stuff, ain't you?"

"Yeah," the first man said, grinning, "we seen you with her. She looks riper than any whore I seen since I been down here. Shit. All these damn Mexicans look alike to me, and smell like pepper. Bet that little *chileña* smells good though, huh? She don't look near as old and used up as the other whores we seen 'round here lately."

Nick stood all loose and easy, letting him talk. The man had a rough look about him, tense and waiting, with a sidearm in a holster and a long, wicked knife hanging in a sheath from his belt. There was a purpose to the drift of his words, more than vulgar admiration of Gisela. He was staring at Nick narrowly, obviously expecting a fight.

Nick shrugged. "She's no *puta*. The lady is a friend."

"Yeah? She looked real friendly, hangin' on to you and all—"

"A word of advice—move on down the street. I'm tired of talking."

"No call to be unfriendly," the taller of the two said in a lazy drawl. "We're Americans like you."

Nick stepped sideways and half-turned, brushing back the edge of his coat to give him free access to his Colt. It was a deliberate act, a warning to most men. Something flashed in the man's eyes, a brief glitter under the shadow of a low-crowned hat, and it came back to Nick where he'd seen him. He pointed to him with the stock of his rifle. "A couple of years ago, you and I had a run-in when you were a sentry at Palo Alto. Corporal—"

"Pickering. Just Kiah Pickering now." He leaned forward slightly to spit a stream of tobacco juice on the ground near Nick's boot, then wiped his mouth on his sleeve, eyeing Nick with a sly smile. "I mustered outa the army. This here's my ridin' partner, Wade Tackett. Yeah, you know me. And I know you. You're Kincade—'scuse me—*Lieutenant* Kincade. You still ride with Hays?"

"Why would you want to know?"

"Thought the Texas Rangers went on back to Texas. Leastways, most of 'em did."

"You sure seem interested in my activities, Pickering." A flash of menace glittered for a moment in the pale eyes staring at him, and Nick realized that Pickering was not a man who forgave a grudge. The incident of their first confrontation obviously still rankled, though now Pickering shrugged carelessly.

"Yeah, as interested as I can git in a man who once held a knife to my throat."

While talking, Pickering edged around, and Tackett moved to the side a little. Nick shifted to keep an eye on both of them.

"Heard you Texas boys are supposed to be pretty tough," Tackett said, still grinning. " 'Take no prisoners' kinda tough, the way I hear it. Well, I'm from Georgia. We grow 'em pretty tough there, too.''

"Don't see nothing to impress me." Nick's slow Texas drawl was accompanied by an equally slow rake of his eyes and dismissing contempt.

Tackett's grin faded and he tensed, looking ugly as he let a hand drop to the butt of a pistol stuck in his belt. "Ain't lookin' to impress you, Kincade," he snarled.

Gil Garcia, who didn't ride with the Rangers but did some scouting for Taylor and often rode with Nick, emerged from the cantina then and stopped in the street, sizing up the situation. A third-generation Texan, Garcia had proven himself very valuable in any kind of situation, keeping a cool head and casual attitude. Now he grinned, but his black eyes were sharp behind a nonchalant shrug. "*Qué pasa, amigo?*"

Nick had seen him step out, but kept his gaze on the two men in front of him, shrugging a little at Gil's question. "*Apuro.*" It was trouble, all right. Pickering was drunk and mean, he figured, because he slurred his words a little, and both of them smelled like they'd been skinning polecats. Growing impatient to get this over with, he growled at Pickering, "Say your piece or pull it, but do one or the other."

Pickering stiffened. "You bastard. Think you're too good to talk to me?"

"Too choosy. Get it over with, Pickering. Draw your piece or walk."

Pickering's eyes thinned into slits, and his hand dropped downward, to the sidearm he wore up high around his waist. His fingers twitched, as if he wanted to pull it, but wasn't sure enough of his aim.

Nick's arm hung loosely at his side. He watched Pickering's face, saw his eyes lose their focus, then sharpen again, as if debating. Nick took a step back, slow and deliberate, letting a smile lift one corner of his mouth. "Go ahead. Try it. You draw first."

Gil Garcia had stepped around in a half-circle, coming up close to where Tackett stood to one side, a little behind Nick and facing Pickering. When the Georgian made a move as if to draw his pistol, Garcia stopped him, teeth flashing in a white grin beneath his thin black mustache. "No, no, I would not do that if I were you, hombre."

Giving a start, Tackett's gaze dropped to the pistol in Garcia's hand, and he shrugged. "Wasn't goin' to."

All this Nick observed with detachment. His attention was trained on Pickering. Sweat beaded the man's face and dampened his pale hair into lank strands plastered to his forehead. Nick waited, calmly and coolly, as if he had all the time in the world.

Still with his back against the wall of the cantina, Pickering flicked a glance from his companion to Garcia, and back to Nick. He licked his lips, shifted his feet, then shrugged. His arms moved slowly out to the sides, and he held up his hands, palms out and empty. "Hell, I don't know what you're talkin' about, Texas. Draw what? I ain't got no quarrel with you. Just makin' conversation."

"I don't like the subject."

"Yeah. So I see. Forget it, then. Thought a Texian who'd killed as many Mexicans as you have might think a little diff'rent, that's all." He looked again at Garcia, smiled a little, and stepped away. "Thought Rangers hated Mexicans. As soon shoot 'em as look at 'em, is what I heard. So it seemed strange that a Texian would cuddle up to a Mex, even a whore."

"You still talking?" Nick casually dropped his hand to the butt of the pistol in his belt. "My ears are gettin' tired."

Wiping a hand across his mouth and looking around at the small crowd that had gathered—mostly American soldiers and a scattering of civilians, all avidly curious at the confrontation—Pickering nodded, surly and flushed with chagrin. "I'm through. For now. Come on, Tackett. Let's go where the air's a little better."

When the two men had gone, moving down the dusty street without looking back, Nick turned to Gil Garcia with a light shrug.

"Reckon they got some bad whiskey."

Gil smiled. "Could be the sun, amigo. Bakes the brain if you ain't careful. You know those two?"

"Met the blond one a couple of years ago. More mouth than sense."

"He'll get it shut for good one day, mouthing off to the wrong man. Thought maybe it'd be today." When Nick just smiled a little, Gil asked, "Would you have risked letting him draw first?"

"It's not always the fastest man who walks away. It's the most accurate."

Gil nodded, looking thoughtful. "Those two could be dangerous. I wouldn't put it past 'em to put a bullet in your back." He paused, then grinned. "But I'd put my money on you, amigo."

"You might lose."

"I do not think so. I have ridden with you, do not forget. Come on. I'll buy you a drink in the cantina, and we will talk of pretty señoritas instead of ugly hombres, heh?"

"Not this time, Gil. I'm riding out today. Going back to Texas. I'm due some back pay, and the fort provost sent word that he's holding it, for some inexplicable reason. You still riding scout?"

"Now that the war is over, I thought about offering my valuable services elsewhere," Gil replied with the easy grin that had charmed many a female on both sides of the border. "California, maybe. Was there once, a few years ago. It's all new territory now, waiting to be taken. Ever been out there?"

"I've stayed awhile in Los Angeles. It's quiet. The sun always shines and the wind is always blowing. But that was a few years back. I hear it's grown almost as big as a town back East."

Garcia pushed his hat to the back of his head, squinting a little in the bright sunlight. "Think of that. There'd be a lot of work out there for a man, money to be made and opportunities to burn."

"Maybe, but I think I'll stick to Texas for a while. Captain Hays made me a damn good offer to ride with him, and he always seems to find enough trouble to suit me."

Garcia laughed, they shook hands, and Nick went on to the provost's office. It took longer than he'd thought it would to get his pay and sign the papers, mainly because the provost had taken up the habit of a noontime siesta, and no one could find him for a while. When the provost emerged, yawning and scratching his belly, he was taken aback to find an irate Texas Ranger waiting on him in his office. By the time Nick left, it was late afternoon, and he knew Gisela would be wondering what happened to him.

And he still had to get his horse from the fort stable. Too many times there was no place to hitch it without the risk of getting it stolen, so he left it in the army stables, a pretty far walk from the hut across the river he shared with Gisela. Late shadows stretched across the road when he finally rode toward the hut; his mount's hooves dug deep into the thick dust of the street. Only a few roads were paved, mostly those in the business district and around the church, and when it rained, the streets were nothing more than quagmires. It had been a while since it had rained, but storm clouds had been lying low on the horizon for the past day and a half, threatening rain. The wind blowing up from the gulf was warm and sticky, with a faint salt tang.

It brought something else with it, a faint drift on the wind that was all too familiar—death. He smelled it. For a long time it had been a constant presence, that smell. Only in the last few weeks had he thought he might go awhile without having it permeate everything around him, but now he smelled it again. He slowed his horse to a walk, looking around at the dark shadows filling the alleys between the adobe huts and stretching over the road and under bare tree branches. A dog howled somewhere close by, and there was a shout to silence it. Then it was still, too still and too quiet for an area that usually seethed with activity.

The late winter sun was almost gone, but where it touched white adobe walls, they gleamed brightly, like sun-bleached bones in the desert. Unaccustomed silence triggered all his alarms. He was too experienced to ignore the warning of complete silence that shrouded the adobe dwelling he shared with

Gisela. Nothing moved around the hut, save the silent crawl of sharp shadows thrown by a Joshua tree against the west wall and flat roof. Then the sun moved below the horizon abruptly, and even that movement ended.

The door was open, but no evening lamp had been lit. Inside, it was dark. The wind picked up a trailing vine and it scratched against the baked mud wall, a faint, eerie whisper. He reined in and dismounted, slowly, his tension rising. His horse snorted and danced nervously as he tied it to a wooden post in front of the hut. He knew what he'd find, somehow, when he went inside, but he didn't want to believe it.

Not even when he stepped over the threshold, found a match, and lit the lamp, did he comprehend it at first. It took a few minutes for it all to sink in, the overturned, shattered table that he'd spent all one day repairing, the smashed gourds and shredded flowers, the torn rugs, wadded up now in one corner like rags.

That was where he found Gisela, in the far corner, half off the mattress they'd shared, discarded like a used rag. She looked so small, defenseless, sprawled and broken as a child's doll. He knelt beside her and lifted her gently into his arms, rearranging her outflung arms and legs, pulling the remnants of a cloth over her naked body. Bruises marked her tawny skin in places, and one of her hands was bloody as if she'd tried to stop the assault. He knelt there, holding her. She'd been inexplicably afraid. He knew she had, yet he'd left her there. Hell, he left her every day, but this day had been different. He'd seen it in her eyes, known there was something that frightened her beyond just his taking her away, but he hadn't stopped to listen or even to ask.

Slowly, he drew his fingers along the curve of her cheek. Her lashes were long, shadowing her face, and he could see tear marks through a fine film of dust on her skin. Iron bands constricted his chest, and he sucked in a deep breath, realizing that he must have been holding it, unwilling to breathe the smell of death that was already heavy and sweet in the small hut.

Sweat drenched his shirt despite the cool air of evening,

clammy against his skin. Nick staggered to his feet, still holding Gisela in his arms, unable to put her down. He saw then that the rag he'd pulled over her was what was left of her skirt, the bright-patterned cotton that had swayed so enticingly around her hips and legs. It hung around her in shreds now, draping down to flutter against his legs. He didn't see her camisa anywhere. Grimly, he studied the small, shadowy interior of the hut, silently filing each clue to who might have done this to her. Who would have harmed her? She bothered no one, mistrusting everyone, and he knew she wouldn't have let strangers too near.

He forced himself to put her on the mattress finally. She was so cold now in his arms, his hot-blooded, passionate little temptress, teasing and coy and sweet and loving all at the same time. Her coarse, silky black hair was matted in places, still wet and sticky, and he pulled it clumsily around her face, combing it with his fingers into neat strands. Then he saw the marks on her neck, red and raw, as if something had been scraped across her skin. Something like—a chain.

The necklace he'd given her was gone. He looked around for it on the hard-packed dirt floor, but it wasn't there. Whoever had done this had taken her necklace, the necklace he'd just given her to keep her safe. The only thing of value she owned . . .

His mouth tightened, and the cold knot inside him ignited into a blazing fire. He would find out who had done this, and they would pay with their own lives.

Nick swore it to her, silently, standing over her while the numbness he'd first felt altered to cold, lethal promise.

The anger didn't lessen when he interrogated the villagers and learned that two men had come to the hut after he'd gone, both of them Americanos, one tall and blond and the other shorter, stocky.

"Señor, forgive me," one of the villagers, a frail old mestizo with shaky hands and a stooped back, said in a quavery voice. "I did not try to stop them. We heard her cries, but—we were afraid."

Fear he understood; inaction was beyond his comprehension.

"I'm sorry, Kincade," the captain in charge of the army post at Fort Brown said when he demanded her killers be arrested, "but there's nothing we can do. We're turning over all authority back to the Mexicans, and after all, she was a Mexican citizen, not one of ours. Let the local police handle it."

"It was Americans who killed her, Captain." Nick was leaning back against the wall, his arms crossed over his chest; some of the coldness he felt inside wove itself into his voice, and he noted the captain's nervous fidgeting through narrowed eyes. "Pickering and Tackett. Army deserters. You're bound to have some jurisdiction there."

"Yes, yes, when we find them. But Matamoros is across the river in Mexico, and this is Texas. Even if we had Pickering and Tackett here now, Mexico would have to file papers to extradite them, and I just don't think any of that's going to happen. Look, I sympathize with you, but—"

"Don't." Nick straightened slowly. His eyes raked over the army captain with contempt. "I don't need your sympathy. Save it for Pickering and Tackett."

"Kincade—"

"Save it, Captain."

Nick had wheeled around and started for the door when it opened after a quick, discreet knock. A man stepped inside, dressed in a natty suit and holding a hat, a faint smile on his mouth. He closed the door gently.

"Lieutenant Kincade, I presume?" he said, eyeing Nick. At Nick's nod, he indicated a chair in front of the desk. "Sorry to intrude, but I've not much time and this is important. If you will sit for a moment, and—"

"I'm on my way out." Nick started to brush past him.

"Before you go, Kincade, I've some papers for you from Colonel Hays," the man said, and held out a folded sheaf. "Read them, please."

It took more patience than he'd thought he had left to read

the papers, then he wished he hadn't. He looked up. "You're Roy Martin?"

"Yes, I am, a marshal for the federal government, as the papers state." Martin turned to the captain. "If you don't mind, I'll need to use your office for confidential government business for a few minutes, Captain."

The captain blinked slightly, looking startled, then jerked his head in a nod. "Certainly." He shot Nick a quick glance, then left the room, shutting the door behind him with unnecessary force.

"The captain seems a bit put out," Martin said, the bland smile still on his rather narrow mouth as he walked to the desk and sat behind it. The chair creaked slightly, and he leaned back, regarding Nick steadily over his steepled hands. "What do you think of the government's offer, Lieutenant?"

Nick tossed the papers to the desk and shrugged. "I'm not interested."

"Really. That's too bad." The smile grew a little tight. "You come highly recommended by Colonel Hays. He says you're his best man."

"I'm flattered. But I'm still not interested. I've got my own business to tend right now."

"Ah yes. The unfortunate murder of that young lady— Gisela Perez, I believe was her name."

Nick's eyes narrowed. "What do you know about that?"

Martin shrugged, his rather colorless eyes studying Nick as he said without inflection, "More than you do at this point."

"All right—you've got my interest."

"Good. Then perhaps we can make a deal, Lieutenant Kincade. Think about it. It's a proposition that can get us both what we want."

"Just what is it you think I want?"

"Pickering and Tackett." Martin smiled. "I happen to know they left Corpus Christi this morning on a steamer. Care to hazard a guess as to their destination?"

"Somehow," Nick said grimly, "I've a feeling they're headed to California." He looked down at the papers, frowning. Silence stretched, and when he looked up at Martin again, he saw that Martin fully expected him to comply. Shaking his head, he shrugged. "I can find them on my own, Mr. Martin. I don't need your help."

"Not to find them, no. But even as a Texas Ranger, your territory is limited, Lieutenant. Killing them outside your jurisdiction would be murder, as I'm sure you must know. However, there is a way you can accomplish your goals, and I can accomplish mine. One hand washes the other, so to speak."

"I'm no goddamn spy," Nick retorted. "I don't have the patience for it."

"Lieutenant, have I asked you to spy? I merely need your connections to gather some information for me, a little polite listening and conversation. This is an offer that I'm afraid you must seriously consider."

There was more than a mere plea or suggestion in his tone, and Nick stared at him narrowly. "And if I refuse?"

"Ah, that would not be in your best interests, I'm afraid. There are those of my superiors who do not look kindly on a man unwilling to serve his country in a capacity of which he is more than capable. There could be a court-martial, or worse."

"You seem to forget I'm not in the U.S. army."

"That could be altered with a few strokes of pen and ink, Lieutenant. Please—don't misunderstand. I'm not threatening you, only appealing to your patriotism."

Nick didn't misunderstand. He understood very well, and knew that a refusal would bring unpleasant consequences. He didn't like being threatened. But if he refused, he'd most likely end up either in jail or dead, as Martin implied, and Pickering and Tackett would get away with murdering Gisela.

He thought about it, about what Martin wanted him to do. Patrick Ryan, suspected of selling munitions to the enemy, had gone back to California; the men he wanted were headed there. Under the guise of renewing an acquaintance with Ryan, he could hunt Pickering and Tackett, while acquiring the information Martin wanted.

How neatly their goals coincided. If he didn't know it was

impossible, he'd think the bland-faced man staring at him so guilelessly had arranged it all.

What the hell. Like Martin said, one hand washes the other, and if he was going to be involved, he would get the best damn deal he could.

"If I agree," he said softly, holding Martin's gaze, "then there are a few details I want specified."

"Of course, Lieutenant." Martin leaned forward, smiling. "I'm certain we can work out a mutually beneficial arrangement . . ."

Part
Two

Four

California
July 1848

Fog wisps curled in tattered shreds around the clumsy steamer, blending with smoke from the tall stacks. Along the shoreline, gauzy mist-shrouds clung in concealing streamers like low-lying clouds. Victoria Ryan leaned against the starboard rail. Oh, the long journey was almost ended, and she was *glad*, for she was so weary of traveling, and now she was here and the mist was so thick, obscuring her first sight of Monterey.

But, gradually, the smudged shoreline grew more distinct as the steamer chugged near land, and she recognized Point Pinos, the headland at the south entrance to Monterey Bay. Pine trees speared the sky, becoming more visible as the sun rose higher and slowly burned off the mists. Familiar shapes gradually appeared through the mist as if by magic. The wide mouth of the bay stretched from Point Pinos to Año Nuevo at the north, with the town of Monterey crouched in the narrow bend of land along the southeast shore.

Clutching the rail with both gloved hands, she strained to see. In the center of town was the open square, the presidio, glistening in the growing light. Four lines of single-story plastered buildings surrounded the square that was dotted with a half-dozen cannon. It should look more familiar than it did, with its red-tiled roofs and white-plastered walls, the tall green pines that spiked the sky in feathery spires twisted by constant winds.

Yet it all seemed so changed. As she was.

She looked down at the tiny bulge beneath the elegant kidskin glove on her left hand. A ring, with minute diamond chips and a small amethyst. Peter Gideon had given it to her two nights before she'd left Boston, a major expenditure for a minister. And when she returned, as she certainly would now, she'd be his wife. *Wife.* She shivered. The wind was brisk and biting coming off the bay; she looked toward the rocky curve of land, blinking away the burn of tears summoned by the wind. It had been so exciting, so . . . unexpected despite her hopes and daring schemes, that at first she hadn't known what to say.

Peter had. If she closed her eyes, she could still hear the echo of his words:

"My dear Miss Ryan, I realize this is impetuous and quite likely rash of me, but I find that I cannot bear your departure unless I know that you will one day return. Say you will. Say you'll come back to Boston when your father has recovered from his illness. Promise to return to me."

Relieved and gratified, not only by the fervent words but by the pale glitter in his eyes, she'd paused to savor her victory, and apparently he'd misread her delay. Grasping her hands so hard she'd gasped, he'd insisted she promise to return to him.

And she had promised. As soon as Papa was better, and no longer needed her in California, she would return to Boston. To the man she loved. Yet, despite her triumph, she'd let a nagging disappointment cloud her joy. Silly, really, but she'd put up her face for Peter's kiss, anticipating a passionate, crushing embrace, and he had brushed her cheek with his lips and murmured his gratitude that she had accepted his proposal.

It had been deflating. She'd felt as if water had been dashed in her face, then immediately scolded herself for being a wanton. He was, after all, a minister, and obviously had much more sense of propriety than she had. He only wanted to spare her gossip, and when they were married, he would hold her as a husband held his wife. She was confident of it.

Yet, somehow, she'd found herself expecting more from him, a kiss that would shake her to her toes, an embrace that would impart his true feelings. Unwillingly, she found herself remembering the kiss she had received almost three years before in a waterfront tavern, and the tall dark man whose face was only a blur now. *His* kiss had shaken her, left her trembling and limp, aching for something without even knowing what it was. It had been a terrifying kiss, so perhaps it was best that Peter's kisses be more sedate and proper. Yes, of course it was. After all, there was a vast difference between real life and the shivering passion of fiction, as everyone knew.

Except for Sean.

Her cousin's irate predictions and sarcastic words still stung when she recalled them: "I can't believe you want to marry that priggish old maid," he'd stormed. "Can't you see the obvious, Tory? All his passion is in his rhetoric. He won't have any to spare for you, and you'll wither away without that kind of love—"

"I hardly think this is the sort of conversation we should be having, Sean Patrick Ryan," she'd said coldly. "And what would you know of love? Your idea of it seems to be tipping the maids behind closed pantry doors . . ."

"Not fair." Blue eyes were accusing when he looked at her, and filled with frustration. "It isn't the same thing at all and you know it."

Fairness demanded that she agree, but she'd added a qualifier: "All right, so it isn't—but neither is comparing Peter's passion for his work with his love for me."

In the end, neither of them had compromised his stand, and when she'd boarded the ship that would bring her to California, there had still been constraint between them, which she hated.

The faint barking of sea lions in the rocks along the coastline penetrated the loud chug of steam engines and the rush of wind. Salty sea spray shot up and over the rail, and Tory took refuge behind a bulkhead to shield herself.

She was the only one above deck this early today, even with the coastline in sight. Most of the passengers were sailing on to the Yankee settlement of Yerba Buena, called now by its mission name of San Francisco, where gold had just been discovered on the nearby American River. Space aboard the steamer was limited, for men frantic to get to the gold fields had bribed, stolen, and almost forced their way aboard at every stop. In May, news had leaked out about a huge gold strike at a place called New Helvetia, or more usually now, Sutter's Fort. As word got out, more and more were coming to California with visions of wealth blinding them.

Gold. Few were immune to the lure, it seemed, and she'd spoken with a number of passengers who were certain they would soon be rich beyond their wildest dreams. Only one or two of the passengers had been entertaining: an older gentleman from France, who was delighted to allow her to practice her schoolroom French on him, and a young army lieutenant named Dave Brock, who was traveling to San Francisco. Not for gold, but to visit his sister who was there with her husband, he'd said, smiling slightly.

After the harrowing riverboat trip and mule train across the isthmus of Panama to the California coast, where she caught the steamer bound for Monterey, she had been grateful for a brief stop at the port of Los Angeles. There she disembarked, going ashore in a small boat, and allowed Lieutenant Brock to escort her on a promenade along the beach, ignoring her maid's remonstrances that she was betrothed. Silly Colette. A stroll along a crowded beach was hardly compromising, and it wasn't at all as if she'd forgotten Peter, she just enjoyed the art of flirtation. She was still young, after all, and enjoyed the glances of admiration she received, the gallant words and pretty bouquets of flowers from hopeful men, even though it was all behind her now. Soon she would realize her ambition and become Peter Gideon's wife—enjoying a life of placid domesticity, no matter *what* Sean thought.

Most days had found her walking the upper deck, preferring even crowded decks to the stuffy confines of her cabin. All the while, Colette, who was rather flighty but quite light-hearted and gay most of the time, clung to her bunk in their cabin, moaning about *mal de mer*. Well, it was almost over. Before long, they'd be on land again with solid ground beneath their feet. Then Colette would cease the almost constant whine of the past weeks and remove her head from a bucket, and life would be bearable again, ending a journey of over two months.

As she'd predicted, Colette's infirmity disappeared shortly after the diligencia carrying them up to the sun-drenched streets of Monterey turned toward the city limits. It was a beautiful day, though a bit windy and cool, and everything was so bright it hurt the eyes.

Red tiled roofs gleamed in the bright air—so many now!—vivid contrast to the white plastered walls of the houses set in jeweled green plots of grass. The wind was a softer breeze, chasing away the more disagreeable smells of the harbor. Long rows of warehouses filled with new and curing cow hides crowded the harbor on each side of the presidio. American sailors called the hides California banknotes, referring to their value as being almost like legal tender—and there were so many stored hides that when the wind was blowing in the right direction, there was a foul odor to the air. Thankfully, the stench faded as they left the harbor behind.

"It is so beautiful!" Colette clapped her hands together; her French accent was still heavy, but her English was getting much better, Tory thought, smiling a little at the maid's glee. "But look at the flowers, mademoiselle. It is like the south of France, where the so-beautiful sun shines all the time, and never is there the cold snow like in Boston."

Tory turned her face up to the wind, not minding at all that the loose ends of her bonnet sash whipped behind her with small popping sounds like streaming banners. She *had* for-

gotten just how balmy the air could be here, with bright pop-
pies strewn across meadows and fields, and sea grasses
bending gracefully in the wind like tiny dancers. Beyond, the
hills were fragrant green with tall pines, cedars, and firs. And
as they passed—the diligencia jolting along roads that were
newly paved in places but still little more than rutted tracks
in others—their driver pointed out the new Custom House,
which had been completed only two years before, and Colton
Hall, which, it was hoped, would soon house California's
Constitutional Convention, the first to be convened since California became a territory of the United States.

This was all so new, but, of course, there were clear frag-
ments of memories that stood out sharply in her mind, and
she was delighted when the diligencia passed the shop in the
marketplace where Papa used to take her and Diego on special
days to purchase confections wrapped in paper, sticky and
sweet, leaving her with a messy face so that Tía Benita would
fuss and scold them all when they returned to the hacienda.

Tía Benita—the title of aunt was just courtesy—was she
still tending Mama and taking care of all the details of the
hacienda? Tory was ashamed, but she had not asked about
her in a long time, yet had thought about her occasionally,
and then always with fondness. Each Christmas, Tory had
selected a small gift for her, a bottle of special scent, or per-
fumed powder, and, once, a beautiful shawl of Irish lace, but
Tía Benita had faded from her mind as had everything else
about California. Now it was coming back to her in bits and
pieces, and for the first time, she felt a sense of rising excitement.

It was only for a little while, after all, until Papa recovered
from his illness, and then she would return to Boston and
Peter. This separation from Peter was probably good for both
of them, for he would realize how much he missed her, and
she would be able to tell Papa personally of her upcoming
marriage. The betrothal had happened so recently, there had
not been time to write Papa; indeed, it had been his letter
summoning her home that had prompted Peter's declaration.
Would Papa object to her betrothal? Surely, he wouldn't, for

after all, Peter was *quite* suitable, and even Uncle Seamus agreed that being wed to a minister who spoke so eloquently and was becoming so well-known in Boston was an excellent choice. It bothered her only a little that Uncle Seamus had gently pointed out a few minor details, such as the fact that Reverend Peter Gideon was not very well off financially, and that being wed to him would mean she would have to learn to be more *frugal* than she was accustomed to being. But at least Aunt Katherine had seemed more pleased by the news, saying that she knew Victoria would be a beautiful bride.

The diligencia rocked suddenly, jolting them, and the driver said something that sounded like an apology for hitting the hole in the road, and pointed ahead of them with his whip. Tory strained, and her heart suddenly leaped. The hacienda spread before them, nestled in a grove of pine trees and spreading oaks, and behind it, rising up a hill, vineyards dotted the landscape. Sunlight glinted from the red-tile roof, and the white-plastered walls glowed with a muted luster behind climbing vines heavy with tiny blue flowers. Buena Vista.

Home.

There, where the front courtyard was fragrant with hibiscus and bougainvillea that Papa had planted, she had played as a child, pretending to serve tea from English bone china to any guest indulgent enough to pause for a moment's play. And in the garden at the far side of the house, there were swings for her and Diego, ropes suspended from a thick-limbed oak at just the right height. Usually, it was Tía Benita who had pushed the swings for them, or sometimes Papa, but never Mama. On the rare occasions Mama left the shadowed confines of her room to come out, she never ventured beyond the tiled patio in the back to the gardens outside.

But it was when the diligencia stopped in front of the hacienda and she was welcomed inside by a delighted Tía Benita, that Tory felt as if she had truly come home. Tears of joy flowed down Tía Benita's broad, unlined face, and she was proudly wearing the shawl of Irish lace Tory had sent her, exclaiming that there had never been a more beautiful gift. There was a flurry of excitement, with faces she'd forgotten appearing to greet Tory, new acquaintances made, and a few reminiscences, and after the first stir of arrival had faded, Tía Benita took her to her father's room.

He was lying in bed, sunlight washing over him, a counterpane across his legs and propped up on fat pillows against the tall, carved headboard. Smiling, he held out his arms, and she rushed to him across the woven straw mats and tiled floor, suddenly so glad she had come.

"Papa," she said, choking slightly on unexpected tears, "I'm home."

"So I see, lass." He patted her clumsily on the back, his fingers reaching up to stroke her head, dislodging her fashionable hat and loosening her hair. "I've made a mess of your bonnet, I'm afraid," he murmured, and she sat down, wiping at the tears on her cheeks and smiling.

"It doesn't matter." He looked so much the same, only older; there were lines and creases in his face that hadn't been there before, but the same bright blue eyes gleamed at her from beneath bushy brows that had gray hairs mixed in with the red. His hair was still thick, though liberally streaked with gray, but age sat on him now, when the last time she'd seen him he'd been robust and hearty. But he was familiar Papa.

In a short time, it was as if they'd never been separated these years, and Tory found herself laughing at his wry comments over the gold strike that had depopulated Monterey, as well as political issues that hadn't seemed to change much even under the new government.

"There are still corrupt officials, still a lack of funds for building streets, yet always enough money to pay politicians," he said, shaking his head. "If I wasn't so damn weak, I'd run for office myself. Could do a better job than the idiots they've elected now, but my legs don't always work properly."

"You wrote of being shot, but that was so long ago, two years or more. Why are you having trouble again?"

"According to my doctor—who's more charlatan than anything else—the bullet moved. I was shot during the first battle of the war, and they never got it out, since it was a field hospital and medicine was limited. It lodged near my spine. I've carried it two years, and I've been lucky till now.''

"Battle? But your letter said—weren't you shot in a duel in New Orleans? Papa, I don't understand . . .''

Smiling wryly, he looked faintly embarrassed. "I probably did write that. I didn't want to worry you at the time. But I wanted to make extra money, maybe strike up a deal with the army for supplies, as I made a lot of profit on leather and beef, so I left New Orleans and went to Point Isabel. While I was there, the fighting started not far away, and I got too curious for my own good. Wanted to watch the battle, because the Mexicans had started bombarding Fort Brown just up the river. I got careless, and the next thing I knew, I was lying in a ditch, left for dead.''

She shuddered. "Papa, you should have told me. All this time, I thought it was only a minor wound from a silly little duel, not something serious like this. I didn't know—'' She stopped, flushing guiltily at the memory of her reluctance to come home. She really could be selfish at times. Sean was right. He always teased her, half-serious, and told her that as long as things went her way, she was the most charming female alive, but God help anyone who crossed her. But was she really that selfish? After all, she'd come home, when she'd wanted badly to stay in Boston with Peter.

Smiling, Patrick said, "*De nada, hijita de mi corazón.* Except for occasional lapses, I am fine. And glad to have you home again, where you belong. I've missed you. And so has your brother. Diego is with your uncle, Don Sebastian, in Los Angeles, but they should be back in a week or two. With the gold strike clogging all the steamers, we weren't quite certain when you would arrive, and there were important matters that must be tended. When you've settled in, there are a few old acquaintances who are anxious to renew friendships with you, so you should soon be very content here. Ah, and when Diego returns, I have a wonderful surprise for you. I'm sure you will be very pleased.''

"A surprise? Tell me now. I love surprises.''

"When it's the right time,'' he said, chuckling, and refused to tell her more, even when she pretended to pout. "You are happy to be here, aren't you, Victoria?" He reached out to take her hand and squeeze it in one of his.

She was dismayed at how cold his fingers were. "Of course, Papa. I look forward to seeing everyone again. It's been a long time."

Ramon, Patrick's manservant, appeared in the doorway, reminding Don Patricio that he must rest. Tory leaned over the counterpane to kiss Papa and promised to return soon. "We'll visit more later. I don't want to tire you out my first day back."

She went to her old room, where she'd slept as a child, and Colette had already unpacked her trunks and put things away. Tía Benita came to the doorway, and said that her mother was resting now but planned to attend the evening meal in the formal dining room. "She gets up a bit more often now," Tía Benita said, "but is still so frail and delicate that she must rest a great deal."

It came as no surprise, and Tory wasn't disappointed but did feel a certain distant sadness. Mama was still a ghost, a nonentity. There were times she wondered if her mother had ever felt the same joy she felt at the prospect of getting married. Had she been excited, with a breathless rush of anticipation when a certain young man smiled? Did she love Papa at all, or had the detached, impersonal relationship between them slowly evolved into what it was now? There was no one to ask, for Tía Benita would never answer questions like that, and she couldn't bring herself to ask Papa. Mama, of course, was too remote a figure to approach with such impertinent queries. Even though Mama had a brother, Don Sebastian, he was not the type of man one could ask questions. Her grandfather, the alcalde, was dead now, and her grandmother was so old she never left her bed in the mission of San Carlos, even for special occasions.

Tory hadn't allowed herself to consider it before, but now she wondered how Papa would feel, knowing his only child was getting married so far away. It had never been said aloud, but she'd always known he expected her to return to Monterey one day to stay, to live at the hacienda with a husband and children. What would he say when she told him about Peter? She looked down at Peter's ring on her finger, and slowly slipped it off. Later. There would be time later to tell Papa, when he was stronger. Now she would put the ring in the carved Chinese puzzle box Papa had given her on her feast day when she was eight, a brightly colored lacquered series of tiny drawers and hidden springs. It would be safe there, tucked out of sight, so no one would ask questions.

When the time was right, she would tell him.

CRSD

Five

Dinner was a silent affair that evening, with Papa sitting at one end of the long, dark, Spanish oak table, drinking too much wine—something Tory had not known him to do before—and, surprisingly, Mama at the other end, a silent, unsmiling ghost, barely illuminated by a tall branch of candles. Perhaps she would have been beautiful if she smiled—miniatures of her when she was young portrayed a lively exuberance and laughing eyes—but Paloma Montoya y Ryan kept a grave countenance. Somber brown eyes regarded her husband and daughter with distant, polite attention, as if she were on her way somewhere else but was too courteous to leave abruptly. Paloma's reply to any question was a faint monosyllable, concise and brusque. Tory wondered if Mama even knew or cared that her only daughter had been away so long.

And then she wished she didn't feel so empty, so forlorn, every time she thought about it.

Tory tried to carry the conversation, but the burden was so taxing, that when the meal was over she had a headache, and she made her excuses not to linger in the parlor, where Papa was expecting a guest. Another one of his boring business acquaintances, she was certain, and pleaded weariness from her journey.

"Of course," Papa said, smiling a little, "I did not think. You must be exhausted. There will be time for you to fulfill the duties of a hostess later." He glanced toward Paloma, who had risen from her chair and was already gliding from the room, a dark, silent shadow, indifferent to anything around her, and his eyes grew a little hard. "God knows, Buena Vista needs a proper hostess."

Rather anxiously, Tory bit her lip, glancing toward her mother's empty chair. "I shall stay if you like, Papa. I am not that tired, truly I'm not."

"No, no. It is not as if this is an affair requiring formality. It is a business matter, and my guest would hardly interest you, I am certain." He smiled slightly, a conspiratorial gleam in his eyes. "I hope to sell him that property up in the mountains."

"Not the barren hill that won't even support a goat, much less a cow?" Tory's mouth curved. "Do you think he'll really buy it?"

"If it is presented in just the right way, I think he will. Now go, do not worry your pretty head with such matters on your first day back."

Gratefully, Tory retreated to her room, where Tía Benita brought her a soothing potion to drink.

"It will help you sleep, niña." Tía Benita smiled a little anxiously.

"Thank you. Please set it down on the table, and I will drink it in a moment." She motioned to the heavy, carved rosewood table at the foot of the bed. Candles burned in branched wall holders, and moonlight streamed through the open doors leading out onto the patio off her room. A cool breeze wafted inside, stirring the draperies. Tía Benita fussed about the room a moment and gave Colette a few instructions, frowning at the girl's insolent stare, then left after bidding Tory good night.

"Good night." Tory managed a smile, feeling a little guilty.

Colette unlaced her gown, then helped her into a silk dressing gown that Papa had sent her from New Orleans. Seated in front of the dresser mirror, she stared at her reflection while Colette brushed out her hair. Her face was hazy in the candlelight, and pale beneath her loose tumble of dark hair, making her look more like a mirage than flesh and blood. Maybe those two old Boston harridans were right: She did look like a gypsy, with high cheekbones and full lips, and her hair all around her face, wild and unruly, defying comb or ribbon most of the time, copper-streaked in the sunlight. In the dim light, her eyes looked almost black, and there was a faint quiver at the corners of her mouth that had nothing to do with weariness.

How silly she was being, to think things would have changed so greatly while she was gone. They hadn't. Not the things that mattered. Not the things that should have changed . . .

When Colette started to braid her hair into a night plait, she stopped her. "I won't need you anymore tonight, Colette. You are free until morning, if there is anything you wish to do."

"*Oui, merci, maîtresse.*" Colette looked faintly surprised, but gave a characteristic Gallic shrug and, pausing only to retrieve her wrap from a chair by the door, let herself out.

Alone, unsettled, Tory wandered out onto the patio. Streamers of moonlight flickered through the tree branches overhead, tiny, silvery shafts that gleamed on the smooth, worn paving stones beneath her bare feet. Her silk dressing gown shifted around her legs, feeling cool and soft and sensuous. It was quiet, peaceful, almost too still. In the distance she heard a dog bark, a burst of laughter, and a few chords on a guitar. The servants, no doubt, in their small cottages situated on the grounds. When they were through with their daily tasks, they would frequently gather at night and play music and dance by the light of a bonfire. Not the more stately dances of Spain that Tory's dancing teacher had taught her, but peasant dances, alive and spirited.

She could remember sneaking from her room as a child and going down to listen, wanting to be a part of them. One night a young girl her own age named Rosita saw her in the bushes and pulled her into the group, laughing and encouraging her to join them. She had, feeling silly at first, and awkward, but soon she had felt the tempo of the music and had begun to dance. It had been exhilarating, a release of energy and spirit, letting her bare feet stamp out rhythms in the dust, tossing her hair and swinging her skirts high above her knees. She'd gone back again and again, reveling in the freedom, in the hot-blooded tempo of the jarabe, jota, and fandango. No one had told, or said anything about the patrón's daughter dancing into the night with the peons. The feeling of freedom hadn't lasted long after Tía Benita had discovered her, and she'd not been allowed to return, though at night, she'd often stood on her patio and listened to the wild, tempestuous music, dancing alone, reckless and willful and rebellious.

It felt odd to think of herself as she had been then, a lonely, unruly child. She'd felt so alone, even with her brother. Diego's world was vastly different from hers, as he was allowed many activities and much more freedom. He attended classes with an old Spaniard who tutored boys from families with enough money to pay, and enjoyed male pursuits such as riding and fencing, coming and going as he pleased even as a youngster. Her world had been much different, composed of needlework—which she detested—and music lessons, dancing with courtly grace, and lectures on the proper deportment of young ladies.

All had changed when she went to Boston. It was a different world entirely, with Aunt Katherine being such a proponent of developing young people's minds. Being among her lively cousins had given her the freedom she would never have had in California. Eventually, she'd learned to curb the more impulsive side of her nature. Though there were times, as now, when an overwhelming need came over her to do something to ease the restless urgings that prodded her. Perhaps Rosita was out in the garden dancing uninhibitedly, her skirts flying up over her knees and her hair sailing out like a black cape . . .

She was so restless, her earlier weariness fading in a rush

of energy. The music from the barrio beckoned, violins and guitars, a siren's song of temptation, and she yielded to the lure.

Not bothering with proper undergarments, she changed into an old cotton skirt she found in the tall, heavy armoire, and a light camisa, peasant-styled, like the women of the village wore. A rebozo hung on a peg, long fringe hanging loosely, and she pulled it around her shoulders. She left her hair loose and slid her feet into soft black slippers, then slipped out through the wrought-iron gate in the patio, feeling rebellious and free.

It was dark where the moonlight couldn't pierce tree branches and brush, and the once-familiar garden paths became a maze in the shadows. A heady fragrance of night-blooming flowers teased her, and the music beckoned her farther along the gravel path. Paving stones had been set into the gravel in places, and she caught her foot on one before realizing it was there, crying out at the sharp pain in her toes.

She bent and removed her shoe to rub her throbbing foot, kneeling on the paving stone that was still warm from the heat of the day.

"What are you doing down there, niña?"

Tory's head jerked up and she found herself staring up at a man silhouetted against moonlight, his broad frame a dark shape that almost blended with the black lace of the bushes. Too startled by his sudden appearance to reply, she stared at him, blinking a little in the dim light.

"Just what I like," the man drawled softly, "a woman who doesn't talk too much. You're a little late, but you'll do just fine."

A small frown knit her brow, and Tory realized that he thought she was someone else; but before she could inform him of his mistake, he had reached out and pulled her up, his hands warm and strong and hard on her wrists.

Moonlight barely penetrated the thick canopy of leaves overhead, but a small, thin reed of light played over rakishly slanted brows and eyes that were a subtle amber-gold, light-tricked and gleaming. His gaze raked over her, bold and assessing and insolently slow, and he smiled suddenly, his teeth a quick flash of white.

"He didn't lie—you're as beautiful as Venus. Maybe there will be some unexpected dividends in this transaction after all."

Still holding her wrists firmly in his strong hands, he pulled her forward unceremoniously, not giving her a chance to protest or rectify his obvious error as he kissed her. Tory gasped in outrage—a mistake, because he took immediate advantage, probing her open mouth with his tongue, shocking her.

She jerked away from him and he let her, but he put out an arm to block her retreat. His shirt was open, stark white against shadow, hanging loosely from broad shoulders. Tory had the impression of dark hair and skin, thick ropes of muscle, and lazy grace as he stepped closer, so close she could feel the animal heat emanating from him. She took an involuntary step away, and backed into a broad tree trunk. He followed, a fluid step, swift and intent, his lazy drawl altering to a more cynical clip.

"Am I going too fast for you? Did you expect wine and conversation first? Tell me, for I regret that I haven't been informed of the proper etiquette here."

Too unsettled to do more than glare at him, she looked pointedly at his arm where it brushed against her breasts, then up at his face again, tilting her head back because he was so tall. Moonlight filtered through the tree branches, dimly lighting his features. Really, he had the most wicked eyes, veiled by impossibly long eyelashes, and his mouth was tucked into a mocking smile that made her fingers itch to claw deep furrows into that lean, square-jawed face. Impossible, but he looked familiar somehow, when she knew she had never before met this man. She would not have forgotten . . .

"Oh no," he said when she tried to push his arm away, "not without an explanation. If I'm being rejected, I would like to know why."

His gaze moved over her languorously, obviously noting the way her skirts draped over hips that had no concealing petticoats, lingering much too long on where her breasts pushed against the thin cotton blouse, before moving finally to her face, studying her. Her rebozo had fallen back and was draped from her arms, covering nothing. Aware of how she must look at this moment, like one of the servant girls instead of the patrón's daughter, she snatched the shawl up and around her, flushing furiously at his bold scrutiny.

Outrage finally loosened her tongue. "I hardly think you want to hear anything I might say to a *presumptuous* man like you!"

He laughed, and when she managed to twist free, he caught her and swung her back around and up against the tree trunk again. This time he leaned forward, his hands planted firmly on the tree above her head and his body pinning hers to the trunk.

"Presumptuous, am I, little beauty? You may be right. But, of course, you didn't have to come out here if you weren't willing. The fact that you're here gives me a right to presume you want to be here." His voice was soft now, a slow drawl accompanied by the increasing pressure of his body against hers, the lowering weight of him a heated persuasion on her breasts, belly, and thighs. It took away her breath, left her flushed and feeling hot inside, as if coals had been banked and were being fanned to life.

"Get . . . away . . . from me," she said through gritted teeth, shrinking back from his touch. He was so close—his face was inches from hers, so that she could almost count each individual eyelash, and she could smell the warm, masculine scent of him—heady and disturbing, and, oh God, what if he kissed her again? She tried to bring up her hands to push him away.

"Was it something I said? Or didn't say? Do you think I won't make it worth your while?" He blew softly at a tendril of hair and it trembled against her cheek, making her shiver. He smiled. "I always pay well for services rendered, little beauty, never fear. And this way is so much more convenient, don't you think? No recriminations later, no disappointment . . ."

Her face flamed with embarrassment, and she was glad it

was dark so he couldn't see it. Dear God, he thought she was a whore! One of the women her father sometimes sent to his male guests as a courtesy . . . Of all the most *infuriating* mistakes—how could he even *consider* it? Did she *look* like a prostitute? And dear Lord, must he lean against her like—like *this*? His entire body was pressed against her from his chest to his hips, unnerving and somehow arousing.

"I am *not* the girl you think I am," she got out in an embarrassingly shaky voice. She cleared her throat, glaring up at him. "You have made a very grave error, sir!"

"Really?" He gave her a thoughtful look, and turned her slightly so that moonlight illuminated her face. Then a flicker of chagrin crossed his face, followed by an impudent grin. "So I seem to have done. Your coloring is similar, but the eyes—my apologies, but you could have pointed out this error a tad earlier, you know. Unless, of course, you were enjoying my rather ardent attentions."

Because it was true, and because she had no intention of admitting it, she brought her heel down hard on his instep, and was momentarily gratified to hear his grunt of pain. Unfortunately, it didn't last. Her thin slippers were no match for his knee-high leather boots, or his reaction.

"Little bitch . . ." His hands closed on her upper arms to lift her, pushing her against the tree until she felt the rough bark press into her spine. Her face was level with his, and as he studied her, the angry glitter in his eyes faded a bit. His brow lifted, and his voice was soft. "Your reaction must mean I was right."

"You . . . you're insane," she got out, her voice much shakier than she would have liked, but there was a strange intensity in his gaze that frightened her. "Put me down."

"I will," he said, softly, "when I'm through."

There was no time to wonder what he meant. His mouth came down on hers, hot and hard, forcing her lips apart with bruising pressure. This wasn't her first kiss, but it was definitely the most aggressive. He didn't just kiss her, he possessed her. Weakness flooded her. She wanted to protest, to struggle, but nothing seemed to be working right, her arms or legs, or even her tongue. He held her pinned against the tree, both hands on her arms, his body a solid, unyielding pressure against her, and brought up his leg, wedging his knee between her thighs. Her thin cotton skirt was no barrier, and her legs parted beneath the force so that she straddled his thigh, her skirt bunching up almost to her hips.

Tory's head began to spin, and waves of dizzy heat shuddered through her. Without undergarments, her bare legs scraped against the rough material of his pants in a slow, abrasive slide. In a haze, she felt him move his hands, skimming them down her sides to her waist to hold her astride him. Dear Lord, what was he doing? No one had ever . . . A shock wave of sensation shot through her when he pulled her forward, dragging her along his steel-muscled thigh in an erotic glide that made her whimper. Blindly, her hands flew out to catch her balance, clutching at him, fingers digging into the muscles of his arm.

Nothing had ever prepared her for this, not Sean's lectures or his warnings, not even the brief glimpses she'd had of the wayward parlormaids. There was no precedent in her life for either this man's actions or her own unexpected responses. Where his hard thigh rubbed between her legs, heat radiated up and outward, ignited in the apex of her thighs like a gigantic inferno. She shuddered, and he rocked her forward again, eliciting the most exquisite tremors.

Then his hands were on her breasts, cupping them, thumbs raking over the hard little buds of her nipples through the thin material of her blouse, and the ache between her legs began to throb. Her mouth opened to . . . protest? surrender? . . . and his tongue slid inside in a sizzling exploration that shocked a moan from her. This wasn't a kiss—it was an invasion. When she would have twisted her head away, he caught her hair at the nape of her neck and held her still, his fingers tangled in the curls. Her head fell back, and all thoughts of resistance faded into something else, strange new emotions he had somehow awakened in her, emotions that made her cling to him, her hands moving up his back to his shoulders, fingers curling into the loose material of his shirt and grazing against the dark, crisp hair growing down over his collar as she kissed him back with growing intensity.

And then, suddenly, just when she thought she would truly swoon, he stopped kissing her and lifted his head to gaze at her with a faint frown. His eyes were hard, narrowed with a brittle light that made them look cold as he pierced her with a thorough glance.

"Ah yes, you are not as immune as you would like to pretend. Are you certain you are not the right girl . . . ?" His last word faded, and his head bent, his mouth taking hers again, this time swiftly and less harshly.

Then he was pushing her from his thigh to stand her upright again, his hand on her shoulder in a light brace. Reeling, she fought for control, feeling dazed. Hazy moonlight was pale, drifting in blurry streamers through tree leaves to light the path and the man staring down at her.

"Next time," he said softly, "just ask for what you want. I'm always willing to oblige a beautiful woman, even when she's not my first choice."

She blinked. Then reaction set in. Instinctively, she brought up her arm, slapping him across the cheek with her palm, and heard a satisfying crack. His head jerked slightly, and for a moment, she thought he would hit her back. Pure, murderous fury blazed in his eyes, but he didn't move.

"Don't overestimate your charms," he grated through clenched teeth. "You might not like the result."

"It's you who have overestimated *your* charms." She was breathless with anger, and amazed at her own daring. "I'd advise you to leave Buena Vista quickly, for I intend to call for the vaqueros, and they are not very tolerant of intruders."

"If that threat is intended to scare me, it doesn't. I've seen the vaqueros here."

His caustic remark made her frown, and the insolent glance he raked over her from head to toe was enraging. Her chin lifted slightly, and her eyes flashed with fury. "If I had a pistol, I'd shoot you myself!"

He grinned. "Now *that* scares me."

She opened her mouth to regale him with a less than flattering opinion of his actions, his attitude, and his morals, but the glint in his eyes stopped her. He was goading her. Why justify his expectation?

She lifted her head to say with just the right amount of contempt, "Run along, while I fetch the vaqueros. I hope the next time I see you, you're full of bullet holes."

"Bloodthirsty little cat." A corner of his mouth twitched with amusement. "Next time we meet, I may take the time to teach you a lesson."

"I cannot think of anything you could teach me." It was a parting shot, a last volley as she turned on her heel to walk away, half-expecting him to follow her.

He didn't. And when she reached the end of the path where it turned toward the house, and glanced back, he was gone. Only spears of moonlight threaded through thick leaves and across paving stones.

The entire experience left her unbearably shaky and bemused, wondering who he was and why he was at Buena Vista. A guest? She hoped not.

But later, when she lay in bed and stared into the darkness while the moonlight faded and night shadows grew paler, she couldn't stop the barrage of memories, nor could she dismiss the unfamiliar sensations he had ignited that left her now feeling a strange, restless disquiet.

She thought of Peter and his pristine kiss. It was hard to envision him holding her the way the man in the garden had, impossible to imagine Peter kissing her the way she had just been kissed. God, she'd not known that any man kissed like that, an invasion more than anything else. And—disloyally— it was hard to imagine Peter displaying any passion. But surely he would feel that way about her once they were wed, would exhibit the same kind of passion, albeit more privately. Of course he would. Despite Sean's rude comments to the contrary, Peter felt most passionately about her. And at least he was a gentleman, not rude and uncouth.

Not at all like the man in the garden. No, Peter was nothing like him. A complete opposite. And she was glad, fiercely glad.

But it didn't help that when she finally fell into a restless sleep, she dreamed of a dark-haired man with amber-gold eyes.

Six

Gil Garcia saw Nick Kincade approaching, and indicated an empty chair with a jab of his thumb. A half-full whiskey bottle stood in the middle of the table next to two dingy glasses, and cigar smoke was thick in the *pulperia*.

Nick's tall, lean good looks garnered interested glances from some of the women he passed, as usual. Women found Nick Kincade fascinating, drawn to him like moths to a flame. And they were usually burned pretty badly for their trouble. Gil had noticed that Nick was inherently selfish in his dealings with women; not cruel, just casually ruthless, using them to satisfy his own needs, bestowing careless affection, then departing before they began to cling and pout, "as women are so frequently prone to do," he'd said caustically on one occasion.

Ignoring the inviting looks from the dark-eyed señoritas who had gathered with their partners to dance on the piazza outside, Nick hooked a chair with his foot, pulled it out, and sat down across the table.

Gil lifted a brow. "What kept you so long, amigo? I was beginning to think that perhaps you had gone to join those looking for gold."

"You know I'm no prospector. I had a previous business engagement."

Gil couldn't help grinning. He was more than familiar with the usual nature of Nick's "previous engagements." "Ah, it was a sweet señorita that kept you, not business."

"You're getting nosy in your old age." Nick returned the grin. "My host insisted that I be smothered in female hospitality, so I considered it business."

"A cynical way of looking at such a profitable venture."

Nick grimaced. "Not if you'd been there. I've conducted more profitable business with an Arkansas mule trader." He rubbed a hand across his cheek, looking restless and a little wary, and his eyes narrowed slightly. "All right. What's going on, Gil?"

He smiled wryly. That was Nick. No beating around the bush, but straight out, so he answered the same way: "Pickering and Tackett are here in Monterey."

Interest flared in Nick's eyes. "I thought they'd be hellbent for Sutter's Fort. Half of Los Angeles and Monterey are up there panning for gold."

"Not those two. They're too lazy to swing a pick or stand in a cold stream with a pan. Stealing gold is more their style, I think."

Nick nodded grimly. "How did you find them?"

"I saw Tackett." Gil leaned forward, voice lowering. "He was drunk, and hooked up with a *puta*. I followed him to a hotel two streets off the presidio."

"Did you talk to him?"

"No. He didn't see me. Hard to miss him, though." He made a gesture of contempt. "*Cabrón!*"

Nick poured a drink into one of the empty glasses, then pushed the bottle toward Gil and looked up. Gil recognized that look—it was intent and vicious, with fine white lines at the corners of his mouth, and his eyes as hot and molten as lava. But Nick's tone was casual, almost indifferent: "How about Pickering? Did you see him, too?"

Gil shook his head. "No luck. Either he's already left town, or he's holed up somewhere with a woman. But wherever

Pickering is, Tackett ain't far behind. He don't piss by himself without Pickering sayin' it's all right.''

Frowning, Nick drank the whiskey, then sat back in his chair. On the piazza outside, guitar music climbed to a crescendo, and violins and castanets filled the air with a lively melody that almost drowned out Nick's soft comment: "I want both of them. Not just one."

Gil nodded agreement. He'd already thought of that, knowing that Kincade wanted both men dead. Not that he blamed him. He'd seen what the bastards had done to a sweet young girl. And he'd recognized the white-hot flare of fury in Nick Kincade's eyes as vengeance. There was a saying about the Texas Rangers, that they'd follow a man to hell for vengeance, and Gil reckoned it was pretty much the truth.

Now he said, "I told Martin about it."

"Martin. Jesus, Gil, why involve him?"

Shrugging, Gil forced himself to meet Nick's suddenly hard gaze. "He's got lots of connections. Admit it. And he wants to see Pickering and Tackett dead as much as you do— well, almost as much. Besides, he's our boss and we have to report to him."

"We report about his business, not mine," Nick said so coldly that Gil looked away.

He'd known Nick wouldn't like it, that's why he'd tried to keep it to himself. But then Roy Martin had shown up, and being the shrewd reader of human nature that he was, he had asked casually if Gil had managed to learn anything more about Pickering or Tackett. One question had led to another, and before he knew it, Gil was reluctantly admitting that he'd seen Tackett in Monterey. Roy Martin had immediately set his own sources into motion, and after that, it was all his game. As usual.

"Martin found out they were hired to work for an outfit going up to Sutter's Fort," Gil said when some of Nick's tension eased. "Claim-jumping, most likely. Hell, half the American sailors in the navy have jumped ship, and left 'em floating in the bay like ghost ships. Once the East Coast hears about the strike, California will be flooded with prospectors."

He shrugged. "It ought to be easy enough to find those two when we want 'em. We can just look in the nearest gold field."

"If we don't lose them in the crowd." Kincade's hand clenched into a fist on the table. He stared down at his empty whiskey glass. After a few minutes, he looked up again. "I'm ready now."

Gil knew what he meant, but felt compelled to try, as he'd promised Martin he would. Why did the government agent always leave him with the dirty work? He knew how much this meant to Nick, and, dammit, he didn't blame him. He'd feel the same way if it had been his woman murdered.

"Nick," he said, a little uneasy, "Martin wants us to wait. He'll be here later, and tell us what he's got in mind, but until then—"

"I don't work for Martin on this, Gil. I'll do it my way. That's the deal."

"But Martin said you agreed to let him handle it."

Nick leaned back in his chair, balancing it on the rear legs. "Not this. Martin knows better. This isn't part of the deal. I agreed to work for them on that condition. It's a trade-off. I impose on my acquaintance with Patrick Ryan to learn what I can about his gun-running operations, and the government looks the other way when I find Pickering and Tackett. One hand washes the other, Martin said. He doesn't need to be telling me what he thinks I should do about Pickering and Tackett."

It was said quietly, and with little emphasis, but there was no mistaking the deadly intent of his words and tone. Gil took another drink, then rolled the glass between his fingers. "I still can't figure out why the government doesn't just go ahead with what they already know about his activities."

"He's not involved in just munitions, but in the old Spanish land grants. A lot of fifth-and sixth-generation Mexicans are losing their property in lawsuits that challenge the validity of the grants. Yet Patrick Ryan has increased his holdings quite a bit. Our government thinks he's buying up the old grants illegally, then selling them at quite a profit. Deeds have been falsified, but so cleverly no one has been able to prove it yet. That's why I'm to purchase land from him. To get proof.'' He shrugged and took another drink, then looked at Gil over the rim of his glass. ''Did Martin say who they were working for?''

Gil's brow lifted. He didn't have to ask who Nick meant. ''Not to me. Wonder how their new boss will feel about you killin' two of his men?''

Nick's cold smile didn't reach his eyes. ''I'll just have to find that out after it's done.''

A fiesta was planned, Tía Benita told Tory, waking her from a fitful sleep. There would be many guests and elaborate entertainment, and everyone in Monterey would be there. ''It's going to be in your honor,'' she said as she flung open the draperies, ignoring Tory's sleepy protest at the bright light, ''and shall be very gay and festive. You are to have a new gown, and the dressmaker is coming here so that you may choose the material and colors, and have your first fitting.''

Irritable at being awakened, Tory muttered something non-committal and pulled a pillow over her head. Tía Benita removed it calmly, urging her up from the bed. Ungraciously, she complied, glaring at Tía Benita.

''Really, if the fiesta is so soon, I cannot possibly have a new gown made in time, and besides, the strain of a fiesta will be too much for Papa.''

''Nonsense.'' Tía Benita began making the bed, looking back at Tory over her shoulder as she smoothed the fine linen sheets and stitched coverlet. ''It is good for him. He has been so melancholy lately. Your return has given him more energy than he's had in months. Besides, it was all planned before your arrival—even Don Mariano Vallejo is to attend! Just think, such a great man—a true Californio and a patriot, no matter what some may say—here in our hacienda. Don Patricio is honored he has accepted the invitation, and so should you be. All that is necessary now is for you to have a new gown, so be quick and drink your chocolate and eat the hot rolls I brought you, for Señora Valdez will be here in a half-hour with her assistants.''

Reluctantly, Tory allowed Señora Valdez—a small, energetic woman who spoke with quick words and fluttering movements of her hands—to show her the satin, brocade, and muslin she brought with her that morning.

''Ah, for you, señorita, I recommend this.'' Señora Valdez unrolled part of a bolt of cloth and spread it across the bed. It was a soft, lavender muslin, pastel and pretty—and very girlish.

''It's perfect.'' Tía Benita clapped her hands with delight. ''And the lace there, next to the feathers . . . sí, that one. It will set off the material—is that a watered silk there, lying next to that bolt of satin?''

Tory looked instead at a bolt still rolled tightly, and pointed to it. ''Spread that out, so that I may see.''

''Oh,'' Tía Benita said with a quick shake of her head, ''that is inappropriate for a young girl. It is not at all permissible.''

''I will be twenty-one my next birthday, and am hardly a child.'' Tory lifted a brow imperatively. ''I want to see that material.''

It was dutifully rolled out, covering the lavender muslin. Tiny metallic threads of silver shot through rich, violet satin, glinting in the light, sparkling. Señora Valdez looked up, smiling. ''It complements your so beautiful eyes perfectly—blue, sí?''

''Violet.'' Tory muttered the correction a bit ungraciously, as she was in some discomfort from the pins pricking her skin, and she'd been standing for what seemed an hour atop a stool while Señora Valdez's assistant fitted her with tapes and pins and strips of paper. She shifted uncomfortably, and the assistant muttered something under her breath as the pin heads popped off, then carefully repinned the paper at the waist.

Tory set her mouth stubbornly, tired of the fitting and the endless chatter of the women. Normally, she enjoyed selecting beautiful materials and colors, but she was tired, having turned and tossed restlessly in her bed the night before. She'd relived the scene in the garden until the sun was a faint glow on the horizon, the horrid memory haunting even her dreams. She should have made good her threat and called out the vaqueros, but she hadn't. Perhaps she should tell Papa, but she knew that in a society where an unmarried female was not allowed to leave her own chamber without a duenna, she would have to explain why she was alone in the garden instead of safely in bed, and where she was going when she'd encountered the strange man. And then she might have to explain why she had not screamed for help or called out, and she wasn't really certain what she could say. That his tongue had been in her mouth so that she couldn't? That would be inviting more trouble than she wanted to confront.

"The muslin, I think," Tía Benita was saying, disapproval lining her face with a little frown, "don't you, Doña Vitoria?"

"No. The satin. It's more suitable for a ball gown." Tory saw the quick glance Tía Benita exchanged with Señora Valdez. It reminded her again that she was no longer in Boston, but in California where the rules were very strict. Everything here was so different, and she realized irritably that ignoring the rigid rules concerning young women was futile. Why, here she was considered a spinster, for she had overheard Tía Benita bemoaning the fact only the night before, and disregarded it. She would not yield in this matter, or in anything else she considered important.

She cleared her throat and repeated: "The satin," but Tía Benita and Señora Valdez were poring over a book of sketched styles the dressmaker had brought with her.

"Feathers would be pretty here." Señora Valdez pointed to a drawing in her pattern book, "And perhaps—"

"No," Tory said, firmly. "No feathers. Silver braid for the bodice. I want the neckline cut lower, as in the new French styles, to be worn off the shoulder, with tiny puffed sleeves. And the flounces must be deep, so that the skirt will bell out gracefully, and not look like wet muslin." She smiled sweetly at Tía Benita—who gazed up at her with thunderous eyes and

lips pressed tightly in disapproval—and added, "I believe I
have some long evening gloves that will go with it very
well."

She stepped down from the stool, grimacing at the stick of
pins in her side, and ignored Señora Valdez's troubled gaze.
"Are you certain you can have it ready by the fiesta, with so
many others to make as well?"

"Yes, yes, of course. Your papa has paid most generously,
and I have three extra assistants to help me. It will be done,
just as you wish."

"Excellent. I am certain that your hard work and effort
will be very well rewarded. If the gown is as I wish, I shall
see that you are paid extra."

Señora Valdez looked extremely pleased, puffing up, and
began to clap her hands vigorously, ordering her assistant to
hurry, that they had so much to do in so little time, and Doña
Vitoria must have the most beautiful gown in all of California.

"Doña Vitoria," Tía Benita said with a little hiss of air
through the space between her front teeth, "you know I cannot allow it!"

"Forgive me, but you are no longer my nursemaid. I respect your right to object, but you must respect my right to
wear what I wish as long as it's respectable."

"Don Patricio will not consider it so respectable, I think."

"Then he will be certain to tell me of his opinion, and if
you are worried that he will blame you in any way, I assure
you that I shall tell him quite plainly that it was at my command."

Throwing up her hands, Tía Benita muttered something under her breath and shook her head, gave Tory a baleful look,
and followed Señora Valdez and her assistant to the door.

When they had gone, and her chamber was peaceful again,
Tory breathed a sigh of relief. At last. She couldn't have
borne another moment of all that fussing about with materials
and patterns. Feathers. Dear God. She'd look like an over-
stuffed peacock if Tía Benita had her way.

A soft breeze swelled out the draperies over her patio

doors, and she went outside to stand on the warm tiles and smell the summer flowers.

There was so much to think about, so much she had forgotten—and it left her feeling at loose ends and restless. With so little sleep the night before, she considered a nap, then discarded the idea. She was too wound up, too full of nervous energy to sleep. In Boston, she would have coaxed Maura or Megan into accompanying her on a sedate ride around the Commons, or even a not so sedate canter around the quad, but here, unless she wished to go into lengthy explanations of her plans, there was very little to do if she wasn't in the mood for reading or writing letters. Men had much more freedom, and it was irritating.

Diego—he should be here by now, shouldn't he? She missed him, his sweetness and even his annoying teasing. As younger brothers went, he was quite acceptable. Besides, anything would be better than being bored to tears and forced to deal with edicts that she had no intention of obeying. Muslin and feathers, indeed.

Because she was only growing more restless with nothing to do, she finally donned a broad-brimmed bonnet and walked down to the corrals. It was another balmy day, with the wind blowing soft and the sun a bright yellow ball in the sky. Old Manuel, who had been head groom since she was three, was still there, and still proud of each and every blooded horse at Buena Vista. Rather stooped now, and stiff, he escorted her through the newly built stables, with a litany of likes and dislikes peculiar to each animal, and gravely allowed her to pat their necks and feed them a bit of apple.

"I can recall my first riding lesson." She stroked the sleek neck of a tall Spanish Andalusian, a breed of horse brought from Spain over a hundred years before, and still bred and reared in California. They were well-muscled, elegant animals, ridden by Spanish royalty and prized for their conformation and the luxurious manes and tails that so frequently dragged the ground. They were beautiful, spirited horses, and she itched to ride one of them.

Now she looked up at Manuel with a faint smile. "You were so worried that I would be thrown."

Grinning, Manuel nodded. "It was the horse I worried about most, that stubborn pony your papa insisted you ride. I did not know who would win—you or the pony—for you were both too hardheaded to give way. In the end, I think you learned much about the other."

She laughed. "I remember—Poco." She gave the bay a final pat on the neck and fed him the last bite of apple, then wiped her hands on her skirt. "I should like to ride today. Do you think you can find me a suitable mount, Manuel? Not a gentle mare, but one with a bit of fire, an animal that I will truly *enjoy* riding."

If he was aware of her ploy, he did not betray it, but merely nodded. "*Sí.* I know just the one."

"Good. Then I shall be back shortly." Smiling her pleasure, she walked back to the house, passing through the grape arbor and beneath the broad, dusty leaves and new fruit. Some of the vines were as thick as her wrist, old vines planted when Buena Vista had still been a one-room house not much bigger than the cottages for the peons. Now vines covered the wooden arbors thickly, bursting with grapes that would soon be ready to pick and make into the wine that Papa sold to the merchant ships always crowding the Monterey harbor. Oak casks of wine were stacked to the ceiling in long cellars dug into the hillside below Buena Vista, waiting to be shipped.

As children, she and Diego had played in the cool gloom of the cellars that were then not so filled with casks of wine; but, of course, that had been long ago. Later, perhaps, she would visit the cellars again, where even in the worst heat of summer it would be cool and pleasant.

The prospect of an outing was exhilarating, and promised a break from what could quickly turn to ennui if she allowed it. No, she would not be submerged in the gloom of the hacienda, not when it was such a lovely day and the sun was shining and the wind blowing up from the ocean smelled so salty and exotic.

Rebelliously, she thought, I cannot allow Papa to mire me

in his plans for me, and I will *not* be Mama's replacement. I am young, and soon I will go back to Boston to marry Peter, and then I will have responsibilities.

Now, for a little while, it would be so nice to forget everything, to immerse herself in the freedom of a bright, promising future. Yes, she would go for a ride, and who knew what might happen? Something exciting, perhaps, something wonderful. There was always time later to confront reality, and it would come quickly enough once she told Papa that she did not intend to remain in California, but was going back to Boston and her betrothed. It was not an ordeal she relished facing.

So, deliberately, she put it to the back of her mind and focused instead on the promised outing, while it was still early morning and cool.

Seven

The early morning sun was barely above the flagpole in the center of the presidio, but shone in the *posado* window brightly enough to hurt Nick Kincade's eyes. He'd stayed in town last night, bunking in Gil's hotel room. Maybe he shouldn't have stayed up so late playing poker and drinking whiskey, but after the meeting with Martin, he'd been too restless to sleep. He'd won a bit of money, but felt like hell now. At least he felt better than Gil looked, and he grinned slightly. The scout looked rough, with bloodshot eyes and a three-day growth of beard, but he'd known Gil long enough to know how quick his reflexes were even when he was dog-drunk and half-asleep. He'd seen Gil come out of a dead sleep with his pistol in his hand and, with one shot, take the head off a rattlesnake as neatly as a butcher's knife.

Nick propped a booted foot atop the worn seat of a chair opposite him, and leaned back against the wall so that the angle of the sun didn't burn his eyes. "I'm not surprised that Pickering got out of Monterey this quick."

Gil looked at him a little strangely, but shrugged. "Can't say I expected it. Maybe someone tipped him off we're in town."

"How about Tackett?"

Already half-lidded, Gil's black eyes narrowed against the curl of smoke from his cigar. "He's still holed up with a plump little *puta* in that hotel I told you about. All we have to do is smoke him out."

"That shouldn't be too hard."

"Martin wants to do it."

Nick's brow rose, and he stared hard at Gil, who shifted a little, uneasily, and looked away. He should have known this would happen if Roy Martin got involved. Usually, he didn't mind when Martin took over, but it was different this time. If it was up to him, he'd confront Tackett in the shabby hotel room and get it over with, but Martin preferred finesse and at least a pretense of legality to his dealings.

"So exactly what does our illustrious leader have planned?" he drawled, and saw from the quick cut of Gil's eyes that he hadn't quite carried off the indifference he'd intended.

But Gil smiled, shaking his head. "Nothing too elaborate. With a little help from the local commandant, he's arranged for Tackett to be in the presidio just before noon. After that, it's all up to you. Oh yeah, and he's drawn up that warrant for murder, just to make it all nice and legal-like, if anybody objects."

"Who's going to complain? Tackett will be dead, and Pickering is hardly likely to stick around and protest," Nick said dryly. "It would make this a lot easier if he would. I'm not looking forward to trailing him into gold country."

"We don't know for sure that's where he's gone."

"That's where he's gone, all right. I'd bet my last dollar on it."

"Hell," Gil said, sounding disgusted, "you'd probably win that bet, too."

Nick grinned. He had a large portion of Gil Garcia's last pay in his pocket, a direct result of drawing three aces and a pair of deuces. "Come on, Gil," he said, swinging his feet to the floor with a thud and standing up. He moved to the hall door and opened it, glancing back at the sleepy-eyed Mexican. "I'll buy you some breakfast. Any man who plays poker as badly as you do deserves a free meal.''

"*Coño!*" The Spanish curse followed Nick down the narrow stairs, but Gil was right behind him.

It didn't take her long to change into a riding habit, and Tory returned to the stables within an hour. True to his word, Manuel had a fine, spirited gray mare saddled and ready. In Boston, she would have had to ride a more docile creature, and be attended by a stable boy or groom, but here, where everyone from small child to the elderly took great pride in his riding abilities, she did not intend to be escorted.

So it was quite annoying when Manuel insisted she wait for her duenna.

Frowning, she shook her head. "I do not wish for a duenna, Manuel."

The old man shrugged. "This is still California, and we still have the old ways, though now we are part of the United States. People would frown if you rode out alone, without a duenna to attend you. I cannot allow it, Doña Vitoria. Don Patricio would banish me from Buena Vista. Where is your maid?"

She thought of Colette, sulky at best, and recalled the one time in Boston she'd taken her riding. Poor Colette had bounced about most brutally, and spent the following week moaning of aches and pains, and that had been the last time she'd gone. Exasperated, she shook her head again. "She is not available, I'm afraid. I shall have to go alone."

"Then I must respectfully decline your request for one of the horses," the old man said with quiet stubbornness. "I cannot have el patrón's wrath upon my head—"

Irritated, but remembering that it was, after all, Manuel who would be blamed if anything dreadful happened, Tory relented rather sullenly. "Very well. I will find Colette, or one of the maids. But I do intend to ride, with or without your permission."

When Manuel lowered his gaze and looked down at the ground, Tory swallowed more hasty words; it wasn't his fault, after all, so she managed a conciliatory smile. "Forgive me,

Manuel, for being rude. I should have known you would re-
quire an escort for me. Please, saddle another horse while I
fetch my maid.''

Colette protested, listing a variety of reasons that she could
not go, but in the end, she was assigned a docile mare, muttering French invectives that Tory was glad she couldn't quite
hear or understand.

Manuel nodded and smiled with relief. ''I will send Pablo
with you as well. Here, come forward, niño—see? He is a
good boy, and strong, though a bit lazy at times.''

She turned, brows lifting as she surveyed the swarthy
young man in his mid-teens. He couldn't be more than an
inch or two taller than she was, and it did not look as if there
had ever been even a suggestion of a whisker on his smooth
face. She scowled. ''Pablo? But he's so young—''

''An excellent vaquero, for all that he is young. He has
been riding since he was an infant, as do most of the young
men here, and has acquitted himself very well in all the
games. Two years in a row now, it has been Pablo who has
won the chicken race.''

Tory smiled slightly, thinking of the wild races conducted
on the beaches, and how the vaqueros would ride their mounts
as fast as possible past a chicken buried in the sand up to its
neck, leaning down to pluck it from the beach. The object,
of course, was to be the first to cross the finish line with a
live chicken—not a mean feat, given the logistics.

As if he sensed her imminent surrender, Manuel added:
''And he knows how to shoot his pistol—albeit a bit wildly—
so you will be safe, Doña Vitoria.''

Hiding her reluctant amusement, she briskly pulled on her
riding gloves. ''Very well. I hope he can keep up with me.''

The maligned Pablo grinned, not at all offended by Manuel's words or her reluctance for his company. ''I will do my
best, Doña Vitoria.''

Placing her fingers in Manuel's outstretched hand, she
mounted swiftly and settled herself in the tall saddle, taking
up her reins. While Pablo was helping Colette mount, Tory
urged her mare forward with a quick nudge of her booted

heels and rode hard toward the gate. She was already out the gate and on the road leading from the hacienda before she heard the clatter of hooves behind her, and smiled.

It was a glorious day, and for the first time since her arrival, she felt relaxed. The sun was bright, the brisk wind tugging at her hair and hat, smelling of the sea. Seabirds sailed gracefully overhead, riding wind currents as easily as ships rode the sea, their lilting cries drifting down and mingling with the crashing surge of ocean foam over black rocks studding the beach below. The steady rhythm of the horse beneath her was familiar and soothing. After letting the mare run a bit on the winding road near the shore, she slowed and allowed Pablo and Colette to catch up.

Colette glared at her, her head bobbing up and down and her lips pressed into a thin line as she clung to the sweat-damp neck of her mount with both hands. The young vaquero didn't seem at all put out about the race, however, though Tory had stayed ahead of him for some distance.

"You ride well, Doña Vitoria," he said, slowing his bay gelding to a walk beside her. Dust drifted in a thin haze above the road, coating horses and boots, settling on broad leaves of plants at the roadside.

"Thank you." She slanted him a reckless smile, feeling alive and free, exulting in her unexpected liberty. "It's been a long time since I've been able to ride like this—I mean out, where there are no paved streets, no carriages to avoid, and people always crossing the road in front of you so that you have to rein in quickly. I didn't realize I'd missed it so much."

His youthful shoulders lifted in a shrug, and black eyes gleamed at her, blinking a little in the sunlight. "Then we will ride as long as you like."

It was the calm, California acceptance of life's inconveniences that she'd forgotten, the easy way of living and appreciation of life. She knew that Easterners considered the Californios to be lazy, indolent; but she rather thought it was an ability to adapt. For years, the Spanish had ruled California, and had been left mainly to their own devices when Mexico had won its independence from Spain, with token service being given to Mexico City in the way of taxes. It should be interesting to see how they fared under the Yankee rule of Americanos, who had a history of being energetic and intolerant.

They took El Camino Real, or Royal Road, into Monterey. It snaked six hundred and fifty miles along the coast, from San Francisco all the way down to San Diego, with Franciscan missions situated at intervals, many of them now fallen into ruin. Even the San Carlos mission at Carmel, three miles south of Monterey, was in need of repair.

Construction on new buildings had been started in Monterey, but the work had been abandoned. Empty scaffolds were propped against half-finished walls, and the carriages, oxcarts, well-laden wagons, and horsemen that usually filled the roads were only a trickle now.

"Gold fever," Pablo replied succinctly when she asked the reason. Monterey had been half-deserted since mid-June, as most of the town's male population went northward to the gold fields.

Tory rode slowly through the town, delighting Colette, who sat up straighter, preening slightly and looking around with great interest. Pablo took his duty as protector very seriously, glaring at any man who gazed too long at his mistress. He was horrified when she suggested stopping at one of the outdoor stalls in the marketplace, and protested vigorously.

"No, no, Doña Vitoria, do not. If you are hungry, or thirsty, I will purchase something for you, but to sit alone in the *mercado* is to invite trouble."

"Nonsense. It's not as if I'm unchaperoned. I have you and Colette." She smiled at him, her brightest smile, the one that would have made Sean shudder with apprehension. Pablo stared at her uncertainly.

And then, as luck would have it, she saw Dave Brock, the young lieutenant who had walked with her on the beach in Los Angeles. He was sitting in the sun on a bench near the presidio, and when he saw her, he leaped up and ran to greet her. She halted her mount to smile down at him.

"Miss Ryan, how wonderful to see you again!" He held her bridle as if he never intended to release it, and looked up at her with admiring blue eyes. "I thought perhaps we would never meet again."

"And I thought you were going on to San Francisco."

"Oh, I am. But our steamer had some mechanical problems, and so we've been sitting in the harbor. Most of the other passengers and crew boarded other ships or bought horses, mules, or whatever would get them north to the gold strike." He shook his head ruefully. "With no one to talk to, I got bored and came into town. Come, sit and talk with me a while. I'd love to have some beautiful, charming company."

Colette snickered, but Tory ignored it. Then Pablo made a rough noise in the back of his throat, and nudged his horse closer, forcing Lieutenant Brock back a step. He looked up, alarmed, and Tory smiled down at him after slanting Pablo a frowning glance.

"My servant is a bit protective, but I appreciate his vigilance. Pablo, this is a friend, and I think I will accept his gracious invitation. I know how it worries you for me to sit unescorted." She disregarded the youth's stricken expression and allowed the lieutenant to help her dismount, though it was irritating the way Brock held her waist a bit too long. Still, she had no intention of ruining her day by allowing a mere slip of a boy to direct her actions, so she tucked her gloved hand into the lieutenant's bent arm and smiled at him, rather enjoying the way his eyes lit up with blatant admiration.

He walked her toward the presidio square where benches had been placed, some of them near mounted cannon. Once the square would have been crowded with soldiers and citizens milling about, but now only a handful lazed in the sun or sat on benches beneath huge old trees. Colette trailed behind them, discreetly, occasionally sparing a sly smile for a handsome caballero riding by.

A breeze blew, and the sun was warm. It was pleasant to talk with the young lieutenant, especially as he was so obviously enamored of her, and she enjoyed a mild flirtation.

Pablo brought cups of *naranjada* for her and Colette, pretending not to hear Dave's request for a cup of the sweet orange liquid, then took up his station less than a yard away.

Water splashed invitingly in a fountain nearby, and the wind was warm enough that she removed her gloves and loosened the sash to her bonnet. It was a stylish hat, blue velvet to match her riding outfit, with a dotted black net sash that tied beneath her chin to keep it firmly atop her head. Now she removed it and pulled the thick mane of her hair over one shoulder in a loose fall, baring her neck to the cool breezes.

Brock watched her every move intently, his gaze shifting from the deep sheen of her hair to her face, lingering. Tory hid a smile. Really, he was so transparent. It would be almost too easy to make him fall in love with her, not that she had any intention of doing so, but still, it was rather gratifying to have him hang on her every word and move.

"Tell me, Lieutenant, what are your plans for the future? Do you intend to stay in California, or will you go back to Pennsylvania?"

A short spray of feathers dyed deep blue to match the color of her habit adorned the crown of her hat, and she toyed idly with them while she listened to Lieutenant Brock's recital of his plans for the future.

"My sister wrote that land is up for the taking out here," he was saying, "and I mean to have some of it. Cattle get fat, and the land is so rich crops almost grow themselves—have I amused you?"

Laughing, she nodded. "Yes. Papa has said the same thing so often, it's like listening to his favorite motto. He was a sea captain when he first came out here almost thirty years ago, and now owns one of the largest ranchos in the area. So I suppose there's something to that."

Dave moved a little closer on the bench, and there was a bright gleam of interest in his eyes. "I'd like to meet your father. I wager we have a lot in common."

Amused, she fanned herself slowly with her hat, letting the feathers drift across her cheek in an idle brush. "Perhaps. But you are going on to San Francisco as soon as your steamer is repaired, so I doubt that will be possible . . .''

"There will always be another steamer, or even a burro if I grow impatient to leave, so it would be no problem—oh, forgive me, Miss Ryan. I'm being precipitate." He flushed slightly. "It's just that I find you so charming, and so beautiful, and I would really love to have the chance to know you better."

The interest in his eyes was genuine and flattering, and Tory allowed herself to bask in it a little. Well, it was always pleasant to be admired, Tory thought, and she was no different from any other young woman. And really, what did it hurt? Lieutenant Brock was quite handsome, with blond good looks and a charming manner, and said just the right things. Their brief acquaintance on the steamer had been only a mild flirtation on her part, for, after all, she loved Peter Gideon, but she felt no disloyalty to him by flirting a bit with Dave. It was not as if there would ever be any more to it. And he looked so lonely, stranded in an unfamiliar city far from home, so, more to be polite than with the thought that he might actually accept, she invited him to Buena Vista for dinner next Wednesday evening.

"Of course, that is almost a week from now," she said, smiling a little at his obvious surprise, "but if you are still in Monterey, and would like to—"

He reached out and clasped his hands over hers, crushing the feathers on her hat. "I shall definitely still be in Monterey, even if my steamer sails in an hour, Miss Ryan! I would not miss such an invitation."

Tory intercepted an amused glance from Colette, and even while she silently cursed the impudent maid, acknowledged a spurt of dismay. It had been only an idle invitation, given because she was certain he would refuse, but it seemed now that she had underestimated the lieutenant. Or overestimated him. Did he not recall that she was to be wed to a man in Boston? But of course he did.

She removed her hands and her hat from his grasp and shrugged lightly. "My father has not been able to get out a lot, so guests are always welcome. He appreciates pleasant company, and I ask only for his sake, Lieutenant.''

"Of course.'' Blue eyes reflected bright sunlight as he nodded. "And I am aware of the honor you do me by inviting me to meet your father.''

"Your *naranjada* is getting warm, Doña Vitoria,'' Pablo said unhappily, moving to stand close. "But please—do not linger here. It is not wise.''

"Don't be ridiculous.'' She tempered her sharp words with a smile, relieved at being rescued from more of the lieutenant's effusive compliments. Was he deliberately misunderstanding her? Her head was beginning to ache, and her pleasant outing was rapidly being ruined, and it made her cross. "Do be seated, Pablo. You're annoying me with all that hovering about. Do you think the lieutenant intends to abduct me?''

"No, it is not that.'' He looked up and past her, frowning.

"Then what on earth is it?''

His dusky face was creased in a frown, and dark eyes squinted across the square. "There is trouble . . . do you not hear?''

Indeed, she hadn't, and she turned to look where he was staring. Several men stood in the sun, facing one another. Aggression was evident in their postures and their rising voices. Her heart suddenly lurched. This was no casual meeting, or disagreement, but something serious. Anger carried on the wind, a little louder now, and she rose to her feet, uncertain whether to flee or stay and watch.

"He may be right.'' Dave rose to his feet. "Perhaps you should go into one of the shops, Miss Ryan. A duel is no sight for a woman.''

Her eyes narrowed. "Nonsense. Just because I'm a woman doesn't mean I'm not as curious as you are—I've never seen a duel.''

Dave looked exasperated and obviously torn between his desire to see her safe and his desire to watch what promised to be a very exciting duel. "At least come over here, behind this stone wall,'' he said after a moment, and she allowed him to lead her and Colette to the wall.

Pablo followed, tense and scowling, his hand resting on the butt of the pistol he carried in the red sash around his waist.

The low wall edged the square and it was much closer, so that she had an excellent view of the men in the middle of the plaza. They were arguing, it was clear. An odd-looking trio, she thought, all clothed differently. A rather nondescript man in a suit stood to one side, as if only an observer of the dispute. Another man was clad in the rough buckskin of a trapper, and kept shaking his head and trying to back away, while the other man looked of Mexican descent, rather dark, slender, and of medium height; he motioned behind them, toward one of the long, low buildings at the plaza's edge.

A man came out of the building; he leaned against a support post of the low porch, and the slatted wood roof cast bars of shadow and light over him. His entire stance was one of lazy indifference, but beneath the outward carelessness, there was a sense of coiled threat.

''*Mon Dieu!*'' Colette gasped, and reached out to curl her fingers around Tory's arm, oblivious to what she was doing.

Without realizing she had, Tory leaned forward, straining to get a better view. It was like a dream, with everything intense and heightened with tension. But this was high drama, a theatrical scene being played before her eyes, and she didn't intend to leave. Not yet. Not until she knew what would happen.

In the square, people began to scatter. There was no sign of soldiers, though earlier there had been a few milling about. Duennas hurried young charges to safety, while some of the men ducked into doorways or behind a white-plastered wall to watch. Tension lay like a thick blanket across the presidio now, when only a few minutes before the square had been basking lazily in the afternoon sun.

Tory looked back at the man leaning against the post, and an ember of recognition sparked. She frowned. There was something familiar about him, but she couldn't see his face for the shadows. He was tall and lean, wearing a fringed buckskin coat over an open shirt, and snug-fitting cord pants tucked into the tops of knee-high boots. A long knife hung from his belt, and a leather holster was on his right hip. Another pistol was stuck into his belt. As she watched, he moved from the shadows of the porch and into the sunlight, his walk slow and measured, like the stalking of a predator. Oh, if only she could see his face, but it was hidden by the brim of his hat, shadowed beneath it.

One of the men in the middle of the plaza smiled slightly and backed away. "Time to take your medicine, Tackett," he said in a soft tone that seemed loud in the sudden hush. "Me and Martin will just wait over here while you and Kincade . . . talk." The two men stepped into the shade of a nearby piazza and leaned against the posts, looking casual and relaxed.

"Garcia—wait!" The man called Tackett looked around, face blanching when he saw the other man coming toward him. He swore as men around him scattered, "Damn cowards—come on back here . . ." He swung back to face the approaching man, poised as if for flight, his tone belligerent.

"I ain't gonna fight you, Kincade. It's all a mistake, I tell you."

"No mistake, Tackett. You're the one I want."

The low, silky voice sent a shiver down her spine, and she gasped with sudden recognition. It was he, the man in the garden—God, what was he doing? What were any of them doing, stalking one another in the square like wolves, moving now in a slow circle? Tackett's hand hovered over the handle of a long knife at his side. He was shorter, stocky, and kept licking his lips nervously, his eyes shifting from side to side as if looking for a way out.

"It's Pickering you want," he said after a moment, hoarsely. "I didn't have nuthin' to do with it. I wasn't even there."

"You were there."

Still walking, his steps careless, almost indolent, Kincade leisurely closed the distance between them. Abruptly, his hand lashed out across Tackett's face, snapping his head back.

Tackett staggered a few steps backward and went to one knee, whining now.

"It ain't me you want, I swear it . . ."

"Where's Pickering?"

"Gone . . ." It came out in a half-sob, "I don't know where—God, you're gonna kill me . . ."

"Tell you what—I'll give you the chance you didn't give Gisela." A little smile touched one corner of his hard mouth as he hauled the sobbing man to his feet. He whipped a black scarf from around his neck, and with swift efficiency, tied his left wrist to Tackett's. "Indian style, Tackett. A fight to the death."

"No . . . no." Shaking his head, straining desperately away, Tackett looked around wildly, as if for help. "Ain't somebody gonna stop him?"

"Pickering ran out on you. No one else gives a damn, so you'd better pretend you're a man and try to help yourself."

The soft voice, taunting, cool and menacing, seemed to seep through Tackett's blind fear, and he swallowed hard, nodding. "All right. Just—give me a chance . . ."

"Pull your knife, or I'll gut you where you stand."

Cold, merciless, the soft words sent chills down Tory's spine. This was a man she had slapped and threatened—and who had held her and kissed her.

It was hard to breathe; the heat pressed down and the wind died. There didn't seem to be any breeze, any movement other than the two men in the middle of the presidio. It was a strange dance, the slow circling, one man steady and certain, the other obviously shaken and terrorized. She began to feel sorry for him.

"Someone should stop this . . ." Her voice was a whisper, her hands clenched into fists atop the low stone wall. "Where is the watch?"

"This isn't Boston," the lieutenant said tersely, his eyes riveted to the scene in the plaza. "The military rules here, and the commandant is probably taking a siesta."

When she half-turned to say something scathing, a blur of motion jerked her head back around, and she saw Kincade

shift, light and as graceful as a dancer. Sunlight flashed on
something metallic, and it was then she saw that Tackett had
pulled out his knife. He lunged forward, aiming at Kincade's
middle, but missed as he sidestepped with an agile twist.

Almost contemptuously, Kincade's blade flickered in the
sunlight, inflicting cuts like the strike of a snake, until Tackett
was bleeding from a dozen different wounds. His cheek
dripped blood, and his buckskin coat hung in tattered ribbons
bright with crimson stains. Panting, stumbling, Tackett tried
again to stab Kincade, but it was painfully obvious he lacked
the skill.

"I'm beat," he whined finally. "Finished. You win."

Kincade looked down at him with contempt, his knife
poised. But then, when Tory was certain he would kill him,
he shook his head grimly and sliced through the scarf binding
them together.

"You're a coward and a murderer, Tackett. You deserve
to hang. It'll give you longer to think about the girl you murdered."

Released, Tackett slumped to the dusty stones of the plaza,
head down as he crouched in defeat. Kincade stepped away
and turned his back to speak to the man she'd heard called
Garcia.

As Tory glanced from Tackett to Kincade, wondering who
the girl had been, Colette gave a little gasp and she looked
back around in time to see Tackett lift his head with sudden
purpose. It happened quickly. His arm rose, the knife blade
glinting in the sunshine, and she knew what he intended.
Without stopping to think, Tory screamed a warning: "Look
out!"

Kincade hardly seemed to move, but suddenly his lean
body was in a half-crouch and he was facing Tackett again.
There was a solid thunk, and a grunt of surprise, and Kincade's blade protruded from Tackett's chest, the long hilt
quivering slightly.

Tackett looked shocked, and one hand lifted to lightly
touch the hilt. He shook his head slightly in disbelief, then
pitched forward to sprawl facedown on the stones.

"You shouldn't have turned your back on him, Nick."
Garcia looked grave, staring down at the body sprawled motionless on the stones.

"It was the only way." Nick Kincade's mouth curled into a ruthless smile. "As long as I was facing him, he wouldn't have the guts to try it. I gave him his chance." He bent and retrieved his knife, then straightened, and wiped it on his pants leg.

"Damn." Garcia shook his head, looking a little stunned. "Damn."

Kincade looked up then, his gaze moving past the crowd that had begun to gather, and straight toward her. Tory realized she was staring at him, but couldn't look away. His eyes held hers coolly, as calm and aloof as an animal. He nodded once, a slight acknowledgment, then pivoted on his heel and walked away.

"Mon Dieu . . . sacre bleu . . ."

As Colette's moans faded into muttered whispers Tory couldn't understand, the enormity of what she'd seen hit her suddenly. A wave of nausea washed over her, and she stared, sickened, at the dead man lying in a pool of blood on the presidio stones. She was barely aware of Lieutenant Brock beside her, of the conversation flowing around them, excited now, when it was safe to be brave.

"God, I ain't never seen nobody so fast with a knife . . ."

"Who's the dead man?"

"Don't know. Tangled with the wrong man, looks like . . ."

"Did you see how quick he was? One of them frontiersmen, I bet, from past the Colorado River . . ."

"Naw, I know who he is. Name's Kincade, from Texas way. A Ranger. *Los diablos Tejanos*, the Mexicans call 'em. Texas devils . . ."

"Come with me, Miss Ryan." Dave was gentle and comforting, but she mumbled an excuse and pulled away.

Colette took her arm and led her away from the presidio and to the horses. She was vaguely aware of Dave's anxious inquiries and her murmured replies; and then she was mounted, with Pablo astride his horse beside her looking thunderous and chagrined, scowling at Brock as he nudged close to Tory, gazing up at her anxiously.

"Yes, yes . . ." Tory looked down at Dave without really seeing him. "Seven Wednesday night is fine . . ."

It had all happened so fast, and now a man was dead and she had warned his killer. She didn't know why, didn't know why she'd been compelled to warn him.

Shivering despite the heat of the July sun, she tried to put the brutality of what she'd just seen behind her. And it struck her that she was more than just a continent away from Boston and Peter now. She was in an entirely different world, where none of the rules was the same, and lives were much more uncertain. And expendable.

Eight

Tory frowned slightly and sat up in her bed. Papa was arguing with someone—a woman, she thought—and their voices had disturbed her afternoon siesta. At first, she'd thought sleepily that she was having a dream, and ignored them. Then, as they'd grown louder, she knew she was not. Rising from her bed, she went to the open doors that led onto the patio.

The voices came from the garden just beyond the stone walls and iron gate. She stepped outside, the patio stones cool against her bare feet, and moved toward the wall; she could hear them much more clearly now.

"I tell you," a woman's voice said harshly, "that I will not allow it."

Papa sounded different, his tone cold and implacable, as she had never before heard it. "You have no choice. I suggest you learn to accept it."

"It is an abomination!"

Tory stepped closer to the tangle of vines swaying over the stones. Heart-shaped leaves rustled when she brushed against them, tickling her cheek as she leaned against the wall. There was a passionate undercurrent in the woman's voice, and she sounded vaguely familiar. If only Tory could see over the wall, or they would pass by the iron gate, so she would know whom Papa was arguing with . . .

"Abomination or not, it will increase my holdings three times what they are now. And it's not as if it's so unusual, now is it?" Papa was saying, his tone heavy with sarcasm. "It's been done since time began, as you should know. Besides, I would never hurt her."

"That is not true—you care nothing for anyone but yourself. It is as it has always been . . . My life may be over, but hers is not. I will stop you if I can, I swear it."

There was a muffled sound, then a little gasp, and a few words she could not hear, and Tory fought a feeling of rising panic. That voice was so familiar, so elusive. She had to see, had to know—

"Doña Vitoria," a voice said behind her, and she turned with a gasp, hand pressing against her mouth. Tía Benita stood in the open doors that led to the patio, a slight frown on her face. "Are you unwell?"

"No. No." She stumbled forward, away from the wall. "I'm fine."

"You look so pale. Are you still thinking of your visit to town last week? Ah, I thought so. You should not have gone like that, and Manuel has been severely reprimanded for allowing it. A proper lady never leaves without her duenna. That flighty maid is not a suitable substitute, and I cannot imagine why you behaved so rashly. Don Patricio may still rebuke you harshly for it, as he should. Such a chance you took!" She paused for breath, and her voice grew kinder. "Ah, but your horse running away with you is punishment enough, I suppose, so I shall not say more about it. Next time, you will think before doing such a thing."

A runaway horse had been given as the excuse for her distress upon their return, and she'd firmly refused to allow Pablo to reveal the real reason. She had no intention of listening to lectures or being forbidden to leave the hacienda again. And remembering the scene at the presidio, she agreed with Tía Benita—she'd been punished enough.

"Now come," Tía Benita was saying, "you must have

your siesta and be rested, for your papa has invited some dinner guests.'' Pausing, she frowned slightly. ''Doña Paloma has taken ill again and will not attend, so it is up to you to be the hostess tonight. What gown will you wear? I cannot find that worthless maid of yours—off flirting with the caballeros, no doubt. Shall I help you choose your gown?''

It wasn't surprising that her mother would not attend. She rarely attended functions, even family meals. It would have been much more comfortable if Diego were back from Los Angeles, but he wasn't due for several more days. Tory managed a smile. ''No, I shall choose a proper gown, thank you, Tía Benita. Who are the guests?''

Tía Benita shrugged. ''I am not certain. Don Luis is coming, for I heard your papa mention him, but I did not hear if there will be other guests. You do remember Don Luis and Doña Dolores?''

''And their obnoxious son Rafael. Yes, I'm afraid I do. I feel a headache coming on,'' she added rather crossly. ''Doesn't Papa remember how I always hated Rafael? He was such a mean little boy. And his sister Maria has never had a thought of her own, but must always echo someone else's opinion . . .''

''Time changes people,'' Tía Benita said placidly. ''You have changed, and so have Rafael and Maria, I am certain. All things change, niña, though we do not want them to at times.''

She looked rather sad, so Tory changed the subject, asking instead about the fiesta. Tía Benita threw up her hands. ''Ah, there is so much to do with the fiesta in only a few weeks, and so many guests will be here—most of the guest houses have not been used in so long that they are in disrepair, but does Ramon do anything about it? No, not that lazy one. He only says that he is to care for Don Patricio, and does not concern himself with cobwebs and musty curtains. Bah. What a lazy good-for-nothing he is!''

Tory only half-listened as Tía Benita rambled on, thinking instead of the scene outside her courtyard. The woman's voice had been so familiar, yet she could not place it. They'd spoken in Spanish; her father's accent, as usual, slightly thick, but the woman's had been flawless. Castilian Spanish, the pure liquid notes as different from her father's as night from day.

". . . and now we have that dangerous-looking man here as a guest, who comes and goes as he pleases, and I do not like it," Tía Benita was saying, capturing Tory's attention.

She turned to look at her. "What dangerous man?"

Tía Benita shrugged. "I do not know his name, if ever I was told it. Your papa met him a few years ago, on one of his business trips. Of course, he invited him to Buena Vista if ever he was in California, and now there are discussions about land purchases, and I have to be certain he is treated politely, for he is, after all, a guest, and—"

"Why have I not seen him if he is a guest?" she interrupted.

"He has been here only twice before, and that was last week, before he went up into the mountains to look at some land Don Patricio has offered to sell. And anyway, he is to stay in the guest house when he is here—only proper, of course, for a single man like that should not be allowed to stay in the same house as the patrón's daughter. It would not be right."

She leaned close, looking worried, her voice lowering. "It worries me that he is allowed the freedom of the grounds very late at night, when all are asleep and it is quiet. That is not all. Though I am not one to interfere in the business of others, I do not like the way the maids look at him. Especially that Rosita. Humph. She is too man-crazy, that one, and one day will end in trouble, mark my words. But when I try to tell your papa, he only smiles a little, and says that she is young and pretty, and of course she likes men, for they like her. I know young men have their . . . needs . . . but really, to allow, even *encourage* such things, is a sin. Even Diego has—but I should not say that."

"Rosita—the same Rosita who is my own age?"

"Yes, that is the one."

Tory thought of the encounter in the garden, and how Kin-

cade had assumed she was sent to him. It must have been
Rosita he was to meet. And if he was Papa's guest, it would
explain how he had so easily moved about the hacienda garden that night, with none to protest his presence. And it explained why he had not feared the vaqueros.

She frowned slightly, and looked at Tía Benita, who had
stepped to the patio doors to pull the draperies closed.

"This guest—is he tall and dark-haired? Handsome?" she
asked, and Tía Benita turned, looking a little surprised.

"Yes. Handsome enough, I suppose, but . . . villainous, if
you comprehend, yes? All I know is, he makes me think twice
about going into dark corners at night."

Tory almost smiled. "You're wiser than you know," she
murmured, and later, when Tía Benita had gone and she was
alone until time for Colette to help her dress for dinner, she
thought of the similarity between the man in the garden and
the killer in the streets. Love words and killing words, spoken
in the same soft, husky tone, as if neither mattered very much.
Maybe it didn't. Not to a man like that, a killer, a ruthless
savage, and God only knows what else.

Oh God—and I let him kiss me, let him touch me, and he
felt my bare legs around him—how humiliating! And
worse—why can I not forget how it felt?

Irritably, she wished she could stop thinking about him,
about the way he'd looked in the soft shadows of night,
darkly handsome, with hot amber eyes—wolf eyes. And she
wished she could forget the way he'd kissed her, so hard
and—yes, she admitted it—intriguing; it was the last that
bothered her most, for she knew that he'd been very well-
aware of her response to him, of her breathless confusion and
yielding. Yes, he was a dangerous man indeed, as Tía Benita
said.

Dinner the night before had been less than pleasant, with
Don Luis regarding her across the snowy-white tablecloth as
if assessing her worth, and Tory had excused herself early,
pleading a headache. Papa had not been pleased, she knew,

but she didn't care. Worse, Don Luis and his entire family were to come for dinner tonight.

Crossly, she had the disturbing suspicion that there was much more to Papa's extended invitations than mere business discussions, for he and Don Luis had deliberately regaled her with glowing descriptions of Rafael—she *did* remember him, didn't she? How handsome he had grown, how manly! He would be a most suitable match for some fortunate young woman . . .

Tory sighed. Her first flush of joy upon arriving home again was fleeting, gone quickly, like mist along the shoreline.

Morning breezes wafted in through the open patio doors of her chamber, bringing the spicy-sweet scent of oranges and lemons that grew in the orchards beyond her courtyard. Disconcerting, how tiny, long-forgotten memories had a way of intruding at times, Tory thought as she stood in the doorway gazing out at the shaded patio. Heart-shaped leaves on the vines tangled up the stone wall and tumbled haphazardly over the iron gates, trembling slightly in the breeze, looking fragile and oh so temporary. As was everything else.

Sagging against the frame of her open door, she thought longingly of the beach, and how peaceful it could be. When they were children, she and Diego had spent many happy hours playing in the narrow strip of sand and dunes, hiding behind the huge humps of black rocks, pretending they were castles or dragons, and the bleached driftwood was dragon bones. Happy times, pleasant memories.

But why should I be gloomy? she thought, straightening. It's not far to the beach, and the wine cellars are cool and inviting this time of year—I will wear a peasant skirt and blouse, and no one will even notice me . . .

Slipping undetected from the house, Tory ambled along the hacienda walls, and wandered through the grape arbors and out past the orchards on the edge of the hacienda boundaries, walking slowly so as not to attract attention and the unwanted company of a duenna or chaperon. It was stifling, *suffocating* to always have someone in attendance, and she wanted some time alone, to think about things, to plan how she would tell

Papa about Peter. He had to know, but the appropriate moment had not seemed to come. Somehow, it was not going to be as easy as she had naively thought before arriving at Buena Vista. Papa *seemed* the same, but he was not. There was something . . . different. An intangible wall between them, a constraint that had not been there when she was a child.

Well, she was a woman now, with a woman's views and a woman's needs, and Papa would just have to understand that she was mature enough to be married. He might be disappointed that it was not to be a man nearby, but after all, she'd been gone for almost ten years and Papa had not missed her so very greatly. Yes, she *must* find a way to remind him that she was no longer a little girl, that she could make her own decisions.

The roar of the surf had grown louder, and the wind tugged at her skirts, smelling of sea slag and salt. A narrow trail led from the high bluffs downward, cutting between haphazard piles of wet black rock gouged with holes from years of exposure to wind and sea. Ruts dug deep into the ground, evidence that heavy carts frequented the road, and she followed it down the curving descent. Here the sound of the surf was deafening; sea spray shot up in frothy cascades over the surface and crest of rocks worn smooth from the pounding of the breakers against them, carried on the wind to dampen her clothes and hair.

To her left stretched a long line of limestone, high as a two-story building, with wind-twisted trees atop, and beneath, it was pocked with caves that reached far back up into the bluffs behind. Steps had been cut into the rock in places, for the men to unload the heavy casks of wine from laden carts and store them far back into the dim, cool recesses. Several yards in front of the caves the ground fell away abruptly, down to a thin ribbon of sandy beach littered with driftwood, too narrow for anything but an occasional boat to launch. It was easier to get the wine to the Monterey harbor by small boats than by wagon, a device Patrick Ryan had been using for years.

Tory made her way down the steep incline to the beach,

blinking a little at the mist stinging her eyes. The sea was heavy today, pounding waves crashing down, undulating swells rolling onto the sand with savage force. She'd never learned to swim; it had been Diego who had learned, daring her to follow, laughing at her when she hung back, furious with herself for not accepting his challenge, but too terrified of the infinite, dangerous sea to drum up her courage.

Yet now she was older; and if she didn't swim, she did have enough courage to wade in the water, though once she had been too frightened to do even that. She sat down on a huge, tortured length of driftwood bleached white by sun and sea to tug off her shoes, then peeled off her stockings and tucked them carefully into the tops of her sand-crusted shoes. At least she was wearing a light skirt, and only one petticoat and no corset, a distinct improvement over the restrictive clothing she'd been forced to wear in Boston.

Now, tucking the hem of her skirt up into the waistband and securing it with the gay red sash she wore, she walked slowly toward the water while the wind whipped at her hair and skirts. Inside she was quivering; the sea looked so black and mysterious, so powerful—a mighty force that could crush her from existence. On the voyage from Boston, a man had fallen overboard in the Atlantic, and his cries for help were quickly swallowed up by the angry waves, until there was no sign of him, and the men who had set out in a small boat to rescue their mate returned saddened and quiet. It had happened so quickly; one moment he'd been clinging to the rigging, laughing at something, and the next, with a faint cry, he was gone, plummeting to the thrashing waves below.

Perhaps she would be like that: a falling star, flaring briefly into existence, then quickly extinguished and forgotten. She shivered.

Her feet sunk deeply into the sand where it was wet, squishing up between her toes, cool and clinging. Tiny froths lapped at her ankles, and she waded farther out, arms outspread for balance as if she were walking a rope strung out high across a ravine, like one of the acts she had seen performed at a small fair in Massachusetts.

Exhilarated by the pounding surf that rose up to her knees, wetting her skirt and thighs, feeling silky and cool against her skin, she stood a moment in the breakers, letting the powerful pull of the ocean mesmerize her. Her hair had come loose and tumbled around her shoulders and in her eyes, obscuring her vision, thrashing about her face like the stinging lash of a carter's whip.

Then her feet slipped a little and she caught herself, heart pounding almost as loudly as the crash of the waves against black rocks and, daring—oh so daring—she took another step, and another, until the water was up to her waist. Her breath came rapidly. This wasn't so difficult. All this time, she had feared the water, feared the ocean, but now she was in it, letting the drag of the current swirl around her—why had she waited?

She felt triumphant, all-powerful—invincible.

When she slogged back to shore, weary from her struggle with the ocean and resistance to the incessant tug of the tides, she saw a figure sitting atop a gnarled and twisted piece of driftwood, dark against the bleached-white wood, looking familiar. Her heart began to pound furiously. It was *he*—the man in the garden—Nick Kincade, and he was waiting for her.

"Birth of Venus," he said when she drew close, smiling a little at her. "All you need is a seashell. Botticelli would be proud."

"I have on too many clothes to pose for that particular painting, thank you." She eyed him narrowly. "What are you doing here? I thought you'd be in jail by now, or hanging from an oak limb."

He shrugged. "It gets boring in town. I decided that country air would be more refreshing."

She lifted a brow. "No doubt it would be healthier for a felon."

"No doubt. Do you know one?"

He was laughing at her! Her eyes narrowed slightly, studying him. There was no outward sign that he had killed a man last week, but she didn't know quite what to expect. A mark, like that of Cain, perhaps? But even that would probably not mar his good looks, and in the bright light of day, she could see that he was *very* handsome, and disturbingly familiar somehow.

Yet there was something intriguing about him, hard and, yes, dangerous, like the sea—an irresistible lure, a challenge.

Deliberately, she let her gaze rake over him as if assessing him, and saw the amusement in his eyes. She tilted her head, surveyed his crisp white linen shirt, the black leather vest, and the dark, snug-fitting pants he wore, then lowered to inspect his knee-high boots. Then she sniffed as if dissatisfied with what she saw, and shrugged slightly.

"If I tell what I know about you, you will no longer be welcome at Buena Vista."

"And will you tell?" One side of his mouth tucked into that annoying smile again, as if a welcome at the hacienda did not matter to him.

"Perhaps. If it amuses me."

"Ah. Are you easily amused?"

"At times." She shot him a glance from the corner of her eyes, and bent slightly, wringing salt water from her hair so that it formed a tiny puddle in the sand at her feet. Why did he make her feel so breathless, as if she had been under water swimming against the current? He was a violent man, and she had seen him kill another human being, ruthlessly and savagely. Just being here with him like this, alone where no one else could see, with only the wind and sea and sky around them, was dangerous. She felt as if she were balanced on the edge of a high precipice, and one false step would send her plummeting over the edge, like the man who had fallen overboard and disappeared into infinity.

But she could not stop her headlong rush into danger, could not prevent the rising surge of excitement that led her to tease him a little, pull the tiger's tail and see if she could escape unharmed.

Her skirt was sodden with sea water, clinging to her legs and the small round curve of her belly, but it was her blouse that revealed the most—soaked through so that the white material was almost transparent, and even her thin undershift did not conceal the thrust of her breasts and the darker circles of her nipples. His gaze had dropped from her face, and even though his eyes were lazy and half-lidded as if the sun was too bright, she knew where he was looking. It made her feel funny inside, all hot and tumultuous; instead of being horrified, she reveled in it, stretched imaginary wings of womanhood and spread them out in a splendid display of brilliance.

It was a mating dance, like that of a peacock, with Kincade's eyes going hot and narrow as she returned his gaze coolly, not trying to hide herself, but staring at him as if daring him to do something about it.

Uncoiling his lean body from atop the driftwood, he stood up, towering over her, sudden intensity written in his dark features and the vibration of his muscles as he reached out to put his hands on her shoulders.

"If this is another game," he said softly, his words almost drowned out by the pounding surf, "I warn you—this time I'll make the rules."

For a moment she was confused, then she remembered the night in the garden, when he had thought she was one of the servant girls being coy and teasing. It was getting too dangerous—she should stop now, laugh lightly, tell him that she had no intention of playing by his rules, and that she was not some servant girl sent to him for his pleasure.

But it was hard to think with him so close, with his hands skimming from her shoulders down her arms, and then around to cup her breasts, his palms heated against her wet, chilled skin. She shuddered at the exquisite contrast, startled by the sudden, deep throbbing low in the pit of her stomach. It spread outward, slow heat, oozing through her veins, rendering her temporarily incapable of anything but yielding to the rousing sensations he was eliciting with his fingers on her nipples.

She should stop him . . . would stop him in a moment, but it felt so good right now, the teasing flick of his fingers, the way he rolled the tight bud of her nipple between his thumb and fingers, and oh God, was that his mouth? Hot, wet, covering the peak of her breast, unbelievably arousing.

And then cool air washed over her, and he had pulled aside the wet material of her blouse, baring her, his tongue laving across her skin in a silky glide that made her moan out loud. It was all so confusing, and she must stop him—really *must* stop him—but then he was lifting her in his arms, telling her how beautiful she was as he trudged through the sand and toward a rocky ledge where a thick tuft of sea grass waved under the press of wind, laying her down gently on the cushion of grass and following her, his lean, hard body an imperative weight . . .

In the shadow of the ledge, it was close and intimate, while the sea was a rhythmic melody that drowned out everything, even her objections, though it seemed as if perhaps she did not say them aloud after all. It all seemed a dream, a slow dissolving of one act into another: the grass beneath her, cool and soft, and him above her, his body hard and hot.

She closed her eyes; he kissed her, his mouth warm and transferring heat to her chilled flesh, until she grew warmer against him and stopped shivering. She found herself kissing him back, lifting her hands to lightly cup his shoulders, sighing softly against his mouth as he shoved his fingers into the tangled mane of her hair and held her head still while he kissed her more fiercely, demanding, consuming.

When his head lifted briefly, she saw his eyes rove over her face, then narrow slightly into a frown. Bewildered, she reached up for him, wanting him to kiss her again, to recreate the searing heat that he'd ignited, and he caught one of her hands in his, bending his lean brown fingers over her palm.

"I don't even know your name, little one. What is it?"

She smiled dreamily. "Venus," she whispered, and pulled his head down to her, her hand on the back of his neck, fingers tangling in the dark, crisp hair that brushed against his collar. With a faint smothered laugh, he stretched his long body across her; his hands roamed over her breasts and down the damp length of her body, stroking her through the material of her wet blouse and skirt.

Gently, with his mouth still on hers, he eased her arms from around his neck, sliding his hands up and over her, and then—so quickly—her wet garments were gone, cast aside into the sand. Naked, shivering again but not from cold, she looked up at him and clutched his arms, her lower lip caught between her teeth as spasms racked her frame.

"Easy, Venus," he murmured, smiling slightly, and lifted to his knees for a moment. She closed her eyes, panicked suddenly, knowing that she had let it go too far. A damnable weakness flooded her, and it seemed as if all her limbs were suddenly limp. She wanted to protest, to stop him, but nothing seemed to be working properly.

Then he was over her again, his lips exploring the curve of her neck, moving down to the deep-rose tips of her breasts. When his tongue circled her nipples, she shuddered, crying out and arching upward, her hands flying up to push against his chest. Ignoring her incoherent protest, he pushed his hand between her legs, opening them to brush gently against the sensitive flesh of her inner thighs.

Even with her eyes closed she knew he had not removed his clothes, and felt the abrasive rub of his trousers against her bare legs. Then, suddenly, he was between her legs, and she felt the heat of bare skin against the tight mat of curls at the vee of her thighs. Whispering to her—love words and sex words, phrases she'd never heard before and could barely decipher—he slipped a finger inside her, making her jerk convulsively and cry out.

"No! Oh God, what are you—"

"Hush," he murmured, moving swiftly to cover her mouth with his, muttering soothing words as if she were a frightened bird, and in a moment, she felt him shift, his hard man's body replacing his hand. He leaned forward until the pressure was almost unbearable, and Tory dug her fingers into his back, bunching his linen shirt into knots, arching upward instinctively.

In a move so quick she could not have anticipated it, he thrust forward, and a deep, searing pain knifed through her. She didn't realize she'd cried out until he lifted slightly, propping his weight on one hand, staring down at her in the faint gloom of the rocky shelter.

"A virgin, Venus?"

She stared up at him, mutinously, suddenly embarrassed by her inexperience, and after a moment, he shook his head slightly and muttered something about incredible odds. She was panting, the breath coming in short, hard gulps of air, and he bent, kissing her lightly on the mouth until the discomfort eased. He laced his fingers through hers and spread her arms out to her sides, behind her head and pressed down into the cushioning grass, and began to move, slowly at first, the friction a bit uncomfortable for the first few strokes. Then, as he moved inside her, the thrust and drag of his body produced a more pleasurable sensation; an excitement that the pain had sharply erased now returned.

It was all so overwhelming, the pounding rhythm of the ocean and the rhythm of him inside her, rising and rising and taking her with him, until she was matching his pace, arching up to receive him, pushing her hips into his thrusts; and then there was an unfamiliar pulsing inside her that radiated outward, spiralling through her body in heated waves that left her breathless and reaching, reaching for that brief, shattering moment when it seemed as if lights exploded behind her eyes and warmth flooded her body in an exquisite release.

And after, when his body stiffened and he thrust deeply, groaning then growing still before he sagged against her, she put her arms around him and held him, still too overwhelmed by it all to speak. It was enough for now that the wild, restless yearning inside her was appeased for once, that the prodding voice was silent. Yes, that was enough for right now.

Later, as if it were a dream, she allowed him to wash her, using a torn piece of his shirt dipped into the ocean, making her gasp at the cold wet cloth over her skin. He helped her dress again, gently pulling on her skirt and blouse, looking for her shoes and stockings, and patiently cleaning off the sand so she could wear them.

"Where do you live, Venus?"

She looked up, blinking a little, still dazed. Reality was

returning slowly, but the harsh little pieces were falling into place as she realized what she'd done. She swallowed hard and managed a smile.

"In a seashell, of course."

He grinned, wickedly handsome, Lucifer in his best role as seducer, only she had done the seducing. A Jezebel. God, those Boston harpies had been right—she was a gypsy, a wild pagan, not proper at all. Oh, what would Aunt Katherine say if she knew? And, God—*Peter*.

He rose lithely to his feet and put out a hand, and she put her fingers in his palm. He pulled her up with him. "Shall I take you home? You look a little unstable, Venus."

"No. No, please—I'm fine. I don't know—what . . . why . . . no, really. I'm fine."

He looked at her critically, and she tried not to meet his eyes, afraid that he would see that she felt like crying. This wasn't the way it was supposed to be. Where were the wonderful emotions that were supposed to follow such a life-altering event? All she felt was a bit foolish, and the wild, wonderful sensations that had swept her along earlier had vanished, leaving her drained and empty.

"You don't sound fine. I'll take you home."

"No!" Her strong refusal made him lift his brow, and the corner of his mouth slanted upward.

"I see."

"No, you don't. You don't see at all." She drew in a shaky breath and managed a weak smile. "It's not at all what you think—and please, don't insult me," she added when he dipped a hand into his vest pocket as if to draw out a coin.

Backing away from him, stumbling slightly, she finally turned and fled, back up the winding trail that led from the shore to the bluffs, tears blinding her. Nothing would ever be the same. Nothing. It was all irrevocably changed in the space of an hour, an instant's indecision, a yielding to impulse and ecstasy.

She wondered if she would still regret it tomorrow.

Nine

Someone was singing in the hacienda garden, a light, clear voice, the French words sweet and sad. Nick paused, leaning against the broad trunk of a Spanish oak to light a thin cigarillo. Smoke curled up from the brown tip, stinging his eyes, rich and aromatic. He inhaled, squinting against the smoke, listening. When the song ended, he dropped the cigarillo to the path and ground it beneath his heel.

"Bon jour," he said softly, startling the singer who swung around, half-rising from the iron bench with a hand at her throat.

"Monsieur," she stammered, looking flustered. The pale hair around her face fell into her eyes as she stood up, looking nervous. "I did not know you were there."

"Any bird who sings so sweetly should not have her songs go unheard, *ma belle.*"

A faint frown knit her brows, and then her eyes widened. "It is you—the man in the plaza . . . oh, *j'avoue que cela est supresant . . .*" She took a step backward and he grinned, following her.

"Approchez, que je vous embrasse." Some of the confusion faded from her face as he spoke in French, and she began to smile, pushing at the hair in her eyes and slanting him a

128

glance from beneath her lashes. She was pretty, and reminded him of a certain *fille de joie* he had once known in New Orleans. Despite his bold invitation and her protests of surprise, the girl's eyes and posture were inviting, not rejecting.

They sat and talked awhile, on a wooden bench beneath a tree at the far side of the garden path. Her name was Colette, she said, and she had recently come to California with her mistress.

"And who is your mistress, pretty one?" He smiled slightly. "Not that Spanish dragon who glares at me every time I see her, I hope."

"Tía Benita?" Colette giggled, a habit he disliked, and shrugged. "Non, not her. My *maîtresse* is young, pretty, and *gai comme un pinson*—but she has not been very gay here, I think."

"Do you?" A warning bell sounded in the recesses of his mind, a presentiment that he was about to learn something he might not like. "Why would she be sad, *petite*?"

Another shrug lifted her slender shoulders, and when she leaned a little closer to him, he could smell the sweet scent of French perfume.

"Because she must leave her betrothed in Boston, and always here, there are people watching, watching, saying, 'Do not go here' or 'Do not go there,' and it is very annoying to be grown and 'ave so many rules."

"But there are rules everywhere in polite society, *petite chou*, not just in Boston. Is that where you lived before coming here?"

"*Oui.* I am glad we left." Her eyelashes lifted, and she leaned forward until her face was close to his. She smiled a little. "I care nothing for polite society. Ffft! I care only for . . . what I like to do."

"And what do you like to do?"

She smiled.

He knew he could have her if he wanted her, for she leaned forward, eyes half-closed, her lips a moist, parted invitation.

"You are very lovely, Colette," he said in French, "but

I'm afraid this is not a good time for pleasant dalliance. Later, perhaps, when there is more privacy.''

Disappointment creased her brow, and her sultry mouth pursed in a pout that took him several moments to ease. It occurred to him that he was passing up a most tempting young woman, and one who was quite upset about his refusal, but oddly enough, he didn't care. Not now. Later he probably would, but now there were more important things to consider.

He would have preferred staying in Monterey at a hotel, but Martin had insisted he return to Buena Vista and Patrick Ryan. Tackett's death had been explained as the mere catching up of justice by government law enforcement, but still, it would be best if Nick stayed out of town for a little while longer, until things died down a bit more. And besides, he still had a job to do with Ryan. Or had he forgotten? Martin had asked with a little arch of his brows.

"Polite conversation is a very effective manner of gathering information," he'd said dryly, looking up at Nick through the thick smoke of a cigar. Leaning forward, Martin had flicked the long ashes into a crystal ashtray on the table between them, then sat back again. "While I realize your impatience, Lieutenant Kincade, I might remind you that you agreed to accept this assignment of your own free will. No one coerced you into a decision."

"Impending court-martial is not considered coercion, I presume," Nick countered mildly, and Martin smiled.

"Preposterous. Why, you were not in the army, Lieutenant Kincade. How could you be court-martialed?"

"That, I believe, was my first question as well." Nick knew well enough that Roy Martin had few scruples when it came to getting what he wanted. And if Martin had to bend a few rules or break them completely, he'd do it with equanimity, citing the overall good of America as reason enough to do so. With his far-reaching connections, Roy Martin could quite conceivably have Nicholas Kincade enlisted in the army, serve, and be court-martialed, all with a few strokes of his pen. Not exactly ethical, he blandly and readily admitted, but when the stakes were as high as the preservation of the newly admitted states, justifiable.

So today he had accepted Patrick Ryan's invitation to stay at Buena Vista while he mulled over the prospect of purchasing land he had inspected, and it had been a wise decision. Already he had managed to glean tidbits of information that might prove to be extremely helpful, once he was able to investigate more thoroughly.

Lanterns were being lit, and the faint light illuminated Colette's pretty face and reminded him that he needed to get ready for what would certainly be a stuffy dinner with Ryan and his other guests. If memory served, the Don Luis who was to attend tonight was also the man Martin suspected of being heavily involved with the munitions scheme. It should be a very interesting evening indeed, though not as rewarding as his afternoon.

He smiled faintly at the fresh memory of a satin-skinned Venus, emerging from the ocean with sultry eyes and an inviting mouth.

Yes, it had been a most rewarding afternoon, and a puzzling one. There was something about the girl, an elusive memory that went farther back than just the hacienda garden. Glimpses of another face with bright, jeweled eyes of amethyst had intruded, interposing between the sand-crusted creature in his arms and a vague memory.

But, matters moving along as swiftly as they had, he'd pushed the intriguing memory aside to attend to the girl at hand. And then the shock of discovering her a virgin had eliminated any other coherent thought so completely, he'd not thought of that odd incident until now.

It couldn't be just coincidence that Colette's mistress was from Boston, and the violet-eyed little brat who had had him arrested was from Boston, could it? Not two such similar coincidences. If that was true—well, he'd find out soon enough, and as Martin was so fond of saying, why borrow trouble? It so frequently found its own way.

*   *   *

Papa had summoned her, Tía Benita had come to say a few minutes earlier, and it was important, so she must see him before the guests arrived. The tone of the message did not bode well, and Tory was uneasy. Everything had seemed to go wrong lately.

The contentment she'd felt so briefly was gone, banished by the incomprehensible events of the day. She'd bathed immediately upon returning to the hacienda, immersing herself deep into a brass tub filled to the brim with hot, scented water, but she could still feel the imprint of his hands on her, the searing places he'd touched with his mouth. Oh God, she must have been crazy, seized with some kind of wild madness, to have offered herself to him like that, like—like a primitive sacrifice.

And he had been quick enough to take her, asking no questions until after, when it was too late. But innate honesty demanded that she acknowledge the powerful attraction she had felt for Kincade from the beginning; from the first time he'd touched her in the garden, she'd found herself thinking of him, imagining his hands on her. Perhaps she didn't really understand the strange, wild yearning that had led her to give herself to him as she had, but it had happened.

She closed her eyes and shuddered. Ever since returning, she'd felt a nagging worry there was something she should know, some important bit of information that eluded her. But what was it? How frustrating, to know there was something she should remember and be unable to retrieve it.

"Maîtresse?"

Tory opened her eyes and turned to see Colette standing just inside her door, half-hidden in the shadows, for the lamps had not yet been lit. It was time to dress for dinner and her meeting with Papa, an evening she dreaded looming ahead of her like a threat.

"Yes, Colette. I know—it's time to get ready."

"Oui. Already there is a guest."

"A guest?"

"Oui. Lieutenant Brock."

"Oh God, I forgot all about Lieutenant Brock!" Tory had

moved to the mirror, and frowned now at Colette's reflection behind her. The French maid was entirely too smug, too insolent, and needed to be chastised when Tory felt more like dealing with her. "Is he already here?"

"*Oui.* Ramon put him in the parlor." She gave her mistress a rather sly glance. "He say that you invite him, and Ramon was so surprised to hear it."

"Well, so I did. Why not? After all, he was always very polite aboard the steamer, and he's aware that I am already betrothed."

"*Oui,* but not your papa. Papa does not know of the so-good Reverend Gideon, does he?"

Tory gave her a cold look. "Not that it's any of your business, but no, he doesn't. Now hurry, Colette, and fasten my gown. Papa also doesn't know I invited Lieutenant Brock to dinner tonight." She turned away from the mirror and looked closely at her maid. Colette was dreamy-eyed and unusually slow tonight. What was the matter with her? It was bad enough that she had been gone all afternoon, and barely returned in time to get ready for dinner, but now she seemed to be all thumbs. "Oh, leave it," Tory finally said, more sharply than usual when Colette had fastened the tiny hooks wrong. "I'll do it myself or ask Tía Benita to help. Just fetch my shawl. Papa is waiting for me in his study, and I must hurry."

Breathless when she reached the study doors, Tory paused in the hall outside to compose herself, smoothed her deep-rose skirts with her hands, then rearranged the lace shawl Tía Benita had insisted she wear for modesty so that it draped becomingly from her shoulders, but left her throat bare. Her hair was swept atop her head and pinned with Spanish combs, with dangling tendrils left in casual curls in front of each ear, down her neck, and on her forehead. A decidedly French style, Colette had said approvingly, though she'd been abysmally slow arranging it. The scooped bodice of Tory's gown becomingly displayed the ruby pendant she wore around her neck; not a large stone, but a deep, rich color that shimmered between her breasts. She was quite fashionable; a bit daring, perhaps, with the low neckline, but stylish. A stunning example of a fallen woman . . .

She knocked on the door, then opened it and slipped inside, managing a smile when her father looked up from his desk with a slight frown that smoothed away when he saw her. "You sent for me, Papa?"

"Yes, I did." He motioned her inside. "Shut the door, please. What I have to say is private."

It sounded serious. Papa rarely used this grave tone with her, and she shut the door, apprehension welling up. *Did he know? Had someone seen?* No, that was ridiculous. She must stop this. After all, she was a grown woman now, and hardly a child. If she had made a mistake, it was her own mistake, and she was adult enough to accept any consequences.

"Are you well, Papa?"

But Papa didn't look as if he was ill, no more so than usual, and even a bit stronger than he'd been since she'd come home. At least he was out of bed, and sitting in his study, a very familiar scene to her. As a child, she'd always known she could find him there, and that he would spare at least a few minutes of his time for her before calling to Tía Benita or one of the maids to take her.

"Is it Mama or Diego?" She moved to stand in front of his desk. It was neat, with a small leather-bound ledger lying open, as if he'd been writing in it. The teakwood caddy that held letters was almost empty. Inkwells and pens were tidily stowed, and a heavy brass paperweight in the shape of a rearing stallion held down a small stack of papers. It was the same paperweight she'd played with as a child. When Papa looked up at her with a brow lifted quizzically, she said, "Mama's all right, isn't she?"

"Your mother is as always," he said tightly. He closed the ledger and tucked it into a drawer, then glanced up at her again, his expression easing. "Here. Sit down, Victoria. I think it's time we had a discussion about your future."

"My future?" She sat slowly in the carved chair by his desk, arranging her skirts and wondering if he meant her inheritance. Surely, he wasn't so ill that—"Papa, it isn't you, is it? You're not going to—"

"Die?" he finished for her with a slight smile. "Sooner or later, but not in the immediate future as far as I know. This isn't about me, niña, it's about you. As you know, the past decade in California has been unsettled, and I had to make arrangements to protect my holdings the best I could. Not just for my sake, but yours and Diego's. Fortunately, I've been lucky. Most of my business dealings have been profitable. I increased the size of my holdings to over twenty thousand acres, and since the annexation of California by the United States, I have increased it even more."

"That's wonderful, but I thought that you were worried about losing some of your land to taxes and the new laws."

"Not anymore." He smiled and leaned back in his leather chair, studying her for a moment. "I'm not certain how much of what you've been told you remember, Victoria, but I came to California as a simple Yankee sea captain. I had a few dollars in my pocket but a willingness to work and learn. And I did. When I married your mother, I married into a family of wealth and prestige. Our wedding gift was this house, though, of course, it was much smaller then. With the first acreage Don Francisco gave me, I planted vineyards and ran cattle. Then ships started to come regularly to Monterey and I had something to sell—wine and leather. With the money I made there, I increased land and vineyards and cattle, and as my business grew, I realized that there is much more money to be made by investing in other interests. Don Luis Reyes became my partner, and for years, we've made an enormous amount of money. For your future."

"By leaving me an inheritance, you mean."

"Indirectly. The house and lands will be Diego's one day. But your legacy is just as much or even more. I've bought property for you, put money back in your name, and sent you to school to prepare you for the future, to give you a solid background on which to draw strength and knowledge." He leaned forward a little, his chair creaking. "Knowledge is power, Victoria, remember that. You cannot be cheated if you know how to cheat.''

This wasn't at all what she'd expected, and she sat stiffly, staring at her father.

"You wrote me of your interest in women's rights,'' he said, smiling a little, "and I was impressed. You're smart, and while it may not yet be the right time for some of the changes women like Elizabeth Stanton and Lucretia Mott are demanding, the time will come. You will be prepared for it. Until then, however, I've made arrangements that will protect you and your dowry."

Head whirling, she anticipated what he would say next and lifted a hand to stop him, but he ignored her, saying, "I've arranged your marriage to Rafael Diaz y Reyes, Don Luis's oldest son. It is a perfect arrangement, as Don Luis is one of my partners, and our moneys will be combined in the distant future—perhaps into an empire. Of course, to protect you there have been several technicalities that I've specified, such as the fact that your husband cannot dispose of your property without your signature, and—"

"Papa . . . Papa, I cannot marry him!" She surged to her feet. "I'm already betrothed to another man."

Patrick stared up at her, unblinking, his expression unchanged. Then he shrugged slightly. "I'm afraid that was unwise, my dear. It shall have to be terminated, of course."

"No." She drew in a deep breath when his eyes narrowed into pinpoint blue flames, her words tumbling over one another: "I love him, Papa. He's a minister, and is vitally interested in women's rights. His name is Peter Gideon, and he loves me, too. Perhaps he could come to California, if you like, so we could be wed here."

He rose to his feet, vibrating with anger, and his voice was the icy cold tone she'd heard him use in the garden outside her patio. "You will marry Rafael. There is no more to be said about it, Victoria. In time, you will see that it is the best thing."

"I won't marry Rafael!" she flared, just as angry as he. "You cannot make me. I don't love him. I don't even *know* him, nor do I want to. I haven't seen him since we were children, and besides—I love Peter.''

Waving a hand in dismissal of that last statement, Patrick said more calmly, ''I realize this is a shock. The banns have been posted, but the wedding is not until next month, and the formal announcement won't be until the fiesta in two weeks. That should give you enough time to become accustomed to it—and to write this Peter and tell him you are no longer betrothed.''

''I won't.'' Her voice was calmer now, too, but no less determined. ''I am an adult, and—''

''You are not yet twenty-one, Victoria. Not that it matters. This is still California, and you are an unmarried female. You have no rights that I do not give you.''

Her chin came up, and her eyes narrowed dangerously. ''I am betrothed. Peter gave me a ring, and more than that—his heart and his love.''

''Love.'' Patrick almost sneered the word. ''None of that matters over time. Don't be foolish. I thought you had better sense, were more aware of what is really important in life. Love doesn't put clothes on your back or food in your mouth, and more often than not, it leaves you empty inside. Don't talk to me of love. You don't know the meaning of the word.''

''Apparently I know more than you . . .'' As hurt by his words as by his biting tone, she voiced her protest in a choked whisper. ''Peter and I need only our love to make us happy.''

God, she felt like the worst kind of a hypocrite! Love—what would Peter say when she told him what she had done? What would he *think* of her?

''Love? I've a notion that if the good Reverend Gideon knew you had not a penny to your name, he would find love elsewhere.'' Papa came from behind his desk, scowling down at her, eyes beneath his bushy brows narrowed and cold. ''Put your foolish notions behind you, girl. I won't allow you to throw away everything I've worked so long for. Do you think I married your mother out of love? I didn't. It was arranged by her parents.''

"Yes, and I see how happy you both are!" She was too angry and hurt and scared to care what she said. "My mother hides in her room waiting to die, and you think only of money and land and cattle. I'd rather starve than marry a man I don't love!"

"That may very well be your fate," he said coldly, and the angrier he grew, the more pronounced was his brogue, until she found it difficult to understand him. "Believe me, girl, you won't like being so hungry your belly meets your backbone, I know that well enough meself. Aye, and I know how it feels to have a man stand to my face and tell me that I'm not good enough for his daughter, I do, that I'll never amount to enough to buy a crust of bread. It cuts deep, girl, deep enough to leave scars, and I swore that I'd never have to hear it again, no, nor none of mine, no matter what I had to do to be sure of it. D'ye think I sent you to Boston to learn rebellion? I sent you to learn what you could not learn here, by God, and now it's time to repay me!"

He took a deep, shuddering breath, his face an alarming shade of red. With each word his voice had risen higher and higher, until now it was a full-scaled roar, reverberating from the dark wood of the study walls, echoing around her.

Just as angry, Tory refused to back down. "I shall go back to Boston on the next ship. Then you will not have to bother with me—"

"Ye'll not go," Patrick said furiously. "There's not a ship's captain will take ye once I alert the port authorities. And don't think I won't."

She had no doubt he'd do what he threatened, and paled. "You cannot keep me a prisoner here!"

"If ye want to think of it that way, it's your choice, but I know I'm only trying to keep ye safe ..." His voice was a low growl, trembling slightly with emotion and fatigue. His hands shook, and he leaned back against the edge of his massive desk, palms propping up his weight as he struggled for breath.

She was quivering, but to relent would be to die, as far as she was concerned. But neither did she want to feel responsible for her father's relapse, and his fury was so great, she worried that he would collapse at any moment. Now was not the time. Later, when he'd grown calm and would be able to listen, she would tell him again that she could not marry Rafael. Until then, she would compromise.

It wasn't easy. She drew in a deep, calming breath, lifting her eyes to her father's flushed face.

"I need time to think."

Papa drew in a deep breath and nodded. "Aye, lass, that you do. Then you'll see that it's for the best. I would not hurt you, don't you know that?"

It wasn't the reassurance it once would have been, but she nodded slowly. "Yes, Papa."

He came to her and put his arms around her, pressing her against his chest, murmuring that she would get over this Peter Gideon soon enough. Arranged marriages were always the best. It was the way of life, and he wanted to protect her.

"Do you remember I told you of a surprise?" He stepped back and curled his finger under her chin to lift her face. "When your brother returns, he is bringing it for you. Your uncle and he should be back from Los Angeles in a day or two, in plenty of time for the fiesta. Ah, you should see Diego. He has grown so tall you will hardly know him . . ."

She managed a faint smile and murmured a reply, but hardly knew what she was saying. Her world was careening out of control with a speed that was astonishing, and she was being swept helplessly along.

CRAD

Ten

Ramon had come to the study door, worried at the sound of el patrón's anger, and Tory excused herself to see to the first guests, who waited for them in the *grande sala*. Any excuse to flee would have sufficed, and she was grateful it had been Ramon, who at least understood the reason. At least she had not cried in front of Papa . . . but this was so *infuriating!*—so unfair—and now there were tears on her cheeks, making tracks in the rice powder she'd applied so carefully to her face.

Angrily, she stopped in front of a mirror lit by hall sconces and peered at her reflection. Carefully, so as not to smudge the light dusting of powder any more than it was, she used the edge of her lace shawl to wipe any trace of tears away. Crystal prisms reflected tiny rainbows of candlelight in a wavering pattern across her face.

Oh, I am so pale, she thought in dismay, and my eyes look almost black in this light. It is so frightening . . . the stuff of nightmares, and I don't know what I can do to stop it . . .

Papa was right when he said she was still under his legal authority. She was. Never had she thought he would be so callous, so completely uncaring about her wishes. This was not the man she had worshipped as a young child, thought of fondly while in Boston, and had been so glad to see when she'd arrived. This Patrick Ryan was a stranger to her, an enigma. This Papa was truly "Don Patricio," his Hispanicized name fitting him as if he had been born to it. Had he always been autocratic? Or was it just that she'd never openly defied him about anything so important to her?

Well, it would do her little good to worry over it now. Later, in the privacy and silence of her bedchamber, she would plan a strategy that would convince Papa she must not be forced to marry Rafael.

But now, Lieutenant Brock was waiting for her in the *sala* and the other guests would soon be arriving, if they had not already. Lord, she hadn't told Papa the lieutenant was coming. Understandable, given the circumstances, but it might be a trifle awkward if Dave stared at her with puppy-dog eyes in front of Papa after her impassioned announcement that she loved Peter and only Peter.

Still unsettled when she reached the *grande sala*, Tory managed to put on a bright smile as she stepped through the open double doors into the room filled with tall potted palms and heavy Spanish furniture. Wrought-iron candelabras illuminated the long room. At the far end, standing before tall windows that opened onto the tiled terrace where a fountain sprayed water and tiny fish swam in the cool, clear blue shallows, two men stood with their backs to her, engrossed in conversation.

They both turned when she entered, as if sensing her arrival, and she held out her hand, moving forward to greet Lieutenant Brock first. Then, as her gaze shifted politely to the other guest, she received a shock: It was Nick Kincade, dressed in elegant black and white dinner clothes that made him look wickedly handsome.

Stunned, she managed to mumble a reply to Dave's effusive greeting, but her attention was on Kincade. Oh, why had Papa invited *him* of all people to attend tonight? After what had happened today, could she behave as if she barely knew him?

Wildly: But I don't know him, not really, even after today,

when he touched me more intimately than any man has ever done . . .

Kincade betrayed no surprise, but merely bowed slightly, looking like a bandit in black and white clothes that did nothing to disguise his menace.

"It's a pleasure to finally meet you, Miss Ryan," he said smoothly, though there was a glint of devilry in his eyes that alarmed her. "Your father has spoken of you so often I feel as if I already know you."

"And . . . and you, sir."

Oblivious to the nuances, Lieutenant Brock took her hand and pressed his lips against the back, staring up at her with unabashed pleasure. "How very good to see you again, Miss Ryan."

"Thank you, Lieutenant." She withdrew her hand as quickly as possible, feeling awkward as silence descended on the *sala*, so that she could even hear the tall case clock in the hallway ticking away the seconds, sounding overloud in the sudden hush. How would she ever be able to conduct herself as a hostess tonight? Not *now*, when she was already on edge after Papa's announcement . . .

Thankfully, her aunt's training came to her rescue, and she flashed a bright smile and turned to greet Don Luis and his wife as they arrived, moving away from Kincade and Brock with relief, her voice light and casual, as if her entire world had not just gone mad.

"Don Luis—and Doña Dolores, how good to see you again after all this time . . . please, have some of our wine, as it's the hacienda's best in ten years . . ."

Maria, Don Luis's daughter, greeted Tory politely, smiling a little and fluttering an ivory lace fan, but it was obvious her attention was elsewhere. Rafael, however, gave her his undivided attention, taking her hand as Dave had done, and fixing his smoldering black eyes on her face.

"You have become a beautiful woman, Doña Vitoria." His smile was polite, but assessing. "I remembered you as a skinny girl with a bad temper."

She smiled sweetly. "I have changed. I'm no longer skinny."

He laughed. "You've still a sharp wit, Doña Vitoria. That has not changed."

"No, it hasn't." The evening promised to be a disaster, and it had hardly begun. Rafael must know of the infamous bargain; he was staring at her too closely, too appraisingly. It was not just the appraisal of changes in a childhood friend, but more calculated, as if she were a horse he intended to acquire. How absolutely *infuriating*!

She tried to ignore Don Rafael and turned her attention instead to Maria, but none of the art of conversation she'd learned in Boston did more than elicit a few noncommittal replies from the girl. Maria had not changed in the least. She'd always been introverted and shy, unlike her brother, but it made polite conversation almost impossible.

All the while, Tory was aware of Kincade, the annoying little smile that lifted one corner of his mouth, the way he stood with casual elegance, indifferent to the undercurrents he had to perceive. She felt flushed, and every time she glanced his way, her stomach did an odd little flip.

Ridiculous! she thought angrily. I should summon Ramon and have him make Kincade leave—quietly of course. But what will I say if he asks why I am making a guest of Don Patricio leave? And, oh God—Kincade might even refuse to go, and then there would be a scene I would have to explain . . . Why on earth is he still here? At Buena Vista?

The answer came with her father's tardy arrival in the *sala*, as he introduced Nicholas Kincade as the man who'd saved his life on a Mexican battlefield two years before. "At great risk to himself, I might add," Patrick Ryan said, smiling at Kincade. "I am in his debt, and my hospitality is always extended to him."

"I shall try not to presume too long on your hospitality, Don Patricio," Kincade said smoothly, "for as soon as we come to agreement on that tract of land you have offered to me, I shall be a neighbor instead of a guest."

"Excellent, excellent! But do not choose too quickly. I

have several possibilities near here, as well as a larger estate in the Sierra foothills. Not near the gold fields, I am afraid, or I would keep it myself . . .''

Tory's brow lifted. A hero. A businessman. A murderer. A seducer. How annoying. And Kincade seemed to perceive her irritation, for the glance he gave her was mocking, his amber-gold eyes glittering at her from beneath long lashes. It was as if he physically touched her, that brief regard, and her nerves tingled.

''So *this* is the man we have to thank for saving you!'' she said, turning her back on Kincade to face her father. ''Then of course, Lieutenant Kincade must be made to feel most welcome.''

She then avoided him assiduously, and spent a tedious quarter-hour talking with Doña Dolores, discussing the merits of French fashions. Maria did not join in, but fidgeted, looking often toward her brother—and Kincade.

Maria wasn't the only one. Tory was sharply aware of Nicholas Kincade as he stood talking to Don Luis and Rafael, switching effortlessly from English to Spanish. Tension vibrated through her, set her teeth on edge, and left her feeling raw and exposed. How did he so easily pretend she did not exist, when her every fiber was quivering because he was so close? It must have meant nothing to him today, the sweet words, the searing sensations he'd generated with his hands and mouth . . . just another casual tumble of a willing girl—oh God, she had made such a *fool* of herself!

In Boston, caught up in the changing dynamics of an embryonic women's movement, she had once declared that she felt it unjust to expect women to adhere to *masculine* notions of proper female behavior. Why accede so blindly to what was expected of them? Why not forge new standards of femininity?

Yet now she wondered if she had been an ingenuous child to ever think that moral standards would change so radically. It was expected that men had base desires, it was acceptable that they cater to them; any woman who did the same would be branded with the epithet of ''harlot.'' Perhaps one day public morality would accept the view of females having as much sexual freedom as men, but it wasn't that way now, and she had been so naive to forget it even for a moment.

In a moment of reckless abandon, she had yielded up that which she should have saved for her husband—for Peter. There had been no words of love, no pretense of courtship, only that wild, impulsive decision that had suddenly changed everything.

And if she'd thought it would mean anything to Nick Kincade, it was obvious she'd been very much mistaken.

She watched him engage in polite conversation with dinner guests as calmly if she were not there, as if he were merely one of her father's California business acquaintances. He even dressed the part, wearing clothes with a Spanish flair: well-fitted trousers that hugged his long legs, a white linen shirt with frilled front and cuffs, a sash around his waist, and the short jacket worn by the Californios. All that was missing was the customary broadcloth cloak of the *gente de razón*, such as the one Don Luis wore, a mark of the aristocracy.

But she would bet ten Spanish reals that a ruthless man like Kincade was wearing a gun or knife, well-hidden of course, but easily accessible.

Almost desperately, she turned her attention to Lieutenant Brock, but Rafael insinuated himself into the conversation, assuming a proprietary air that she found very irritating. Several times, he took her arm or her hand, giving Brock a warning look that could not be misinterpreted. Her irritation grew until she found it difficult to be polite, and she was on the verge of saying something sharp when dinner was announced. At last—a diversion.

In a juggling of dinner guests to accommodate the unexpected Lieutenant Brock, Tory was seated between Dave and Rafael, while Rafael's mousy younger sister Maria flirted shamelessly with Kincade, who sat beside her and was very attentive.

By the time the second course had been served, Tory's hand tightly clenched her gold-trimmed fork. *Foolish girl . . . perhaps I should inform her of his recent activities—tell her* what a rake he is, and a killer as well. Then perhaps Maria will not stare up at him with such big, shining brown eyes, or laugh quite so gaily at his every comment, sounding like a simpleminded schoolgirl, she thought viciously.

How could Papa even consider marrying her into this family? Don Luis and Doña Dolores were so boring, preferring to talk of local gossip rather than world events, women's rights, or even politics. What did *she* care if the local dressmaker had run off with a Yankee ship captain to look for gold? Or if—

"Pardon?" Surprised, she turned to look at Doña Dolores, "did you say it was a Señora *Valdez* who has left Monterey?"

"*Sí.* With a Yankee ship captain." Doña Dolores's broad face reflected her vicarious enjoyment, and she nodded eagerly. "It is a great scandal, for the Yankee captain was the one who delivered all the bolts of material to her to make the dresses, and now there are many who will not receive gowns they have ordered. He has the gold fever, like so many others. There are so many I know who have left suddenly, abandoned everything to go north and dig in the dirt and water to find gold, when they should stay here in Monterey . . ."

Tory stopped listening at that point, focusing instead on her own inner turmoil. After all, what did she care if Señora Valdez had not made a silly ball gown, when Papa had transformed into a coldly determined autocrat who had no sympathy or regard for her feelings? While she regretted the estrangement it had caused between them, a chasm that she wasn't certain would ever be crossed, Papa had hardly looked at her since arriving in the *sala*, as if she no longer existed for him. Did he think his decision would be the end of it? That she would acquiesce without another word?

To hide the sudden resentment in her eyes, she stared down at her plate, pushing at a thin slice of beef with the tines of her fork but unable to work up even a pretense of an appetite. When she glanced up, she caught Kincade's gaze on her and flushed angrily, her chin lifting in a gesture of defiance. As if he understood, he smiled slightly, that swift tucking of one side of his mouth in a mocking salute.

Damn him! But what could she expect with a man like Nick Kincade, who acted as if he'd never seen her before, as if nothing had happened between them? She might have been a fly on the wall for all the notice he gave her. Contradicting her first reaction, now she was irritated that he did no more than nod politely in her direction and turn away, bending his head to Maria again, smiling at something she said, his eyes crinkling at the corners with amusement.

Tory fumed. Her efforts to ignore him went largely unnoticed, and it was vexing that he seemed pleased enough to ignore *her* and devote so much attention to that sallow-faced little Maria. And really, she didn't care at all, except that he should at least be remorseful over what he'd done, and a little shamefaced about it.

The only reason she was so aware of him—of his low conversation and soft laughter, the way he smiled at poor Maria so often—was purely protective, of course. It would hardly do for him to try with the shy and naive Maria what he had done with *her,* would it?

And what would Papa say if he knew about that? Kincade would hardly be so welcome at the dinner table, she was certain, and might even find himself facing the vaqueros' guns, as she had once threatened. It would not be the first time an irate father had taken matters into his own hands when a man had ruined his daughter.

Ruin. Oh she *was* ruined, ruined for the purpose of marriage to Don Rafael, anyway, and what would happen if that was discovered? She shuddered to think. No Californio would wed his son and heir to an unchaste bride. It was beyond discussion, beyond decency . . .

"I was at the presidio last week, Lieutenant Kincade, and witnessed your duel," Brock said, catching Tory's attention so that she looked up at him with sudden apprehension. But he wasn't even looking at her, gazing instead at Nick Kincade with a faint sheen of admiration in his eyes, as if it had been a wonderful thing to slice a man to bloody ribbons in front of an entire town.

Kincade nodded politely, his brow lifting slightly. "A

rather sordid incident to discuss in front of ladies, don't you think, Lieutenant Brock?''

Flushing slightly, Dave nodded with a quick glance at his host. "Of course. My apologies. I should not have mentioned it in front of the ladies.''

"Definitely not,'' Tory heard herself say sharply, cutting a glance at Nick Kincade's impassive face. "Discussing murder at the dinner table is hardly a polite topic of conversation.''

She didn't know why she felt compelled to goad him, even at poor Brock's expense, but she did, and could not seem to stop herself.

"Really, I find it most distasteful to even countenance the fact that such vile occurrences and people exist in today's society. It's deplorable.''

If she had expected to embarrass Kincade with the wealth of contempt in her tone and words, she was disappointed. At least she gained his undivided attention, however, and his amber-gilt gaze shifted from Maria to her, resting on her with polite regard.

"Victoria!'' Papa sounded appalled, and she knew she had committed a serious breach of etiquette, but perhaps it was her third glass of wine, or the disturbing effect Kincade had on her when he was so near—just across the table with his attention so focused on Maria—and why should she care? Let Papa get angry. It was his fault for creating such havoc in her life, for being so heartless.

Stubbornly, she turned her gaze to her father. "I am positive that Lieutenant Kincade agrees with me, even if he is too polite—or cautious—to admit to murder.''

As shocked tension hummed in the air above the ornately set dinner table, and wineglasses hovered as if frozen into immobility, Dave Brock stepped manfully into the breach, looking uncomfortable and confused.

"Please, this is my fault for even bringing up such an unsuitable subject, and I beg your apologies for shocking the ladies into nervous reaction as I so obviously have done. It was unforgivable of me.''

"Of course, Lieutenant Brock.'' Papa sounded furious,

though his words were polite. "Though it seems as if my daughter has become overwrought by such conversation, I assure you she will be just fine. Victoria, shall I ask Tía Benita to escort you to your room to lie down?"

Carefully, not meeting Kincade's eyes, she shook her head. "No, Papa. I am sure that I will be fine in a moment, once the conversation changes to a more agreeable subject."

Don Luis cleared his throat and turned tactfully to his host, asking if the grapes promised to be as good a harvest this year as the last. "I understand your wine has once again been judged the best in our area, Don Patricio, and I congratulate you."

"Thank you, Don Luis. I attribute our success to the new techniques I have tried, and will be delighted to give you a tour of the vineyards and cellars at your convenience . . ."

Fully aware of Nick Kincade's somewhat bemused regard, Tory turned her attention to Dave again, sighing a heartfelt apology for her rudeness. "I just find it so distasteful to consort with criminals," she added in a loud whisper, and ignored Brock's uneasy glance toward Kincade. "But enough of that—I am certain you would also benefit from a tour of the vineyards. And you must visit the cellars where the wine casks are stored. It's quite remarkable how cool it is there, no matter the weather."

Papa spoke up then, his brow lifted and a strained smile on his face. "Alas, the cellars are being repaired at the moment, Lieutenant. Erosion has escalated, but another time, you will be welcome to visit them."

From there, the topic of conversation drifted to the new laws that were being made now that California was a territory of the United States, and Tory's outburst was carefully ignored.

It was a relief when the meal was over and the men retired to Papa's study to drink brandy, smoke cigars, and talk about the gold strike that was creating such a stir; but her ordeal was not ended. Now she must sit in the *sala* and be polite to Doña Dolores and Maria, pretending that she enjoyed their company. Not even Aunt Katherine's training had prepared her for the hour and a half of pure boredom she endured. Finally, while Dolores and her daughter embarked on a discussion of Spanish mantillas and Irish lace, Tory excused herself with a murmur. She left the small *sala* under the guise of using the convenience, and escaped onto the terrace for some precious privacy.

A ragged August moon shimmered in the sky overhead, and a night bird called softly. The heady fragrance of climbing roses filled the air, and gardenias smelled strong and sweet. Water splashed in the fountain. Beyond the garden, someone was playing a guitar, and the music sounded impassioned and reckless, a throbbing echo of her mood.

Wandering by the profusion of roses that tumbled over a trellis and ran haphazardly over the stones, she plucked a fiery blossom, cradling it in her palm while she struggled to reconcile the problems that faced her. There didn't seem to be an easy solution to any of it. But it was her life, wasn't it? If Papa was unhappy or angry with her, then *he* would just have to live with that. She would do what she must do to make herself happy; marrying Rafael was definitely not a viable consideration.

All during the disaster that was dinner, Rafael had sat beside her, slanting her an occasional glance, his dark eyes half-hidden by his lashes. He'd been polite, but beneath the cool exterior, she'd discerned an extremely possessive streak, evident in the proprietary glances he gave her and the way he observed Brock, as if he were an adversary—or her lover. Really, it was enough to make her recklessly contemplate ways to prick his conceit!

Caught up in her own internal chaos, Tory did not hear anyone come up behind her, not until a soft voice jerked her around, and she found herself staring up at Nick Kincade.

"Who are you hiding from, Venus?"

She drew in a sharp, irritated breath. "Don't call me that. And I'd appreciate it if you'd just go back inside and find someone who desires your company. Try Maria. She looked ready to fall into your arms at dinner. Maybe you can take *her* out to the garden tonight."

He laughed softly. "Loaded for bear, aren't you? Does Papa know what his little girl does when no one is watching?"

"Maybe the question is, Does Papa know what his honored guest does when *everyone* is watching!" She sucked in a steadying breath. "I would hardly equate public murder with a duel, but apparently, I'm the only one here tonight who has that opinion."

"Apparently." His brow quirked upward. "But you don't really care about that. That's not the reason you're so angry, is it?"

"What would you know about my reasons? You don't know anything at all about me—nothing!"

"Ah, there you are wrong, Venus. I know how soft your skin is and how sweet you taste, even with salt water on your mouth—"

"Stop it!" She was shaking, quivering with emotion and fear and yes, even shame that she had been so easy, and that he, of all people, should have been the one to discover her weakness.

He laughed softly and said carelessly, "I even know that you have a penchant for visiting Boston taverns—or once did."

When her head jerked up with eyes blinking in confusion and mounting horror, he grinned, teeth white in the murky light of lanterns strung in the trees over the terrace. "I'd almost forgotten you, Venus, until today, when I saw you clearly in the light and remembered your eyes. A man could never forget those eyes, even when they belong to an impudent brat with a disagreeable tendency to have good Samaritans arrested for their efforts."

"It was *you*—" She stumbled to a halt, flushing and compelled to defend herself, though she had no idea why. "It wasn't me who had you arrested, but my uncle—and anyway, you probably deserved it," she ended tartly when he laughed at her. "I'm sure Uncle Seamus only did Boston a service by having you removed as quickly as possible."

"Yes, so I was told as I was put aboard a ship in chains.

A unique experience, and one I'm not eager to repeat."

Crossly, "Well, don't blame *me!* You seem to have a tendency toward trouble anyway, as you have so readily proven in Monterey. I wouldn't be a bit surprised to hear soon that you have been hanged for it, or at the very least, chained in the hold of a ship bound for the Sandwich Islands."

"Not a bad fate. I rather fancy the bare-breasted native girls, with their dusky skin and clever little hands—"

"Degenerate!"

"Most assuredly. And where do you fit in?"

His soft words hung in the air for a moment, and Tory felt the heat of humiliation and self-loathing shrivel any scathing response she could have made. Her humiliation was complete when he murmured: "Beautiful Venus, I think you made a mistake today. If I had realized you were a virgin, I would not have allowed you to do it."

Unable to bear his pity, she managed a careless shrug. "It was no mistake. I intended to give myself to a total stranger, and I have no intention of divulging my reasons for it. It just happened to be you who came along at a propitious moment, that's all. Don't flatter yourself that it was anything more, because it wasn't."

"I see."

"No, as usual, I'm certain you don't see at all. But that's really not my concern. I got what I wanted, and that's the end of it." She curved her mouth into a mocking smile that made his eyes narrow. "You were used, Lieutenant Kincade, but I have no more use for you now."

He didn't reply, but stood gazing down at her, his eyes slightly narrowed and a faint smile tucking one corner of his mouth. His lazy speculation made her heart begin to beat crazily, and the breath grew short in her lungs, so that she felt a little lightheaded. What on earth was the matter with her? The man was totally dissolute, yet in the blink of an eye, her mood had switched from furious to this breathless anticipation, as if she thought he might kiss her just to prove her wrong—and then she was suddenly fearful he wouldn't.

There was a knowing gleam in his gaze that made her flush,

as if he knew what she expected, knew that she was almost daring him to kiss her, and she drew in a sharp breath. His eyes changed subtly, veiled suddenly by the length of his lashes, and he looked away from her, frowning a little.

"This isn't the time or place for this little experiment, Miss Ryan. And I'm not at all certain you want the truth anyway."

"As if a man like you would know the truth." Her fan clicked open and shut, open and shut, making a clacking noise as she fidgeted with it nervously.

Nick shrugged, recognizing her uncertainty.

During dinner, he'd observed with cynical amusement that the poor lieutenant practically turned himself inside out to be witty and charming, his gaze almost desperate every time he looked at Victoria Ryan. Poor bastard. She'd discard him in an instant; it was obvious that Brock was only a very minor event in her life, while Rafael Reyes glared daggers at him. The future husband, no doubt, and faced with the prospect of wedding a Boston belle who would not be the tractable, obedient wife he had every right to expect. How had Patrick Ryan convinced Don Luis to sacrifice his son? And what kind of advantage would there be to them for the bargain? Maybe Martin was more right than he knew when he said that Ryan would sell his mother if he smelled a profit in it.

But now Victoria Ryan was fuming, trying to provoke a reaction from him she obviously couldn't handle when she got it. He stared down at her, into jeweled eyes fringed with sooty lashes, and recalled an ugly hat and defiant eyes gazing up at him, belonging to a young girl who had no business being in a Boston tavern. He should have recognized her immediately, but it had been dark that night in the garden, and he'd had other things on his mind on the beach today, where her wet clothes had revealed more than they'd hidden from his interested gaze.

After a moment, when her magnificent violet eyes were still flashing with anger, he said softly, "Here comes one of your suitors, Miss Ryan. Try to be respectable."

"Really! You are the most impossible, insufferable, *evil* man I've ever had the misfortune to meet—"

"Somehow, I doubt it."

It was faintly amusing to watch her control her temper with an effort, then turn toward her *novio* as if nothing was the matter, putting a smile on her face that could curdle milk.

Rafael Reyes—probably under duress—was approaching across the patio, looking rather grim when he saw Victoria with Nick. Poor fellow. Married life would be hell for him.

The slim Californio smiled when he reached them, though his eyes were wary. "I do not think you should be out here without your duenna, Doña Vitoria," Rafael said stiffly. "Is she nearby?"

Victoria stared at Don Rafael, and Nick saw the flash of resentment in her eyes at the implied reproof. No, not a young lady who would take kindly to being dominated by her husband, that was plain. After a moment of sizzling silence, she pointed toward the house.

"Tía Benita is not far, since you seem worried about her. *I* am entertaining our honored guest."

Amused, Nick wondered if Don Rafael would catch the subtle sarcasm in her tone. He seemed a little confused, as well as disapproving.

"*Alone*, Doña Vitoria?" Rafael's lifted eyebrow and cool glance toward Nick was displeased. "It is not at all proper to entertain a man alone."

Victoria smiled, but behind the sugary facade, her voice and eyes were sharp. "I'm certain you don't mean to criticize me, Don Rafael. After all, I am not a child, and am quite capable of assessing situations and conducting myself properly."

Anger simmered in the young Californio's eyes, and his demeanor was stiff and offended, but it was apparent he had no idea how to handle this temperamental young woman challenging him to try. Silence fell, thick and heavy, before Rafael cleared his throat, his words deliberately calm, though a deaf man could have heard his fury: "Doña Vitoria, perhaps you will allow me to speak with you in private for a moment."

This was a good time, Nick decided, to take his leave.

But Victoria Ryan was stubbornly determined to tweak

Don Rafael's nose, it seemed, for she reached out and put a detaining hand on Nick's arm when he turned go to, smiling brightly at him. "I would not dream of being so rude as to ask my father's honored guest to leave, Don Rafael, and I find myself amazed that you would do so after seeming so concerned with the finer points of etiquette." Violet eyes gleamed with temper as she fluttered a lace and ivory fan with quick, agitated movements, stirring tendrils of fire-dark hair at the sides of her face.

"Señor," Don Rafael said harshly, turning to Nick, "will you excuse us while I speak with my *novia*?"

"Of course." Nick grinned at the quick dark look she threw him, and gently removed her hand from where it still rested on his arm. Stepping back under the rosy glow of a lamp, he paused to say: "I enjoyed the dinner and the conversation, Miss Ryan. It's been a pleasant evening, but a long day. I'll leave you two to enjoy the privacy of the garden. I'm told it is very romantic at night."

He didn't look at her again, knowing he would see fury in her eyes and the set of her jaw at his final words. Too bad Rafael didn't seem eager to civilize his future bride; he'd bet it would be anything but boring.

Eleven

Tory stared at Nick Kincade's departing back. Unbelievable. Why had she not known him at once? How had she forgotten that day almost three years ago in a Boston tavern, when she had been so terrified, and stood helplessly while a strange man kissed her thoroughly and ruthlessly? For weeks afterward she could not forget it, dreamed of it at night, and when she awoke, felt so flushed and funny inside, disturbed by the restless yearning that the dreams always left. Even Aunt Katherine had remarked that her experience had changed her, and worried that she had somehow been scarred by the dreadful incident with that horrible stranger.

But it had been Sean who had suspected the truth, that it was much more than just the terror of being involved in a tavern brawl that had affected her. Afterward, he had patiently and kindly explained to her some of the truth about what happened between men and women, and how an experienced man could take advantage of a young girl's inexperience. Then she had understood more, and after a while, the dreams had disappeared and she had managed to put the entire sordid incident out of her mind.

Until now.

Until he had just reminded her of it, his eyes gleaming at

her with a trace of mockery . . . God, she was so humiliated!

"I demand to know the meaning of your improper behavior, Doña Vitoria," Rafael was saying harshly, his hand hard on her arm.

Tory shook it loose and turned her attention to the young Californio. "Don't you ever talk to me like that again!" She didn't bother to hide her anger with Rafael, though she kept her voice low. "You are not my *novio*, and it is unlikely that you will ever be, no matter what my father and yours may have decided. I will never be the meek, docile little wife that you want and need. And besides—I'm in love with someone else."

Rafael swore softly in Spanish, and his dark eyes gleamed angrily. "I shall speak to your father about this . . . I will not accept soiled goods, no matter the dowry."

Tory started to correct him, then stopped and smiled. "Really? I'm relieved to hear it. Perhaps—"

"Doña Vitoria," Tía Benita said from the doorway, looking angry and upset, "I have been searching for you."

"As you can see, I am here." Tory nodded coolly at Rafael, who moved angrily aside to let her pass.

She left him standing on the patio, rigid with fury, grim purpose glaring at her from his dark eyes. There was no doubt in her mind that soon there would be repercussions, but she didn't care. She had endured enough for one evening, and it wasn't over yet.

Dave Brock cornered her as soon as she entered the *sala* again, looking a little nervously at Tía Benita, who hovered close behind like a hungry hawk. "Miss Ryan, may I speak to your father about calling on you again?"

A little embarrassed, Tory stiffly informed him that her father had decided she was to marry Don Luis's son, and that she was sure he would not give permission.

"But that can't be!" Dave's blue eyes were dark with distress. "On the ship you said you were to marry a man in Boston, but I thought—"

"Please, don't make things worse." Her head throbbed, and she knew Tía Benita had no intention of allowing them private conversation. Her voice lowered. "My father had no idea that I am already betrothed, and this promises to be a terrible mess. I don't think I can bear any more confusion, so just go on to San Francisco." She could barely force the words out now, and saw that Tía Benita was descending upon them as if she suspected a mutiny. "Please, Lieutenant—just *go*!" she said almost desperately.

Stiffening with hurt pride, Dave nodded. "Very well. I'll go."

"Oh, do forgive me, but it is all such a terrible strain." She put an impulsive hand on his arm and forced a smile. "I'm at my wit's end. I don't know what to do, or how to get out of this mess, and I'm afraid I've offended you needlessly. I don't want you to leave angry, Lieutenant, or feeling that you have erred in some way, please."

Dave was silent for a moment, then nodded. "I think I understand. If you need me, I'll be in Monterey for another week, or at least until I can find a horse to buy. There's a shortage of them since the gold strike, with everyone buying them up to ride out of town or use as pack animals. At any rate, I'm staying at the hotel off the east side of the presidio."

"Thank you, but I'm afraid there's nothing you can do. I'll just have to work this out as best I can—if it can be salvaged at all."

Tía Benita moved closer, watching and listening, and there was nothing else she could say, so she silently endured until enough time lapsed that she could plead a headache without causing any more comment than she already had. It was bad enough that she had verbally assaulted Nick Kincade in front of the entire assemblage of guests, but then to be forced to sit in their company knowing they must think her rude at the very least, while Nick Kincade—who was the cause—appeared as a much maligned guest, was more than she could bear.

Thankfully, she soon escaped, stingingly aware that Tía Benita's escort was more for her confinement than for her comfort. Once back in her room, she was too tense to sleep, and tossed and turned restlessly in her wide bed, staring out her opened draperies at the soft night shadows in her court-yard.

Was there no way to convince Papa how set against the marriage she was? She went over their confrontation word by word, replaying it in her mind until she was exhausted. Yet nothing changed, and in retrospect, her father's words were even more determined than she'd realized at the time.

In the cool gray hours before dawn, she bitterly resigned herself to the fact that her father had no intention of changing his mind, and every intention of forcing her to keep the agreement he had made with Don Luis. That there had been an advantageous bargain, she had no doubt. Not for one moment did she believe that he had just her happiness in mind; there were too many unexplained questions for that to be true.

What had happened to the loving father she remembered? Had the years changed him, or had her child's perception been warped? It was inconceivable that he could always have been this calculating, but the evidence was before her in his cold, unyielding edict that she marry Don Rafael.

Their interview after breakfast was even more unpleasant than the first had been, and despite his threat, Tory was shocked to discover that Papa had already alerted the port authorities that she was not to be allowed to leave Monterey by ship.

"For your own protection." He averted his eyes, looking down at the pristine surface of his desk. For a moment, he toyed with the paperweight, fingers sliding restlessly over the bronze stallion. Then he looked up at her, and his eyes were cool and remote. "And I have arranged for my personal physician to attend you tomorrow afternoon. An examination has been requested by Don Luis."

A chill raked her, and she couldn't speak for a moment. Apparently, Rafael had gone straight to his father, and Don Luis to Papa. Well, she had known the risk, even if she had not considered this result.

Her chin lifted defiantly. "I refuse to allow it. I am not a mare in heat, but a woman. Your daughter, in case you've forgotten."

He met her eyes coldly. "I've not forgotten. Apparently you have. It doesn't matter. If you are found to be . . . defiled . . . you will leave this house in disgrace, and spend the rest of your days in the convent of Santa Lucia."

Hot tears clogged her throat, but she would not allow them to fall, and managed to keep her voice steady. "And if I am not *defiled*?"

"Then you will wed Don Rafael, as has been planned."

Bitterly, she said, "Then perhaps I should save us all a great deal of trouble and announce that my trunks should be packed for my journey to Santa Lucia."

Patrick's mouth thinned, and his blue eyes were flinty and hard. He stared at her for a long moment, and then, with no warning, jerked up the heavy bronze paperweight and flung it across the room. There was the brittle sound of breaking glass as it struck a window, and shards flew into the air like tiny missiles. Tory did not move, but stood holding his gaze, though her hands were clenched into tight fists at her sides.

"Maldito!" he swore in Spanish, staring hard at her. "Do you know what you have done? There is a debt I must pay, a debt of honor as well as of gold. It was borrowed with the understanding that you would marry Don Luis's son, and now you have ruined it . . . all my plans destroyed if this is true . . ."

Tiny veins stood out on his forehead, and his complexion altered to an alarming red, but his voice was fairly steady: "As you have shown yourself to be unreliable, I shall *insist* that an examination be performed, so that I will be able to assure myself that you have had so little regard for your own welfare as to conduct yourself like a common strumpet. Now go. *Go!*"

Without a word, Tory turned and left his study.

Shaking with reaction, she thought angrily, How can I forgive this? He has gone too far. Whatever might have been before is forgotten now. Now she knew she could not stay, *would* not stay, and would take whatever steps she must to escape Monterey and her father's determined plans. But how? It had to be soon. Once the examination was completed, Papa was perfectly capable of having her locked in her room until he could make the arrangements to send her to a convent.

Night shadows were long when she finally formed a desperate plan, a wild clutching at straws, and she went to her writing desk and pulled out a clean sheet of paper and pen and ink. Several discarded attempts later, she finally had penned what she hoped would succeed.

"Word has come to me that Señora Valdez almost finished my ball gown before she left Monterey," she told Tía Benita the next morning, "and I must hurry to be certain that it is the right gown before it is sold to someone else. It is paid for, and perhaps I can finish it."

Tía Benita insisted that she would accompany her into town. "Perhaps your mama will take a long nap today, so that I may go with you. I have been told not to allow you out of my sight."

"Am I a prisoner?"

Hesitating, Tía Benita shook her head. "No. But you are to be escorted every moment, I am told." Her eyes were worried, and there were deep lines on each side of her mouth; after a moment, she shook her head again, sighing. "You are so stubborn, niña, like your brother. Can you not resign yourself to the marriage? It is customary for parents to arrange marriages, as you must know."

"It is a feudal custom. This is the nineteenth century, not the ninth. And I am not a mare to be *sold* to the highest bidder." She paused, bit her lip to hold back any more bitter, betraying words. "It looks as if I will have to yield in the end, though it makes me sad. I intend to do my best to talk Papa out of it."

Tía Benita smiled a little. "I expected that much. So I will see if it is possible for me to escort you into town, though if I cannot, you must still have an escort. You do understand?"

"Yes, of course. And if you think that I try to avoid it, I can tell you that I don't mind an escort."

That was not at *all* what she wanted, but fortunately, Mama was restless that day, and insisted Tía Benita remain with her. It was Colette who accompanied Tory into Monterey, as well as Pablo and two other vaqueros as their escort—or guards, she thought resentfully, as if I am a criminal!

It was a cloudy day, with rain on the horizon, a long gray line coming off the ocean and bringing strong winds with it as the chaise sped along the winding road that curved beside the ocean.

Colette was delighted to be out from under the shadows of the hacienda walls and the tension that permeated it of late, while Tory was too nervous to pay much attention to anything but her own inner turmoil. If her plan worked, it would offer her the opportunity she needed; if it did not, she might very well find herself an unwilling bride. Or a nun.

"Wait outside," Tory said to Pablo when the chaise was halted at the stone curb in front of Señora Valdez's shop, and when he frowned, she added with just the right touch of derision, "Unless you have a fondness for silk and lace undergarments?"

Coloring, Pablo muttered a warning that she not take too long, for he would have to come inside with her, as Don Patricio had told him to do if she was out of his sight for longer than a few moments.

"I shall stand in the shop window where you can see me if you like," Tory offered as Tomás, one of the vaqueros, helped her down from the chaise, his broad face impassive.

Relief flooded Pablo's dark features. "Then you may take your time, Doña Vitoria."

Once inside the shop that smelled of musty wool and the dyes they used for laces and threads, while a bewildered clerk tried to explain that Señora Valdez had gone and she did not know which gowns were complete, Colette slipped silently out the rear of the shop as Tory had instructed her. Nervous, clasping and unclasping her gloved hands, Tory stood in front of the wide square shop window as she had promised Pablo, and argued lengthily with the clerk.

The clerk, a rather frazzled woman, looked nonplussed when Tory insisted that she search for the gown.

"I know it is here, Señora Sanchez. It is almost ready, for I was told that it was. You must search for it."

Finally, in exasperation, Señora Sanchez went upstairs to the sewing rooms to look for the gown Tory described, muttering to herself in Spanish about the crazy Americana as she climbed the rickety flight of stairs.

Tory glanced out the window; Pablo was patiently waiting, as she had expected. Of course. He would manfully strive to do his duty, as he had sworn to Ramon he would.

If it was not so terrible to be trapped, like a rabbit in a barrel, she would find it vaguely amusing that such a young man had been entrusted to be her jailor. Perhaps he was still trying to overcome the cloud that had shadowed his reputation after the day he had accompanied her to the presidio; she was sorry for that, but she had been so shaken by what she had seen, the terrible, brutal death of a man in the square, that she had said the first thing she could think of when asked why she was so distraught upon her return, and poor Pablo had been blamed for her horse running away with her.

Another dark deed to lay at the feet of Nick Kincade, who had as little regard for human life as he did for the impressionable emotions of a young woman he found on the beach. It had occurred to her since to wonder what he had been doing down there that day but then, she had not thought to ask.

By the time the clerk found the gown for her, Colette returned, breathless and triumphant, her usual insolence replaced by the excitement of being part of a secret plan.

Standing behind a row of laces, Colette whispered, "The lieutenant says he will do what you ask in the letter, if you will only let him know when you wish for him to help you."

Tory nodded. Lieutenant Brock promised to be very helpful after all. Perhaps she should feel a little guilty for taking advantage of him, but he had offered, after all, and she was desperate. Besides, she would pay him well, as she had said in the note Colette delivered, so it was not as if she was being totally heartless.

She turned her attention to the distraught clerk, who was

pointing out to her the unfinished hem and sleeves, and how it was not fit to be worn.

"See here? The hem is pinned but not sewn, and the sleeves are not yet puffed—"

"I'll take it anyway." Tory lifted a brow when Señora Sanchez stared at her, aghast. "Señora Valdez took my father's money for it, and it is to be my wedding gown. Box it for me, please."

"But . . . it is not finished!"

"Box it," she said so coldly that Señora Sanchez quailed, nodded, and did as she was told. When they left the shop, Colette carried the gown in a large box, and gave it to Tomás to put into the chaise.

It might work after all, Tory thought, almost feverishly. Lieutenant Brock could escort her to San Francisco, and there she would board a ship for Boston. For home—and Peter Gideon.

On the way back to Buena Vista, scattered drops of rain began to fall, leaving a dusty smell in the air where it struck the road. Leaves of roadside plants shuddered under the increasing impact. By the time the chaise arrived at the hacienda, the leather roof was slick with rain and the horses were wet, as well as the vaqueros, who looked drenched and uncomfortable.

Manuel came out to greet them with an umbrella so the ladies would not get wet coming into the house, but his expression was so grave Tory had an instant's fear someone knew what she intended to do. But that was impossible. She had not even told Colette what she planned, only given her a sealed envelope to deliver to Brock.

Rain was a steady rattle against the tautly stretched material between the metal spines of the umbrella as she stepped beneath its shelter, frowning a little. In the distance, thunder rumbled.

"What is it, Manuel?"

"Doña Vitoria," he began, his voice quavering, "I am afraid that something evil has befallen. You must go inside at once, for you are needed."

"Needed?" She stepped across a widening puddle in front of the porch and under the protection of the low roof, fumbling with the sash of her hat to shake the feathers free of rain. "What do you mean?"

Shaking his head, the old man lowered the umbrella and looked down at the ground for a moment, then up at her. "Your father has taken very ill. Please. Go inside."

It was then she noticed the strange carriage in front of the hacienda, and as she went inside, she passed a weeping housemaid just inside the door. Ramon stood wringing his hands in the hallway, not looking at her. Dear God—it must be terrible, if the servants were so upset.

Tía Benita met her in the hallway outside her father's room, and her eyes were red with weeping. "Niña," she said, choking a little on her tears, "your papa . . . your papa . . ."

"Papa? What is the matter? Tell me at once, Tía! You're frightening me."

"He's dead, niña," she said softly, and reached out to pull Tory close to her, her arms warm and comforting against the sudden chills that racked Tory's body. "Your papa is dead."

Twelve

Heavy black linen shrouded the front door and windows; wooden shutters were closed, and it was dark and cool in her father's study, shadows crouching like ravenous beasts in the far corners, making Tory shudder at the comparison. *Ravenous beasts* . . . Like her uncle—

Don Sebastian gazed at her coolly. "Nothing has changed. Your father's death is unfortunate, but the wedding to Don Rafael will be as planned."

In the corner of Papa's study, Diego shifted from one foot to the other; autumn sunlight slanted through the shutters over the window and across his youthfully handsome face. Tory stiffened with outrage and looked back at her uncle. Don Sebastian Montoya, Mama's brother, had taken over household affairs since Papa's death. Now he sat at Papa's desk, in Papa's leather chair, acting for all the world as if he intended to take Papa's place.

Oh no, not if she could help it!

Lifting her chin, Tory matched his coolness. "You are not my father. This is insupportable. He's hardly in the ground before you come in here and announce that you're going to take over. As the oldest child, I am fully capable of arranging my own life, and I resent your interference. I will not tolerate it.''

Sebastian's hooded eyes regarded her steadily. "You are female, and have no rights. I act in your behalf, as your father would do.''

"Papa is dead.'' She choked slightly on the words. *A stroke,* the physician had said, *probably brought on by some kind of stress* . . . "You are not my guardian, and I refuse to allow your interference, is that understood?''

"You have no choice.'' Sebastian rose from the chair. He faced her with narrowed eyes. "Your father allowed you too much freedom. I have no intention of doing the same. As your guardian, I shall see that you recall proper manners and behavior. If Don Patricio had forbidden your wild ways, he would not now be lying in a grave.''

Tory blanched. Her throat ached with suppressed pain and fury. It was bad enough that Papa was dead, and she felt such regret for their final words, but to be reminded of it so cruelly . . . ! She refused to let her uncle intimidate her anymore, as he had been doing since Papa's funeral, and stepped angrily forward.

"How dare you—!''

"I dare what I please.'' He lifted a dark brow and pushed several papers across the desk toward her. After dipping a pen in the inkwell, he held it out to her. "You will obey, or I will have you locked in your room until you are no longer my responsibility. I'm certain you don't want that, do you? No, I thought not.'' A faint smile curved his thin lips, a cruel smile, as if he enjoyed her agitation. "Now sign the papers as you were told.''

Tory looked down at the stack of papers. Something to do with her inheritance, he'd said, a mere formality. But how can I think of business when Papa is dead and I am *still* being forced to marry against my will? Oh, it is insufferable to be completely dependent and helpless . . .

She looked up at Don Sebastian. "I will not sign anything, even if you lock me in the calabozo, is that clear enough? You won't intimidate me with this bluff. No priest would perform a ceremony for a woman brought to the altar in chains, not even in California. Do not test me, Tío Sebastian—I think you will lose.''

His hand curled into a fist around the pen, snapping it in two with a brittle pop. He held it up, staring coldly at her. ''I will break you in half just so if you are fool enough to challenge me. And you *will* sign these papers, whether willing or not.''

''Enough of this!'' Diego's sudden words were the first he'd spoken since Tory had confronted their uncle. ''My father is hardly cold in the ground and you are quarreling like two dogs. I refuse to allow it.''

Tory looked at him with surprise. Diego sounded so mature, so very much in command, and she realized that he had grown into a man while she was away. His dark blue eyes were angry, his mouth a taut line.

Diego came forward, putting himself physically between them. He put a hand on his sister's shoulder. ''Go see to Mama while I speak with Tío Sebastian. Please,'' he added when she glared at him, and after a slight hesitation, she nodded and left the room.

As she shut the door behind her, she heard her brother say, ''Fool! Don't you know better than to provoke her like that? Tory will never sign those papers if you try to force her . . .''

At least Diego had sense enough to recognize that she could not be so easily intimidated. Perhaps he would be an ally in her resistance against their uncle. He would be the only one, for she had no one else. Not even her mother.

Mama. Oddly enough, Paloma seemed to have grown stronger in the week since Papa's death. Now she could more frequently be found out on her shaded patio, or in the *grande sala,* and at the dining table of an evening. It was as if her husband's death had freed her, and Tory felt vaguely uneasy around her. But, after all, it was not as if she had ever been close to her mother.

Doña Paloma was out on the verandah, sitting in a patch of warm sunshine. Her dark hair was piled atop her head and held with Spanish combs that glittered in the light, and she looked up when Tory approached. A faint smile curved her mouth, but her brow was lifted in surprise.

"Please, sit." She indicated a wrought-iron chair with a wave of her arm. "It is a pleasant day."

Rather taken aback, Tory sat down opposite her mother, feeling awkward and uncertain. There were no traces of grief on Paloma's face, or even melancholy, and Tory resented her indifference. Perhaps Papa hadn't been the best husband, but his daughter had once loved him—or loved the man she had always thought he was. That was the Papa she would miss, not the coldly autocratic man he had been at the last. Somehow, that part was forgotten in the sorrow over his death.

"You came to me for a reason," Paloma said after several moments of silence. "What is it you wish?"

Conversation with her mother was so rare that Tory blurted, "I want to leave Monterey. I want to go back to Boston, but Don Sebastian says I must marry Rafael."

Paloma's brow lifted slightly. "Did you expect differently because your father is dead? Men do not care for our wishes. We are expected to obey, not think."

She spoke calmly, but there was an underlying note of bitterness that did not escape Tory's notice, and she leaned forward to gaze intently at her mother.

"But we don't *have* to always obey like mindless sheep, do we?"

The suggestion of a smile quivered at one corner of Paloma's mouth. "The answer depends on who is asked the question."

"I'm asking *you*. Do you think women should be treated as slaves, forced to marry whomever is chosen for them, and then considered as undisciplined children if daring to object?"

"I'm not the one to ask that question," Paloma said after a long interval of silence. "I did as I was bid, and offered no objections. I behaved as I was reared to conduct myself, as a lady, quiet and meek and submissive."

"Yes, and spent the next twenty years of your life hiding

in a dark room because you hated it so badly,'' Tory retorted.
"Did you not ever wish you had said *no*?''

For the first time that she could remember, her mother
looked at her as if she was really seeing her. She stared at
her for a long moment, then blinked slightly; her large dark
eyes were shiny with a misty sheen of unshed tears. "Every
day of my life, I wished that I had the courage to say no,''
she said finally, her voice a bare whisper, "that I had run
away with my Roberto instead of—''

She halted and looked away, her words drifting into silence. Tory suddenly realized how hard life must have been
for her mother. How dreadful, to love one man and be wed
to another, to look down the long, lonely years and realize
that it would never be any better. It was no small wonder that
Paloma had chosen to shut herself away rather than face the
reality of her life.

But it was not a choice Tory intended to make. Perhaps
her mother had not had the courage, but she did. Or determination would better describe what she felt, a tenacity that
refused to allow her to meekly submit to the autocratic de-
mands of another.

Leaning forward, she caught her mother's attention. "I,
too, have a Roberto. In Boston. His name is Peter Gideon,
and I am betrothed to him.''

Paloma nodded slowly. "I warned your father that you
were not the weak child I had been, but he would not listen.
I told him it was an abomination, but he was so determined—
the agreement with Don Luis, you see, was more important
than anything else . . .''

Tory stared at her. Echoes of words in the garden outside
her room came back to her. *It is an abomination . . . you care
nothing for anyone but yourself . . . my life may be over but
hers is not . . .*

"It was you, wasn't it . . .'' When her mother lifted a puzzled brow, she explained, "In the garden a few weeks ago,
outside my gate. I heard you arguing with Papa. I didn't recognize your voice, it was so—''

"Determined?'' Paloma smiled bitterly. "Yes, I am rarely

given to spurts of defiance. I discovered years ago how use-less and exhausting it can be.''

"Not for me.''

Paloma regarded her closely for a moment, then smiled. She lifted a hand as if she would caress Tory's face, but let it drop back to her lap. She looked away, frowning a little, then turned back to her daughter as if seized with sudden determination.

"There is something I must tell you—there are moneys deposited in your name in several banks, and Diego's as well. It was a way of hiding money that your father made by selling weapons to foreign countries.''

"Weapons? Oh, sales of munitions. I suppose someone has to do it, have war materials manufactured and—''

"No, no, Victoria—it is not as you think. These weapons, these instruments of destruction, are sold to any band of mer-cenaries who have the money to buy them, not just legitimate sales to foreign powers. Do you know what that means? Ah, I see by your face that you do. Yes, if a group of criminals offered money for rifles, pistols, ammunition—even cannons and artillery—your papa would sell them at a high price.'' She sank back into her chair and put a hand over her eyes for a moment, then looked up at Tory again. "You say noth-ing. Does it distress you, or do you also consider it a suitable manner of gaining a fortune?''

She felt cold suddenly, and shivered, putting her arms close to her body. "No. It's . . . I hate it. All this time, the money he sent for my education and support—now I know why Un-cle Seamus never wished to discuss business with Papa. He never said, but I always knew there was something, and I just thought . . . Dear God, how I hate even the thought that he did such things!''

"Yes, as did I. Listen to me, *mi hija,* for what I will tell you next is very important—there is much money hidden away, for your papa did not trust Don Luis or my brother. If Sebastian discovers it, he will continue with this despicable trade, the dealing of death to innocents. He must not be al-lowed to retrieve the moneys, do you understand?''

"But what can I do?"

"You must get to the accounts first and empty them."

Tory shuddered. "I could not—knowing that it's evil money, I would always feel as if it was stained with blood."

"Use it for good then, but do not allow my brother to have it."

She stared at her mother, at the face that now held more fire and passion than she had ever seen in it. "But Mama, why do *you* not do it?"

Paloma's mouth twisted bitterly. "There are reasons and— reasons, my child. I am old now, and too weary to fight. I cannot bring shame upon my family by going to the authorities with what I know, and Diego—he has always been so close to your father, and God forgive me, but I do not know him. He is aloof, very male, and men seem to think so differently from women that I do not know if I could trust him not to do the wrong thing. Even if he intended good, he might very well play right into Sebastian's hands. My brother is clever, which is why your father went to such lengths to hide money and information from him. If he can, Sebastian will rule the world."

"You can't mean that."

"I do mean it. Ah, child, there are things you do not know, things that happened so long ago . . . but to talk of them now is pointless. Tell me, will you take the money before your uncle can get it?"

"If I can. But . . . how?"

"You wish to leave Monterey, yes?"

"Of course, and I had even planned a way to do it, but then Papa died, and I thought there would be no need, that I could just go back to Boston after all the affairs here were settled. I've always assumed that Diego would inherit the house and land, as is customary."

"You must get away. I will tell you how, but you must do it. If I do too much, Sebastian will grow suspicious. Is there someone you can ask to help you?"

"Yes, the man I met on the steamer, Lieutenant Brock. I think he will help. I don't trust anyone else," she added darkly, thinking of Nick Kincade. Why, he was probably one of the mercenaries her father sold his weapons to, and would like nothing better than to get his hands on the money! Oh, how could she have ever been so foolish as to think even for a moment that he was exciting?

"Good. Then I will make arrangements once you have gotten a message to this lieutenant. I will have Rámon deliver it to him, for he would never suspect me of betraying the family." Her eyes glittered darkly, and the smile on her mouth was exultant. "Yes. You are strong, niña. You will be able to do what I never was able to do. Ah, the wasted years . . . perhaps one day you will forgive me, but seclusion was my only salvation. And perhaps if I tell you a little of my past, you will be able to forgive me for not being strong now, either . . ." She took a deep breath and looked off into the distance, gazing at the folded green hills beyond the hacienda, her voice a low, sad murmur as she related the events of her past.

Paloma's story wasn't unusual for the times, Tory thought later when she was alone in her room, but it was worthy of a Greek tragedy. In a rare display of defiance, fourteen-year-old Paloma had fallen in love with Roberto, son of a small *hacendado*. Don Francisco, Paloma's father, was embroiled in a feud with Roberto's father, and forbade the marriage. Events escalated, ending with Roberto's death. An accident, it was said, but Paloma knew better. Don Francisco was horrified to learn that his daughter was carrying Roberto's child, and made plans to send her to a convent in Mexico.

Then Patrick Ryan had arrived, a Yankee sea captain who had done business with Francisco—and was willing to marry a girl carrying another man's child in exchange for land grants and money. There hadn't been much choice for the grieving Paloma—a convent or marriage to a stranger. When her baby was stillborn a few months after the marriage, she retreated into herself. Not even the eventual births of her children abated her grief, and after a time her husband stopped coming to her room at all. It suited her. She withdrew even more, allowing only Tía Benita to be close to her. Until now, when she confided in her daughter.

It explained a great many things, and Tory found she could forgive her mother at last for the years of seeming indifference.

Thirteen

A week had passed since the unpleasant interview with Sebastian, and Tory had forced herself to pretend meekness and compliance, though she thought at moments that she would like to fling Tío Sebastian's sneering regard into his face, tell him that she knew the truth.

But she could not, not without exposing the careful plans that she was devising with her mother's help. Paloma was still a surprise, and if not for her counsel, Tory knew she might very well be married or in a convent by this time. It was Paloma who somehow persuaded Sebastian to allow time to pass before forcing an issue that might prove to be embarrassing and awkward with Don Luis, and so Tory was largely left alone, though watched much more closely than she would have liked. Always there was someone with her, patrolling the garden outside her small vine-shaded courtyard, or even in the long corridor outside her chamber door, footsteps echoing in the long night hours.

It was enough to drive her to the very brink of rebellion, and it took great effort to keep her temper and exhibit only outward complacence.

It had been two weeks now since Papa's death and the funeral procession through the grounds of the hacienda and past the small chapel on the hill, up to the burying ground atop a high bluff that overlooked the ocean. There, towering, wind-distorted trees stood guard, trunks and limbs blasted by years of wind and salt air into silent, bleached sentinels. The family crypt was made of stone and carved with angels and vines and celestial scenes, and the mourners stood silently while the priest waved the holy chalice and intoned prayers for the dead, and Tory had tried to pay attention but found herself thinking instead of her future.

It had been useless, a waste of time to think that perhaps she could forget what had happened between her and Papa, for immediately after the funeral Tío Sebastian had begun to dictate his own wishes. To escape him, she had fled with Colette to the hacienda, pleading a headache, catching a glimpse of Nick Kincade standing solemnly beside a slender Mexican who looked vaguely familiar. Driven by the almost frantic need to get away from her uncle, she had not paused to speak, but barely nodded as she passed. Even when Lieutenant Brock stopped her to offer condolences, his expression sympathetic while he held her hand in his much longer than necessary, she'd been aware of Nick Kincade watching them, scowling slightly when she allowed Brock to escort her to the hacienda.

Nick had not come to visit her, not even to offer his condolences since then, and she thought bitterly that it was just as well. When she thought of him, a strange, almost feverish reaction swept over her, leaving her helplessly wondering if she would see him again. And the nights . . . the nights were the worst, when she lay in her bed and tossed restlessly, remembering his lips on her breasts like burning brands, the insistent thrust of his tongue into her mouth, demanding and possessive, making her shiver with an urgent need that she'd instinctively known he could assuage. Oh, that was the worst, the really worst, that he had stoked the fires and then slaked them with his body, and she had wanted it.

The same restlessness filled her now, as she stood in the open door of her room and watched the sunlight slowly dissolve into long deep shadows, while the air grew cool and abundant with the sweet scent of night-blooming flowers and the hum of insects. A bird called, liquid song lifting to heaven, and in the distance she heard the plaintive melody of an old Spanish ballad soaring above the other familiar sounds of the hacienda.

Music again, down in the barrio where Rosita and the others would be dancing, the first time since el patrón had died. Life went on.

In the still night air, the music was easily heard, and when the ballad altered to a more lively tune, she closed her eyes, shivering slightly. Several minutes passed, and almost without conscious thought or will, she found herself swaying to the music of fiddle, guitar, and horn, her body instinctively reacting to the lure of the rhythm. Her feet were bare, her silk dressing gown flowing and loosely tied around her waist with a sash, and the thick, dark-fire mane of her hair defiantly unruly about her head and shoulder, streaming down her back almost to her waist.

Evening air cooled skin soon flushed with her exertions, and the slap of her bare feet on stones still warm from the day's heat was in time with the tempo of the Spanish fandango. The silk hem whirled about her legs, up over her knees, and she tossed her hair and clapped her hands, losing herself in the dance, in the compelling seduction of the music.

All the pent-up frustration and pain of the past weeks, and the unfamiliar restless yearnings of her body were alleviated with her swift, swaying movements, the release that she needed being expressed in the dance. It was benediction, it was completion, it was a farewell, for her determination was forged by the release of suffocating doubts.

It was time. There would be no more delays. Her course was set, and Monterey would soon be behind her, as well as dark memories that she would abandon with all the other barriers to her happiness. Eyes closed, body misted with perspiration that made her silk dressing gown cling to her damply, Tory smiled slightly as she whirled to a halt and dropped to one knee on the courtyard stones, panting from her exertions, and filled with renewed conviction.

''Why do you dance alone, Venus?''

Her eyes flew open. She recognized the faintly mocking drawl, and her head turned slowly to see Nick Kincade watching her through the iron bars of her courtyard gate. He was smiling slightly, his white shirt faintly luminescent in the deep shadows that cloaked the garden beyond her patio. Slowly, she rose from her knee, holding his gaze, and walked to the gate.

She stared at him through the iron bars. ''I often dance alone.''

''It's much more fun with a partner.''

A faint smile tugged at one corner of her mouth, and she had no idea why she was even talking to him as if they were seated in the *grande sala* with proper chaperons instead of alone, and her in a silk dressing gown that hid very little of her from his steady and, yes, admiring, gaze.

''But I rarely have a partner.''

''A pity. Venus without a mate.''

Was that a reminder of the day on the beach? When he had lifted her in his arms and taken her to a grassy bower to make love to her? Her lungs were depleted of air, and the blood beat through her veins so loudly that it sounded like the ocean surf washing over black rocks.

''*You're* here,'' she heard herself say with detached amazement, and was only vaguely surprised when without further conversation, Nick scaled the gate with an agile twist of his body. There was a faint rattle of the gate on its hinges, and the padlock thumped softly against stone.

''Locked away like a fairy princess, Venus? I saw your guard earlier. Are they afraid you will escape, or that someone will spirit you away? Take you to a crystal palace and ply you with magical dreams?''

She would have answered his rather nonsensical query, for it was obviously meant to be teasing and idle, but then he was reaching out for her, and as if she had known all along that he would, she put her face up for his kiss. There was the briefest of hesitations, then with a sound that faintly resembled a groan, he took her face between his hands and brushed her lips with his mouth.

He tasted of wine and tobacco, a heady mixture, slightly sweet and definitely warm, and she leaned into him with a sigh as his kiss deepened. It was absolutely insane, of course, and she knew it in that distant logical part of her brain that was screaming at her to be sensible, but the past weeks of vague yearnings and restless insomnia rendered her incapable of heeding the warnings.

And besides, whispered a tiny little voice, if she did not grasp at this now, she would be gone soon and never see him again. Nick Kincade had already erased any reason for restraint that afternoon on the beach, and so much had happened since then, who knew what might be just ahead?

Nick's hand tangled in her loose hair, pulling her head back to give him access to her throat, and his mouth moved along the arch in a slow, heated glide as he gently parted the front of her dressing gown with one hand. She shivered when his fingers found the taut aching peak of her nipple, teasing it between thumb and fingers until she felt a low, throbbing ache ignite.

How long he held her there, his hands summoning the most exquisite sensations while his mouth tasted her throat, lips, the curve of her ears, she did not know, but soon—a moment? two?—he was lifting her in his arms again as he had that day on the beach, crossing the square stones of the courtyard and stepping inside her chamber to move to the high, wide bed against one wall. Only one branch of candles had been lit against the encroaching night, and now cast a faint flicker of light and shadow across the wall and bed. Ropes creaked as he placed her on the mattress and knelt over her, a dark shape against fuzzy light behind him, his features sharp with desire.

Oh, she was insane, she thought wildly, but never had she dreamed that she would be caught up in so consuming a flood of passion. It seemed that he had only to look at her a certain way and she turned into a shuddering bundle of aching flesh that ached for his touch. There was no denying it, and she would be the worst kind of hypocrite if she tried.

Forgetting her reservations, everything but the arousing
sensation of his hands on her breasts, belly, between her
thighs, Tory eagerly embraced him, vaguely aware when her
silk dressing gown was removed, acutely conscious of the
bronze sheen of his bare chest and shoulders, the smooth flow
of taut muscle and skin as he removed his shirt. Bed ropes
creaked slightly as he bent over her, and then he was kissing
her again while she shivered with reaction.

Whispering soft words, sex words and love words, he lav-
ished attention on parts of her body she had never considered
a man would even see, and she blushed to think that she was
so sinful as to not offer a single protest, but yield up gladly.
It wasn't until he slid down slightly, his hands parting her
thighs for the light, feathery brush of his fingers over the very
center of the throbbing ache, that she saw what he intended
and cried out.

"No! Oh, whatever are you . . . but that is indecent!"

He ignored her, and his tongue traced quivering circles over
the mat of curls between her thighs, flicking over the exqui-
sitely sensitive peak in a way that made her moan and the
breath catch in the back of her throat, and then somehow her
hands were tangled in the dark wealth of his hair and holding
him, while someone was making soft cries—her, perhaps?—
and the candlelight flickered erratically.

But conjecture was forgotten in the next moment, as a
warm, shivering pulsation careened through her in a rush and
she was arching upward with a convulsing grip on him as the
waves overtook her, drowning her like ocean currents in a
flood of release.

She was still lying bewildered and breathless, not quite sure
what had happened, when he slid up and over her, and this
time there was no discomfort when he entered her, nothing
but a damp, heated welcome as her body accepted him slowly.
For a moment he was still, then he began moving in the way
he had before, creating incredible friction that kindled another
kind of fire, until she was moving with him, eagerly thrusting
her hips up to receive him, her fingers sliding down over his

back while his breath was warm against her ear and coming in short, hard pants for air.

Gradually, while the tension in her increased to an almost unbearable tautness, Tory felt Nick's cadence accelerate in pace with his breathing, until the tension was so taut that she felt as if she must explode. When it came, the eruption was shattering, tearing into her, and he covered her mouth with his to muffle her cries, though she could feel as well as hear his own groan of release.

They lay there afterward, and he laced his hands through hers and held them over her head, pressed down into the fat pillow plump with goosefeathers, his body still a heavy weight atop her. As their breathing slowed, he shifted to one side, a leg still thrown atop her. As their breathing slowed, he shifted to one side, a leg still thrown atop her thighs, his chest rising and falling in quick motions.

Drowsy, replete, Tory smiled hazily up at him, gratified somehow that he looked as relaxed and boneless as she felt.

"Beautiful Venus," he said against her cheek, his face nestled into the curve of her neck and shoulder so that his breath was a warm drift over her ear. "You are surprising, as always."

"Surprising?"

"Um. Unpredictable. We must both be insane. Do you realize that if I'm found in your bed, I'm liable to be shot out of hand?"

She nuzzled his neck and felt the slight roughness of his evening beard against her cheek. "You lead a dangerous life," she whispered.

He found her mouth, traced the outline with his tongue, and nodded. "But at the moment, I have no complaints."

"And later?"

"Later, I'll probably break into a cold sweat."

He kissed her again, and soon—too soon—he said regretfully that he had better leave, that any moment someone could come to check on her.

"Will I see you again tomorrow?" She caught herself when he frowned a little, his eyes cooling. She bit her lip, irritated that she had sounded so needy, so desperate. "Not that I think I will be able to manage to slip away, but perhaps something could be arranged."

There was a short, tense silence, then he caressed her cheek with a finger, smiling a little wryly. "I came to tell you I'm leaving tomorrow, Venus."

"Leaving?"

"I've stayed longer than I should anyway. My business here is finished. I had intended to leave this morning, but spent most of the day trying to find a way to say goodbye to you before I left." His mouth kicked up at one corner. "Perhaps I should have mentioned it earlier, but things got . . . out of hand."

There was a lump in her throat, and a sudden icy chill in the pit of her stomach that felt as if she had swallowed a block of ice. But she managed a careless shrug, and tried to match his insouciance.

"Oh, that does not matter. So you are leaving. I wish you a safe journey. Perhaps one day we will meet again somewhere, though I doubt it unless you plan on visiting Boston, for I intend to rejoin my betrothed, you know."

His eyes narrowed slightly, but he looked indifferent enough when he said, "I thought you were to wed Don Rafael."

"Oh, since Papa's death, things have changed. Actually, Diego and I were discussing my plans a few days ago, and nothing has been settled. Why, I may just decide to tour the Continent for a time before I make any decisions that I may regret. But you—I am certain, Lieutenant, that you have many things to do, and places to go to take care of your business."

She sat up, and as his arm fell away and he rolled to one side, his body a long, lean shadow on the mattress, she began to pull her hair over her shoulder and comb it with her fingers, braiding it as if the entire affair had not affected her at all. But inside, she was sick with the knowledge that she had once more ignored convention and wisdom and decency to throw herself at a man who took her casually and then discarded her just as casually. But what had she thought? That he would

declare himself in love with her? That he would beg her to
go away with him? No, that sort of thing happened only in
romantic tales, not in real life. And really, whyever would
she want to go away with a rough, uncouth man like Nick
Kincade, when she had Peter Gideon and his fine sensibilities
waiting on her in Boston?

Laughing gaily when Nick said slowly that he might linger
at Buena Vista for another day or two, Tory shrugged off his
suggestion. "Oh, that would be nice, but I have remembered
that I promised to go riding with Lieutenant Brock, and, of
course, Don Rafael is always *so* attentive, even though I have
told him that we need no longer pretend to be betrothed."

She reached for her silk dressing gown, wadded up at the
foot of the bed, and pulled it around her, talking of vague,
unimportant things while Nick dressed. It wasn't until he
kissed her goodbye, a brief, cool touch of his lips against hers,
that she thought she might betray herself and burst into tears,
but she managed to hold them back until he had gone, striding
lithely from the chamber and across the patio to vault the iron
gate and disappear into the soft night shadows.

And only then did she turn and bury her face in her pillows
to weep, inhaling the scent of wine and tobacco that made
her feel as if he were still there.

Diego strode into the study that had so recently been his
father's, long strides taking him across the room to where his
uncle still sat behind the massive desk.

"You said this was all decided, that there would be no
trouble. Yet now my sister wishes to inspect the marriage
contracts, or she will protest the marriage to even the pope."

"That would take more time than she has, Diego. Bah, let
her rant and rail, for all the good it will do."

"But she is very set against the marriage, Uncle."

"And since when has that ever mattered?" Sebastian's
brow rose, and the thin lips beneath his aquiline nose
stretched into a cold smile. "She is a woman. Her wishes are
of no matter."

Diego leaned forward, his palms flat against the surface of

the desk so that his eyes were almost level with Sebastian's.
For a moment, he saw a flicker of disquiet in his uncle's eyes,
and smiled.

"They are important to me."

"Bah! You have grown soft. This is necessary, I tell you.
If your father had listened to me, he would not have allowed
her to go off to Boston and learn radical ideas. She would
know her place, and not think that she has rights equal to a
man's."

"Tory is my sister." Diego straightened. "I would like to
know that she will be happy in her marriage—as I was told
she would be."

"Don't be foolish. I did not raise a fuss when *my* sister
protested her marriage, and neither should you."

Diego looked coolly at his uncle, disliking him very much
at this moment. "You are speaking of my mother, I presume."

Sebastian's mouth curled into a mocking smile. "Perhaps.
And perhaps I am just trying to remind you that there is more
at stake than your sister's happiness. The agreement with Don
Luis must be kept. And soon, before Vitoria reaches her
twenty-first birthday. Ah, I told your father not to do such a
foolish thing, not to make arrangements so favorable to Don
Luis just for the loan, but he would not listen, would not wait
until I could find the funds elsewhere. Now, it is too late.
Now, unless she is wed to Rafael before her birthday, we
stand to lose everything."

He paused, dark eyes narrowing into cold slits. "You
should know that the guns we had so carefully hidden away
have been found. Hundreds of them, concealed in empty wine
casks, were taken by intruders. It is a disaster. When Tomás
went down to the cellars to retrieve some for delivery to our
friends in Mexico, he discovered that raiders had been there.
There was evidence of boats and even a few boot prints in
the sand, and most of our supply is missing."

"Gone! Do you think it was Don Luis?"

"Bah. He would never soil his hands or risk exposure, not
that one. He will take the money, but it must be others who

take the risks. No, he cannot have been the one to remove the weapons from the cellars. It must be someone else, a rival, perhaps. Or even . . . someone closer.''

"What are you suggesting, Uncle?"

Sebastian shrugged expansively. "Who might bear a grudge toward Don Patricio? Or Don Luis and Rafael?''

"If you are suggesting it might be Tory—"

"It is a possibility, Diego. She is angry, stubborn, and very impulsive. If she knew of the weapons, might she not take matters into her own hands, perhaps? It would be so easy to betray us to our competitors, and there are many who would like to steal our supply, if they were assured it could be done.''

"Certainly, she is capable—if she knew of the weapons. She does not.''

"Can you be certain?''

Diego hesitated. Just how well did he really know his sister anymore? She was so changed since returning, but, of course, he had not seen her until after their father's death, and then any young woman could be distraught and unreasonable. Still, if Tía Benita was to be taken seriously, Tory had made many mistakes since her return, and behaved very impulsively. Yes, it was entirely possible that she would know of the weapons, but he did not think she would know where they were.

"It's possible," he said after a moment, grudgingly, "but I still do not think so. And anyway, why would it matter if she did know? What could she do? Selling weapons is not against the law.''

For a moment, Sebastian stared at him from hooded eyes, then smiled, a thin curling of his lips. "You are nineteen now, Diego, old enough to know some truths that may not be what you want to hear. The weapons that we sell are not to honest foreign governments as you think. We sell to guerrillas, mercenaries, any faction capable of paying well for them. If Victoria knows this, and wanted to betray us, it would be disastrous. Ah, I see by your face that you really did not know. Foolish Don Patricio. He thought you would always be naive, I suppose. But that is of no consequence now—you are as deeply involved in this as are the rest of us. If one is betrayed, *all* are betrayed. *Now* do you understand the vital necessity in wedding your sister to Don Rafael as soon as possible? We must at all costs ensure her cooperation.''

Diego stared at him in stunned silence, and his face went pale beneath skin burned dark by exposure to the sun. All his preconceived notions, his ideals and convictions, spun into a shattering arc of disbelief.

''This cannot be true . . . Why, I have met some of the men who come to buy weapons from us, and while it is true that Papa was always very secretive about these sales, I always thought it was because there was only a limited amount of weapons and an unlimited number of governments wishing to purchase them.''

Sebastian snorted. ''True enough, I suppose. In a way. But we were not as selective in our choice of customers, perhaps, as you assumed. So you agree that Victoria must be wed as soon as possible?''

''I still do not think she would betray us, even if she knows the truth behind the munitions.'' Diego swallowed bitter words, fully aware now that he truly had been naive, and had chosen too many times to look away when there were little incidents that were not quite right.

''*Dios,* Diego,'' Sebastian said irritably. ''It is obvious you are very inexperienced in the ways of women. They are versatile creatures, with devious methods that would astound the ordinary man. I assure you, your charming sister could be very dangerous to our plans if we allowed it.''

''*We?* I'm not certain I want to be considered a part of this, Tío Sebastian. Not until I know exactly what is involved.''

Sebastian leaned back in the leather chair, making the springs creak slightly as he studied his nephew. ''I think you do know what is involved, Diego. And you are too late—you are already committed.''

Angry now, Diego glared down at his uncle, but there was no mistaking the subtle gleam of triumph in Sebastian's dark eyes. He was right, dammit. He was already obligated, whether he wanted to be or not.

But that did not mean Tory had to be involved in what looked to be an increasingly dangerous situation, and maybe he should do what he could to get her away from Monterey before things got worse. If he did nothing and allowed her to be married against her will to Rafael Reyes, then he might very well be plunging her even more deeply into a quandary she might never escape.

But how did he avoid it?

Nick leaned back in his chair across the table from Roy Martin, regarding the government agent with irritation. A bottle of tequila sat on the table between them, and in the corner of the *pulperia*, three musicians struggled to coax recognizable music from two fiddles and a guitar.

"Patrick Ryan is dead. I found the hidden cache of weapons in the wine cellars, and we seized over five hundred rifles, pistols, and rounds of ammunition, the largest seizure of illegal weapons ever made in Monterey, maybe the United States. And now you tell me we aren't even going to arrest the men responsible. What else do you want?"

"There's the land grants—"

"The land I bought up in the Sierras has turned out to be legally purchased so we have no case there, and I'm stuck with a thousand acres of scrub and rock that wouldn't support a single cow. If I had any intention of ranching—which I don't—I'd die of starvation up there. I could have stayed in Texas for this."

"You might keep in mind that the government offered a generous loan for you to buy the land," Martin reminded mildly.

"An offer I intend to enforce once their interminable paperwork is done, don't think I won't. Not that I have any illusions I'll see the money again soon, but I'd like to remind you of the debt. It's the least our government can do, since I've been delayed so long in my own business."

"Ah yes, the villainous Mr. Pickering." Martin smiled. "It

has come to my attention that his pursuit of honest employ-
ment has led him to Sutter's Fort of late. I understand he has
been employed in the very earnest endeavor of gold panning
along the American River."

"If he is—which I doubt—he won't be doing it long. He'll
be robbing the miners rather than performing honest labor."

"Precisely my point." Martin coughed politely and lifted
an eyebrow. "By the way—I understand that Ryan left behind a son and daughter, as well as his widow."

Nick's eyes narrowed. Martin rarely made casual conversation. He was leading up to something, and he had a distinct
feeling that it wasn't going to be something he wanted to hear.

"Get to the real point of this discussion, Martin. I'm tired
of waiting for the axe to fall."

Fingering a few papers on the table, Martin frowned
slightly as if in deep thought, then looked up at Nick again,
eyes cool and assessing. "There is a considerable amount of
money illegally gained by Patrick Ryan. It would be very
much to your advantage to discover what you could about
it."

"You mean to your advantage," Nick said bluntly. "Stop
beating around the bush and say what you mean."

"Very well. Since you insist on being straightforward, as
usual, I'll abandon diplomacy. We have not yet made any
arrests because we want more than just a few guns and one
or two of the men responsible. There is a lot more at stake
here. The government knows that Ryan has hidden a large
sum of money somewhere, but we have not found it. We want
it. This money is intended to be used to purchase more weapons to be sold to foreign powers, and, of course, that is very
dangerous.

"I don't need to tell you what it could do to our rather
shaky recovery from the Mexican War if this news leaks out.
It has come to the attention of California Territory's provi-
sional governor, Richard Mason, that Don Sebastian is also
involved in this scheme, along with Don Luis. The governor
expressed concern that with the recent hostilities still leaving
a certain faction with ill-will, it might be best that we . . .

curtail . . . Ryan's activities. Of course, the perpetrators have set up a company that is innocent enough in appearances, but only a cover to conceal their illegal operations. Ryan's death puts a rather severe hindrance to our investigation. His books show nothing out of the ordinary. It all appears legal.''

"But you know it's not.''

"Precisely. And we are certain his heirs and partners know it as well. Which brings us back to a very pertinent point—once we find it, how do we retrieve the money without losing the malefactors?''

"I see your problem. If you take the money, no one will be able to claim it and you'll have no proof where it came from. If you don't seize it, they might be able to get to it without being caught. A tidy little mess indeed, Martin.''

"Which is why I thought of you, Lieutenant.''

His eyes narrowed slightly. Most of the time he liked Martin, and even enjoyed his rather dry sense of humor and colorless observations, but there were definite times the man irritated him.

"I've got other business.''

"As a friend of the family, you would be able to find a means to discover what we wish to know, I am certain.''

"I'm hardly a friend. I've never met his widow. Ryan's son seems cordial enough, but the daughter and I had a . . . ah, little misunderstanding, you could say. I'm not at all certain she'll even talk to me anymore.''

Martin's lips curved in a humorless smile. "I didn't say we care how you acquired the information, only that you do. I just offered a suggestion.''

Irritated, Nick stood up and tossed a coin to the table's surface. "For my meal. I would rather not be obligated to you bastards.''

"Lieutenant, you are being precipitate. I merely suggested that you assist us in this small matter. And if it helps, I might add that the daughter has made arrangements to leave California without the knowledge or assistance of her family. She has asked a Lieutenant Dave Brock to come to her aid by smuggling her from Monterey up to San Francisco, and there to arrange passage on a ship for Boston. As she offered to pay him most handsomely, it is our opinion that Miss Ryan has knowledge of the location of the money, and intends to retrieve it alone.''

''Then it ought to be fairly simple for you. Just be waiting on her when she does.'' Why did it irritate him so to hear that Victoria Ryan was mired in this entire mess? It shouldn't bother him at all, but it did.

''But Miss Ryan is not the one we want. We want the men behind all this, the men who planned it and have executed it for the past five years, growing rich off the blood of others. It is a shame that Miss Ryan is involved at all, for we do not believe she really comprehends the enormity of the intrigue, but she is at the moment our only hope of luring the true perpetrators from their sanctuary of anonymity. I have a suggestion.''

Martin made a steeple of his hands, fingertips to fingertips, gazing up at Nick over them, one of his favorite postures. It usually preceded a preposterous suggestion, Nick had learned.

It was no different this time.

''We intercepted a short message sent to Lieutenant Brock by Miss Ryan, and he is to meet her at a specific location Friday night, there to proceed with her daring departure. I propose that instead of Lieutenant Brock being her escort, you take his place.''

''Her powers of observation seem quite keen, and I think she will realize I am not Lieutenant Brock very quickly,'' Nick pointed out dryly.

''That fact could work in your favor. Yes, I realize there is some constraint between you, but I have every confidence that you can overcome her reluctance quite satisfactorily. Especially if you propose to perform the same service—more or less.'' A sly smile curved his thin lips. ''And along the way to San Francisco, I think there should be lengthy delays that will provide ample opportunity to have extensive conversations and, I am sure, confidences. Also, we want to be certain the leaders are waiting on her when she gets there, so we can draw the net around them before they realize it is a trap."

"What makes you think she'd tell me anything? If she's as involved as you think she is, I hardly think she'll share the information with me." He leaned forward, palms against the table. "In case you've forgotten, I have my own business, and I've wasted enough time."

A bland smile curved Martin's mouth. "You'll be traveling in that direction anyway. Did I mention that Kiah Pickering is working for Don Sebastian Montoya? Don Sebastian confiscated some land on the American River, and is paying men to mine it for him—and kill anyone who protests his claim. Montoya is the girl's uncle, you know. On her mother's side. It seems that Montoya has a few business ventures that his brother-in-law was not aware had been authorized . . . it would be killing two birds with one stone."

Martin waited expectantly, as if he knew Nick would agree, and it was hardly consoling to know he was right. He'd take her along, even against his better judgment. He didn't doubt for a moment that Martin suspected the reason for Victoria Ryan's aversion to him; the man usually knew everything. But Nick also knew that it would make absolutely no difference to Martin as long as his goals were attained.

What complicated the matter was the way *he* felt about the violet-eyed little temptress; for some reason, he found himself thinking about her too often. It was annoying, this unwanted lust for the girl, and it could turn out to be damn inconvenient if he allowed it to interfere.

Rather slyly, Martin said, "It might prove to be a very interesting situation, I think."

Nick lifted a brow. In his opinion, Martin was addicted to understatement.

Part
Three

Fourteen

Midnight shadows shrouded the streets of Monterey. It was deserted and still, where once there would have been much gay music and laughter, and dancing on vine-shrouded piazzas outside the cantinas and *pulperias*. It was eerily quiet now, with only muffled hoofbeats and footfalls, and sounds like the scuttling of rats in the narrow alley. Tory shivered in the brisk air. Oh, what if she was making a mistake? But she had no other choice, did she? No, not after everything that had happened. She still flushed with chagrin when she thought of Nick Kincade and how carelessly he had used her, still raged silently at his casual cruelty. And of course, it was *so* humiliating to admit to herself how easy she had made it all for him, how quickly she had fallen into his arms. Yes, this was best. Besides, it was done now. She and Colette had left the sprawling hacienda behind them. There was no going back.

They'd dismounted to lead their horses through the close passageway littered with refuse and obstacles, and Tory wrinkled her nose at the stench. A gust of wind down the narrow alley made her shiver. She pulled the warm rebozo more tightly around her head and shoulders. A peasant skirt blew around her legs, and beneath the loose camisa, she wore a plain shift but no restraining corset, as much for comfort as a disguise. They were to resemble simple peons, so no one would mark their passage. Who would pay attention to poor laborers leaving Buena Vista in the night?

And, as a precaution, she had a heavy pistol tucked into the sash at her waist, hidden beneath the long loose folds of her rebozo, a difficult weapon to steal from her father's gun case, but she had managed it after several nerve-racking minutes of jiggling the lock. She knew how to load and shoot, though it had been years since she had attempted it, but still she felt safer with the pistol at her side. Most difficult had been securing the horses, an intricate feat of manipulation, with Colette distracting poor Pablo in the little hut behind the corrals while she caught the horses. Thank God the animals were no longer allowed to run free with only lassoes around their necks, but were penned in corrals. Saddling them in the dark had not been easy, as the ragged equipment she'd hidden in the bushes outside the walls earlier was missing some of the necessary straps and buckles, but serviceable. And it had gotten them this far, skulking in the alley that led to the rear of the hotel where she was to meet Lieutenant Brock. Oh God, where was he? What if he'd decided not to come? Or been unavoidably detained? What would she do then?

Colette nudged closer, her voice quavering and sounding as uncertain as Tory felt. A tiny square of yellow light from an overhead window slanted across the girl's face. "*Maîtresse,* this is very dangerous."

A loud clatter interrupted Colette's whispered misgivings, and they both gasped; when it sounded again, Tory looked up to see a second-story wooden shutter banging against the wall. It flapped noisily back and forth.

Heart pounding, she rested her cheek against the cool adobe of a building. She was flushed, and her throat was so tight and aching. Doubts clawed at her like hungry beasts, and she thought briefly of her brother and mother. Oh, Diego would be furious, but Mama understood. After all, it had been Mama who arranged things, hadn't it? So surprising, Mama's sudden change after years of remaining in the background like a shadow. But she was right. This was best. Leaving Monterey was the only solution. Peter was waiting for her, would be so glad to see her, and she would explain everything to him, confess what she had done, and surely he would understand. Weren't forgiveness and mercy some of the sterling qualities of a minister? He would forgive her and she would be his wife, as was meant to be. And with the trust fund set up in her name, there would be no money worries, either, as Uncle Seamus feared. No, all would be well, once she returned to Boston.

"*Maîtresse*," Colette hissed again with a wild flap of one hand, and Tory straightened, giving her a swift, harsh look.

"Stop it. You're frightening the horses." She held hard to her mare's reins to keep it from sidling away, and put a hand over the animal's nose to still its muffled nicker. "What *is* it, Colette?

Colette stepped close, and in the muted light from the overhead window Tory could see how pale her face was.

"I 'ear men talking—is it your so wicked uncle?"

Thrusting the mare's reins into Colette's cold hand, Tory took a few cautious steps from the shadows. She craned her neck and strained to see, but detected no one. Only a few leaves skittered across the deserted street with a dry, rustling sound. Rain threatened, and in the distance, she could hear the sullen rumble of thunder.

"I hear nothing." She returned to Colette and took the reins again. "It's just the wind, perhaps, or the coming storm. We must hurry, for we're already late, and Lieutenant Brock may not wait much longer."

"He'll wait," Colette muttered irritably. "There is no need to hurry so. He is a fool, that one."

Tory's gaze narrowed slightly; she had considered leaving the maid behind. Colette had expressed a preference to stay in California, saying it was so warm, but in the end, Tory had insisted she come. Even in Boston, decent females did not travel without at least one servant, and anyway, she wasn't certain she could fully trust Colette not to somehow betray her plans before she was safely away.

"We can't be certain he'll wait long, Colette. Come along and stop being so laggard, as if we had all the time in the world."

Still, despite her outward composure, Tory's heart was thumping, her stomach in knots, and her throat tight with apprehension as they made their way through the dark, quiet alley to the rear of the hotel. It was a distinct relief when she saw a shadow against the north wall, a vague outline of a man against the dull ocher background of adobe. The shape shifted and separated, and there were two silhouettes, men both of them, with horses tucked into the shadows. *Two* of them—? But of course, Dave did not know the area well, and had probably hired a guide; he was more foresighted than she'd supposed him to be, and she was suddenly glad she had seized the opportunity and asked him to help her.

They must have made a noise somehow, though Tory thought she was being exceedingly silent as they traversed the alley, for one of the men turned while they were still several yards away, and she saw the faint gleam of his eyes in the deep shadows.

"It's about time." The tallest shadow moved, separating from the other nebulous forms, striding toward them. "You're late."

Rather startled, Tory frowned. The voice was low-pitched, gruff, and vaguely familiar, but didn't sound at all like Dave Brock. And the lieutenant had never spoken to her like that, so . . . *rudely*, as if he was angry with her. But, of course, these were hardly ordinary circumstances, and her nerves were frayed as well, making her voice a hoarse whisper.

"It couldn't be helped. Getting the horses out of the stable was more difficult than I anticipated. And we're not so very late. Only an hour."

There was no answer to that, only silence as the lieutenant reached out for her mare's reins, while his companion—a Mexican wearing a broad sombrero and faded serape—did the same for Colette's horse. Silent, they led the animals deeper into the shadows of the alley, where little light filtered down from window or ragged moon. Tory followed, practically dragging Colette with her when the maid hung back, muttering to herself in French.

There was no tangible reason for it, but Tory was uneasy. Maybe it was only her nerves, which were stretched tautly with the daring and danger and finality of what she was doing, yet . . . yet she *knew* something was amiss. It couldn't be just her imagination that the lieutenant was taller than she remembered him, and leaner. But, of course, she never really paid *close* attention to his height, or much else about him, to be truthful. Yet there was something indefinable that bothered her, made her unsure of the situation. It was his walk, maybe, the silent, predatory tread that made her think of a wild animal in the dark, a panther keeping to the shadows, lithe and dangerous. Somehow, she'd never associated danger with Dave Brock, for all that he'd mentioned serving in the recent Mexican War. She'd envisioned him as a clerk in some general's office, not fighting in the trenches. Could the tense situation have brought out the primitive side of his nature?

An image of his rather round, cherubic face briefly flashed through her mind. It seemed unlikely.

When the lieutenant halted at the corner of the building and put up a hand to stop them, Tory set her jaw and moved toward him, determined to ease her mind or find out the truth, whatever it might be. She peered up at his face, but it was hidden by night shadows and the brim of his hat. No, Dave Brock was not this tall—he was only a few inches taller than she, and more solid, not towering above her like a dark, lean threat.

Surreptitiously, she slid one hand beneath the fluttering fringe of her rebozo, and rested her palm on the butt of the pistol in the sash around her waist. It felt solid and heavy— comforting—in her hand. Apprehension thickened her throat and her words.

"Show me your face, Lieutenant Brock."

A soft laugh vibrated in the deep shadows, sounding mocking and unnervingly familiar. Clouds shifted, allowing moonlight to illuminate the alley with a dim hazy glow that cast long shadows against the dull adobe walls and threw the men into sharp relief. Tory surged to her toes; her free hand flashed up to grab the brim of his hat, but he caught her arm.

Steely fingers pinched her wrist, hard but not hurting, then released her.

"Relax, little cat. It doesn't really matter who gets you to San Francisco, does it?"

Behind them, Colette caught up, and now she gave a little gasp and soft cry: *"Il le faut—Kincade."*

"Oui, ma chérie."

Tory's eyes widened. She would have known that mocking drawl anywhere, and at his first words, had recognized the unexpected—the unbelievable!

"You—I should have known! But why would *you* be here?" Tory looked sharply from Kincade to where her maid stood in the shadows, and caught a glimpse of Colette's delighted face. Surely not—had she been betrayed?

Stepping back, she curled her fingers solidly around the butt of the pistol, and before she lost her nerve, drew it. The muzzle wavered slightly, gleaming dully in the pale light, and she wrapped both hands around the smooth wooden grip to steady it. "Stop right there," she said when Kincade swore softly and took a step toward her, "or I'll shoot, so help me God, I will!"

"Little fool. A shot will bring out the entire militia. And you don't want that. Or do you? I thought you wanted to go to San Francisco."

"How do you know about that?" Her grip tightened a little, though even in the chill night air her palms were damp and sweaty and the heavy pistol tended to slid a bit. Tossing her head so that the rebozo slipped away from her face and arm, she steadied the weapon, pointing it directly at Nick Kincade's broad chest.

"It doesn't matter how I know. Obviously, I do." He sounded impatient; he hadn't moved after that first angry step, but stood still and wary, his eyes focused on the pistol she held.

Moonlight worked its way through an iron balcony on the second floor of the hotel, forming a bar of light that illuminated Kincade, and she had the distracted thought that he resembled an image of Satan she had once seen in a museum painting. Cold, beautiful, and utterly wicked, a seducer of women and consort of evil, a lethal lure to destruction.

She swallowed hard and flicked a glance toward Colette, who stood at one side looking terrified.

"Did *she* tell you?" The pistol swayed slightly in Colette's direction, and Tory ignored the maid's sudden angry exclamation in French, keeping her attention trained on the more serious threat in front of her. "It's obvious you two have met before—did my own maid betray me?"

"Why do you think you have been betrayed?" A shrug accompanied his casual question, followed by: "You may not think you have any more use for me, but I can get you to your destination much more safely and quickly than Brock could ever do."

"Where is he? What have you *done* with him? My God—" A terrible thought struck her. "You haven't killed him, have you? *Have you?*"

Kincade stared at her, and she saw that he hadn't shaved and a dark stubble shadowed his face, reminding her of a pirate. All he needed was a cutlass to complete the impression, not that he looked any less dangerous garbed in buckskins and gunbelts. Dear God, he looked like the worst kind of outlaw, with his eyes flashing fury at her and his features set and hard, a rakehell face.

"I assure you, ma'am, your gallant lieutenant was very much alive when I left him, though a bit—restrained."

Was that mockery in his drawling voice? She fixed her eyes on him, trying to decide if he was being truthful, and in the deep silence that fell she heard the scrape of boots on the alley floor and Colette's quickly in-drawn breath.

The Mexican—she'd forgotten him, somehow, in the confusion of discovering that it was Nick Kincade and not Dave Brock waiting for her—had slipped up behind her, swift and silent as a striking snake, his hand lashing out to slam down across her wrists, knocking the gun from her fingers with a numbing blow.

"Ah, I am sorry, señorita," he said in her ear, catching her when she tried to dive for the gun, his wiry-muscled arm around her waist, holding her up against him while Kincade stepped forward and scooped up the pistol from the ground in a smooth motion. "But you might have been hurt, no?"

"No!" She jerked away from him, giving him an angry look over her shoulder, pushing at the tangled mane of her hair and rebozo so that she could see clearly, then turned to Kincade, her chin jutting up at him defiantly. "What do you intend to do with us?"

Nick Kincade stuck her pistol into the belt around his lean waist and cocked a brow at her. "Take you to San Francisco. That's what you're willing to pay for, isn't it?"

She stared at him uncertainly. He sounded so ironic, so . . . angry . . . and his eyes were like chips of amber stone, studying her so coldly that she suppressed the urge to step backward.

"The money? You want the *money* I will pay?"

"What do you think I want—the pleasure of your company? Think again, Venus. Escorting young women with a penchant for waving loaded pistols has never intrigued me. Try it again and I'll make you regret it."

His words and obvious disdain stung like the lash of a whip. Drawing herself up, she strove to retrieve her dignity, to keep anyone from seeing how painful she found his rebuff.

"But why go to so much trouble for *me*, Lieutenant? I thought you had left Monterey. And really, I'm not at all certain I want to risk my safety with you, when Lieutenant Brock is so *reliable*, so competent."

There was a noisy rattle of curb chains and metal bits as one of the horses shook, and the Mexican went to calm the animal with soothing words and a hand on its nose, while Nick Kincade's brows lowered and he shrugged with obvious impatience.

"Sorry if you were expecting your gallant lieutenant, but Brock has been unavoidably detained. Now do you want to get to San Francisco or don't you? You'd better come up with a damn answer quickly, Miss Ryan, for my patience is at its limit.''

''You needn't swear at me, Lieutenant Kincade. I am perfectly capable of comprehending the situation if it is clearly explained.'' She drew herself up and took a deep, steadying breath to calm the race of her heart and the nervous tightening in her stomach. What else could she do? To delay too much longer was risky, and she *had* to leave Monterey. If Nick Kincade was willing to take her—

''Very well. I will allow you to escort us to San Francisco, but only on the same terms as I offered Lieutenant Brock. A hundred dollars and expenses, and no more. Is that understood?''

Instead of answering, Kincade pivoted on his heel and joined the Mexican; he led the horses to the mouth of the alley and stopped. He stood there a moment, and Tory flushed as she realized he had no intention of replying to her terms. Either she could go quietly and hope that he would acquiesce, or she could go back to Buena Vista and hope that no one had missed her yet.

But it was getting very late, and soon it would be dawn, and if she did not leave now—

''Come along, Colette. They are waiting on us.''

In much too short a time—should she have thought about it more?—they were riding out of Monterey, with the wind kicking up dust and blowing tree limbs, sending clouds scudding over the bright, silvery globe of the moon. Behind her, clinging to her mare with both hands, Colette muttered in French, and every time Tory glanced back at her, she was met with a malevolent glare. It would not surprise her to discover that Colette had betrayed her, but it couldn't be helped now.

And only time would prove if she had made the right decision.

Gil Garcia heard Nick cursing under his breath as he nudged his horse into a steady canter, and understood the reason for it.

If he knew Victoria Ryan well enough, he would warn her not to tread too harshly with Nick. But at the same time, he knew how useless it would be to try. Maybe he didn't know her very well, but he had four sisters and he'd pretty well figured out how the female mind worked. For all Victoria Ryan's education, manners, and social graces, she was obviously naive about men. Behind her anger and insults was a definite attraction, and one she probably didn't even understand herself. But it was there, in the oblique glances, the slightly breathless awareness of Nick, and even her sharp words.

As they left the few faint lights of Monterey behind, climbing steadily up through brush and trees into the hills, Gil glanced at Nick where he rode slightly ahead of them and wondered if his partner's temper was because he wanted the girl or because he didn't want her. It was hard to tell with Nick for usually he was pretty careless about the women they met. But for some reason, it was different with the Ryan girl, and Gil sensed that perhaps there were things he did not know.

Had something happened between them? He had no intention of asking any questions, but it was pretty obvious there were some unresolved problems. Ah well, it was not *his* problem he was glad to say, and anyway, the pretty French maid—who cast more than one or two interested glances at Nick herself—might prove to be a most intriguing diversion if he could persuade her to ride a little closer to him, maybe talk a bit.

Talking to women came easily to Gil, probably because he had grown up in a house full of women and was familiar with their interests. It should not be so very hard to coax Colette into easy conversation, learn things that otherwise she might not say, being on her guard against him because of her mistress. And even if he learned nothing, it would be a pleasant way to while away the time, for it was almost a hundred miles to San Francisco, and Roy Martin had stressed that they were to take their time to give any pursuers ample opportunity to reach the town first.

No, this was not a bad assignment at all, Gil thought, nudging his horse into a trot to come up alongside Colette. Not at all.

༄

Fifteen

Diego Montoya smiled at the lush young woman flirting with him; her dark eyes flashed an invitation that he couldn't—didn't want to—ignore. It had been a long time since he had been with Rosita, and she was the prettiest and sultriest of the servant girls working at Buena Vista. He'd heard the music from the barrios and left his room, restless and unable to sleep with so much on his mind. He'd arrived in time to see Rosita dancing, her firm young body misted with perspiration from her efforts, her low-necked camisa damply clinging to breasts that he remembered very well. It had been Rosita who had introduced him to the delights of sex a long time ago, when they were both very young. Then she'd been much more experienced than he.

But now—it had been a while, and his body ached for release, so he straightened from where he'd been leaning against a low stone wall and held out a hand, and Rosita came to him immediately, eyes gleaming with triumph.

"You have missed me, I think, Don Diego."

Her sultry purr heated his blood, and the tempting glimpse of her cone-shaped breasts beneath the blouse only stoked the fire higher. He could hardly wait for her, and impatience led him to stop beneath the shrouding leaves and heavy limbs covering the arbor. Set in the garden near the fish pond, the arbor was a favorite spot with lovers, and he'd used it himself more than once. As he intended to do now.

Holding her hand, he took a backward step up into the leafy seclusion, and she came with him, laughing huskily. "You are so impetuous, Don Diego. Do you not worry someone will find us?"

He was already pulling her to him, fingers curling into the edge of her cotton blouse to tug it down and release the pouty swell of her nipples to the night air. "No. I do not worry about things that do not matter." His hands covered her breasts, and he could feel her nipples harden against his palms. He bent, sucking in a beaded nipple, rolling it on his tongue until he heard her moan, felt her lean closer into him, head back so that her long, loose hair grazed her hips, her eyes half-closed, her lips parted and moist, gleaming in the fitful moonlight that barely pierced the thickly twisted vines overhead. Her hands gripped his upper arms, clinging to him, offering her bare breasts to him eagerly.

Impatient, his blood beating hot and fast through his body, Diego moved from one breast to the other, then bent to kiss her mouth, her throat, one arm moving behind her to gently lower her to the smooth stone floor of the arbor. He knelt over her, discarded her clothes with swift, efficient motions, and unbuttoned his pants to release the hard, aching swell. Rosita squirmed slightly atop the cushioning mound of her skirt, panting in soft little moans as she spread her thighs for him. She reached for him eagerly as he moved between her legs, and he slid inside her with a luxurious glide.

"Dios!" His mutter was lost in her soft moan, and in the lilting cries against his ear as he found a rhythm, moving in and out with heated strokes that brought him quickly to his own release. He couldn't help the swiftness of his reaction, but wasn't so selfish as to leave her unsatisfied, and after a moment, began to move again. Her muscles tightened around him, and she sighed into his ear, her hands moving up and down his back, sliding under his shirt to caress his bare skin, then around the front to wedge between their bodies, cupping

him in her palm. As she caressed him, he grew harder and his thrusts stronger, until she was squirming beneath him. Her hands moved to grab at his shoulders, and her legs lifted to wrap around him, arching upward with little pants for air. Even when he heard her groan in his ear, felt her hands raking at him as she reached her own release, he did not stop, but kept moving until she had climaxed again, this time with a loud, keening cry that he quickly muffled with his mouth over her lips.

Finally, panting and clinging to him weakly, Rosita pushed at a damp strand of hair in her eyes, smiling. "You have learned much since that first time, Don Diego. I think that now, you are no longer a pupil, but a teacher."

He laughed softly. "And you are, as always, a facile liar, Rosita. Do you say that to all the men you lie with like this?"

She pretended hurt, but her lips were curved into a smile. "Why, you know I am true to you always, Diego."

He rolled over to lie beside her, one arm thrown carelessly across her naked body. He idly stroked the damp, tawny flesh of her belly, propped up on one arm to smile down at her. Dim moonlight barely lit her face, giving it a sheen like old Spanish coins.

"I do not ask celibacy from you, Rosita, nor do I want it. You have always been as you are now, free to do as you like with whomever you like, just as I am."

"Sí, I know this." She trailed a fingertip down his cheek to his jaw; her eyes glistened in the murky gloom. "It is not easy for a woman to resist such a fine man as yourself, you know."

Clasping her hand in his, he kissed her fingertips. "I didn't know you had tried to resist me."

"I have not, it is true." Rosita shifted slightly and turned to peer up into his face as if trying to pierce the gloom and see him better. "Do you think your sister would resist a man she thought fine and handsome?"

Faintly surprised, he shrugged. "I have not thought about it. I do not think she would look much at a strange man. Why?"

After a moment, Rosita sighed softly. "It is only because I know she is not wise in the ways of men that I say this, Don Diego, but your sister was out here in the garden with Nick Kincade not long after she arrived at Buena Vista."

Diego scowled. "That is not true. Why would you think it?"

"Because I saw her." Rosita twisted, and her voice was uneasy. "But perhaps I was mistaken—"

"No. Tell me what you saw. I want to know." He sat up, jerking Rosita upright, ignoring her squeal of alarm. "And if you are lying to me—"

"No! I am not lying, I swear by the blood of my mother that I am not lying, Don Diego . . . I do not know why I said what I did, but it does not matter. As you said, your sister is not one to look at a man, so—"

His fingers tightened around her wrist, crushing her hand until she cried out. "You saw something. Tell me."

"You are hurting me . . . please . . . I will tell what I know . . . It was the night she returned . . . you were in Los Angeles and I was lonesome, Don Diego, for you were gone so long . . . Yes, yes, I will continue. I was summoned, for there was a very handsome man here that el patrón wanted me to entertain, if you understand what I mean . . . you know how your father liked to please his guests. So I met him, as I was asked, and I liked him, so I came here to the arbor to meet with him, for I knew that he wanted me."

She paused, drawing in a deep breath, her voice anxious, and Diego nodded coldly. "Go on." It was no surprise that his father provided willing women for his guests; it was an old custom. And the women were never forced to accommodate the men, but if they chose to do so, it was their own choice.

Rosita pushed at a strand of hair from her eyes, her hand shaking slightly. "I waited and waited, but he never came, and in a little while I heard voices, and thought perhaps he had gotten lost, so went to investigate. I saw them. He was holding Doña Vitoria in his arms, and kissing her. She . . . Her blouse was down, and she did not look as if she was fighting him, but was holding him . . . Are you very angry with me for telling you, Don Diego? Perhaps I should not, but as it is rumored that she is to wed Don Rafael, I thought—''

Diego did not wait to hear more, but rose to his feet in a lithe, swift uncoiling of his body, buttoning his pants as he left the arbor and Rosita behind.

When he reached Tory's room, he found it empty, and knew with sudden certainty what she had done. By God, he could not let her ruin herself that way, running off with a man like Nick Kincade. And Kincade—he'd not thought him foolish enough to take a young virgin from under the very noses of her family, but perhaps *he* was being the foolish one. Perhaps Tory was not so virginal. After all, she spoke of a betrothal in Boston, yet met Kincade in the garden and allowed him liberties no decent young woman would permit.

He wrestled with the problem all night, wondering bitterly if he could force his sister to marry a man like Don Rafael, or—God forgive him for even thinking it—Nick Kincade, if indeed, it had been he who had seduced her. But then Tory had never been very pliable, and her years in Boston had made her only more intractable and impossible to control. Ah *Dios*, what was he to do? He was the man of the family now, despite Tío Sebastian's usurping the role—which he intended to put an end to very quickly—and he had an obligation to Tory that he must fulfill. He would go after her and bring her back, and learn the truth. Then he would decide what must be done with her.

Having decided, Diego left his bedchamber just as the sun was rising above the ocean cliffs to gild the mountains with pale light, his mouth set in a taut line as he strode down the corridor to his uncle's chamber.

After several hours of hard riding, Tory was numb, and even Colette's moaning whimpers had subsided into an occasional groan. They had been traveling all night, with the ocean to their left and rocky trails and brush to their right; sometimes they left the road to ride up into the hills that ran alongside it. For the longest time, there was only the sound of distant surf washing over black rocks, hoofbeats, and the creak of saddle leather. The early doubts seemed unimportant now that Monterey was behind them. All that was important was getting to San Francisco, taking the money deposited there before Sebastian could get his greedy hands on it, then boarding a ship to Boston—and safety.

Boston. Uncle Seamus and Aunt Katherine—and, of course, Peter. Strange, how now she could barely summon up his image in her mind, even when she closed her eyes tightly and tried. Peter was so vague, a pale blur with golden hair and spiritual smile, a distant memory. Except for his ring, of course. She wore it again, on the third finger of her left hand, a reminder and a promise. The tiny diamond chips and amethyst held more hope for her than anything else right now, except perhaps the small ledger she had wrapped in oilcloth and stuffed into a hidden pocket in her saddlebag.

The ledger, written in Papa's familiar neat hand, detailed deposits in several banks—two in San Francisco, one in Monterey, two in Los Angeles, and a huge deposit in different names at a Boston bank—adding up to over three hundred thousand dollars. A hefty dowry, indeed. It made her slightly uneasy to think of it.

Mama had insisted on helping arrange her escape by claiming Tía Benita's attendance on her, had even had old Manuel called away from the stables and his beloved horses so he wouldn't be there when she and Colette took the horses. Mama seemed so glad, almost . . . triumphant. As if it were *she* escaping Monterey and the confining bonds of Tío Sebastian . . .

Oh God, everything was so confused, so chaotic. Nothing had gone as she'd wanted. Her entire life was turned upside down in such a short time. It had been less than three months since her return to California, a month since her father had died. Never had she thought her return home would end this way, fleeing Monterey in the dark of night in the company of a man like Nick Kincade.

And it was galling to know that he found it so easy to

dismiss her, to regard what had happened between them so casually, when she remembered every detail with such clarity. There had been no declarations of love, only whispered words of seduction before he had left her bed with words of careless farewell. Oh, *how* could she have been so naive? So foolish? It didn't bear thinking about.

Night shadows had slowly given way to the first misty streamers of pale light beyond the hills when Nick Kincade called a halt in the hills up above Monterey, stopping on the narrow banks of the Salinas River. They had followed it for some time, keeping the winding contours on their left, traveling swiftly at times in a circuitous route. It was vaguely surprising to Tory that they had not yet crossed, for the Salinas River was only ten or so miles from the outskirts of Monterey.

"Is there a reason we're stopping here, Lieutenant Kincade?"

"Horses need rest and water. Dismount for a while."

Her brow lifted at his terse reply, but she was admittedly grateful for a respite. And she'd thought herself an experienced rider—there wasn't a muscle that didn't ache, she reflected as she dismounted, flinching. It was a bit irritating that Kincade showed no effects; indeed, he made her think of one of the Plains Indians, the way he rode his horse, effortlessly, seeming a part of the huge black animal. He was even dressed like an Indian, she thought, sliding a surreptitious glance at him in the rising light, with supple buckskin trousers and a deerskin shirt, and some sort of leather thong around his neck with a long, gleaming animal bone dangling on his chest. Barbaric. As barbaric as he was . . .

Gil Garcia helped Colette down, his teeth flashing in a white grin beneath his black mustache when she collapsed in his arms, whimpering pitifully in French. Tory spared them the briefest of glances, frowning a little when Colette seemed to lean a bit too long in the handsome Mexican's arms. As if she felt her gaze, Colette glanced her way, then slid a sly glance toward Kincade, who had his back to them, tending his horse.

Her inference was obvious, and Tory's mouth tightened. She had no intention of allowing that kind of insolence, and really, the girl was becoming impossible. She should have left her in Boston and brought instead sweet little Marie, but Colette had begged, saying how she hated the cold northern climate, and couldn't she please go with her to where it was warm?

At the first opportunity, Tory would have to speak to Colette about her behavior, but now she settled for giving her a frosty stare that had little or no effect on the impudent maid. Since arriving in California, Colette had become increasingly insolent, and if not for the fact that it would be too obvious, not to mention dangerous to travel alone, she would have left her at Buena Vista.

Irritated—by Colette and by her own wayward thoughts—Tory led her mount to a patch of thick green grass beneath the stunted, twisted branches of a scrub oak to let the mare graze. Not far from her, Kincade didn't even seem to know any of them were there as he tended his horse, checking the girth and bridle straps, seeming absorbed in the animal.

After a few minutes, he glanced up and saw her, and his brow lifted in that knowing, arrogant manner he had, as if she had just done something foolish. It never failed to grate on her nerves, and she looked away, angry and feeling as if he was right—she had been very foolish by ever allowing him the liberties she had.

The air had grown much lighter, a soft glow spreading over the horizon and pinkening the sky and clouds. Instead of washed grays and blacks, the world began to take on color again. Kincade walked his horse past her, taking it down to the edge of the river for water. He stripped off his deerskin shirt and knelt on the bank, one knee pressed into the mud, while he scooped up water to wash his face and wet his hair. Shifting light gleamed on the smooth, sun-bronzed skin of his shoulders and back, and glittered with subtle blue glints in the deep black of the wet hair he tied back with a strip of cloth, looking for all the world like a savage Indian.

Tory stood indecisively holding her mare's reins. Should

she join him? He'd not said more than two words directly to
her since they'd left Monterey. Then she thought, This is ridiculous. Why should I be afraid of what he might say or
think? He is, after all, being *paid* to take me to San Francisco,
isn't he? He's no more than a hired guide, and that's all. I'm
the one in charge here, and perhaps it's time I reminded him
of that fact!

She led her mare down to the water's edge, and stood there
while the horse blew softly in the water, sending ripples out
in widening circles before drinking noisily. Kincade ignored
her. He'd finished washing his face, and was sitting back on
his heels, still crouched at the water's edge, his arms resting
on his bent knees while he sharpened his knife against a small
chunk of flint. It made a rasping sound that was almost louder
than the rushing of the river through the reeds and over
smooth gray stones.

"Mind if I join you?" She didn't wait for a reply, but
chose a cushion of grass and sat down only a few feet from
him. When he didn't reply, she cleared her throat, driven by
some nameless force to *make* him look at her, *make* him acknowledge her. "How quickly do you think you'll be able to
get me to San Francisco, Lieutenant?"

The blade turned slightly against the piece of flint, catching
a vagrant ray of sunlight that skittered along the edge in a
quick flash of light. He turned the knife in a smooth arc,
inspected it briefly, then tucked away the flint and slid the
knife back into the leather sheath on his belt; he rose to his
feet in a lithe uncoiling of his lean body. Towering over her,
rugged and very male, with bands of hard muscle on his chest
and stomach that made her remember things she shouldn't,
he shrugged.

"Depends."

Tory averted her eyes, unsettled by his proximity, by the
way he looked at her, and the slightly breathless feeling that
overcame her when he did. To counteract her confusion, she
retreated to sarcasm.

"Depends on *what*, may I ask? You needn't pretend you
are being put upon, Lieutenant, because if you will recall,

you're being paid *very* well to get me to San Francisco. And I didn't *ask* you to be my guide—you took it upon yourself to steal the opportunity from Lieutenant Brock, when it is quite obvious—''

In a move so swift she could not avoid it, he reached for her, his hands clamping down on her arms to drag her to her feet, pulling her up so that her toes barely grazed the ground. She flattened her hands against his warm bare chest, felt his heart thud strong and steady beneath her palms as she braced herself. He stared down at her, with water drops still clinging to the dark length of his lashes.

"You seem to be laboring under a misconception, Miss Ryan. You are not in charge. I am. If you have a problem with the hierarchy, feel free to protest—to Mr. Garcia. I have no intention of listening to your whining or your complaints. And if you get on my nerves, I'm liable to leave you behind. Do we understand each other?''

Dumbfounded—and unnerved—she nodded tightly. It wasn't until he released her, and she stood rubbing at her wrists, that she said sullenly: "Is it whining or complaining if I ask how long it will take to get there, Lieutenant Kincade?''

"Borderline.'' His eyes narrowed slightly, but one corner of his mouth kicked up the tiniest bit. "A few days, depending on weather and pursuit. It's only ninety or so miles, but unless we risk unwanted company, we'll have to use old paths that will take us deeper into the foothills at times. Does that answer your question well enough?''

"For now.'' She wasn't about to relent too much, not when he was looking at her that way, the rising sun tangling in his dark lashes and glinting in his eyes, making them shine like copper coins. "If I need further explanation, I'll be more than glad to ask Mr. Garcia.''

"Suit yourself.''

With that, he turned on his heel and walked away; a short whistle summoned his horse to follow. Tory watched silently, and frowned when Colette approached Kincade with her fair hair shining in the early light, looking up at him with a faint, intimate smile that left Tory wondering if there was anything between them.

Her hands clenched into fists at her sides, and she felt an irrational anger. How dare Colette flaunt her tawdry affairs like this! Look at her, behaving like a slut, smiling up at Kincade, laughing a little, putting one hand on her hip and swaying toward him flirtatiously, reaching out to drag her fingertips lightly over his bare chest, touching the amulet around his neck. They conversed in fluent French, and she was surprised that Kincade spoke the language. She couldn't hear what they were saying but it didn't matter. She could just imagine the conversation, the provocative comments, the reminders—

"Miss Ryan?" Gil Garcia approached. His large hat was pushed back, dangling down his back by a thin cord around his neck, and he was smiling at her. He indicated a flat rock beside the road where he had set a jug and some food on a small cloth. "Perhaps you would like to eat something now. I'll water the horses, while you and Miss Poirier eat and tend to any needs you might have."

She colored slightly, unaccustomed to having her *needs* spoken of so casually by a strange man. She nodded stiffly. "Thank you, Mr. Garcia. At least *you* are considerate."

He grinned and lifted his shoulders in a light shrug. "Not really. We will not stop again until dark. This will be your only chance." He looked behind him, where Kincade was still talking to Colette, laughing a little at something she said, then Gil turned back to look at Tory with something like perception in his gaze. It made her flush and lift her chin.

"Perhaps my maid will join me when she is through speaking to Lieutenant Kincade, Mr. Garcia. I, however, intend to take advantage of your offer, since this will be my only opportunity today."

"You are very wise, señorita."

When Colette joined her on the rock, shivering a little as the wind rose higher, Tory held out a chunk of hard brown bread and some cheese, not speaking. Colette's gaze was averted as she took the food and began eating. They ate in silence, and when they were through, went into the bushes to take care of their private needs.

"Hurry, *maîtresse,*" Colette looked anxiously over her shoulder while Tory crouched in the bushes. "They are calling for us again."

"I don't care. Just keep holding that shawl up as a screen, and stop worrying about what they want."

Let them wait, she thought irritably, irrationally. She knew they should hurry, that Tío Sebastian might have discovered her gone already, and at this very moment might be close behind them. But, perversely, she thought an extra minute or two would hardly make that much difference, would it?

Colette kept glancing over her shoulder, the red drape of rebozo shaking in her grasp. Then she gasped out a warning that someone was coming, and Tory barely managed to rise and straighten her garments before Nick Kincade pushed through the bushes. He stopped, looking at Tory as she fumbled with her skirts; her face heated with embarrassment and outrage.

"How dare you—"

"Come now or be left."

"What a despot you are, Lieutenant. I shudder to think what you'd do if you had any real power."

She shoved past him, but she'd gone only a few steps when he caught up to her, grabbing her by one arm to swing her around.

"This is not a game, Miss Ryan. If you are so determined to be contrary, then I suggest you just sit out in the middle of the Camino Real and wait for your uncle."

"Release my arm, please. Or am I supposed to ask Mr. Garcia to do that, too?"

His mouth thinned, and there was a hard glitter in his eyes that made her wonder if she had pushed him too far. Oh, why did she have this compelling need to test him, when all it did was make matters worse? It defied logic, and she couldn't explain it, even to herself.

But he didn't say anything, just released her arm and walked away, preceding her down the slope studded with brush and little gullies made by water washing down to the river.

It was Colette who said, a little nervously, "If you make him too angry, he will quit, yes?"

"I could not possibly predict what a man like Nick Kincade will do, Colette."

"But if he quits, what will we do out here alone, *maîtresse*? It is dangerous, and we could become lost—we should have stayed at the hacienda, that is what we should have done, I know it!"

Tory flashed her a furious look and descended the slope, stepping over prickly clumps of bunchgrass and vowing silently that no matter what Nick did next, she would not protest. Colette was right, much as she hated to admit it, and if Kincade quit, she would find herself alone in the foothills with no idea which way to go. She would have to put her resentment and embarrassment behind her, and behave like the mature woman she was, not continue with this unwanted hostility.

"We'll cross here." Kincade was talking more to Gil Garcia than to the two women, but Tory couldn't help a nervous exclamation.

"Is it safe?"

He looked at her finally, the first direct glance since their confrontation early that morning.

"Safe enough. We'll swim the horses across. Just dismount and swim beside. If you hold on to the reins and let the animal do most of the work, you'll be fine."

Shivering, she blurted, "I can't swim!"

His brow lifted, and she saw that she had his complete attention. "I seem to recall a dip in the ocean in your past, Miss Ryan. Or do you intend to pretend that didn't happen, either?"

His inference was obvious, and she tried to stem the betraying flush that heated her cheeks. "No, I am well aware that you observed me wading in the ocean, but if you'll recall, it was hardly a swim."

For a moment he was silent, and then nodded thoughtfully. "It's not very wide here. I'll take you across."

She thought of him so close to her, and shook her head, taking a deep breath.

"That's not necessary. I can manage. Just tell me what to do, and I'll get my horse across like the rest of you."

"And slow us down when we have to rescue you downriver? No, I'd rather not waste the time, Miss Ryan. I'll swim you across."

"Pray, what is the difference in my holding on to you, or to my horse? Unless, of course, you just *want* to carry me, Lieutenant Kincade?"

His mouth tightened, and after a short pause, he shrugged. "Fine. Hold on to the horse, then."

But when he took her to the water's edge, insisting she remove her petticoat and tie her skirt up between her legs for greater mobility, and she looked across the river that seemed huge and black now, with water rising along the marshy banks, she began to wonder if she had made a mistake.

Colette had already tucked up the hem of her skirt, and her bare legs gleamed palely in the morning light. Tossing her pale hair, the maid slid Tory a smug glance of superiority and urged her horse toward the water with no hesitation.

It was that action that forged Tory's grim determination, and with a deep breath and a silent prayer, she gripped the saddle horn of her tall mare with both hands and eased the animal into the water that quickly swirled up to her knees. Gil Garcia had already crossed, swimming his rangy sorrel across the river and carrying a length of rope that he quickly tied to a sturdy tree at the river's edge. The rope swayed over the rushing current in a drooping swag, providing guideline and, if necessary, lifeline.

"Follow the rope," Kincade said behind her when she hesitated, "and grab on to it if you have to. Both ends are tied securely, and should hold you if necessary. I'd fashion a safety rope for you, but that can be more dangerous than crossing this way if debris washes down the current."

She nodded silently and looked up, to where Gil stood on

the opposite side and shouted encouragement to both of them, while Nick Kincade stood watch behind them on the banks. It didn't help that Colette seemed not to mind it at all, but swam strongly beside her little dun mare, heedless of the water around her.

Terrified but determined not to show it, Tory tried not to panic when the water reached her waist, then her chest, and then the mare gave a soft little snort of surprise as the bottom slid away, and began swimming, pulling Tory with her. The horse's legs pumped smoothly in the water, and it held its head above the surface as the current swirled around them with a strong suction. Panting with fear and effort, Tory clung tightly to the saddle horn, glad she'd had the good fortune to choose one of the vaquero's old roping saddles, for the saddle horns were made broad to afford greater ease in lassoing the cattle that ran free across the pastures, and now gave her a larger handle to hold.

Water blurred her vision, and above her she could see the rough texture of the thick rope shaking in the drafts caused by the swiftly rushing water.

Over the rushing sound of the water around her and the mare's labored breathing and thrash of her legs in the river, Tory could hear Gil shouting at her and looked up, blinking at the water in her eyes. The constant drag of the current made her arms ache as she clung to the saddle, yet she dared not relax her grip to wipe away the water so she could see. Even her hair, which she had tied back tightly on the nape of her neck, had come loose and was clinging to her face in places, obscuring her vision. Vaguely, she could tell that Gil was pointing at something, and turned her head slightly.

She saw it an instant before it struck, a thick tree limb bobbing in the current, branches thrusting up like skeletal fingers to the sky, catching her a glancing blow. It wasn't hard, and only stung, but in reflex, she put up a hand to ward off the limb and lost her grip on the saddle horn. Frantically, she tried to catch the rope overhead, but slid past it so quickly with the mare's strong, smooth strokes through the water that she missed.

Panicked now, she grabbed at the mare's tail, fingers tangling in the streaming filaments with desperation. Clinging to the very tip of the tail, she found herself sinking beneath the water's surface, while at the same time she was being pulled inexorably forward, so that water rushed into her nose, her mouth, and over her head, choking her.

Black currents swirled over her, a suffocating tide, and she knew she was going to drown. She'd heard stories about people who had almost drowned, and how it was actually said to be a rather pleasant death once one gave up the struggle and yielded to the inevitable. But, of course, the very people who claimed that as truth were the ones who had clung to life and so could not quite be trusted for veracity.

She would never give up, and struggled to the surface, gasping for air, clawing her way upward only to be pulled under again by the forward motion of the horse and the river's tenacious pull. She thought of the sailor who had fallen into the Atlantic, and wondered vaguely if he had struggled against his fate or yielded to it.

Then the conjecture did not matter, because she felt a strong arm circle her waist and heard a familiar welcome voice in her ear, telling her to let go of the tail and trust him to help her. She wanted to believe, to trust, but the panic compelled her to keep her grip on the only solid thing she could find, and until Nick Kincade forcibly uncurled her fingers from the mare's tail, she could not let go.

"I've got you, Venus. It's all right—you're safe now. Hold on to me . . . see? Air. Breathe quickly, before another wave comes . . . that's right."

His reassuring voice, calm and steady and constant, coaxed her the rest of the way across the river, until he found his footing on the bottom and hauled her, coughing and choking, onto the solid bank. He sagged down beside her where she sprawled in the mud, breathing heavily, while Gil knelt beside them and began pushing on her back with both hands, forcing water from her lungs in explosive bursts.

Gasping, Tory finally looked up, sucking in a deep gulp of sweet, pure air. Her hands were splayed in the mud, fingers

clutching at the ground as if afraid to let go, and wet ropes
of her hair snaked down over her face and into her eyes so
that she could hardly see, but she was alive and on solid
footing. Between snorting gasps for air, she laughed exul-
tantly.

"I did it!"

She rolled to her back and pushed the hair from her eyes
with a muddy hand, staring up at the cloud-streaked sky and
flirting sun through narrowed eyes, blinking a little as Nick's
face bobbed into view above her. He was smiling, not the
usual mocking smile, but a genuine slant of appreciation.

"By God, you did do it, Venus," he said, and laughed
when she agreed.

"Didn't I?"

As he sat smiling at her, blinking water from his lashes,
his eyes drifted slowly over her, and she saw in them a faint
explosion of light, a quick yellow flare of response that was
gone so quickly she wasn't certain she'd actually seen it. It
could have been reflected bows of sunlight, but she didn't
think so. It had been too similar to the gleam she had seen
in his eyes that day on the beach, and again on her patio,
when he'd reached out for her and taken her in his arms,
saying things that still made her heart race when she remembered them. Made her feel things that still kept her awake at
night.

Nick looked away for a moment, and when he looked back,
the familiar detachment was in his gaze, and she swallowed
her disappointment. How could he make her feel this way?
So breathless? Hoping for—for what? Another casual inter-
lude that meant nothing to him and much more than it should
to her? Oh no, hadn't she suffered enough? And still chastised
herself for being so weak, for wanting something she should
not want.

He rose to his feet smoothly, eyes shuttered by his lashes
now, his face impassive. "You'll need a change of clothes.
Make it quick, because when I return, we'll be riding again."

There was no time to reply. He wheeled around to the river
and plunged back into the currents. Tory watched for a mo-

ment as he swam with swift, strong strokes across the swirling dark water, and when he reached the opposite bank and his horse, she got up, wringing the water out of her hair as calmly as if she had only taken a bath in a shallow tub and not almost drowned.

"Colette, bring my saddlebags, please. I'll need to hurry if I'm to be ready when he returns."

Sixteen

When dusk fell, they were far from the river and the ocean, high up into the hills, where tall pines and thickets slowed the horses but hid them from pursuit. Hooves were muffled by thick layers of pine needles and years' accumulations of fallen leaves, only occasionally making any noise by stepping on a brittle limb or fat pine cone.

Exhausted by lack of sleep and unaccustomed riding, Tory was too numb to do more than cling to her saddle. All she wanted was food and sleep. And maybe a fire. The brisk air chilled her, and her hair was still damp on the nape of her neck where she'd tied it back with a ribbon. Soon it would be too dark to see her hand in front of her face, and the moon, if it was even high enough to rise above the tips of the pines, was obscured by fitful, racing clouds.

Her mare followed the horse in front, blindly, the pace slower now that they were higher up. Trees that were twisted into fantastic, grotesque shapes squatted like black gnomes among the rocks of a trail. They rode a bit higher, until they came to a rocky ledge protected from the wind by a high stone monolith. Numbly, Tory realized they had stopped, and slumped over her horse's neck gratefully. Was there any part of her body that did not ache?

She hadn't the vaguest idea where they were, or how far they had ridden, but for the moment, it had ceased to matter. All she could think of was a fire, food, and sleep. Her eyelids felt scratchy, and she was shivering from the chill that had descended upon them with sunset. A light fog had begun to settle, damp enough to penetrate even the wool serape Gil had given her earlier when he'd noticed her shivering.

After her near-disaster in the river, she'd noticed that both Gil and Nick had seemed to be more patient with her, and in turn, she had abandoned her animosity and cooperated with whatever she was expected to do. It was certainly easier and took much less energy than the constant fueling of her anger. And besides, it was foolish to continue when she was so dependent on both of them to get her to her destination, wasn't it?

Even Colette, never loath to complain of discomfort, had voiced only scattered objections throughout the day, and now sagged just as wearily atop her horse, obviously too exhausted to dismount. She looked at Tory blearily and managed a faint shrug, as if to admit her misery.

Biting back a groan, Tory eased down from her horse, glad she'd abandoned any notion of maintaining decorum by using a sidesaddle. It would have been impossible to ride sidesaddle for this long, keeping her balance in such an awkward position. Only a man could have ever decided that it would be more feminine to ride in that particular manner, she thought, wincing slightly as her feet found the ground and scrambled to gain solid purchase.

Coming to her, Gil took her mount's reins and Colette's, and told them both to unroll their blankets beneath the ledge, that he would tend the horses.

"There will be only bread and cheese again, for we do not risk a fire at night," he said, smiling slightly when Colette moaned. "But it is better than being apprehended, don't you think?"

It didn't matter to Tory, and she stumbled toward the ledge Gil had pointed out with her blanket clutched against her chest. Within minutes after she'd choked down the dry bread and thick hunk of cheese, followed by water from a canteen, she was rolled up in her blankets and asleep, exhaustion quickly claiming her.

Morning seemed to come in only minutes, and she was being awakened with a hand on her shoulder, shaking her firmly.

"Get up, señorita. It is morning, and we have a fire and some hot food."

Groggy, she sat up, wiping the sleep from her eyes with one hand, looking toward the cheerful blaze that burned only a few feet away. A flat black skillet was atop a wire grate stretched over the fire, and she could smell coffee and bacon.

With the blanket wrapped around her, she stumbled to the fire and gratefully accepted a hot tin mug of steaming coffee, inhaling deeply as she held it gingerly to her lips.

"It might be a little too hot right now," Nick warned, looking up at her over the bacon sizzling in the skillet. "Give it a minute to cool."

But even several minutes later she still burned her tongue, and winced. With coffee, bacon, and beans fortifying her, she felt much better, and began to twist her hair into a thick gleaming braid to fall down her back. She was aware of Nick Kincade's eyes on her, and knew that he had been watching her obliquely ever since she'd awakened.

Nothing was said for several minutes, and in the gracefully fanning branches of firs and pines, birds chirruped and twittered noisily, greeting the morning with enthusiasm.

"This is where we split up for a while," Nick said, still watching her closely, and saw her chin come up and eyes widen with surprise. "Gil did some scouting this morning, and cut sign of someone behind us."

"Who?" She put out her tongue to lick her lips, looking uncertain and nervous. "Did he see who it was?"

"He isn't certain, but he's pretty sure it's your uncle and brother. They're following the main road mostly, but have about a dozen vaqueros with them, so it's better not to take any chances."

"Yes. Yes, you're right . . . but why split up? I mean, why not just keep off the main road?"

"The horses can only go so fast and so far without having to stop, and the same holds true for us. If we split up for a little while, we have even odds of making it to San Francisco without being forced to make a stand."

"Make a stand—" Her eyes were huge violet pools now, shadowed by the length of her lashes, staring at him with growing realization. "Do you mean—there might be *shooting*?"

His mouth twisted. "It's possible. Unless you just want to surrender if they get close enough to demand it. I'll warn you now, you can do what you like, but I've no intention of giving myself up to be shot or hanged. I wasn't guilty of abduction in Boston, but this is a damn sight different."

She colored slightly, nodding. "Yes, I know."

He stared at her a moment, at the deep sheen of her hair where it curled wantonly around her face, framing features that belonged in a Caravaggio painting, rich and textured, with glowing color and perfection. He'd thought of her every night since first kissing her in the garden, and found it damn inconvenient that his body always responded with a familiar tightening, as it was now, when he was just sitting across a fire from her, with Gil and the French maid only a short distance away.

It was even more irritating that her surprising virginity and sweet abandon only made the memories more insistent. When Martin had suggested Nick be her escort to San Francisco, it had been self-preservation that made him object.

Now he was to gain her confidence, allow her to betray the location of her father's money and to be bait for Sebastian Montoya and his confederates, when the trouble was, his conviction that she was a selfish little wanton with few redeeming qualities had slightly altered. It had been the incident in the river; she'd exhibited a streak of stubborn courage that had surprised him, and earned his grudging admiration.

None of which lessened his desire for her in the least.

Rising to his feet, he glanced toward Gil, who had saddled

the horses and was standing talking quietly to Colette. The French maid had made it plain she was willing to comply with what she was asked, and would offer no resistance when told to go with Garcia. He hadn't been certain Tory would be as acquiescent, and still wasn't certain she would not balk when she realized the separation would be for longer than a few hours.

It was easier not to tell her too much, and in a short time, Gil and Colette had ridden into the thick ridge of pines to the west, while he turned toward the east. An unnecessary delay, in his opinion, but Martin planned carefully, leaving any unexpected problems to Nick's discretion.

"That's the reason I hired you," he'd said once, smiling faintly, "because you are fully capable of overcoming the unexpected obstacles that usually arise. I trust your judgment implicitly, Lieutenant."

Rather cynically, Nick had observed that Martin too frequently interfered for that to be always true.

"Though the unexpected never fails to happen," he'd added then.

It was true. Who would have thought it would be necessary to guide Victoria Ryan to San Francisco just to keep stockpiles of new weapons out of enemy hands? A ready supply of modern munitions in the hands of the Mexicans could ignite another war, and he'd already witnessed too many good men die fighting for the lands now relinquished to the United States. If he could help prevent another war, he would.

Tory Ryan knew where her father's money was, and if he had to use her to get to it before the money could be spent to buy more weapons for the enemy, he would. He'd searched her saddlebags while she was asleep and discovered a leatherbound ledger. A quick glance through it had given him the information he needed, and he'd replaced it carefully so she would not know he'd even seen it. All that was needed now was the culmination in San Francisco.

Glancing behind him, he frowned a little when Tory smiled at him, her face lit by an elusive shaft of sunlight that filtered through the thick canopy of pine needles overhead. Ironically, he wondered if it would eventually bother him to so callously use a woman. Maybe, if it turned out that she was a pawn in her father's scheme. He still wasn't certain about that. Whichever way it turned out, he had decided that he would not touch Victoria Ryan again.

Not even to test her barbed assurance that she had no more use for him. Apparently, she didn't. She'd certainly turned to Lieutenant Brock quickly enough, probably using her sweet body and bewitching smiles to elicit his help. Brock was the kind of man who would idolize a woman; a patient, loving man—all the things that Nick wasn't and didn't intend to be. He was the kind of man who could use her when it was necessary, and leave her behind when it was over, and he knew it.

They rode all day, moving fast enough to outdistance pursuers—if there were any—but slow enough to pace the horses. Shadows had begun to lengthen, turning the cerulean haze draping the tops of mountain ridges into a deep, deep blue, and the air was crisp and cool, feeling a bit damp as they rode into a corridor of towering pines and cedars with interlocking branches that formed a natural tunnel.

Tory looked weary; her slender shoulders drooped a bit, and the thick mane of her hair tumbled over one shoulder in a ragged clump that had escaped the confines of her braid. She flipped it behind her and arched her back, stretching a little before she spoke.

"Where are we going?"

"East first, then back west."

"Oh. To confuse any pursuers?"

"It should work well enough, don't you think?"

"You're the expert, lieutenant. I'm sure you know what you're doing."

An errant ray of sun lit her eyes with tiny spangles that bleached them to almost blue in the diffused glow, and he turned away, unwilling to tell her just yet of the change of plan. That would come soon enough, and there would likely be hell to pay when she discovered what he was doing.

It was almost dark when they stopped, and the promise of

rain was heavy in the air. It started lightly at first, then with a sudden downpour, so that by the time he found a natural cave beneath a high rock ledge as shelter and they got the horses inside, they were soaked to the bone, and Tory was shivering uncontrollably. He gave her a brief, assessing glance.

"Take off your clothes. I'll build a fire."

He knelt on the dirt and rock floor of the cave. Taking a small pile of leaves and limbs that weren't too wet, he added a few twigs he picked up at the mouth of the cave, then lit a fire. It smoked terribly, as he'd known it would, but he was in a hurry to get heat to Tory before she took chill.

Coughing, he looked up and saw Victoria Ryan staring at him, her hands twisted in front of her, holding tightly to the edges of her blouse as if he intended to attack her. It was vaguely irritating, after all that was behind them, and he scowled.

"Maybe you don't mind staying wet all night, but I'm getting out of these clothes."

When she took a wary step backward, he swore disgustedly.

"*Mierda!*—what do you think I'm going to do? You have a pretty high opinion of yourself if you think all I have to do is catch a glimpse of skinny legs to lose control."

A deep flush rode the high arch of her cheekbones as she stared at him mutely, and he could see the uncertainty in her slanted eyes, as well as a faint flicker of defiance like that he'd seen when she'd gazed at the dangerous currents of the river. Was that how she viewed him—as a challenge? But he shouldn't feel too sorry for her; this experience would be an excellent example of what could happen to unwise little city girls who tried to run off with a fortune in illegally obtained money.

And if she was lucky, the money would be all she would lose before this was over.

In the leaping light of the fire, she looked like a gypsy, a tawny-skinned vagabond with unruly hair waving about her face, wary and suspicious. He stood up and began unbuckling his gunbelt, his eyes on her face.

She made a short, rude sound that he didn't need to interpret, and lifted her chin in a stubborn gesture.

"I fully intend to change into dry garments, Lieutenant, but hardly while you stand there staring at me like a . . . a vulture! Please, if you have any decency, you'll allow me some privacy."

"If you think I'm going back out in the rain while you take your precious time changing clothes, you're very much mistaken. For Christ's sake, stop behaving like an adolescent. We both know I've already seen you without your clothes, even if you prefer pretending otherwise."

Her eyes narrowed, and her lips thinned into a mutinous line.

"My first opinion of you was quite accurate, it seems. You are little more than a degenerate and a villain."

"Yet you didn't mind experimenting with me on the beach that day, did you? Ah, I see you aren't ready to forgive me yet for taking the precious virginity you were so anxious to lose. It never fails to amaze me how irrational females can be. Tell me—did Brock mind that he wasn't the first?"

"You bastard!"

"Such language, Miss Ryan. And you so prim and proper now."

He didn't know why he was so angry, unless it was because she had made it obvious she had no more use for him. Even that wouldn't have bothered him if not for the stinging memory of his noble desire to overcome Sebastian's guards so he could tell her goodbye, and the shrugging indifference that met his efforts. After making love again—which he had not intended at all—she had been so casual, her voice a light, cutting whip as she chattered about riding with Lieutenant Brock and expecting Don Rafael's company, as if he had not been the first man to have her and it meant nothing to her. It shouldn't bother him, and he was damned if he knew why it did.

And he was damned if he knew why it was so easy for her

to make him hard just thinking about her, remembering how soft her skin was, and how tightly she fit around him—

"Don't think I would ever allow you to touch me again, Nick Kincade. As I told you, my reasons for it were my own, but I've no more use for you *that* way."

Her eyes gleamed like dark amethysts in the light of the low fire, with black lashes half-lowered, looking provocative as she cast him a sidelong glance, tossing her dark-fire hair over her shoulder, standing there with her clothes wet and clinging to her, almost transparent so that he could see the dark circle of her nipples and the shadowy triangle at the juncture of her thighs. Her tongue darted out, wetting her lips, the expression on her face almost challenging as she watched him.

His eyes narrowed, and he let his gunbelt fall to the cave floor while his hands went to the buttons of his pants, flicking them open with deft movements.

"What—?" The color drained from her face and her eyes widened as she took a stumbling step backward, realizing from the hard set of his mouth and the flinty hardness of his eyes that he had every intention of disrobing. "Do you have no shame at all! Isn't it bad enough that you feel it necessary to *remind* me of what happened? How you . . . how you—"

"Such belated modesty, Venus. I'd almost think you want me to override your objections for you. Is that it?"

"You flatter yourself, Nick Kincade."

"Do I?" A mocking smile kicked up one corner of his mouth, and he shrugged out of his shirt as if she weren't standing there, letting it drape over the rugged hump of a rock.

Using the toe of one foot against his opposite heel, he wedged off his boots. With his pants unbuttoned so that she had a glimpse of dark curls arrowing down from his navel, he turned and shook out a blanket on the cave floor, ignoring her.

The air in the cave had grown smothering, and she could smell the burning leaves and even the wet, steaming hides of the horses tethered at the mouth of the cave. It had to explain why she was so lightheaded, why she felt as if there was a shortage of air. Her hands ached, and she realized she'd curled her fingers so tightly into her palms that her nails were digging into her skin. She should never have come with him, and wouldn't have if there had been any other choice.

Drawing in a deep breath of damp, smoky air, she tried to subdue the urge to slap him again as she had that night in the garden.

"I'm certain you would like an excuse to do what you want, but I can assure you that I have no hidden yearnings for you, Lieutenant. My little . . . *experiment* . . . was hardly a success, and I regret that I lowered myself to involve a man of your caliber. But, of course, it was necessary."

She'd meant to be so cutting that he would be vanquished by her scorn, by the same brutal rejection she had felt when he'd so casually departed Buena Vista without a word of regret, or even a vague promise that he would return for her.

But she knew immediately from the sudden opacity of his eyes and the white lines bracketing his mouth that she had erred. His reaction was swift and harsh, catching her by surprise as he came toward her. She threw up her hands as if to hold him off, but it was useless, and she knew that even as she attempted to shove him away from her.

His hands tangled in her hair, jerking her head back so hard that tears sprang to her eyes.

"Damn you for a teasing little bitch," he ground out softly, and she swallowed a sudden whimper at the angry glitter in his eyes. "You know exactly what you're doing, don't you? I thought you were a bit naive in all this, thought maybe you were too innocent to realize exactly what was happening, but now I know I was wrong. You deliberately set out to catch my attention that day on the beach. How did you know I would be down there looking for the damn guns? Were you supposed to be a distraction? It almost worked. By the time you left I sure as hell wasn't thinking about illegal weapons.

"And now this—another diversion, maybe? This supposed flight from Buena Vista—is it real or contrived? Am I supposed to be distracted again? Or is there another reason I can't seem to get rid of you?''

"Please—" She forced the words out through stiff lips. "I don't know what you're talking about—you're hurting me . . .''

"Not nearly as bad as I could, Venus. You know that, don't you? That I could make you wish you'd never been part of your father's little enterprise?''

He knew! She'd been right—he was one of Papa's *clients*, one of the mercenaries who purchased illegal guns and started wars . . . Oh God, what could she do now? It would have been better to stay and take her chances at Buena Vista than be used by Nick Kincade, and she was suddenly more afraid than she had ever been before. Of him, of the white-hot fury she saw in his eyes. Oh, why had she even been tempted to tease him so? To taunt and goad him into this frightening reaction?

There was none of the casual mockery she was used to in his voice or his expression, only this savage, brutal anger, and Tory began to struggle, even knowing that it was futile.

"Let me go! You—brute! You beast! Oh, why won't you let go of me?''

He was pushing her backward, swearing when she wrenched an arm free and lashed out at him, her nails raking over the bare expanse of his chest and leaving long, bloody furrows.

"Bloodthirsty little cat,'' he muttered harshly, and caught her hand again, then threw her down on the cave floor atop the blanket only half-spread over the cold rock. He pinioned her easily, using his weight as leverage as he pressed her against the rough wool. "Be still, dammit. And stop screaming. You're only scaring the horses.''

Driven by fear and anger and wild despair, Tory ignored his warnings and even his threats, struggling breathlessly and furiously against him until finally he swore again and jammed his mouth down over hers, smothering her screams of rage. Instinctively, she bit him, and had the brief satisfaction of hearing him swear some more as he jerked back, staring down at her with narrowed eyes like pinpoints of yellow flame.

With one hand, he wiped blood from his torn lip, pushing back to regard her more warily. His body was still over hers, a muscular leg pinned over her thighs, while his bare chest pressed into her rib cage. She felt the heat of his skin against her even through her wet clothes, and realized with sudden panic that her skirts had somehow become twisted around her legs, leaving her bare almost to the waist.

And she knew, as she glanced up into his eyes, that he was also aware of it.

"I *hate* you!" she said, almost meaning it, desperate to divert his attention.

"Do you, Venus?" One corner of his mouth flicked up. His anger seemed to have cooled into determination now, and she strained away from him, seeing in his eyes a different kind of intensity. His leg shifted slightly, and his knee thrust suddenly between her thighs, parting them. "How much do you hate me? No, I wouldn't try that again, if I were you. I might break your pretty little arm if you do . . ."

He'd caught her arm as she swung a closed fist at his head, easily pushing it back against the cave floor, stretched above her head so that the backs of her fingers grazed against his gunbelt lying where he'd carelessly tossed it. His action had brought him even closer against her, so that she could feel the heated press of his body from her breasts to her thighs. Panting, she locked her eyes with his, and she knew from the hard thrust of his groin against her what he wanted.

There was little to prevent it; certainly not her puny strength.

Unless . . .

Arching her back until her breasts flattened against his bare chest, she heard his surprised grunt. His eyes narrowed slightly, and this time when he kissed her she did not struggle, but opened her lips for the thrust of his tongue between them. God, she had not expected to respond, had not thought that it would be so arousing, and she strained desperately, uncurling her fingers behind her until she felt cold metal.

It wasn't until she had a firm grip on Nick's pistol that she tore her mouth away from his, bringing up the weapon with a trembling hand as she did. But her hand was shaking and her thumb slipped off the hammer as she tried to fire, and then he was knocking it from her grip with a brutal slash of the side of his hand against her wrist. There was a clatter and a loud report that reverberated in a deafening roar inside the cave, waves assaulting her ears so that she only barely heard Nick's furious curses and the startled whinnying of the horses.

Blinking, she looked up at him, and saw something like amazement in his eyes.

"You would have shot me."

"I'm sorry I didn't!"

If she'd thought he would be angry, she was wrong. After a pause, he said mildly, "Next time, take aim first."

"Bastard!"

"Did you stop to think what you'd do out here alone? Or do you think you can find your way by yourself—"

"I'd rather be lost than have to be here with you! Do you think I want your kisses? Your touch? I don't!"

"Little liar," he said softly after a moment, and as if to prove his point, drew a hand over the swell of her breast, smiling when she shivered. "See? Maybe the partner doesn't make much difference to you, but you can't deny you like it when I touch you here . . . or here . . . Your clothes are still so wet, Venus, and you're shaking . . . wouldn't it be better if they were gone? No, don't try to hit me again. I'm getting tired of that, and I think that maybe you are, too."

In a daze, panting and half-sobbing with frustrated rage, Tory made a futile effort to keep her clothes on, but soon they were stripped from her and tossed aside. She lay naked on the rough wool blanket, squirming under the insistent touch of his hands until he took her wrists in one of his fists and held her arms above her head again, giving him free access to her breasts, belly, and the sensitive cleft between her thighs.

"Oh, won't you leave me alone?" she begged in a shaky gasp when he drew a hand over her body, but shuddered weakly when his fingers caressed her in a lingering glide.

Somehow, she thought dimly that a rape would have been

more acceptable, but this—this slow, teasing torture, was much worse. For now she could not pretend that she was immune to him, could not stop the shivering response he elicited from her, and he knew it.

"Why won't you leave me alone?" she whispered, but he only laughed huskily.

"You'd never forgive me if I did, and you know it."

Nothing she said mattered, and even she recognized that her struggles were only halfhearted, and that despite her first resistance, she was kissing him back, opening her thighs for him, arching upward for the strokes of his hand and quivering when his mouth moved to her breasts. Oh, it was all so intolerable, but she could not help herself when he was touching her like that, saying things in Spanish and French that she only half-heard and understood, and anyway, what did it matter? She was no longer a virgin, and it could hardly make any difference now.

And, oh God, but it was so exciting when he kissed her like this, rough and demanding, ruthless and yet strangely gentle, leaving her no option but to give him what he was demanding of her. Her own body betrayed her, and it was only pride that prompted her to a resistance that he easily overcame before he spread her legs and moved between them.

He entered her swiftly and she arched her hips up to take him, blindly, helplessly swept along on the overwhelming tides that compelled her to meet his thrusts. This time, there was a savage hunger in him—in both of them—and wildly, she thought that it had been this she had glimpsed so long ago, this searing need that had driven her so relentlessly until she had found Nick Kincade and somehow known that he would know how to appease it.

Perhaps Sean had been right after all, and a quiet, safe love would never have satisfied her.

Seventeen

It was just after dawn when they left the cave the next morning, and Tory sat sullenly atop her mare while Nick led the way along a narrow, rutted track that she could barely see. She had asked him bluntly, her voice sharp, if he was involved with the illegal trade of munitions, and he'd given her a strange, cool glance but only replied that she would know soon enough.

Damn him! How intolerable to be kept unaware of what was going on, and wonder if she had somehow immersed herself in a predicament that could be very dangerous.

As if Nick Kincade were not dangerous enough.

God, it was humiliating to recall how she had responded to him, despite all her protests and vows of hatred. And worse, that he knew how he affected her.

"When do we meet Mr. Garcia and Colette again?" she asked when the afternoon sun trickled through the tops of giant redwoods that blotted out the sky. "Today?"

They had stopped for a moment in the narrow road that was little more than a faint path through the trees, and the horses stood quietly, tails flicking at an occasional pesky fly. Tilting back his dark head, Nick drank deeply from his canteen, then lowered it and shrugged.

"Not for a while."

"Not for—! But San Francisco is not that far away, and it shouldn't take more than a few days at the most to get there—you *are* taking me to San Francisco, aren't you? Oh damn you, answer me!"

His eyes were hard when he looked at her, leaning forward with his forearm draped casually over his saddle horn.

She had thought for a while the day before that he'd looked at her with something akin to respect in his gaze, but there was no sign of it now. Now there was nothing but cold hostility and wary regard in his eyes.

"I'll get you to San Francisco," he said after a moment. "It just won't be as quickly as you want it."

"But why?"

He sat up and nudged his huge black forward again into a walk. "Don't be so damn impatient, Tory. Unless you want to risk being caught by your uncle."

"I'm not sure I haven't leaped out of the frying pan into the fire," she retorted, staring hard at his back, and clenched her teeth together when he shrugged.

"Then head west, and you're bound to run into Don Sebastian on the main road."

Because she wasn't really certain she could *find* the main road, and because she had a suspicion Nick would not let her go anyway and there would only be another confrontation that she would lose, she pressed her lips tightly together and followed him. At the first opportunity, she would get away from him. And when she was safely in San Francisco, she would think of a way to turn him over to the authorities. It would serve him right.

They kept riding, until Tory was beginning to think they were going in circles. When night fell and Nick made camp in a copse of trees, fashioning a crude shelter with feathery branches of cedar boughs, saplings, and rope, she half-expected him to repeat his actions of the night before.

So it was vaguely surprising when he didn't, but only rolled up silently in his blankets beside her and told her tersely to be still. For a long time she lay stiffly, starting at his every movement, but as the night dragged on she fell asleep, and did not wake until he shook her roughly the next morning.

"Get up, Tory. We'd better keep moving."

It was another day like the last, and she settled into a routine of sorts, plodding along behind him, her mind drifting. She thought of Boston and Peter, and then Sean, and wondered with a trace of bitterness what he would think of his cousin now if he saw her, dirty and ragged, her skirts sunfaded and filthy despite an effort to wash them in a stream, and her hair—which he had always stroked so admiringly—wadded now into a shapeless knot on the nape of her neck to keep it out of her face.

Poor Sean, he had always worried so about her, scolding her that she was too wild, too impulsive, but underneath, she had known that he took great pleasure in some of her escapades, for she had heard him laughing to one of his friends about it.

"It will take a strong man to tame Tory," he'd said, "if ever she can be considered conquered, which I doubt. Ah, but what exhilaration to even try!"

Sean's friend had agreed, and they had laughed, and Tory—who had been standing just inside the front door and overheard their conversation on the porch—pretended she heard nothing when she joined them. Part of her had been a bit miffed that Sean would discuss her as if she were a wild animal or dog to be trained, but part had rather enjoyed his speculation as to her strength of character.

Yes, what would he think now?

Now she had to pretend acquiescence while riding with Kincade, when she knew that as soon as the opportunity arose, she would abandon him without a qualm. She'd begun to suspect that he had no intention of getting her quickly to San Francisco, though she could not fathom the reason for his delay. It certainly wasn't because he enjoyed her company!

When he spoke to her now, it was curtly, and his face remained as impassive as an Indian's, his eyes remote when he looked at her. And perversely, it was annoying that he could detach himself from her like that, as if she was nothing to him. Which, of course, she was. She was no more to him than he was to her.

Sagging wearily in her saddle, as night shadows began to fall and tiny insects stung her exposed skin unmercifully, she could hardly believe it when Nick reined in atop a rocky crest and pointed.

"We'll stay in town tonight."

She stared in the direction he indicated, thankful and relieved to see what could hardly be considered a "town" but was more of a settlement. Not that it mattered. She could sleep in a bed, eat hot food, and perhaps get a clean change of clothes—and keep away from Nick Kincade.

"It's about time," she said tartly, and saw his eyes narrow at her tone. She didn't care. What did it matter what he thought? Once they reached the town, she fully intended to inform him that his guidance was no longer needed. And if she had to wait a *month* to find another guide, it would still be better than this!

From atop the high ridge, the town had looked close, but as they started riding down the sloping hill studded with juniper and rocks, she realized that it was a lot farther than she'd thought. Tiny lights were strung out in a twinkling scythe, and never seemed to get any closer. It was late when they finally reached level ground in the small valley, and dogs set up a commotion as they rode slowly down the main— only—street.

Music played, a tinny sound coming from a rough, ramshackle building flanked by two or three smaller structures, and outside, several horses had been tied to a sagging bar nailed across two posts. There was the sound of rough laughter.

"Where have you brought me?" she demanded to know, and grew irritated when he wouldn't reply. "Nick Kincade, I have no intention of staying in some . . . some *whorehouse*, so don't even think to try it."

He turned to look at her then, and light from one of the

square windows briefly illuminated his face, reflecting in his eyes with a yellow gleam.

"In your present state, I don't think any decent whorehouse would have you, Tory. Of course, if you want to ask—"

"Damn you!"

Nick laughed, a mocking sound that grated on her nerves, and she ground her teeth together to hold back any comments that would only fuel the fire. Soon, she promised herself, she would be rid of him. And then she wouldn't have to think about him anymore, wouldn't have to worry that he would touch her, or kiss her, or make her debase herself so low as to actually *dream* of him as she'd been doing—

Oh damn, what was the matter with her? Why did she have to think of him like that? To be so weak? It was ridiculous, and she was desperate to get away from him.

It wasn't a whorehouse that he took her to, but she had the dismal thought that perhaps she would have been more comfortable in one. The rooming house was little more than a rambling shack, and the room so tiny that two people would barely fit inside at the same time. But it had a bed, and a rickety table with a cracked pitcher of water and equally shabby washbowl, and even a neat pile of thin cloths next to it for washing.

Nick surveyed the room with a single shrugging glance, and lifted a brow when she asked where he intended to sleep.

"Here. Where did you think? The stable? I'm not that self-less. Of course, if you're unhappy with the arrangements, you're welcome to try the stable yourself. Or even the whore-house. Once you're washed up, you might be presentable enough. Just don't expect to command a high price. Even in this backwater town, it's expected that the whores smell better than wet dogs."

Earlier, his jibes would have summoned a nasty response, but now she was too tired and dirty and hungry to care. She shrugged a shoulder.

"I suppose I should be insulted, but at this moment, I don't really care what you say. Or think. Just be gallant enough to give me a little bit of privacy for washing, if you will, and I'll be grateful.''

There was a moment of surprised silence, then Nick shrugged, and she didn't look up when she heard his boots scrape over the bare wooden floor as he crossed to the door.

''I've got some errands to do anyway, so the room is yours. But don't try to lock me out. A three-year-old child could kick this door open.''

She looked up, but he was already out the door, and it closed behind him with a soft click. For several minutes, she sat there on the thin, sagging mattress and listened to the silence that was broken occasionally by laughter and music drifting in through the window left open to allow in a desultory breeze that barely stirred the curtains.

When she turned her head, she thought for a startled instant that a strange woman was in the room with her. Then she realized it was her own reflection in a small, tarnished mirror that hung on the wall across from the bed. She rose slowly to step across the room and peer into the mirror.

Good God, was it really she? This stranger? This huge-eyed creature with a sunburned nose and untidy mop of tangled hair? She felt like laughing, and then, strangely, like crying. The hairbrush and few toiletries she'd brought in her saddlebags would hardly help *this* slovenly appearance! It would take a miracle to make her presentable again.

A light tap on the door sounded, and she gave permission to enter, curiously eyeing the gray-haired woman who swung the door open a crack.

''Excuse me, ma'am, but your husband said as how you're to have this.''

''Oh, but he's not—'' Tory halted, realizing that it would be a grave mistake to tell the boardinghouse owner that she was not married to the man who would share her room. She managed a smile. ''Have what?''

But then she saw the wiry, young boy in the hallway, and recognized his bulky burden as a tub. Of sorts. Wooden, and not very large, but much better than the cracked pitcher and washbowl.

"It costs fifteen cents extra," Mrs. Brady was saying, waving the boy into the room, "and another nickel for soap, but your husband is a mighty persuasive man. Told him it was too late to stoke up the fire for bathwater, but he said as how it would mean so much to you and all to be able to take a bath. Ah, I've birthed three of my own, so I know how it is. And riding as far as you done can't help none, so if this'll bring you some relief, I guess it can't do no harm to burn a little more wood."

Tory stood silently during this speech, her first surprise giving way to shock, then amusement. Not only was she Nick Kincade's wife, but pregnant as well! How droll. And it didn't matter to her that Mrs. Brady was laboring under a misconception. If a little fraud would get her a hot bath, she'd enter into it most wholeheartedly.

"You are very kind, Mrs. Brady. A hot bath will certainly help me in my . . . er . . . condition."

The blush she managed was genuine enough to be very believable, and after a few moments of casual conversation and general advice on what to eat and how to manage with an infant, Mrs. Brady signaled to the perspiring boy lugging water buckets that it was enough and withdrew, closing the door behind her with a last bit of advice on waiting until the water cooled a bit so as not to take *too* hot a bath, or the baby would be born with red scald marks.

"Happened to my husband's niece. Oh, the soap is there on the table. Call when you want the tub taken out."

Tory stared with appreciation at the tub that had probably been a whiskey barrel at one time, and smiled. Red baby or not, she was climbing into that tub while curls of steam still rose into the air.

She had to climb across the bed to get the cloths, then back again to undress and step into the tub, and she sank down into the water with a sigh of pure delight. Still smiling, she washed her hair first, then the rest of her, not even caring that the tub was so small she had to bend over to rinse. Perhaps Nick Kincade had his good side. It's just that this was the first time she'd seen it.

It was the first decent thing that Nick had done for her, and she wondered cynically what it would end up costing.

The saloon was the most elegant building in Bear Creek. It boasted a bar, a dozen tables and chairs, a wooden floor, and even a painted nude in a gilt frame on one wall, a well-fleshed woman draped over a red velvet couch.

Nick ordered whiskey and frowned into his glass as he rolled it between his palms. He didn't know what had come over him, but seeing Tory's shoulders slumped in obvious exhaustion, and hearing the weariness in her voice, he'd been compelled to ease her discomfort. And it really hadn't cost him much, considering that he was supposed to bill her for all expenses when they reached San Francisco anyway.

Grimly, he thought that it would hardly be too soon. It had shocked him the way he'd lost control in the cave that night, even knowing she was deliberately pushing him to the edge. He hadn't expected the fury that raked him when she'd so blatantly betrayed her involvement in her father's scheme. Why should he care if she was involved?

But, somehow, he did, and it rankled that he'd let her push him as far as she had.

"Hey," someone said, and he looked up from his drink, brows lifting at the man standing beside him. "Don't I know you?"

"I don't think so."

"Yeah, wait—I know where I know you from. Monterey. A couple months or more ago, I saw you in the presidio. That was some fancy knife work."

Nick didn't reply, but gazed coolly at the man until he looked away, frowning a little. The silence stretched until the stranger coughed, looked uncomfortable, then mumbled something about another drink as he moved away. The brief moment did not go unnoticed, and Nick saw from the corner of his eye that another man was listening, gazing at him from the far end of the bar.

But no one else approached, and when he finished his drink, he flipped a coin onto the surface of the bar and left the saloon, stepping out into the street. A brisk wind had arisen and blew dust and some loose paper down the rutted avenue, grit stinging his eyes a little. The smell of steak and onions hung in the air, and not far away, a dog barked.

He'd given her plenty of time. Tory should be through with her bath by now, and if he timed it right, he might get there while the water was still warm enough for him to use. No point in wasting a tub full of water.

When he knocked sharply on the locked door of the rented room, he heard her inside, and thought for a moment she intended to refuse him entry. But then there was the sound of a key grating in the lock and the door swung open, framing her. He blinked. Instead of ragged clothes and hair pulled back into a clumsy braid, Tory was dressed in a clean white blouse and patterned skirt, with her hair loose and waving around her face in still-damp ringlets. A fine mist made her tawny skin glow, and light from the oil lamp on the table played over her.

She smiled. "An improvement, I hope."

"Definitely."

"It was very considerate of you, and I appreciate your thoughtfulness in securing the bath for me."

Resting his shoulder against the door frame, he lazily surveyed her from head to toe. If a bath could sweeten her temper like this, maybe a hot meal would work miracles.

"Are you hungry, Venus?"

"Famished!"

He grinned at the fervor in the one word. "Then let me use the tub and water, and we'll walk down to a little place I saw on the other side of the saloon. I smelled steak and onions earlier."

She hesitated, then nodded. "I'll wait in the sitting room downstairs for you."

"Sitting room? A fancy name for a dark corner. It won't take me long."

By the time he joined her, Mrs. Brady was regaling Tory with graphic tales of the rigors of childbirth, and beneath the dusky peach of her skin, Tory was beginning to turn pale.

"Come along, love," he said smoothly, crossing to her and taking her hand to lift her to her feet, "we must feed two now."

Mrs. Brady rose to her feet as well, nodding vigorously. "Oh yes, be certain you eat healthily! If only you hadn't arrived so late—I served chicken and dumplings at my evening meal, but, of course, the other boarders ate it right up, so there's not even a spoonful left. But go down to Harry Stark's little place, and I know he'll fix you right up. Mercy, I hope he's still open, because he's been closing early lately. Gout, I think. I serve breakfast early, so be sure and come down soon enough to get a chair."

With her admonitions and advice still ringing in their ears, Nick escorted Tory to the front door and out onto the tiny porch, solicitously, as if she really were pregnant.

"Whatever made you tell a lie like that?" she asked when the boardinghouse was behind them. "I had to listen to the most *gruesome* tales—I'm certain I shall never be a mother. It sounds much too—dreadful."

His brow rose, and he slanted her an amused glance. "A hearty meal should hasten your recovery. And remember—you're eating for two."

When she laughed, he had the thought that he'd not heard her laugh before, not like this, with rich amusement. It was a nice sound. Too bad there would be little reason for her to laugh much in the future. Once they reached San Francisco and she discovered that he was responsible for seizing her money, he doubted he'd ever get close enough to her again to hear her laugh—or even cry.

Eighteen

He woke her just before dawn, slipping inside her to rock gently back and forth until she began to respond, and still half-asleep, she put her arms around his neck, giving herself up to the rising sensations: sweet dispossession of the senses, the drowsy awakening, sensual whispers in the gray half-light of dawn, the aching sense of urgency he provoked with his hands and mouth, taking her once again to that weightless sense of insubstantiality. And then the release, that searing, burning detachment that took her out of herself, made her feel as if she had touched the sun.

She slept again, and was awakened when Nick shook her gently. "Come on, Venus. We've got to go. Better hurry, or Mrs. Brady will give away your breakfast."

Her eyes opened, and she smiled almost shyly, feeling a little awkward after everything that had transpired between them. He handed her a wet cloth to wash the sleep from her eyes, silent, with an almost grudging smile.

Somehow, a transition had taken place, and she thought it must have been last night, when they had eaten at the tiny, surprisingly adequate cantina, and it had seemed as if everything was almost normal. At first, it had been a bit awkward, but when the garrulous, cheerful owner passed casual conversation with them—talking about the gold strike, and how because of it he had more customers passing through Bear Creek now, though few stayed—she began to relax.

And later, walking back in the dark, soft night where only the lights from the saloon streamed onto the dusty street, and even the laughter seemed more subdued, she'd felt almost close to Nick. Perhaps it was the decent meal, but he grew a little more expansive, and actually answered some of her curious questions about him. It wasn't surprising to learn that he came from Texas, nor was it as big a surprise as it once might have been to learn that he was educated, having attended an eastern university and even having toured Europe. Somehow, it fit. There were times his drawling comments definitely betrayed him.

By the time they returned to the boardinghouse and ascended the steep, narrow stairs to the tiny second-floor room, the resentment and anger she'd felt for him had coalesced into some sort of uncertain, unwilling acceptance. It couldn't be called trust yet, and definitely not affection, but out of the turmoil of her emotions, she was able to extract and name at least *that* particular response.

Now her earlier resolve to abandon him at the first opportunity had also changed—to indecision. Could she trust him? What if he altered again, became that hard-eyed man in the cave? And, oh God, could she trust herself not to be a credulous fool where he was concerned? *Why* must she be so confused, when a part of her knew that he was as changeable as a chameleon, as predictable as the wind?

But really, did she have much choice? Bear Creek was not exactly a thriving metropolis, and the few characters she'd seen lounging around didn't look as if they could find the end of town, much less San Francisco. So it didn't seem to matter if she could trust him or not. For the moment, he was all she had.

After eating a substantial morning meal, they bid Mrs. Brady farewell and left Bear Creek behind.

They rode up into the deep woods again, where towering redwood trees blocked out the light below, leaving the ground shadowed and cool, as silent and solemn as a cathedral. Birds twittered overhead, and branches shifted slightly in the wind, high up, where it could still reach. It was quiet, hooves muffled against decades of undergrowth and fallen leaves that smelled musty.

Nick rode ahead of her on the narrow path, seeming a part of the long-legged black under him. He didn't bother with the cruel-roweled spurs so many Spaniards and Californians wore, but guided his mount with his knees. Like an Indian, looking as if he belonged on a horse. She could almost visualize him riding across the Texas plains, wearing little more than a breechclout, his long legs wrapped around his horse and his black hair pushed back by the wind.

The amulet she'd seen before gleamed dully against his chest, and she asked him about it, not really expecting that he would answer, but he did. It was not at all surprising to learn that once he had stayed with the Comanche, years before when he was a teenager and rebellious.

"My father was pushing me to take on responsibility," he said, his mouth twisting in self-mockery, "and I thought I would stay with a Comanche friend of mine on the plains, where life was free and there were no rules."

"So did you enjoy your freedom?"

He looked away, ahead of them on the path, and his gaze was remote and cool.

"I found out that there are all different kinds of rules, and some of them can mean the difference between life and death. I grew up where life could be hard, but always there was food on the table, and protection from the elements, and security in knowing there would always be someone to back me up when it came to trouble. But living with the Comanche, I learned that the only certain thing in life is that it can be snatched away in the blink of an eye. It was a momentous discovery."

Tory didn't ask any more, and for a while they rode silently, each lost in his own thoughts. She'd had her own momentous discoveries of late, and knew what he meant. How shocking—and painful—to learn things about her father that she'd never guessed, and even about her mother. The only person who had not shocked her was Diego, but perhaps if she had stayed at Buena Vista, he would have also.

Oh, she wished she knew what to think, what to do. Everything was so confused, when once her life had seemed so orderly and arranged, and she'd thought it would all fall into place as it was supposed to do. But now her emotions were so shaky and unclear, veering from one extreme to the other, and she felt like a thistle drifting at the mercy of the wind.

When they reached Pescadero Creek where Nick said they were supposed to meet Gil and Colette, he told her to wait in a copse of willows at the water's edge with the horses, while he set off to find them.

"But why? Why can't I stay with you?" Tory frowned. "I don't want to wait here alone."

Nick's brow rose, and one corner of his mouth tucked into that slightly mocking smile that always irritated her.

"Since you seem well-acquainted with firearms, Venus, I'll leave you one if it will make you feel better."

"Are you sure you trust me not to shoot *you*?" she muttered a bit resentfully, but took the revolver he held out, frowning a little at its heavy weight.

"A Walker Colt," Nick said, laughing when she exclaimed at the cumbersome pistol. "It's a six-shot, and may be a bit long, but if you point it in the right direction, it'll work well enough."

"I don't know how anyone can hit anything with this!"

"Believe me, it'll do the job. I ought to know. Remember my abortive Boston visit? Yes, I see that you do. I'd gone up there for a reason, to check out firearm patents. Before I was so prematurely ejected from your fine city, I was able to find out useful information. And when the Mexican War started, Sam Walker of the Texas Rangers looked up Mr. Colt in New Jersey, and together they worked out the refinements. Pistols like this one were used to fight the Mexicans, and it's a damn fine weapon."

"Wonderful. I hope I don't have to use it."

"I don't anticipate that you will, but if you do, take your

time and be sure of your target. I still have your claw mark.
on me, and don't need any more wounds any time soon.''

She refused to apologize. After all, he had not exactly been
a gentleman that night, and deserved whatever he'd gotten,
in her opinion.

"If you hadn't frightened me, I would not have scratched
you.''

"Ah, but I wasn't talking about *those* claw marks, little
wildcat.''

His grin was infuriating, and she flushed at his obvious
allusion to their passion of the morning.

"You needn't be so vulgar, Nick Kincade.''

He nudged his horse closer and, leaning out, grasped her
chin in his palm, kissing her so thoroughly that when he released her, her head was spinning and she hoped dazedly that
she didn't drop the revolver.

"Stay here,'' he said, pulling away and reining his horse
around to clamber up the bank. "It's not a likely watering
spot, so you should be safe while I check things out, find Gil,
and see if he's managed to lose our pursuers.''

When he'd gone, it was quiet, and Tory stared into the
rushing brown water, the pistol growing heavier in her grasp.
She dismounted and sat down on a rock to wait, blinking a
little at the bright glare of the sun on the muddy creek. Dun-
colored currents washed lazily over rocks and reeds. After a
recent storm, everything was scrubbed clean, but the water
here had been stirred up instead of freshened by mountain
torrents. Farther west, it flowed into the ocean, Nick had said,
but up here it was still little more than a sluggish trough.

It was warm, with the sunlight beating down and the wind
soft, and the rushing sound of the water made her sleepy.

Tory was drowsing when she heard an alien noise and
opened her eyes, squinting against sunlight reflecting from the
water. Willow branches shifted in the breeze; leaves rustled
in a rough whisper, some of them falling to spin away in the
creek water. It was late September, and already autumn added
a crisp bite to the air. She shivered and sat up, touching the
pistol in her lap to reassure herself.

A crack split the air, and she lurched to her feet, almost dropping the pistol in her haste. The burst of noise was quickly followed by several more shots, and she scrambled up the rocky bank to where her horse was tethered and grazing on lush grass watered by the creek. She slipped on a stretch of mud, caught herself, and snagged the leather reins, pulling up her horse's head. The willow copse was thick and provided excellent shelter, and she put a calming hand over the horse's nose to keep it quiet as she huddled into the branches.

Blind fear seized her, and she gripped the pistol tightly in one hand, damning the way her fingers shook so. Oh, what am I doing out here like this? she thought wildly. I should have stayed in Boston, where at least it's civilized, and the worst danger that can befall is being run over by a beer wagon . . . and damn Nick Kincade for leaving me here like this while he runs all over Creation, doing God only knows what . . .

More shots pierced the air, and then she heard shouts, wild, undulating whoops that made her shiver, closer now. Her mouth was dry and her heart beating so fast she could hear the pounding of blood in her ears, and even her knees began to collapse, so that she had to curl her fingers into her horse's bridle and hold on to stay upright.

What was it he'd said? Take careful aim, and be certain of her target, she thought, or words to that effect.

So when she heard the crashing in the bushes a dozen yards away, and caught glimpses of movement, she steadied the pistol in her hand and brought it up, her thumb resting on the hammer. The long, heavy barrel wavered slightly, and she took a deep breath, squinting along the dull bluish gleam of the muzzle, carefully waiting, waiting . . .

And then through the tall, waving grasses and clumps of trees came horses, and she saw Gil and Colette, with Nick Kincade behind them, half-turned in his saddle, firing his rifle over his shoulder. The sharp smell of gunpowder was in the air, with thin strands of smoke rising in puffs, and Tory realized she'd emerged from the willow copse when Gil yelled at her to mount up.

Stumbling slightly, still holding the revolver, she managed to climb aboard her snorting, shying mare, and by then they were abreast of her, and she saw the reckless, dangerous light in Nick's eyes as he paused, his black gelding half-rearing.

"Ride, dammit!"

She didn't need another warning, and dug her heels into her mare's sides so that it sprang forward, hooves digging into the marshy ground and mud flying up around them. She followed Gil and Colette and behind her could hear Nick, sounding like one of their pursuers, whooping as wildly as they were. Looking back once, she saw bare brown bodies and knew then that Indians were chasing them, though she had no idea why. Normally, they were rather peaceful, in her experience, though at times they raided one another, or remote settlements, for horses and cattle.

But now, with murderous, chilling howls, the Indians gave hot pursuit, and Tory thought frantically that they would all be killed.

Then, as suddenly as it had begun, the pursuit ended, and she looked back again, fearfully, her throat tightening as she didn't see Nick anywhere.

"Where is he?" she screamed, but Gil would not let her stop, reaching out to snag her reins and jerk her with him when she tried.

"He can take care of himself. Don't worry about Nick."

But she did worry, and it was with a huge sense of relief that she saw him finally riding toward them through the brush, his lathered mount moving along at an easy trot, and Nick looking like an Indian himself with a red cloth tied around his forehead and his shirt gone, bare chest gleaming brown in the sunlight. Tory's mouth tightened when she saw streaks of blood on him, and she looked away for a moment, swallowing hard.

"I don't think they'll try that again," he said, reining his mount to a halt beside Gil. "Not with us, anyway."

"Didn't think the Nez Percé were so warlike," Gil muttered as he raked his hat from his head to drag his sleeve over his sweating forehead. "Guess they thought we were after the cow they were butchering."

"They're Shoshone. A little out of their usual stomping grounds, I think. Maybe on a hunting trip before winter hits. There's three less of 'em now, so it'll take a while to see to their dead."

Nick uncorked his canteen and tilted back his head, drinking deeply and then pouring the rest of the water over his face so that it dripped onto his chest.

Venting her fear, Tory burst out, "I could have been killed, and you seem to regard this as some kind of lark!"

Nick's eyes cooled, and his brow lifted. "We all could have been killed. Am I supposed to apologize?"

Because some of her fear had been for him, and he was too reckless to even care about the danger he'd been in, Tory glared at him.

"No, but you were almost killed! If you had any sense, you'd at least be a little frightened!"

"And what good would that do? It's over now. And when it was happening, I was a little too busy to be scared, Venus." An impudent grin squared his mouth, and he nudged his black close, so that she could see the water droplets still on his lashes. "Would you miss me?"

"Like a wart!" She turned her horse away before he could reach out for her, fully aware of Gil and Colette staring at them, and knowing what they must be thinking.

Nick's low laughter followed her, and she rode stiffly, avoiding looking at either Gil or Colette. Her cheeks burned. Of course, they probably guessed what was between them now, but she had no intention of validating their suspicions. It was too embarrassing, especially after all the things she'd said in the past.

And anyway, it was obvious at least Colette had come to the correct assessment, because when they made camp that evening, spreading blankets under rough shelters of pine boughs and saplings lashed together, the maid glanced at Tory slyly, a brow lifting.

Gil Garcia intercepted the glance and understood it for what it was. Later, when the women were asleep by the fire, he took Nick aside, shaking his head. "It might be best to keep those two apart, amigo."

Nick glanced at the women wrapped in their blankets, and gave a light shrug.

"That would be a bit difficult, since Colette is Tory's maid."

"Maybe so, but I've a feeling there will be trouble if you don't." Gil rubbed a hand across his jaw, his beard scratching his palm. It was a thorny issue, and normally he wouldn't stick his nose into another man's business, especially where women were concerned, but this was different. He took a deep breath. "Colette's got a burr under her saddle about the Ryan girl. She resents her, and it's pretty obvious she thinks there's something going on between you two."

"That's none of her business."

"I agree, but she doesn't seem to look at it that way."

Nick's brow rose. "Interfering, Gil? That's not like you."

"I'd just like to keep this little game together until we get to San Francisco and can get the money and get rid of both women. Hell, Nick, I don't give a damn what you do with Miss Ryan, but we both know how this is going to end."

A branch in the fire popped and sent a shower of sparks skyward, and in the faint glow, Gil saw the quick glitter in Nick's eyes and was surprised. Maybe the girl meant more to him than he'd thought . . . and in that case, he was definitely treading where he shouldn't.

"Never mind, Nick. You know what you're doing. I shouldn't have said anything."

Nothing else was said, and in the trees overhead an owl hooted, the sound soft and plaintive.

By silent mutual consent, Nick Kincade and Tory kept their distance from each other in the days that followed, slipping back into polite formality. But this time it was not as easy for Tory to pretend an indifference she didn't feel, and she found herself glancing at him too often, remembering how he had held her, his mouth against hers, calling her *love, amor, amante* while his body summoned incredible sensations from her quivering flesh. And then she would look away, telling herself that once they were in San Francisco, things would be different.

Arriving at their destination was more than just a hope now, and Gil had said that Don Sebastian and Diego had taken the Camino Real along the coastline up to San Francisco.

"Apparently, they know where you intend to go, Miss Ryan," he said one night when they camped, his black eyes studying her.

Frustrated, Tory stared back at him. "I can't help that. I *have* to go there. And Tío Sebastian has no authority there, I am certain, so I shall still be able to purchase passage aboard a ship for Boston."

Across from her, Nick Kincade was silent, though she felt him looking at her in the firelight. They hadn't talked much since joining Gil and Colette again, and now she wished that they had. What was he thinking? Did he want her to go? Or did he even care if she left California? Turning her head, she caught his gaze and held it, her breath suspended as she wondered if he would protest now.

But then he rose to his feet and stretched lazily, and said that he was going to stand guard.

"Relieve me in four hours, Gil. We start out before first light in the morning."

Tory watched him go, his lithe strides taking him quickly from the camp into the trees where he was to stand guard, and tried to ignore a tremor of despair. But then she turned back toward the fire, and sitting beside Gil, her pale eyes a faint sheen in the fireglow, Colette was staring at her with something like derision. It was as if she *knew* how Tory felt, how Tory ached to hear Nick say he wanted her, not just for a few hours, or even a night, but forever, to be his and only his.

And since it was obvious he had not, Colette considered Nick Kincade fair game.

Tory accidentally came upon them in a dense thicket the next morning, where sunlight weakly filtered through high, tossing tree branches and dappled the ground in shifting patches of light and shadow. She came to an abrupt halt, watching with a frown as Colette flirted outrageously with Nick, tossing her loose blond hair, tilting her head at him and smiling, even putting out a hand to touch his chest, her fingers lightly grazing the bare skin beneath his open shirt. His hair was still wet, apparently from a morning swim or bath, and the shirt clung damply to the contours of his chest. He carried the looping coil of his holster and pistols in one hand, and his pants were unbuttoned, as if he'd dressed hurriedly.

It was hard to hear them, and without betraying her presence, Tory had to stay where she was, straining to listen to what appeared to be a very cozy discussion conducted in low, rapid French. Smiling archly, Colette ran a fingertip up the open edge of Nick's shirt to explore the square set of his jaw, then played lightly over his mouth until he caught her hand, holding it.

His eyes were crinkled at the corners, and he was smiling. When Colette slid a bold hand down his chest, he didn't try to stop her or move it even when she brazenly shifted her hand to the front of his pants, caressing him through the material. First hot, then cold with rage and nausea, Tory watched as Colette rubbed her palm over Nick's obvious arousal. Colette laughed softly, and then, shockingly, she swiftly bent, her hair draping down as she knelt in front of him, and Tory heard Nick mutter something under his breath.

Fury flashed through Tory, followed by a wild urge to yank out handfuls of Colette's pretty blond hair. But she should really be mad at Nick, too, though he was grinning now, pulling Colette up, laughing at her disappointed protests.

"This isn't the time or place, *chérie*. Not that I don't appreciate your efforts."

Then he turned her around in the direction of the camp and gave her a little shove, smacking her playfully on her bottom as she stepped forward with an arch glance over her shoulder, her mouth pursed in a provocative pout. Slyly, Colette said something in French, obviously using street slang that Tory couldn't follow, and Nick's grin widened, though he shook his head.

Undeterred, Colette shrugged a shapely shoulder. "There will be time later, *non*?"

"Maybe," Nick said, buttoning his pants, his eyes still amused and his arousal still evident. "Go back to camp before you're missed."

Not waiting to hear more, Tory turned and fled. It didn't help that he had not done what Colette obviously wanted—this time. She felt sick, uncertain. His body had made his true wishes quite evident, and she thought of the other women he must have known. Casual women, women he'd left behind and never thought of again. Was that all *she* was to him? Was she just one more in a long line of conquests? It made her feel ill to think that she was, that she was not even the last, and that he would allow another woman to touch him like *that*, so intimately, so . . . perverted. That's what it was, of course, a perversion, not normal. It was not anything she could ever do, and no decent man would expect it.

So then why did she feel so . . . *inexperienced?* Awkward and wondering if he had thought her a novice, too clumsy and inexpert to want again?

By the time she returned to camp, Colette was sitting cross-legged on her blankets, looking quite smug when Tory walked past, her eyes behind pale lashes gleaming with triumph. Tory did not give her the satisfaction of noticing, didn't pay any attention to the French *puta*. Let her do what she wanted. And Kincade, too, damn him!

For the rest of the day, Tory and Colette kept a sort of armed truce, speaking when necessary, wary and guarded the rest of the time. Tension stretched between them, sparking only on occasion, until that night, when Gil said they would arrive in San Francisco the next day.

They were camped on a small rise, still far from the main road, but in the distance Tory could see the light blue haze that marked the ocean, a long line on the horizon.

"Tomorrow?"

Gil flicked her a glance, nodding. "Maybe late, but it is not so very far now. And the men who were following us are gone, so perhaps you are safe."

Leaning against a tree, where he was repairing the buckle on his horse's bridle, Nick seemed not to hear but kept working, his lean brown fingers deftly slicing apart leather and fashioning a new strap. After a moment, Tory looked away again, feeling depressed and uncertain.

So it was to be over now. She would arrive in the city, use the ledger to retrieve her father's money, and leave for Boston. Would Nick go with her? Would he want to go? And, oh God, what if he didn't?

Perhaps it was just as well. The emotions she felt for Nick Kincade were so involved and complicated that she was exhausted from dealing with them. Even a glance from him could set her heart to fluttering, and make her blood beat fiercely through her veins. She was sick of it, sick of wanting, of not knowing—and he had retreated back into a remote, casual stranger again, his gaze polite but distant, his conversation general, as if she were someone he had just met.

Yes, it was best this way. It would all be behind her soon, and if matters went well, perhaps by tomorrow night she would be on a ship back to Boston. And civilization, where she did not have to bathe in streams and flee Indian attacks, where men did not wear guns and knives but treated women with respectful deference.

Now she was weary and filthy and longing for a bath; it would be terrible to ride into San Francisco looking like a vagabond.

"Where are my saddlebags?" she asked Gil, and he waved a hand.

"I put them over there with the others when I unsaddled the horses. They are still there, I think."

Busy preparing the evening meal—beans and bacon again—Gil only glanced up at her with a quick, flashing smile before he turned back to his task, and Tory didn't have the heart to tell him she'd already looked. Another search did not reveal them, and it took her several frustrating minutes to realize that Colette must have picked up the wrong bags to take into the woods with her.

Nick had told them he'd found a small stream tumbling over smooth, gray rocks and down a hill, forming a shallow pool that was perfect for bathing. Scooping up Colette's bags, Tory went into the woods and followed the marked trail of bent and broken branches Nick had made for them to find it without getting lost. She could hear the rush of water, and despite her weariness, looked forward to a bath. Now that the weather was so cool, the water would be icy, but refreshing.

Stripped to her chemise and lace-trimmed drawers, Colette perched on the edge of a flat rock above the natural pool, looking up when Tory arrived in the wooded niche. Her expression altered slightly, her eyes narrowing and her mouth thinning.

"What is it, *maîtresse*?"

It was said sullenly, her resentment obvious, but Tory ignored the undercurrents as she set the girl's bags on the ground next to her.

"You have the wrong saddlebags. Where are mine?"

Colette paused, and a sly look crept over her face. "*Non*, I do not. I 'ave mine."

"They look alike, Colette, but I assure you that you took the wrong bags. I'm not accusing you of anything. I just want my saddlebags."

Coming to her feet, the maid threw back her loose hair over her shoulder to face Tory belligerently. Her hands rested on her slender hips. "Always you want something from me. I am sick of it, me, and do not want to work for you anymore. I will stay here, in California, and not go back to that cold Boston. It is not me who is a liar and thief, and I will not take the risks that you take!"

Blinking, Tory followed her rapid French slowly, eyes widening when she understood the last. She stepped forward, angry now.

"I have no idea what you are talking about, you little slut. I don't care if you work for me, or if you stay here or drop into the Pacific, but you have my saddlebags, and I *do* care about that. Tell me where they are.''

Colette's eyes flashed. ''I tell you nothing. You think you are so smart, to hide things, but they know, foolish one. I tell you they *know* what you are about. I heard them talking when they thought I was asleep, and know it all.'' She laughed scornfully. ''You think Kincade love you, heh? You think because he make love to you that he will stay with you? Do you? *Non*, I tell you he will not, that he only want what you have in your saddlebag, the little book I found that tells them what they want to know.''

A chill of horror seeped through Tory, ice forming in the pit of her stomach. *The bank ledger . . .*

''What are you talking about?''

''The book with numbers in it. I cannot read it, but I know it must be important, for you take such good care of it, keep it in the oiled cloth where it will not be wetted, hide it so careful in the secret bottom. Ah, I see that I am right, heh? It is important to you. And I wonder, me, just how important it is, and what it might be worth to you to have back . . .''

Tory took a deep breath. Rage displaced dismay, thundering through her, melting the ice in her stomach and filling her with heated wrath. She took two steps forward, until she was within an arm's length of Colette.

''You don't want to do this,'' she said quietly, slightly amazed at her control when she was shaking so badly inside with the need to slap the maid's sneering face. ''Just give me my bags, and I'll pretend this has not happened.''

''*Non, maîtresse*, you will do more than that. Much more. I know that there is a great deal of money at stake, more than I could ever dream of getting by working for you, or anyone else. A domestic does well just to have food and a roof, heh? But you, you have manage to steal from your own family a fortune, enough to share with me and not miss it. I will not be greedy. Let us say—five thousand dollar? A small amount compared to what you will have left, and much better than letting your uncle or those men take it away from you. And they will, I promise you.''

Quietly, feeling the fury build up inside her until she wondered that she did not explode with it, Tory listened to every word, translating the mixture of French and English carefully, and knew with sickening dismay that Colette was right. *Fool*, to have trusted Nick Kincade for even a moment! She should have followed her first instincts and refused to allow him to guide her, should have trusted herself more. She'd known what he was, had seen him kill a man, for heaven's sake, but she'd been so blinded by that aching, breathless need inside her, she had not paid attention.

But that didn't matter now. Now she had to retrieve the precious ledger before this foolish girl gave it to Nick and everything was ruined. If he knew about the ledger, then it stood to reason that he intended to steal the money from her. After all, he knew about the illegal guns, and was probably one of the mercenaries who purchased them. It was a great deal of money, and any mercenary would be anxious to get his hands on it.

Outwardly calm, Tory surveyed Colette for a moment. "Where are my saddlebags?"

Colette laughed. "I will not say, not until you write on a piece of paper and sign it that I am to have the five thousand dollar."

"It would be worthless, even if you could read it."

"*Non*, you will write it in French, and it will be worth five thousand dollar, for you cannot afford to betray me. I will tell Kincade about the book if I do not have the money as soon as we get to San Francisco, and then you will not have it, either."

"Five thousand dollars is a lot of money. It may take me a while to get it." Tory stepped to the side, staring coolly at Colette. Oh, if it was true, if he did know about the money— and there was no reason to believe otherwise—he would simply take it, as the girl said. Unless she could get the ledger away and hide it somewhere. Oh God, then how would she pay for her passage to Boston? The possibilities flashed through her mind with lightning speed, and after a moment she said calmly, "If you tell Kincade about the ledger, you won't get your five thousand dollars."

"But I will have not lost as much as you, heh? I will be as the same, but you—what will you do? Go back to Monterey and marry Don Rafael? He would not have you now, even if your uncle did not kill you."

Tory's hands curled into fists at her sides; her fingernails dug half-moons into her palms, but her voice was steady.

"Don't be an idiot. All I have to do is write Uncle Seamus for passage to Boston."

"And how long will that take? Three months? Four?" Colette laughed. "How will you eat until he sends the money, *maîtresse*? Where will you stay?"

"Very well, Colette. I will write you a promissory note for five thousand dollars. But only if you give me the ledger."

"*Non.* I will give it to you when we are in San Francisco." A sly smile curved her mouth, triumphant, gloating. "Do not be sad, *maîtresse*. You still get to keep most of the money. Unless your uncle find you."

"You'd better hope he doesn't," Tory said, unable to keep the bitterness from her voice. "Or we'll both be without any money."

It wasn't a pleasant thought, and she wondered what would be worse—facing Sebastian's wrath or Nick Kincade's duplicity. She could have forgiven Nick another woman—she could not forgive this betrayal.

Nineteen

San Francisco was a surprise, despite the reports of booming enterprise and an influx of prospectors and entrepreneurs. During the five months since word had leaked out about the gold found on the American River, the once sleepy town of Yerba Buena had undergone vast changes. Canvas tents, wooden shacks, and even quickly constructed adobe buildings crowded the vast mudflat of North Beach. Abandoned ships clogged the harbor waters, most with unloaded cargo still in the holds, while wharves were crammed with exposed goods. Streets that were little more than rutted tracks teemed with disembarking passengers, oxcarts, and mule-drawn wagons. Overall, the growing town exuded a sense of anticipation.

Tory felt none of that. Her emotions were more akin to anxiety and apprehension as she followed Kincade past a run-down mission to turn on the rutted track of a road that bore the unassuming name of Market Street. Below, dipping sharply, lay the harbor and clutches of ramshackle dwellings, while a forest of swaying masts with furled sails clustered in the bay edging North Beach.

Gil found them rooms in a hotel off Portsmouth Square, but she didn't even want to ask the price. Everything here was exorbitant, and as she'd passed shops, she'd been amazed that merchants could find anyone willing to pay a dollar apiece for a raw egg, or fifty dollars for a shovel.

The hotel was crude, with only six rooms, but better than some she had seen, the one-story structures with weatherboard walls and roofs of cotton sheeting. The accommodations inside could hardly be any better.

Nick Kincade stopped her, one hand on her arm, before she went up the narrow, musty stairs to the second-floor room of their hotel. She jerked her arm from his grasp as if burned, staring up at him. Something flashed behind his eyes, then they turned cool again.

"Gil and I got you here, like we said."

"And now you want to be paid your hundred dollars, no doubt." Her tart, almost contemptuous comment didn't seem to affect him. He just nodded, his expression impassive and unreadable.

"That's right. All we want is our money."

"Really, Lieutenant, where are your manners? Can't you be courteous enough to allow my maid and me to rest a bit before you demand your money? Besides, I must go to the bank to get it, and I'm much too tired to do that today. Won't morning be soon enough for you?"

"Morning will be fine, Miss Ryan." His gaze flicked to Colette, who stood back a little, watching and listening. "Gil and I will be tending to some business of our own, so we'll just leave you ladies to rest. If you need anything, the clerk will get it for you. Just ask him. And if I were you, Miss Ryan, I wouldn't go out alone. It's not exactly safe on these streets, what with all those shiploads of gold hunters coming in every day. If you want to leave, Gil or I will escort you."

"Thank you for your warning, Lieutenant. I'm sure we have no intention of leaving our room. This journey was much too exhausting."

A faint smile touched one corner of his mouth, and he nodded, lifting his hand to brush a finger against the brim of his hat, as if she were merely a woman he was passing in the street, not someone whose body he'd slipped into while a storm raged outside . . . God, she shouldn't even think of that anymore, shouldn't even care. His only interest was the money, while hers—?

"Good night, Miss Ryan. Mademoiselle Poirier."

A boy took up their saddlebags, and she and Colette followed him, Tory resisting the urge to turn around and glance at Nick, to see if he was still looking at her, or if he had left the tiny entrance hall the desk clerk had grandiosely referred to as a lobby.

When she and Colette were alone in the small, dingy hotel room, Tory lifted her saddlebags to the narrow cot that would serve as a bed and turned to face the maid, eyes narrowed.

"Give me the ledger. Now."

"Not yet." Colette backed away a step, looking nervous and defiant. "You promised a paper."

"And you'll get it, but not until I see that the ledger is safe. For all I know, you've lost it. Now give it to me. My patience is almost gone, and I'm about ready to just tell Kincade myself and get it over with. I hate this suspense. And who knows—he might even be generous enough to give me enough money for passage to Boston."

Colette considered, her pale lashes flickering over her eyes, then she shrugged, a Gallic gesture of nonchalance.

"Very well. I will show it to you. Then you must give it back to me until I 'ave my money."

"You little fool. I can't get the money without the ledger, don't you know that?"

There was no point in telling her most of the money was in a Boston bank. She'd just have to deal with that when it was no longer avoidable. Right now, she had to have the ledger, had to have the name and numbers of the banks where Papa had put some of the money. Oh, *damn* this tangled deception he had contrived! Hiding money like some kind of packrat, sticking it here and there, so that now she was obliged to collect it as if she was gathering chicken eggs from haystacks.

But she would do it. She would get the money, then decide what to do. There wasn't much time, not if Kincade knew about it, and if her uncle had guessed where Papa had secreted his funds.

Reluctantly, warily, Colette brought out the ledger, yielding it to Tory as if it were made of spun glass, gingerly placing it in her palm. As well she might treat it. The small book represented more money than either of them had ever seen, or were likely to see if Kincade learned of it.

"Fetch me some paper," Tory said. "And pen and ink." When Colette hesitated, she lifted a brow. "You want your promissory note, don't you?"

"Will I be able to trade it for the money?" Colette's suspicious hesitation wasn't surprising, and Tory nodded.

"Yes, of course. Don't you know *anything*?"

"I know enough to get five thousand dollar from you," the maid returned tartly, and because it was true and infuriating, Tory didn't reply.

The note was written out, the numbers Tory needed gleaned from the book, and the ledger was tucked into a small velvet purse.

"They expect us to rest," Tory said, meaning Kincade and Garcia, "so we must hurry if we hope to escape their notice. I saw a flight of back stairs that we can use to avoid them. Now come, help me make myself presentable, or no bank officer will consider for a moment allowing me inside his establishment, much less allow me access to these accounts."

In a much shorter time than she'd thought possible, Tory stood outside the hotel, blinking in the bright sunshine and the crisp, salty wind that swept up from the bay over Portsmouth Square. She wasn't impressed by the town, though it was obviously growing quickly. Hand-lettered bills were tacked to wooden storefronts advertising real estate and city lots for sale, priced as high as six hundred dollars. Outrageous.

How could Papa have ever entrusted money to a bank in this town? she wondered acidly as she picked her way carefully down the wide street, avoiding huge holes and puddles. Of course, it was probably an excellent diversion, for Sebastian would *surely* never have considered that he would do such a thing. Even so, it would be best to be cautious, though she had seen no sign of her uncle.

She pulled her shawl more closely around her against the brisk air, ignoring as best she could Colette, who appeared a demure lady's maid at her elbow, solicitous and obedient, instead of the scheming little bitch that she really was.

The precious book was snugly fit into the purse dangling from Colette's arm—a precaution, of course, should "*la bellâtre* wish to be treacherous and cheat poor Colette."

Tory wished viciously that she could push the maid into one of the puddles of mud and stagnant water standing in the street. But she had no desire to call any more attention to them than they were already receiving as they made their way down the street. Men stared at them, some touching their hats respectfully, others gawking rudely, as if they had never seen a woman before. While it was true that the women she had seen here dressed more simply, her garments weren't *that* daring. She was wearing the simple blue velvet gown with ruched bodice; it fit snugly from her bosom to her waist, then flared out very prettily into full skirts that, after being wadded up in her saddlebags, had dozens of creases that required the skilled attention of a maid and hot flatiron. With Kincade and Garcia likely to check on them, there hadn't been time to remove the wrinkles. Still, it would have to do.

The bank stood on a corner of Montgomery Street, near the plaza. Hardly an imposing structure, but rather one that looked as if it had been built hastily, while all around it construction was going on, scaffolds raised, men shouting, and wagons rumbling past. Inside, business was brisk. She found it amazing, and a bit gratifying. Perhaps Papa hadn't made such a mistake after all, putting his money here. Though fairly crude, there were bank teller's cubicles, a table, and some offices in the back, and she headed directly for the door with the title of president.

In a very short time, the president, Mr. Carroll, had expressed his delight at meeting such an important investor's beautiful daughter, and of course he remembered her father, a lovely man, and how terrible it was that he had died so young. He stroked his short, thick mustache with one finger, smiling at her, obviously trying not to be too bold when he let his gaze drop down the line of her throat to where her skin gleamed above the scooped bodice of her gown.

"Ahem, I will do everything I can for you in this time of grief, Miss Ryan. Though your father did not do business with us very long—indeed, only three months—he was very well-liked."

Tory smiled with just the right amount of sadness, looking down, thinking that Mr. Carroll really meant Papa's money had been well-liked, and murmured her gratitude. She looked up in time to catch his gaze riveted on the shadow between her breasts, and smiled when he flushed.

"Then I'm certain you will understand, Mr. Carroll, that I must withdraw Papa's money from your bank." She sighed and dabbed at her lashes with the edge of a handkerchief. "It's unavoidable."

"My dear Miss Ryan . . ." Pausing, he looked nonplussed, and cleared his throat before smiling again. "I understand your need for funds at this time, but to withdraw such a large amount . . . surely you meant only a portion of it, and not the whole."

"Oh no. I meant the whole amount. And of course, I am fully aware of the requirements for withdrawal, and have with me the necessary account numbers." She pushed the bank-book across his desk toward him and leaned forward. "It's all written right there. Those are your initials—LC?"

"Yes, yes they are—" He looked unhappy, and his fingers drummed against the desktop. "But you see, it's not so easy to remove such a vast sum as this. It's not as if I had the actual cash tucked away in a drawer. The money is being used, invested wisely, of course, in new enterprises all over town. Your father understood this."

"Am I to understand that if my father had come in here and demanded back the cash money he gave you, you would refuse him?"

"Refuse? No, no, I did not mean to give you that impression. I am not refusing. I am just explaining that it will take time to gather the funds for you.''

"Very well.'' She heard Colette mutter something under her breath, and slanted her a quick, harsh glance before turning back to Mr. Carroll. "I will give you until tomorrow morning.''

"Tomor—Miss Ryan, I'm afraid you still don't understand.''

"No, Mr. Carroll, I'm afraid it is *you* who does not understand. This is my money, left to me by my father—and here you have the documents as proof—and I shall be back to collect it in the morning.''

In the end, Mr. Carroll finally agreed to have the money for her by the day after, but certainly no sooner than that, as he had to call in bonds and liquidate some holdings, and really, couldn't she take just a portion of it . . . perhaps transfer funds to several different accounts?

When they left the bank, Tory had five hundred dollars tucked into her velvet purse, not exactly a fortune, but enough to purchase passage to Boston—and some time. If it was so very difficult for her to get the money, then might it not be even more so for Tío Sebastián? And he did not have the ledger and account numbers that were required for withdrawal, while she, of course, did. Perhaps this would not be as complicated an ordeal as she had feared, and if she could only manage to delay matters until the transaction was completed, she might very well be able to sail out of the San Francisco harbor with the entire fortune tucked away.

But now there was Colette, who was furious, and even when Tory told her coldly that there was obviously nothing she could have done about it, as she herself had heard, the French girl continued to mutter angrily about the small sum she'd been given.

"A 'undred dollar? For how long will that last me? Ah, I should 'ave done as I first thought, and tell Kincade. I would 'ave more money than this—''

"Your trust in Lieutenant Kincade is remarkable, considering that you claim he intends to steal the entire amount.''

A brisk wind tugged at her skirts, and she held them down with one hand, looking impatiently toward Colette, who stood on the edge of a shallow stone curb at the bank's front door, glaring at her. "If you're so unhappy—tell him. I don't care. But if you do, don't be surprised when you're left with not even that hundred dollars."

"You sign the paper—"

"And when I get the rest of the money, I'll redeem the note." Her eyes narrowed at the girl. Damn her. *Damn* all of them . . . this was impossible, a frustrating, infuriating situation, and she wished she had never allowed herself to be coaxed into returning to California.

"Maîtresse . . ."

Colette's voice sounded strangled and a little odd, but Tory was too angry and unsettled to care, flicking her a dark look before she turned away to step into the street. There were no sidewalks, not even wooden ones in most places, but just dirt extending beyond shops and buildings. How am I ever supposed to navigate such a mess? she thought distractedly, lifting her skirts and stepping gingerly around a still-steaming mound of horse manure.

And then she lifted her head, and her stomach did an odd little flip as she saw them coming toward her—her uncle and brother at the head of a group of mounted vaqueros were crossing Montgomery Street with grim purpose. An instant of panic gripped her, when she felt her limbs freeze and her heart begin to race, and then a wagon rumbled past, momentarily blocking her uncle from her view. Tory whirled, saw that Colette had already begun to flee, her skirts lifted to show ankles and calves as she sprinted down the rutted street with more energy than Tory had ever known her to possess.

Oh God, what could she do? She heard Diego call her name, but ran blindly, not caring which direction, only that it be away from them. She had to escape, had to get away, or she would be taken back to Monterey and whatever they might do to her, and there would never be another chance, no matter what she might say or do.

Tory could hear the clattering sound of her feet against a

short wood porch, then the softer thud when she reached the street, slipping a little on the slick surface. Her breath was loud in her ears, sounding like a steam bellows as she ran, feeling like hunted prey. Hampered by her long skirts, she lifted them in her fists, vaguely aware of startled glances from pedestrians as she fled along a sloping street, trying to keep her balance and half-sliding along the ruts.

Her hair came loose from the chignon she had fashioned earlier, flying into her eyes, half-blinding her so that the steep ascent of the hillside street grew even more difficult to traverse. And all the while the pounding in her ears was like that of a heavy surf, a crashing sound, drowning out everything but her fear and urgency, the flailing beat of her heart.

As her feet began to drag and her muscles to weaken, her breath growing short and painful, she heard shouts behind her, hoofbeats, Diego's voice, angry and demanding, and knew that it was hopeless. A sharp pain jabbed her side, making it difficult to breathe, but she could not stop yet, could not yet admit defeat, though she saw the futility of it.

All for nothing, the flight in the dark of night, the torturous journey into the hills and across swollen rivers—and Kincade. She should have listened to him, though not for the reason he had given. Strangers could be no less dangerous than her own family.

She turned into an alley, then ran between picket fences made of barrel staves, feet sinking into mud and muck, and emerged onto Market Street. She paused in the shadowed doorway of a building to catch her breath, the pain in her side sharp. After a moment, she cautiously made her way from the doorway, her pace much slower; hope began to surface again when she looked behind her and did not see her uncle or brother. No vaqueros were in sight. Wagons crossed in front of her, and she darted out into the street and ran alongside a cart, trying to blend in with the pedestrians.

As the traffic thinned out, she pushed herself onward, spurred by fear and desperation, not knowing how close they were, or if they would come this far to look for her. Surely not. They would think she had gone back, maybe, or be looking for her in a hotel, or even the bank. Panting, she climbed the steep hill doggedly.

Ahead of her lay the old mission they had passed on the way in, and Tory realized she had come much farther than she'd thought. It was built in rambling adobe, the style that was so common in California. It looked abandoned, and when she got closer, she saw that it had fallen into some disrepair. A few chickens pecked around a yard choked with weeds, and she made her way toward the two-story building at one end, where an arched doorway opened between stone columns that held up a second-floor balcony.

Movement flickered inside, and hoping it was a priest or someone who could give her sanctuary, she stumbled through the open doors, blinking in the hazy light. Candle-scented and gloomy, the wide aisle down the middle of the room was flanked with statues, and a reliquary stood on a small dais at the front. It was empty, she saw when she drew near, as the entire place seemed to be. Her labored breathing grew easier, and she leaned gratefully against the reliquary to catch her breath. Several minutes passed in the quiet peace of the high-ceilinged chapel, and slowly, her heart resumed its normal pace, and the heated flush of exertion began to fade.

She shivered and wished she had a rebozo to wrap around her, something other than this thin little daydress she'd worn to impress a banker. She could not return to the hotel, of course. It would be too dangerous. What would Kincade say when Colette told her story? Or would he bother to ask once he realized that Sebastian and Diego had found them? Oh God, and how would she manage to purchase passage without being discovered, for it was certain that her uncle would think of that, just as Papa had done . . .

A noise at one side startled her and she whirled, gasping as a figure filled the doorway, shadowy and threatening.

"Who is there?" Her voice sounded tremulous and frightened. No one answered. Outside, she could hear the muffled squawk of a chicken, and a dog barked, sounding far away. She moved, and her feet scuffed over the stone floor much too loudly. "Who . . . who is there?"

The shadowed figure moved forward, stepping into the room, and behind ranged more figures. Don Sebastian strode into a thin ray of light that filtered through the doorway, smiling. Behind him, she recognized Diego, and knew that the other shadows would be the vaqueros. Her hopes sank.

As Don Sebastian walked toward her, she sagged to her knees on the floor in front of the reliquary. It was old and wooden, scarred with age and dusty, with large cracks in the joints. Folding her arms against the side, Tory leaned against the shabby structure and pressed her face into her sleeves. The velvet purse was wound tight around one wrist, and she eased open the cords that bound it, sliding the small ledger from it. Just as she tucked the book into one of the cracks of the reliquary, Don Sebastian reached her, and curled his hand around her arm to lift her up.

"So," he said in a voice thick with satisfaction, "you have arrived in San Francisco at last. I've been waiting for you. We have much to discuss."

Twenty

Diego Montoya y Ryan regarded his sister and uncle with narrow, speculative eyes. Tory had changed, much more than he had first considered when he'd seen her again. But, of course, it had been a long time, and she was a woman now, where once she had been only an annoying girl. Perhaps his uncle was right, and her willfulness should be sharply curbed.

Now, watching as Sebastian pulled Tory to her feet, shaking her a little, he did not protest, but waited to see what she would say. Even as a child she had been rebellious and full of surprises, such as the times she had stolen down to the barrios with the servants and danced with great abandon, her hair flying loose about her face, skirts swirling up around her bare legs, looking for all the world like a Spanish gypsy. Or when she had ridden off into the hills alone on her pony, making everyone worry and search for her, and then would come back, more often than not on foot, bruised and disheveled because she'd been thrown. He'd thought her reckless then, even as a child, and looking at her now, as she faced their uncle with her loose hair thrown back and chin tilted defiantly, he knew that had not changed.

"Release me," Tory said coldly, eyes flashing rage, "I have no wish to go with you."

"And do you think anyone here cares for your wishes?" Don Sebastian's lips curled. "You are disobedient, and should be punished for running away as you did. We have come to take you home. Your *novio* waits."

Tory's arm twisted in his grip, and her eyes clashed with his, sparks flying between them. "Let him wait. I told you that I would not marry him, and I won't. Now release me."

Ah, not surprising that his sister was such a defiant little cat . . . Didn't he recall how she had always been? And he admired it, even while he deplored her foolishness in tweaking their uncle so boldly.

Diego moved forward, recognizing that neither of them intended to yield.

"Enough. Let her go, Uncle. I wish to speak with my sister."

To his faint surprise, Sebastian did not release her but instead beckoned the vaqueros forward with a quick jerk of his hand.

"I cannot do that, Diego. Forgive me, but I do not intend to risk her escape."

Outraged, Diego put up a hand to stop the vaqueros, and when they ignored him, swore softly. "*Dios!* This is an insult. If you do not obey me, I will dismiss you from Buena Vista!"

Unhappily, Tomás, who had been at Buena Vista as long as Diego could remember, said, "Pardon, Don Diego, but we must obey your uncle. It has been told to us that you are not yet the master, but still under his guidance, and we have no choice."

Drawing himself up, Diego fixed Sebastian with a furious gaze. "My uncle is mistaken."

"I'm afraid not, Diego." Sebastian looked amused. "These men know that if they do not obey me, they will face much worse consequences than being dismissed from your employ. Ah, I see that you still do not understand. There is much more here at stake than the mere willful disobedience of your sister, or even the stolen munitions. The book is gone."

Diego's eyes narrowed. His suspicions were right. His uncle was fully aware of the book and its importance. He drew in a deep breath, and glanced at Tory. She was staring at him, her eyes wary, and he wondered then if she had taken it. Surely not. How could she know? Papa had never intended that she know, had intended that she quietly marry Rafael and solidify their families without being involved in the business beyond the transferral of her portion. No, she had fled to avoid marriage to Don Rafael, not because she had stolen their father's account book. It was a trick, a ruse to see if he would admit the existence of the ledger, and he didn't trust his uncle not to use the information against him.

"What has some book to do with my sister?" he demanded as he stepped forward, half-tempted to draw the sword at his side and command Tory's release.

But Sebastian Montoya was pulling her forth, still holding tightly to her arm, and looking quite certain. "Ask her. I think she will tell us what we want to know soon enough."

In a swift motion, Sebastian curled his fingers into the straps holding Tory's purse around her wrist, yanking it free. She cried out and aimed a blow at his head, but her uncle swept an arm back, his hand catching her across the face and slamming her back against the wooden reliquary.

Furious, Diego lunged for him and caught Sebastian by his shirtfront, his fists tangling in the fine linen of his white shirt. "*Dios!* I will not allow you to hurt my sister!"

Staggering, Sebastian held up the velvet scrap of purse; his eyes were wary in the murky light, and Diego felt a fierce spurt of satisfaction at his uncle's apprehension and quick, almost frightened response.

"Diego—the missing ledger. Do not pretend that you do not know of it, for I am well-aware that you do. I have known of it for months, but your father was too crafty for me, and hid it well. How she got it, I do not know, but I assure you, your sister has the ledger with all the accounts and amounts listed."

Slowly, Diego released his hold on Sebastian's shirt, setting him free. "Ledger?" His eyes narrowed on his uncle. "Which ledger is this, uncle?"

"The ledger from Don Patricio's office. I have been told that Vitoria has taken it."

"Told by whom?"

Don Sebastian took a step backward, straightened his shirt where Diego had crumpled it, and flicked Tory a glance before he half-turned and gave a swift order. In a moment, Tomás dragged someone into the chapel and swung her into the shaft of light. Colette, Tory's maid, stared up at Diego, her bruised face frightened and still wet with tears.

"It is true, Don Diego, that my *maîtresse*'as the book you seek. It is in the little purse . . ."

"Is it, *mozalbete*?" Tory laughed angrily. "Then look for it in there, if you are so certain. *Ramera!*"

Diego lifted a brow at Tory's harsh curses, and wondered where she had picked up such language. After studying his sister's face, he wasn't too surprised that the ledger was not where the maid claimed, though his uncle ripped the cloth bag apart, scattering money carelessly on the floor. It was only when Sebastian raged and blustered and made threats Diego would never have allowed to happen while Tory stood silently contemptuous, that he began to suspect she might have taken the ledger.

A faint, caustic smile curled her mouth as Tory watched Sebastian rage, but it was her coolly lifted brow that finally convinced her brother she knew where it was.

After a few moments, when Sebastian's threats began to turn very nasty, Diego interrupted in an attempt to defuse the volatile situation.

"Enough, Tío. It is obvious to me her maid is lying."

"Am I?" Colette's laugh was a little strangled, and she pushed at a strand of pale hair in her eyes. "*Non*, m'sieur, I am not. Where do you think the money on the floor came from, if not the bank? Eh? And me, I 'ave a 'undred dollar that I was given, to keep me from telling Kincade . . ."

"Kincade? What does he have to do with this?" Sebastian's sharp question went unanswered as Colette just shrugged and lapsed into frightened silence.

Diego watched Tory, and she stared back at him, her eyes

a cool violet, and the tumble of her hair over her shoulders shifting with every angry breath she took. A red mark marred one side of her face, where Sebastian had struck her.

He had to get her out of here. Sebastian was in a fury, and he had seen his uncle's rages vented on hapless victims before, never a pretty sight. If Tory would not save herself by confessing, he must do what he could to defuse the explosive situation.

"I came here to retrieve my sister, not a supposedly missing ledger," Diego said finally. "It is probably just misplaced, and we will find it when we arrive home. Come, Tory. We will go home, and discuss this."

Sebastian stepped in front of him when he reached out for her, blocking his path, his eyes narrowed and dangerous.

"No, Diego. She will tell us where she put the ledger. I will not risk it escaping me again."

A faint clink and shuffle behind him indicated that the vaqueros had stepped forward, weapons raised, and Diego swore silently, angry that he had put himself in this position, and angry with his sister for behaving so foolishly. She should have told him, trusted him, and perhaps together they could have devised a scheme to allay their uncle's plans, but it was too late now.

And the missing ledger—it must be true that she had taken it, or she would not now be so defiant. The little fool! Did she not know how angry Sebastian would be, how cruel he could become? He would do whatever he felt he must to get the ledger, to get the money that was a fortune. Bitterly, he thought of the times he had told his father not to trust Sebastian, had warned him that steps should be taken to protect the money, but Papa had been so certain it was safe, and always there would be more time, always it was *mañana*. Now it was too late.

Sebastian gave an order, and the vaqueros came forward, two of them taking Diego by the arms, not meeting his eyes, quailing a little at the icy promise he made them: "You will live to regret this—if only for a little while."

When Diego was taken outside, Sebastian turned to Tory.

His mouth curled into a ruthless smile, and his dark eyes were cold. "Now. You will tell me what I want to know, or you will soon wish you had. The ledger—where is it?"

Her mind was whirling. She was terrified, it was true, more terrified than she had ever been, but if she told Sebastian what he wanted to know, he had no more reason to keep her. It was Don Sebastian who controlled the vaqueros, and Diego was as much a prisoner as she. Poor Diego—perhaps she should have confided in him, but it was too late now, too late for anything but desperate measures. Would her uncle do something drastic? She would not put it past him, yet if he did, he would have to kill them both, her and Diego, for it was obvious her brother was not willing to hurt her.

"You are taking too long to remember where you put it," Sebastian said softly. "Perhaps I should help you. Is it on your person, maybe? Shall I have you remove your clothes?"

Her chin jerked up. He is capable of anything! she thought then, frightened but determined not to let him see it. With slow, deliberate motions, she ran a hand over her tight-fitting sleeves, then shook her skirts vigorously. "As you can see— nothing. I assure you there is no ledger on me."

"You are lying, Vitoria."

"*Pendejo!* Do not call me a liar—" A faint gleam caught her eye, and she looked down, gasping a little at the knife her uncle held in his hand. A surge of fear cut through her as cold as any knife blade, icy and making her shiver.

"Are you reconsidering, Vitoria? You should, before I must cut away your garments. It would be too bad were you to have an ugly scar on your cheek, eh? Or perhaps lower, across that slender neck of yours, and if my blade should slip a little, go too deep . . ."

"You wouldn't dare."

"Would I not? What would I have to lose? If you were dead, and your foolish, reckless brother as well, then all would be mine."

"You're forgetting my mother."

Sebastian laughed, lifting his shoulders in a shrug. "Paloma is much wiser than you. She does as she is told, as she has always done. She learned a long time ago that it is useless to be defiant, that it only causes much sadness. And death.''

Tory looked at him, at the cold, cruel light in his eyes, and suddenly knew. The words tumbled out before she could stop them—''You killed Mama's Roberto, didn't you?''

Looking surprised, Sebastian stared at her, then shrugged again, carelessly.

''It surprises me that you know about that. It was so long ago . . . ah, but I suppose you have heard the talk, the suspicions. No one ever knew for certain, and still do not know. Roberto was stupid, and too careless of his own life. He should never have forced himself upon a daughter of a Montoya. It was inevitable that someone would kill him.''

He advanced several steps, dark and menacing, his eyes just slits in his face, the knife a lethal threat, catching light from the doorway and gleaming softly as he held it up. The reliquary was behind her, the wood pressed into the back of her thighs where she leaned against it, and Tory put her hands behind her and grabbed hold of the frame. Part of it came loose, a thin strip of splintered wood no bigger around than her thumb, and her fingers immediately curled around it, prompted by some primitive animal instinct of defense.

If he touches me, I will kill him . . . I don't know how I can manage it, but this will not be so easy for him, she thought, fiercely.

Don Sebastian pointed the blade toward her, lightly touching the tip of it with his finger, a mere flicker, but it was sharp enough that a drop of blood sprouted where the tip touched, crimson and sliding down his finger to the knuckle.

''You see, I keep my weapons honed,'' he said in a grating purr, and there was no mistaking his meaning.

Her hands tightened around the piece of wood that had come free; holding it behind her, hidden in her skirts, Tory edged to one side; her palms were damp, her throat tight. Her heart beat loud and rapid, seeming to fill her ears with a dull roar.

Sebastian turned with an amused expression on his thin, hawk's face. ''No, do not think to get away from me that

easy, Vitoria. Now come, my patience wanes. Tell me what
I want to know before I must hurt you.''

She wet her lips, panting slightly with fear. ''You are mad
. . . I know nothing.''

''And you are very foolish . . .''

When he lunged for her, the knife blade sliced through the
shoulder of her gown before she twisted out of the way more
agilely than she thought possible. Then she was turning back,
everything a blur, her arm lifting, bringing up the piece of
wood, glimpsing the short iron nail jutting from the end as
she brought it down with all her force on her uncle's arm. It
stuck, the nail digging deeply into the fleshy part, and he
dropped the knife to grab at his arm, screaming, cursing her,
and shouting for the vaqueros.

It was all so quick . . . shouts and curses, and the sound of
running feet as the vaqueros came through the door. Tory
sprinted for the back of the chapel, her skirts flying up about
her knees.

There has to be another way out, oh God, let there be . . .

The shouting grew louder, along with more cursing, and
she thought that Diego must somehow have managed to sway
the vaqueros to his side. But she did not dare stop, even when
she heard the shattering reports of guns being fired that
sounded much too loud inside the chapel, reverberating from
the walls and high ceiling, showering the air with powdery
white bursts of plaster, ear-shattering cracks that sounded as
if fifty guns were being fired all at once.

As she reached the back of the chapel, a curtain flickered
over a doorway, and she saw a thin thread of light and darted
for it, heart in her throat, not daring to look back. It was such
a slender hope, such a risky chance, and it might all be futile,
they might catch her before she could get away, could flee to
the commandant of the presidio, perhaps, and throw herself
on the mercy of the government.

Anything would be better than letting Sebastian win . . .

Dust flew up in a choking cloud when she yanked back the
faded blanket that served as a covering, and she flung herself
out the opening into a small courtyard behind the building.

She had crossed only half the yard, chickens squawking and
fluttering from her path, when she heard the sound of pursuit.
Gunfire was a constant noise now, terrifying and loud, seeming to come from all sides. Everything was such a blur, the
blinding, suffocating fear, the hard impact of her feet against
soggy ground as she ran, not knowing where, just running
afraid and desperate, toward the hills beyond.

Appearing out of nowhere, it seemed, a serape-clad figure
loomed directly in front of her, and she screamed, veering
away. But she got only two steps before she was caught, a
strong arm around her waist that lifted her off her feet, holding her.

"Quiet," a voice growled in Spanish next to her ear, but
in her fear and panic, she screamed and struggled, twisting
uselessly. Finally, harsher: "*Cállate!*" He held her fast, hands
like iron bands around her arms, pushing her in front of him
mercilessly, back toward the mission.

Half-sobbing with frustration and fear, Tory caught a
glimpse of her brother ahead of her, surrounded by armed
men, looking grim as he stood in the shadow of the mission.
His jacket was torn, and a livid bruise reddened one side of
his face. When she drew near, stumbling a little as her captor
propelled her forward, she saw that the vaqueros who had
come with Diego and Don Sebastian were also looking grim,
and several of them were bleeding, including Tomás, while
some lay unmoving on the ground.

A rapid exchange in Spanish followed, conducted by the
man behind her and another at one side who held a rifle on
Diego. All these men were armed to the teeth, ammunition
belts slung over their shoulders, wide-brimmed hats hiding
their faces, and some wearing the blanket-style serape around
them.

Confused, Tory slowly realized that they had stopped, and
that her captor was still holding her tightly while he spoke.
In the midst of her confusion, she realized that they were
speaking a form of Spanish she didn't understand, but had
heard the Indians who lived near Monterey speak. She looked
at Diego, and saw that he understood, for his eyes were filled

with angry frustration and his mouth set in a taut slash.

"You have no right to do this," he said furiously, speaking to the man behind her. "This is not your business."

"I'm making it my business," was the cool reply, and Tory frowned, twisting to see behind her. But he gave her a rough push, holding her so that she could not turn, could not see, and she was forced forward.

He gave another order, speaking in the Indian dialect, and a man came to take her by the arm. She pulled away, eyes flashing.

"Don't you dare touch me!"

"Do what they say, Tory," Diego said then, with a note of contempt that she didn't quite understand. "These men are serious and dangerous, I'm afraid. Perhaps your instincts were right, after all."

"I don't understand—what is going on?"

"We're being robbed." Diego's mouth twitched with sardonic amusement. "Or at least, our uncle is being robbed."

Tory looked around and saw Tío Sebastian leaning against a post, holding his bleeding arm, arrogant and furious. She looked back at her brother, angry confusion drawing her brows down over her eyes.

"A robbery—for God's sake, this is insanity. What could they want?" She half-turned to look at the man in the shadows behind her, the one who had followed her outside and brought her back. He stood beneath the overhang of a porch that still had vines clinging to it; the few leaves that indicated grapes had once grown up the post and rotting wood fluttered in a slight breeze. "Are you mad?" she demanded.

"No, not mad at all." Lifting his rifle, he pointed to Don Sebastian with the muzzle. "There is something that we want."

"And what is that?" Her voice was scathing as fury overrode the numbing fear, and she pushed angrily at hair scattered in front of her eyes, fixing the bandit with a scornful stare. "What do you want, for God's sake!"

Sebastian laughed harshly. "Well you should ask, little

bruja. If you had given it to me as I told you, we would be on our way now, instead of at their mercy.''

"Given you . . .'' She paused, sucking in a deep breath before glancing at Diego, who gave an almost imperceptible shake of his head.

Apparently the bandit leader saw it, and he said something again in that guttural language that made one of his men step forward and club Diego with the butt of his rifle, knocking him down. Diego sprawled in the dirt, groaning.

Tory screamed his name and lunged forward, but was grabbed by the arm, swung back around to face the leader, who was staring down at her impassively. She froze when their eyes met, for even beneath the wide brim of his hat, she could easily see his face now. He made no attempt to hide, but lifted a mocking brow.

"So you still have it, do you, Venus? I should have known. Give it to me, and we'll go on our way and leave you with your loving family.''

Behind the taunting smile, Nick Kincade's narrowed gaze was coolly assessing, as if gauging how far he could push her. She should have recognized him at once, would have probably, if she had not been so frightened and confused, but now she felt the fury bubbling up from deep inside her, the knowledge that he had used her to gain only money a pricking, hurtful barb.

Without conscious thought, she launched herself at him, fingers curved into clawing talons that raked at his face, managing to strip furrows into his cheek before he brought up an arm to defend himself, swearing at her as he held her at bay, his hands hard around her wrists.

"*Mierda!* Be sensible, dammit, Tory!''

"Sensible!'' It came out a shriek, breathless and incoherent as she added several panting oaths that only made him grin. "You're nothing but a thief . . . Let go of me . . .''

But he held her firmly by the wrists so that she would not scratch him again and, looking over her head, spoke to another man that she now recognized as Gil Garcia beneath a wide-brimmed sombrero, using the Indian dialect. After a moment, Nick looked back down at her.

"Give me the ledger and we'll leave you in peace to tend your wounded and go home. It's the only choice you've got, so don't bother arguing."

When she remained stubbornly silent, he swore under his breath again, fingers tightening. This time his words were short and impatient. "I don't have much time and you're wasting it. Tell me where it is, Tory."

Gil said something to him, sounding urgent, and in the distance, Tory could hear the sound of hoofbeats. She lifted her head, saw the faint haze of dust rising up along the road from San Francisco. Someone muttered *soldados*, and she knew it must be soldiers from the presidio, who had heard the gunfire, perhaps, and were coming to investigate.

From where he still lay sprawled on the ground, Don Sebastian looked up at Kincade, his eyes exultant in the fading light.

"I am personally acquainted with Governor Mason, señor, and you are in much more trouble than you could have dreamed. Give over your weapons to my vaqueros, and I may persuade the soldiers to be lenient with you, and not shoot you on sight . . ."

"Save it." Nick's grip moved up to tighten on her arms, digging painfully into her flesh. "Tell me where you hid the ledger, Tory, or I'll be forced to do something you won't like."

Panting a little with strain and fear and uncertainty, she looked beyond him, at the men he had with him and her uncle's vaqueros, and then at her brother, where he still lay sprawled in the dirt of the plaza. When Nick gave her a shake that whipped her head forward so that her hair fell into her eyes, she knew he was at the end of his patience and might really do something terrible. She forced her eyes to his face.

Fine white lines bracketed the corners of his mouth, and his eyes were hard. "I've given you enough time to decide." He raked her with a contemptuous glance before looking up to give a sharp order to one of his men.

The man crossed to Diego in two strides and jerked him up. Late sunlight gleamed along the wicked edge of a knife blade as he held it to Diego's throat, and Tory screamed.

"No! Oh no, don't! Please, don't hurt him. He doesn't know where it is, I swear it . . . Oh, God, please . . . Nick, don't let him hurt my brother."

"Tell me, Tory." Mixed with the urgency in his tone was a soft coaxing note, and she nodded finally, half-sobbing.

"All right. I'll tell you. I'll tell you . . ."

He sent one of his men into the chapel and he came back out quickly, grinning, holding up the small ledger in his hand.

"You made the right decision," Nick said, and released his grip on her arms at the same time that the bandit holding the knife to Diego's throat removed it and shoved him to the ground. The bandits moved quickly among Don Sebastian's men, gathering the vaqueros' weapons with them.

"You'll find your guns in the well once we are gone," Gil said to Diego, "but do not follow us. We will shoot any man fool enough to try."

Tory stood frozen, watching Kincade, listening to Colette's whimpering sobs and Diego's curses, dazed, almost numb with it all. They were mounting their horses, the bandits, ten or fifteen of them, all looking as wicked and dangerous as their leader. Nick Kincade was mounting his horse as well, a lithe vault into the saddle, and turning it to speak to her brother, quietly, words she could not hear.

Diego was in no position to help her. Sebastian had made that clear enough. And now she knew without a doubt that her uncle would use her cruelly, and there was little she could do about it. No one could help her, not even her mother, who had already done all she could. Sick, slightly swaying, Tory dragged her gaze from her brother to her uncle, and saw in his dark, burning eyes that he would be without mercy. He had lost not only the ledger, but any hope of retrieving the money now.

Kincade urged his horse forward in a trot, toward the small iron gate in the church courtyard, glancing once in her direction.

Without pausing to think it through, Tory lurched forward and grabbed Nick's boot as he passed, holding on, running beside the snorting, wild-eyed horse, her hands slipping on the leather. He reined in and looked down at her, cold and polite.

"I'm in rather a hurry, Miss Ryan, so if you don't mind—"

"Take me with you." She inhaled deeply when his eyes narrowed and one brow shot up, tasting dust and her own fear—and desperation. "Don't leave me here. You don't know what it will be like, don't know—oh God—just take me with you. I could be your hostage. You know my uncle will follow you, and the soldiers are almost here . . ."

It was humiliating to plead like that, but the alternative was even more horrifying.

She heard Diego swear at her, and Sebastian howled a threat, but she stubbornly kept her gaze turned up to Nick, willing him to agree, thinking dizzily—fearfully—that he would refuse. He was staring at her with narrowed, speculative eyes, unsmiling, his face impassive, and her heart sank. Then he smiled slightly, that familiar lopsided tilt of his mouth that looked more dangerous than amused.

Kicking his foot free of the stirrup, he held out his hand, palm up. "All right, Venus, I'll take you . . ."

Part
Four

Twenty-one

Dark had fallen hours before. Tory shivered but bit her lip to keep from complaining, sensing that Nick would hardly be amenable to female frailties. Not that he'd paid much attention to her since leaving Mission Dolores. With her brother's furious entreaties ringing in her ears, Tory had looked back only once, and seen Diego standing in the dirt plaza in front of the mission.

They had stopped when the mission was out of sight, and Tory was given a horse to ride, Kincade swinging her down, barely looking at her, acknowledging her with only a faint nod of his head. She had been put in the care of Gil Garcia, who rode nearby, her guide in the night.

Now, riding a trail she couldn't even see behind several men she didn't know, she wondered if she had made the right choice. There had seemed little else to do then, with Sebastian staring at her with cold, evil promise and certain reprisal. It had been a matter of choosing poisons, and with Kincade, at least there might be a chance.

The cause of her uncle's wrath and pursuit, the small leather-bound ledger, was now safely in Kincade's hands. He'd looked through it, flipping the pages, then glanced up at her, a faint smile tugging at one corner of his mouth.

"Good thing for you it didn't get lost or destroyed, wouldn't you say? What would you have had to barter with?"

She had not answered but looked away, too unsettled and apprehensive to think of a reply. She could not forget Diego's angry pleas with her as she'd mounted Kincade's horse, or his parting threats to have Nick arrested and hanged for the crime of abduction. With her holding on to him, her arms around his waist, Nick had laughed. It would hardly be abduction when she had begged to be taken, would it?

For a while, it had looked as if the soldiers might actually catch up to them, but then Nick had insisted she exchange clothes with one of the bandits, a young boy who looked only about fourteen. Perplexed, she had agreed, grimacing as she donned Gustavo's dusty thin cotton shirt and wide-legged pants. Gustavo just grinned at her as he paraded in her blue dress, dragging the hem in the dirt, mincing and making his companions laugh, as well as her. Then they'd mounted again, some bandits including Gustavo splitting from the group to ride in another direction. From a high rock, she had watched as the soldiers pursued them, until they'd disappeared from sight in the rocks and trees. It had been hours now, with no sign of pursuit. They were far from the mission and any sign of civilization, riding relentlessly onward.

Gil Garcia rode close to her in the deep shadows of a mountain ridge, sounding sympathetic. "Here, *pobrecitá*. A serape to keep you warm."

Remembering another time he had come to her rescue with a warm covering, she took the wool garment and slipped it over her head gratefully. It settled around her, warm and enveloping, smelling of dust and tobacco.

"Thank you, Mr. Garcia."

"Gil." He laughed softly. "I am not used to being so formal, and we have ridden together before, eh?"

"Yes." She subsided into silence, too weary to think of pleasantries, and after a moment asked, "Where are we going?"

"Ah, that I cannot say. We are to meet someone, but after that—you are to have passage to Boston, I understand."

"Am I? No one told me." Her hands slipped on the leather reins and the horse picked up its pace, so that she had to fumble for control. Her pretty mare was sorely missed, but this plain little dun was far more suitable. And really, its gait wasn't so bad, though not as smooth as her mare's.

Gil rode beside her for a little while longer, talking softly, his easy conversation keeping her awake and more alert than she might have been. She was so tired, and remembered that she had eaten nothing but a biscuit one of the bandits had given her earlier. It had been hard and flat, but edible, and she'd devoured it quickly, half-afraid he might take it back if she complained.

These hard-faced men were aloof for the most part, Gil being the only one to talk easily, with the others riding in silence. They were obviously accustomed to this kind of riding, hard and fast, building no fires to alert pursuers, grim and deliberate. Up ahead somewhere rode Nick Kincade. Since leaving the mission, he had barely acknowledged her presence other than a brief nod of his head in her direction, and his indifference was maddening.

She felt betrayed, and though she reasoned that she'd suspected him all along of dealing guns with her father, the stark truth of his perfidy was painful. It was one thing to be a mercenary, and quite another to use her to steal her father's money. She didn't know why, for both were criminal acts, but the latter hurt the most.

By the time they stopped to rest, Tory was reeling in her saddle with exhaustion, and it was Gil Garcia who helped her down, his hands gentle on her as he half-carried her to a rocky shelf. Some of the men were cutting brush and forming it into shelter, weaving branches together and then throwing an oil-cloth of India rubber over them. Gil escorted her to one of them, giving her two blankets and some cold biscuits and bacon.

She regarded the biscuit unenthusiastically, but bit off a hard chunk and began to chew. Gil smiled slightly and stood up to leave. "There will be no fire tonight, but if you wrap up in your serape and blanket, you will be warm enough."

She nodded dully. She remembered enough not to expect a fire. Wasn't the thought of Don Sebastian catching up to them before she could secure passage aboard a Boston-bound vessel unnerving enough without taking any risks? Hunched in her blankets beneath the crude shelter, she looked up at Gil where he stood, silhouetted against the rocky forest around them.

"I don't suppose you'd want to tell me what is going to happen to the money in my father's bank accounts."

It wasn't very surprising when he shook his head. "No, I cannot say. But do not distress yourself, señorita, for it will be used well for the good of many."

"I suspect there's a vast difference in my estimations of the proper use of so much money, and your leader's," she couldn't help saying, more sharply than she'd meant. Why let them know it bothered her? Or that she was devastated to discover that Nick Kincade was little more than an outlaw? A mercenary thief? And those were only a few of his qualifications, if she let herself think about them, about the dead man in the presidio, and the Indians he had killed, and, dear Lord, probably many more than that.

Gil crouched down beside her, his dark eyes fixed on her face and a faintly amused smile curving his mouth beneath the thin, black mustache. His voice was soft and sympathetic.

"You must understand that our plans were ruined when your uncle did not take the ledger and go to the bank to retrieve the money. Now we do what we must. You did not have to come, you know."

"I know." She shrugged carelessly, ignoring the thickening lump in her throat that had nothing to do with the cold, dry biscuit. "But I had little choice, as I'm certain you recognized. My uncle bears me no love, and would not have hesitated to wed me to Don Rafael or confine me in a convent for the rest of my life. At least now I can go back to Boston and those who . . . who care about me."

If Gil noticed the way her voice trembled slightly, he did not betray it, but merely nodded understanding. "It is always

best to be with those who care about you. And your brother—
he would not help you, you think?"

"Diego . . . oh, I don't know. Diego's changed so much
since last I saw him. He's no longer a boy, but a man I don't
really know anymore. Once, I would have sworn he would
not allow me to be mistreated, but—but he was with Tío
Sebastian, and though he did try to stop him from hurting me,
he did nothing to save me."

"It did not look to me, when we got there, that your brother
was in any position to help," Gil said dryly. "But I admit, I
was not paying too much attention, with the bullets flying so
fast about my head like angry bees. If you don't mind me
saying, Miss Ryan, it might be best if you were to contact
your brother somehow. I think he would help you."

"It's too late for that. And I'm not as sure as you seem to
be that he would be able to help."

"Don Sebastian had him at a disadvantage, true, but it was
most likely a shock to Don Diego that the vaqueros refused
to heed his wishes. I have a feeling that once back at Buena
Vista, Don Sebastian may find himself with an angry man on
his hands instead of a boy, as he thinks. Your brother will
find a way to strike back."

Tory shivered. "For Diego's sake, I hope you're right."

Rising to his feet, Gil looked down at her. "It is late, and
there is much to do yet. Get some rest while you can. We
will ride again before first light tomorrow."

He turned, took a step away, then looked back to say softly,
"Vaya con Dios"—a very strange good night, she thought.

It felt as if she had only just fallen asleep when she was
awakened by a rough hand on her shoulder, shaking her, telling her in Spanish to get up for they must ride, *andale!* She
sat up, blinking sleep from her eyes, frowning a little and
pushing the hair from her eyes. One of the bandits stood there,
staring at her, his face hidden by the wide brim of his sombrero.

"All right, I'm getting up."

He left, and she sat there a moment, struggling to wake,
hugging the wool serape around her shivering body. Sounds

of horses being saddled and men talking in a low murmur filled the air, and she heard hooves on rock, and then on the softer debris beneath the tall trees. It was still dark, with visibility limited to a foot or two in front of her face, the only light provided by starshine and a tiny piece of moon still high in the sky.

Nick Kincade came to stand in front of her, his boots straddling the edge of her blankets as he pushed back the brush roof of her shelter. "Hurry up, Tory. We can't wait on you to leisurely wake."

Because she had no intention of allowing him to know that she was tired—giving him an excuse to berate her—she stumbled to her feet, still clutching the edges of the serape with her hands tucked inside it.

"Do I have time to tend my needs before we leave?"

"If you hurry."

Once she would have stammered and blushed, hating to ask such a question, but now it came out naturally, and she thought with a trace of irony that she had come far in the past weeks. By the time she returned from the privacy of the bushes, her blankets were rolled and horse waiting, with Kincade shifting impatiently from one foot to the other. He was alone, all the others having disappeared, the only sign that they'd even been there the hastily erected shelters still leaning against rock and trees.

Silent, he handed her a small cloth pouch and her reins, and when she had mounted and was following him up the winding trail through the deep forest where it seemed as if he couldn't possibly see his way, she discovered some more of the flat biscuits and a piece of bacon tucked into the cloth. She ate silently as they rode, her horse's nose almost bumping the flanks of his black gelding.

They rode for some time this way, and she actually began to doze in the saddle despite the rather rugged terrain, waking sharply when her horse stumbled. She blinked and saw that it had grown light, seeping slowly down through the tangled tops of tall pines, spruce, and cedars. Kincade was a yard or two ahead of her, crosswise on the path, leaning on his saddle horn and watching her with mild amusement.

"If you'd fallen, you'd have gone right down that slope."

She looked, shuddering when she saw the steep, brush-studded decline that fell away at a sharp angle from the narrow path. Looking back at him, she managed a nonchalant shrug, hoping she sounded calmer than she felt at this moment.

"But I didn't fall."

"No." He reined his horse around, the smile still on his mouth. "Not yet."

This was more familiar, and she found herself settling back into a similar routine that they had established before. When they rode out of the trees finally and into a small, more level plain, she nudged her mare up beside him.

"Where are the others? They can't have gotten that far ahead of us."

"They're not ahead of us."

When he didn't say anything else or expound on that terse comment, she had a sudden spurt of foreboding. "They *are* waiting for us, aren't they?"

"What would it matter if they were?"

"*If*—oh God, what do you mean? I thought—Gil said—aren't you taking me to a seaport? Where did they go? Where's Gil Garcia?"

The glance he gave her was hard, devoid of his earlier amusement and tolerance. "Gone. Sorry, Venus, you didn't specify who was to be your guide. I assumed you meant me, as you begged me to take you."

"Yes, of course, but that is not at all what I mean. It's—" She stopped. It would be useless to press him if he didn't want to answer, and so she switched tactics. "Where are you taking me?"

He surprised her by answering: "Sutter's Fort."

"You can't be serious!"

"Dead serious. Do you have a better idea?"

"But that's so far away—and inland, not on the coast at all, I'm sure. Why, we'll have to cross the bay to get there, or go all the way around, and it will take days, maybe weeks!''

"Only a few days if you can keep up. I have to go south first, then we'll cut around, ride up to Sacramento City. From there you can board a steamer that will take you down the river and out into the bay, then past San Francisco to the Pacific. It takes about four or five days, and after that, you'll be on your way to Boston. Your only other choice is to wait at one of the seaports on the coast, and I can guarantee you that your uncle will have men looking for you there.''

She grew quiet. It made sense, she supposed, but was not at all what she'd expected or wanted. It meant she would be with Nick much longer, and somehow, the thought was terrifying.

"You seem to have thought this out thoroughly,'' she said after a few moments. "Are you certain it will work?''

"You'd better hope so.''

It began to rain before dark, and rained steadily for the next few hours. Nick was supposed to meet Roy Martin at Mission Santa Clara de Asis, nearly thirty miles south of where they'd camped the first night. The weather slowed him down, but he couldn't go too fast with Victoria Ryan dragging behind. Her first flare of resistance had waned finally. Except for a few comments here and there, she didn't whimper and complain, other than to tell him once, breathlessly, her face flushed with fury and eyes as dark purple and soft as pansies, that he was deliberately trying to make her miserable.

"Don't push your luck, Miss Ryan,'' he warned her softly, and she had looked at him more closely and subsided, turning her face away but not offering any more provoking observations.

She stayed quiet until they reached the edge of a creek that ran parallel to a rocky hill studded with natural caves. "Can't we stop for a while? I'm tired, and this rain is so cold . . . The horses are exhausted as well. Last time, you told me we had to pace the animals. Isn't that true?''

"You're not very subtle.'' He pointed up the hill, where a

scraggly cottonwood grove hid the entrance to a shallow depression in the rock. Rain dripped from branches and leaves, forming small pools on the ground, running in narrow rivulets down the slope to the creek. "We'll camp there."

When he had the horses unsaddled and brushed down—checking hooves for splitting and damage, running his hand over withers, croup, down hocks to fetlocks and back up—he hobbled them near the front of the cave, then went to squat by the fire. Surprisingly, Tory had a skillet of beans and bacon almost ready and, in a moment, silently shoved a plate toward him. He ate just as silently, studying her in the flickering light.

Maybe he should have left the girl with her brother. Nothing would have happened to her. Diego was not likely to allow it, despite Sebastian's control. But she'd looked so desperate, so terrified, with her big eyes and that loose cloud of dark-fire hair tumbling all around her shoulders, down over the low, scooped front of her blue dress, not quite hiding the tempting rise of her breasts. And he'd remembered how she'd tasted, felt, sounded when she moaned in his ear, and let that override common sense.

There had been no need to take her with him. He had possession of the ledger, which was all that could be salvaged from the botched assignment. It grated on his temper that the plan had gone awry, and he intended to remind Roy Martin when he saw him next that he had suggested being less subtle and more forceful. Not that it mattered now. Martin would have to work with what he had, which was the ledger listing account numbers and amounts. Maybe they didn't have Don Sebastian and his confederates, but at least the government would have control of the illegally obtained money.

And he had responsibility for Victoria Ryan.

She was only three feet away, pretending not to notice him when he knew she did. It was too obvious in the way she sat so self-consciously, toying with her hair, fiddling with the sleeves of her borrowed shirt. The serape was a wool heap at her back, and she had removed her shoes and stockings and was wiggling her bare toes against one of the blankets. Her glances were quick darts of her eyes toward him, then away, as if unwilling to meet his eyes.

It was irritating. And arousing, and he was damned if he intended to let her get to him again.

Twenty-two

They arrived at Mission Santa Clara late the next day. Never, Tory thought, had she seen a more beautiful valley than the one in which the mission was situated. The Sierras rose majestically toward the sky, blue-tinted and hazy with dark green trees, jutting up from the valley floor in an abrupt, elongated barrier. It was warmer in the green basin than it had been in the mountains, and the sun beat down on her face and bare arms with welcome heat.

At one end of the mission rose a high, vaulted chapel, with a bell tower and tiled roof bearing a huge cross; a small iron fence edged the courtyard in front of arched double doors leading inside. Long, low buildings formed an ell to the left, in crumbling disrepair as were most of the missions she had seen. Ahead, just beyond the sprawling buildings of the Franciscan mission, was the settlement of San José, a collection of frame houses scattered in a pretty pattern across the valley floor.

Travelers were welcomed, and in the broad plaza fronting the mission, children played and dogs barked. Father Michael was not there, they were told when they dismounted, but they were invited to stay.

''There is no charge, of course,'' the postulant said, smiling

301

a little, "but you are welcome to make charitable donations if you like."

"I'm supposed to meet someone here," Nick said as he dismounted and helped Tory down, ignoring her curious glance. "Roy Martin."

"Ah yes. He is waiting for you, señor. I will show you to him, while Juana escorts your wife to your room."

"Oh no," Tory began, but the friar was already beckoning a young girl toward him, telling her to take the lady to the room off the rear courtyard. Nick just grinned mockingly, and remarked that his wife was very tired, indeed.

Before she could summon a response that was sufficiently withering, Nick was leading the horses away, and she had only the girl to deal with, a young, lively creature with big brown eyes and shiny black hair. The girl smiled at her, and though her eyes widened a little when she noticed that Tory was wearing men's trousers beneath the enveloping serape, she did not comment, other than to beckon her toward the mission dormitory.

Tory was shown to a tiny room that was spartan clean and had a narrow cot, with a wooden cross hanging on one wall the only decoration. A small niche held a lamp, and several candle stubs were placed neatly on the small table. On a chair next to the bed, a cracked pitcher and washbowl held a folded square of thick cloth.

"Shall I fetch you some water to wash, señora?" the girl Juana asked. "And perhaps have your baggage brought to the room?"

She had no baggage, of course, but there was no reason to tell this pert girl looking at her with inquisitive eyes something like that, and she shook her head.

"I'm certain the baggage will be brought later, but you may bring water, or show me the well so that I may get it."

"Sí, I will be glad to show you the well, if you like. It is not far, but only in the small courtyard nearby."

Tory took the pitcher and followed her along the covered porch hung with flowering vines, and out into a small, tiled courtyard bursting with pots of bright flowers and a small garden patch of herbs. An oak tree spread ancient limbs over part of the enclosure. Wooden beams formed a slatted roof next to the buildings, and a few tables were scattered about, with some benches along a low stone wall.

"Sometimes, at night, we come out here to play music and dance a bit," Juana said as she led the way to the well in the center. A low wall circled it, and a bucket was attached by a long rope to an iron ring set into the stone. She lowered the bucket into the well with a splash, and began drawing it up, smiling slightly. "The padre does not always like for us to play our music, but when he is gone, as he is now, up into the mountains to give last rites to a poor, dying soul, we can do as we please. The others do not care, as long as the men do not drink too much and become difficult. And sometimes, they even come to watch, and listen to the music. You should come. My brother plays the guitar very well."

"It sounds very . . . entertaining," Tory said, and leaned forward to fill the pitcher from the bucket. "Perhaps I will come and listen to the music sometime."

They lingered for a time in the late afternoon sunshine, and when Tory returned to the room, she found that Nick's saddlebags had been placed in one corner. Her mouth tightened. Did he think he was going to stay in here with her? As if they were truly husband and wife? No, she would not agree to that again, and she didn't care what he had to say about it. Staying in a cave with him was one thing, but sleeping in the same small room in a mission, with a cross on one wall and a chapel only a few yards away, was insupportable. She would not do it. It was profane, and even if he grew angry and his eyes turned to those hot yellow flames again, she would refuse. It was unthinkable.

She pushed the cot in front of the door and set the chair atop it for good measure, then undressed and washed herself in the tepid water, using a small piece of soap she found in the washbowl with the cloth. Afterward, she washed her undergarments and wrung them out, then draped them over the table to dry. Her clothes were tattered in places, the sleeves rolled up to her elbows, and she brushed them as clean as she could before putting them back on again.

There was a knock on the door, and she stiffened, head jerking up. "Who is it?"

"Juana, señora. Your husband had me bring you clean clothes since your baggage was lost. Shall I open the door?"

"Just a moment." Feeling a little foolish, she pulled the cot away from the door, wondering if Juana heard and what she made of it, then swung open the door. The girl was looking at her a little oddly, but held out clean garments, a simple loose camisa like the peasants wore, and a bright, patterned skirt.

Tory didn't meet her eyes, but took the garments, thanked her, and shut the door, leaning against it. The wood was cool against her back. It was stuffy in the small room, the only window covered with shutters, and she moved to swing them open and allow in a cool, refreshing breeze. It was dusk, and the mountains ringing the valley were blue-hazed and beautiful, with the setting sun outlining them in lacy patterns against a rose-gold sky. Rainbow colors, beautiful enough to make her throat ache, shimmered in the air as the sun sank slowly in the west, in the ocean beyond Monterey.

She thought of her brother then, and her mother, and wondered if Paloma had known how important the ledger would be to Don Sebastian. But of course she had. She'd said he wanted it, had wanted to thwart him as he had done her so long ago. Did Paloma suspect that her own brother was responsible for Roberto's death? Or did she only seek vengeance against the men in her family who had caused her so much unhappiness?

And, most painful of all, did she not care that her daughter would suffer for it?

The question had haunted her since she'd realized how determined her uncle was to get the ledger, since she'd discovered that even Nick Kincade wanted it, and God only knew who else. It was a lot of money, after all, and there were men who would do anything for it.

Through the unshuttered window, she watched night fall;

insects hummed, but fewer now that it was so cool at night. Soon it would be winter in the high mountain ranges, for already leaves were beginning to scatter below the oak trees, in colors of bright red, orange, and yellow. Where would she be when spring came? Boston? Or here, where it always came early with warm days and frosty nights? Nights so cool that it would be comforting to lie next to a man?

Oh, why did she let Nick torment her so? Always he was a presence, in her thoughts, her dreams, even when she did not want him there. Now, when she knew he was close, she found herself listening for his footfall outside the door, his familiar stride and mocking voice, and it made her despair. Why should she make it easy for him?—be waiting as if she was one of those unfortunate women she'd glimpsed in whorehouse windows? And why did she sometimes feel like that, as if she were one of them?

La perdida—the lost one.

A genteel name for a whore, she thought, and fitting.

Restless and hungry, she lit one of the candle stubs and left the room, moving along the covered corridor to the court-yard she'd visited earlier with Juana. She could hear the music before she arrived, the throbbing passion of the guitars and wild beauty of violins that soared into the soft night sky. It was an old peasant tune, one that she remembered from long ago, vibrant and rhythmic, tempestuous.

Lanterns had been lit and hung from the beams, swaying light over tables filled with laughing men, and women dressed in colorful calico and cotton. The men were costumed as usual, with open-necked shirts, short jackets of silk or figured calico, and straight-legged trousers, with bright sashes around their waists. The women wore silver jewelry, huge hoop ear-rings and necklaces, their long hair worn loose for the most part, except for the married women who had done their hair up with wide Spanish combs. All were gay and laughing, some passing around tequila, and another more potent drink, the native pulqué. The smell of roast meat was in the air, and her stomach growled.

As the music grew louder and faster, some of them got up

to dance, hands held over their heads, fingers snapping in tempo and feet stomping briskly against the stones of the courtyard. Tory stood uncertainly, watching from the shadows of the covered passageway. There was something primitive and unrestrained about their dancing, making her think of those nights so long ago when she had stolen away from the house to go down to the servant barrio and lose herself in the same driving music. It had been a release, an outlet for her frustrations, and even as a child, she had recognized an elemental need.

Perhaps it was the promise of music that had brought her out here tonight, or the strange, restless yearning inside her that drove her to seek escape, seek relief. Everything was so confused, her life turned upside down, and she wanted to forget, for a while, that nothing would ever be the same.

Without conscious will or consent, when a young man appeared before her, dark and lithe and smiling, urging her into the dance, she went silent and unsmiling with him. She wore the loose cotton camisa Nick had sent, low-necked and tucked into the waistband of the bright, full skirt that swirled around her bare legs, her hair caught in a loose braid on the nape of her neck and tied with a ribbon taken from her chemise. Her kid slippers were low-heeled and soft, skimming lightly over the stones as she moved with her partner to the courtyard. Half-closing her eyes, feeling reckless and daring, she stood for a moment, snapping her fingers in time to the music, a faint smile curving her mouth. This she knew, this wild music coursing through the night, released and releasing, freeing her.

The sweeping gaze her young partner raked over her was speculative, as if wondering if she could dance, and then the musicians changed into the jarabe, and her feet found the rhythm. She did not dance as proper ladies should dance, arms held stiffly at her sides, eyes downcast and only her feet moving beneath the hem of her gown, but as the peasants danced, as the Spanish gypsies danced, with her heart and soul and entire body all caught up in the music. Slowly, her hips moving in a sinuous twist, she let the rhythm take her, faster and faster, her feet flying, her skirts soaring up above her knees, dancing as if for a man, a lover.

"Dios mío!" her partner muttered, his eyes hot, glued to her body as she moved sensuously, eyes still half-closed, and her hair loose now, the ribbon lost as it came free and whipped around her face, into her eyes, dark and gleaming with copper lights in the glow of lanterns.

Tory heard hands take up a clapping rhythm, heard murmurs of appreciation and admiration, and dancers moved aside as she lost herself, dancing as if she had never danced before, dancing as if she had not danced since she was a lonely child in the chill, solitary moonlight of her patio. But now, there was a difference, somehow, as she let the music seep inside her, felt almost as if it was passion that moved her, made her blood run hot and the pulses beat so strong . . . and her hips swayed of their own volition, the teasing dance of courtship, of invitation and seduction, wanton and wild and knowing. Now her body knew the touch of a man, and she showed it in her provocative movements, in the way she tossed her hair, feeling the eyes of the men on her like hot caresses, pretending that it was Nick who touched her, caressed her . . .

The jarabe ended and a corrido began, and still she danced, with her hair wild about her shoulders, her body growing damp and the pulsing beat swift and compelling. She forgot about her partner, the young man who had pulled her into the dance, and another took his place, his lean, lithe form moving about hers with pantherish grace, his bootheels clicking hard against the stones, his eyes intent. A bottle of tequila was thrust into her hand and she tilted it up, drank, then passed it along, the unaccustomed sear of fiery liquid burning down her throat and into her stomach. And as she swirled, her gaze skimmed those around her, noting distractedly that it wasn't just Mexicans here, but Americans too, even a tall blond man at the far end of the courtyard beneath the shadow of an oak, watching.

But she didn't care. Didn't care who was there, or who wasn't there, or if she was alone. It didn't matter who danced with her, or if the bottle of tequila was passed again, all that mattered was the release of the dance. Lanterns swayed overhead, the musicians played, and there was laughter and gaiety, and she could lose herself, for a time, and think of nothing, remember nothing, not even Nick Kincade and his betrayal . . .

In the shadows beneath the beams next to the building, Nick watched with narrowed, furious eyes as Tory swayed like a wanton to the throb of guitars and violins, stamped her feet to the clicking snap of castanets. Damn her, the little bitch, what the hell did she think she was doing? This was hardly the way to be inconspicuous.

Beside him, Roy Martin cleared his throat and coughed. "She doesn't look very upset, Lieutenant. Could you have underestimated the restorative powers of your attentions?"

Nick shot him an angry look, but his tone and words were neutral. "She just makes a quick recovery, it seems."

"Yes. So it seems." Martin's dry tone was infuriating, and he lifted his glass of tequila, sipping as he watched Tory over the rim of his glass. "Her presence makes things awkward now, I'm afraid. Don Diego has alerted the commandant, and his uncle registered a complaint with the office of the governor. Both have their own agendas, though I believe the brother is truly worried about Miss Ryan's safety. She should have been left."

"I agree. She should have been left at Buena Vista. We had the guns, but you got greedy. Now we have nothing but the ledger I gave you."

A short silence fell, then Martin nodded. "You are right, of course. Perhaps I should have given more consideration to your suggestions, but what is done now is done. Well, we will recover the money, of course, but regretfully, Don Sebastian and his nephew are still free, as are Don Luis and his son. They are searching not only for Miss Ryan, but also for you, believing, of course, that you have stolen their money."

Nick smiled wryly. "Of course."

"It's unfortunate, but there is also a warrant out for your arrest on abduction charges, signed by Governor Mason. You must remain out of sight as much as possible until we are successful. Without revealing our strategy to the governor it will be difficult to nullify it, but I assure you that we are working swiftly to do so.''

''I feel so much better.''

Roy Martin frowned. ''Sebastian Montoya can be dangerous, since he has certain connections at his disposal—powerful men who have little compunction about using their power for a price. But it is Don Diego who worries me the most. He's young and hotheaded, and I'm afraid that he has offered an enormous sum of money for your apprehension and the safe return of his sister. Have you thought of a safe method to handle her return?''

''I'm not returning her.'' He met Martin's frowning gaze coolly. ''I still have business of my own, remember? Pickering has been seen near Sacramento City. Since I'm headed there anyway, I intend to put our charming little problem on the first steamer headed for Boston.''

Martin's face cleared, and he nodded. ''Excellent notion. As always, you have solved a difficult situation with ingenuity and enterprise. Your expertise is always in great demand. There are few men with your stellar qualifications—''

''Flattery won't work, Roy.'' When Martin merely lifted a brown in feigned surprise, Nick shook his head. ''I'm not taking any more assignments until I have finished my own business, so whatever you may be planning, forget it for now.''

''You amaze me, Nick.'' Something like amusement flickered in Martin's face. ''I only wanted to mention the recent explorations of John Charles Fremont—have you heard of him? Ah, of course you have. A famous explorer of his caliber could hardly escape your notice.''

A burst of laughter from the patio distracted Nick, and his gaze shifted to the crowded dancers beneath swaying lanterns.

Martin's gaze also shifted to the courtyard, lingering, his brow lifted. ''Miss Ryan is very beautiful. And capable of attracting a lot of unnecessary attention, don't you think?''

''Yeah. Guess I better do something.''

Nick shoved his chair back from the table, the scraping of the legs over stones lost in the loud throbbing of guitars. Tory was still dancing, beads of perspiration making the bare skin of her throat and face glow, her eyes half-closed in abandon and her mouth a sensual curve. Martin was right. He should have left her. It would be amazing if she didn't start a riot the way she was dancing.

He was briefly aware of Martin's quizzical gaze as he started across the crowded courtyard to Tory, then focused only on the slender, swaying woman who danced much too close to her partner. The man was engrossed in her, his eyes dark slits in his face, his teeth gleaming white beneath a thick mustache as he snapped his fingers over his head, one hand on his hip, concentrating on the steps that brought Tory close to him. He put a hand on her waist, swung her around, and brought her up hard against him, her body pressed close to his from breast to knee, so that her skirts swirled around him in a provocative cape.

Seeing all that as he advanced, Nick scowled when she did not push the man away, but instead leaned back, her slender arms lifted over her head, twining, fingers snapping and her head thrown back so that her hair whipped behind her like silk tendrils. It brought her body into closer contact with her partner, and her breasts grazed the white cotton of his shirt for the briefest moment before Nick grabbed him, spinning him around and giving him a little shove away.

"Find another partner."

"*Hijo de puta!* It is you who should find another partner—" A knife gleamed suddenly in the hazy lantern light, and the man smiled behind the blade. "I do not like to be interrupted."

Dammit, he had no patience for this. Nick turned away with an exclamation of contempt and reached for Tory. Surprised fury creased the man's face and he sprang at him, but Nick sidestepped easily, coolly bringing down the side of his hand on the back of the man's neck as he passed. It sent him sprawling, while the knife clattered to the stones some distance away. The music ended with a crash, and Tory stopped, her eyes wide and her mouth a round little O of shock. He reached out in the sudden silence, a hand around her wrist, and pulled her to him.

To the stunned people around them, he said calmly, "My wife no longer wishes to dance."

No one said a word, not even Tory as he half-pulled her across the courtyard and into the dark shadows of the passageway. She was breathing hard, her breath little pants for air as he dragged her with him. A lantern gleamed smokily over their heads, dangling, and he saw by the fitful light that her eyes were hazy and glittering with rage.

"Don't say it," he warned when she opened her mouth, but he could have saved his breath.

"How *dare* you! You *hijo de puta!* Thief! Murderer . . ."

That was as far as she got before he put his hand over her mouth and dragged her along, his temper rising. She could infuriate him in an instant, no matter how hard he tried to keep his temper.

When he reached the room, he kicked the door open with his foot, and it slammed back against the wall with a loud crack. He slung Tory inside and closed the door behind them, leaning against it to stare at her in the feeble light of a single candle. She stood uncertainly, swaying slightly, one hand on the small table for balance. She smelled like lye soap and tequila, and he knew from the glaze of her eyes that the potent liquor had affected her. Not that her judgment was ever the best.

"Get out of here!"

"And leave you alone?" He lifted a brow mockingly and saw her eyes narrow with rage. "I wouldn't dream of it. Not with the display you gave out there, all that passionate dancing, like a gypsy, all wild and sensual—who were you dancing for?"

"Certainly not you!" She took a step away from the table and paused, chin flung up defiantly as she glared at him. "You had no right to stop me. I was enjoying myself, and for the first time since I've come back to California, too. I wish I'd never come back. I wish I was still in Boston, and I wish I had never met you . . .''

He watched her dispassionately, gauged the moment when her tirade would subside, and tried to reason with her. ''If you want to get to a seaport without attracting your uncle's attention, making a spectacle of yourself is no way to be discreet. For God's sake, what got into you out there?''

She pushed at the hair in her face and gave him a sullen glance. ''I don't know. I just felt like dancing.''

''And drinking tequila. Have you eaten? I didn't think so. No wonder it went to your head. You'll feel like hell in the morning.''

''I don't care.''

''You will.'' He watched her move slowly to the small chair beside the bed, casting an oblique look at him from the corners of her eyes. All claws and calculation, a teasing little schemer that would have him dancing at the end of a rope if he wasn't careful.

Rather clumsily, Tory sat down in the chair, her skirts hiked up over her knees and giving him an interesting view of bare legs all the way up to slender thighs. No undergarments, the little minx. She saw where he was looking and got mad, pushing at the calico skirt, glaring at him.

''Degenerate!''

He shrugged. ''On occasion. You can't be complaining. Not after that performance you gave for everyone. Every man out there was wondering what it would be like to have you, to strip away your clothes and run his hands over your bare breasts, touch you between your legs and listen to you yowl like a cat in heat, clawing and scratching—and they were all wondering if you would be as wild and wanton in bed as you are when you dance, Tory, didn't you see that? Of course you did. Don't bother to deny it. You knew what you were doing.''

She was staring at him, eyes like purple bruises against dusky skin, her hair still loose and curling around her face. The tip of her tongue flicked out to wet her lips, and her mouth quivered slightly. Desire hit him then, making him ache. His gaze slid over her, down to where her breasts pushed against the thin material of her blouse, and he thought of how sweet she tasted, her tight little nipples filling his mouth and his hands. He should give her what she'd been asking for out there, take her and hear her voice in his ear again, those sweet husky pleas and moans of need.

But he wouldn't. Not now. She'd had too much to drink and needed to sleep it off.

He pushed away from the door, and Tory's eyes widened. She didn't protest when he reached her, didn't resist when he pulled her up from the chair, his hands around her wrists as he turned her and backed her toward the bed. The edge caught her behind the knees and she swayed slightly, so that he held her suspended, her weight dragging on him, slight as a child's, her slender body willowy and graceful.

She was breathing rapidly, chest lifting and falling, her lips parted slightly and her eyes still wide and dark with an emotion he couldn't read. Something moved inside him, a weakening of his resolve, the memory of her beneath him returning with swift, savage force. She seemed to sense it, and leaned into him, her breasts pressing against his chest. Damn her. But he wanted her, here and now, so badly he was hurting with it—unexpected, unwanted desire that made him curse her and himself in the same silent breath, thundering through his body and making his movements less gentle than he meant.

When he pushed her back on the narrow bed, she lay still, staring up at him, with the blouse slipped low, revealing the high, rounded curve of her breast, tempting and flawless. Her hair spread across the bed under her, a carpet of dark-fire silk, cradling her pale face and framing the smooth curve of her bare shoulders. Drawn by a force stronger than he'd guessed, he reached down, pulled away the blouse to bare her breasts, caught his breath at the taut, aching perfection of them. She had the most tempting body. He swore, soft and violent under his breath, recognizing his unwilling need for this one woman, something he had not thought would ever happen. It wasn't just because she'd been virgin the first time, though he'd thought for a while maybe that was the reason he couldn't stop thinking about her; it was a hundred other reasons, beginning with the first night in the garden.

Like now, when she was lying back on the bed, propped up on her elbows, her eyes wide and as startled as a doe's confronted by a grizzly, staring up at him with softly trembling lips and breasts as bare as an Amazon's, making him so damn hard that if he didn't do something quick, he'd explode with it.

He pushed her skirt up, and she started, grabbing his wrist. His eyes met hers. A whisper: "Spread your legs for me, chica."

"Nick . . . I'm not . . . you shouldn't . . . I don't want to do this."

"You know you don't mean that." His hand slid up her thigh, fingers grazing the bare skin and making her shiver, wedging between her legs with firm insistence, until she shuddered. He smiled. "Open for me, love. Like that. Yes, like that . . . you like that, don't you? Don't you?"

Soft, husky, he told her how beautiful she was, how much he wanted her, and what he wanted to do to her, how he could make her feel if she let him. All the while his hands moved between her legs, fingers sliding inside her hot, wet sheath, his thumb caressing the tight little nub at the top of her sex until she was shivering, shaking, crying out and spreading her thighs wide for him. He bent, his mouth on her nipple, tugging, while his hand stayed inside her, his thumb still rubbing over her until she was writhing, arching upward, her hands in his hair to hold his head to her breast. He felt her clench around his fingers, convulsive heat, and moved lower, until his head was between her thighs, his tongue replacing the erotic flick of his thumb, and heard her soft cry.

"Oh God no, what are you doing?" Her hands tightened in his hair, pulling sharply until he swore at her.

"*Maldito*, relax, will you? You can't deny it feels good . . . and you're beautiful there, soft and sweet . . . You like that, don't you? Like the way my hand feels? I can make it feel better, Tory, if you'll let me like before . . ."

Little sobbing breaths racked her body, but her hands relaxed their grip in his hair, and he bent again, tongue raking over her and inside her, until he felt her shudder, felt her hips lift for him; then her hands were on him and she was whimpering, noises like a kitten at first, growing higher and more urgent, and her fingers raked over his back and bunched his shirt in her fists and she was crying out, sobbing his name over and over as her climax exploded, and he tasted her sweet ecstasy on his tongue.

As she clung to him, shivering, he lifted, tearing off his shirt and unbuckling his belt, unbuttoning his pants and releasing himself, sliding inside her hot, wet body in a luxurious glide, shuddering as she tightened around him. God, she was tight . . . so tight and hot . . . clenching him, velvet contractions that made him hold fast to his resolve and hold back his own release until he could take her again to that shuddering peak, wanting to feel her convulse around him.

Withdrawing, thrusting, withdrawing again, each stroke a long slide of pleasure, until his breath felt locked in his throat and she was looking up at him with glazed eyes, panting. He lifted, braced his weight on his palms, holding her gaze, and pushed deep, shuddering a little at the tight soft heat around him like a glove. He kissed her again and tasted tequila on her lips, a heady residue no more intoxicating than the taste of her on his tongue. And all the while he was moving inside her, the thrust and drag of his body eliciting exquisite tremors from her, making all the nerves in his groin tighten with anticipated release, until he wasn't sure he could hold out much longer, wasn't sure he could wait for her to find her release before he exploded inside her. Vaguely aware of her moans, of the hands clawing at his back, he moved faster and faster, the culmination so close now, so close . . . a whisper away, another stroke, burying himself so hard and deep and fast that she sobbed, but not with pain, for she was thrusting her hips up at him to meet his furious strokes, her legs lifted and curved around his back, holding, holding . . . and then, when he knew he couldn't last any longer, heard her wild, keening cry and erupted into a long, shuddering release of his own.

After, when she was still quivering, her legs trembling around him and her face wet with tears, he kissed her, tasting the salt on her cheeks, then pressed his face into the fragrant curve of her neck and shoulder. Damp hair tickled his jaw; he was still shaking inside, breath coming in harsh little gusts of air between his teeth.

As the storm of reaction passed, she began to shiver, and he lifted his head to stare down at her, at this wild, surprising, passionate little cat in his arms. He was still hard inside her, throbbing slightly, and his mouth twisted into a grimace. What was it about this one woman that so intrigued him? She was spoiled, willful, irritating, yet he found himself grudgingly thinking of her when he should be concentrating instead on more important things. That he thought of her at all was amazing in itself. He'd thought once he had tasted her, had eased himself inside her, he would be able to forget about her.

The fact that she was here with him disproved that theory.

Gil had warned him, had sensed that she would be trouble. He should have listened. Dammit, what did he do now?

When she opened her eyes and smiled dreamily, her arms lifting to curve around his neck and draw his head down for a kiss, Nick thought that for the moment, he knew what he would do. He had to get rid of her, put her on a boat—any boat—and get her away from him. Tomorrow he would do what must be done. *Mañana*. But this was now and she was here and warm and willing and sweet, and he was already moving inside her again, incredibly aroused, ignoring caution.

Twenty-three

Streamers of pale gray light came through the unshuttered window and slanted across Tory's face, waking her. She blinked, groaning a little at the dull pounding in her head, and tried to sit up. Her hair was caught, and as she half-turned, memory of the night before flooded back at the same instant she saw Nick Kincade beside her. Her hair was pinned beneath one of his shoulders, and he lay atop the blankets, naked now, his long body bare and reminding her of how she'd behaved last night.

Oh God, when she thought of the things he'd said to her, the things he'd done—acts she'd not known existed but he said were normal—the heat rose to her cheeks in a burning surge. He'd kissed her everywhere, in the most intimate places imaginable, turning her over on her stomach, licking his way from her calves to her neck, then turning her on her back and doing the same to her front. He'd even kissed the bends of her knees and arms, tongue laving across her skin in fiery strokes.

It made her feel odd when she thought about it, when she remembered how she had let him do anything he wanted with her, had felt as if she was watching it from outside her body, a sweet dispossession of restraint taking over. And then, when he had explored every inch of her, returning again and again to some spots, he wanted her to do the same to him.

Cheeks flaming, she'd refused, but he'd taken her hands and put them on him, had shown her what he liked, inexorable yet oddly gentle, until she wanted to please him, wanted to hear the breath come through his teeth in a hiss of pleasure. But then he had wanted her to do what she had seen Colette attempt that day, and she'd been shocked and angry, jerking away from him and refusing.

For a moment he'd been quiet, then he'd shrugged and begun kissing her again, soon easing her anger with another kind of emotion, one that left her weak just to think about it.

God, she must be insane, but after everything—her suspicions, his betrayal—she thought she was falling in love with him. *Amor de corazón*—did she feel that way? Why else would she let him do what he had done? It wasn't the tequila, though perhaps it had helped remove some of her inhibitions, but something deep inside her, some aching need that he had sparked. It was different from what she felt for Peter Gideon . . . Peter, oh God, what would she do about him? But he was so far away, and really, every time she thought of him, Nick's face bled into the mental image, supplanting blond hair with black, blue eyes with yellow eyes like flame, until nothing was left but Nick. And what did she have? There had been no promises, no words of love, only sex words, and she was probably being such a fool, but—

"How's your head?"

Nick's voice startled her, and she glanced down at him. His eyes were open, glittering beneath the dark brush of his lashes as he looked at her. Her heart gave a sharp tug, and she looked away and shrugged.

"Not as bad as I deserve."

"That explains the frown, I guess." He sat up, raking a hand through his hair, the familiar half-smile on his mouth.

She couldn't help looking at him, couldn't help the odd little wrench inside that was so disturbing. Why did he have to look at her like that, as if . . . as if he knew how she felt? He would use it against her, she knew, if she let him know that she felt any tenderness toward him, felt anything but an acknowledgment of the passion they had shared. She couldn't hide *that*. There were red marks on him where she'd scratched him, faint but obvious, and she remembered clawing at him like a cat in heat—his phrase—arching upward and crying out her pleasure.

He rubbed a hand across the rough stubble of beard on his jaw, grimacing. "I need a shave."

"When do we leave?" she asked, more abruptly than she intended, desperate to retain some sense of control; the wariness came back into his eyes.

After a moment, he shrugged. "Soon. You in a hurry?"

"You know I am. If I don't get on a steamer out of California, I'll end up married to Rafael or worse." Her head hurt so . . . and he was looking at her, cool speculation in his gaze, the familiar detached regard that she was so used to seeing . . . but what can I do? she thought, almost despairing. He hasn't said he loves me, hasn't said he wants me with him . . . Will he say it now? If I say I'm leaving, will he ask me to stay?

But he was getting up from the narrow bed, moving across her in a lithe twist of his long body, and she had the dispassionate thought that he was so beautiful, with long muscles in his shoulders and arms and legs, the flat, ridged belly, and that chameleon part of him that changed from soft and harmless to hard and lethal so quickly. Never had she thought she'd consider a man's body beautiful, but she did this man's.

Nick began to dress, and while he buttoned his pants, he looked up at her, a brow lifting. "I thought you were in a hurry."

"Yes." She swung her legs over the edge of the bed, feeling awkward again, uncomfortable as she held the blanket up over her naked breasts, not meeting his eyes. "I am."

He was silent, and when he was completely dressed, with gunbelts around his lean waist and heaven only knew how many other weapons on him, he strode to the door and pulled it open, looking back at her over his shoulder. "Be ready in fifteen minutes."

The door shut behind him, not loudly, but firmly. Tory stared at it. Unexpected tears stung her eyes, and her throat ached. She'd not really thought he would ask her to stay. And really, she didn't belong out here. Not anymore. California was no longer home. Her home was in Boston. With her aunt and uncle, and Sean. With Peter. If he still wanted her.

It was well past dark when they rode into the outskirts of Sacramento City three days later, having made excellent time. Tory was exhausted and bedraggled and cold, for it had begun to rain again, a fine, steady drizzle. This was Sutter's Mill, Nick said, his voice the same, flat tone that he'd used with her since leaving Mission Santa Clara.

Blearily, blinking at the rain clogging her vision, she peered at the collection of crude tents beneath trees, white and gray and shuddering under the rattle of rain. She clung to the saddle rather than sat it, too weary to do more than nod when he said he would find them some sort of shelter for the night.

Even with the rain, men moved about, slogging through mud on what she supposed were streets, though they looked more like goat tracks. When Nick dismounted and disappeared into the wet shadows, she sat her mount with head drooping, the oilcloth he'd given her doing a poor job of keeping her dry. Her little dun snorted and sidled to one side, and Tory lifted her head.

In the shadows beyond a sagging tent, someone moved, a furtive shape briefly silhouetted against the lantern light inside the canvas. Tory sat up straight, skin prickling and nerves stretching taut.

"Who's there?"

No one answered; the wind snapped a loose edge of canvas tent with a loud, popping sound. The shadow moved again, coming closer, and she tensed, suddenly wide awake and afraid.

"Show yourself, or I'll shoot. I swear I will!"

Panicked, she brought up her arm as if pointing a gun, wishing she had one, even the heavy Colt. God, if he came toward her, what would she do? From down the row of tents there was a muffled burst of laughter, then voices, and through the soupy weather she saw Nick returning, his head bent against the rain and wind. When she glanced back, the shadow was gone.

"No room here," Nick said when he reached her, his voice muffled by the sound of rain and the wind coming through the trees. "We'll try Sutter's Fort. It's not far, and has a hotel and hospital."

"Nick—someone was watching me."

He glanced around, a quick slice of his eyes, and his mouth thinned. "Wouldn't have anything to do with the fact that you're in front of the latrine, would it?"

She flushed and lapsed into silence. It would be amusing if it weren't so embarrassing, and she wondered what the poor man who'd come out into the rain to use the convenience had thought.

Silent, she followed Nick through the night, hooves squelching in the thick mud, tree limbs dripping rain on them as they wove through the scattered tents to miss the worst of the mud puddles. There were so many tents, so many who had come to find gold, and ramshackle dwellings boasted signs listing goods for sale, shovels and picks and pans.

They left the remnants of settlement behind them, moving through trees again. Tory was stiff when Nick finally halted, dazed and barely aware when he pulled her from her saddle, swearing under his breath that she was a lot of damn trouble as she sagged against him, unable to stand. She didn't have the energy to defend herself, or remind him that he'd awakened her before daylight and forced her atop her horse, and they'd had only two brief rest stops during the day. It would take too much effort, and gain her nothing. He'd only tell her again in that cold, impatient tone she was so used to hearing that she shouldn't complain since she was the one who was in a hurry to leave California.

Because it was true, and because she didn't understand why she'd been driven to say it as she had, she'd lapsed into a sullen silence.

Now, as someone took the horses and he half-carried her, she looked up through the misty rain and saw to her shock an actual house, with lights in the windows and a door held open wide to admit them, and beyond that, warmth and laughter and music. Senses dulled by weariness and turbulent emotions, she'd not even noticed where they were, but saw now around them a town of sorts, bigger than the last, this one with wooden buildings and streets that looked more like streets instead of rutted tracks. It was still all mud, but more civilized-looking.

And then Nick carried her inside and swung her to her feet in a room that smelled of kerosene and whiskey, and he was laughing softly at a surprised greeting from someone.

"Nick Kincade! My God, man, what are you doing up here?" a male voice boomed. "Don't tell me you're prospecting for gold!"

"Not exactly, Casey. Looks like you've got a gold mine right here. They told me down the road you had a place. Any room for one more?"

Tory pushed back the oilcloth over her head, blinking at the bright light from several lamps. Tobacco smoke filled the air, and the room was crowded with tables and roughly dressed men.

"Only one? Or is that someone you've brought with you, Nick?"

Tory turned her head, eyes widening a little. A portly man stood smiling at her, his genial face covered with whiskers, and dressed as if he had just exited a sartorial parlor of the highest quality. Crisp serge covered his generous frame in excellent lines, and his high collar and neat tie were nearly covered by the thick beard that reached to the middle of his chest.

"Two guests, if you've got room." Nick pulled her forward a little bit. "She looks like a half-drowned cat right now, but she cleans up all right."

Angry and embarrassed, she jerked her arm away, lifting her chin. "I don't think we've been introduced, sir."

"Ah, that we haven't. But I'm not surprised, as Nick has been known to forget his manners."

The comment drew a wry laugh from Nick. "Thanks, Casey. This is Miss Smith, from Oregon Territory. Miss Smith, this is Matthew Casey, a beau of the first water, as you can see."

Rather startled by the introduction, she then realized that it would be foolish to give her real name, and nodded. "It's nice to make your acquaintance, Mr. Casey."

"And it is always nice to meet a beautiful woman, Miss Smith, even one with so rude a man as your companion. Has he also forgotten to feed you?"

The smile directed at her was genuine, and despite the uncertain situation, Tory smiled back. "Among other things. One of his many failings, I've noticed."

Flicking an amused glance toward Nick, Casey shook his head. "I think she knows you fairly well, my friend. But come, you are both wet and tired, I can see, and hungry as well. While I have you some food prepared, Tom can evict the boarders in the back room so you'll have a place to sleep."

"Oh, but you shouldn't," Tory began, and Casey tut-tutted and said of course he should, that they'd taken up too much space and didn't pay on time anyway.

"And besides, a lady should not have to sleep in a tavern corner." As he talked, he clapped his hands sharply together, and a young woman came from behind a curtain at one end of the room, wiping her hands on her apron. "Sally, please show this young lady to our master suite as soon as Tom has removed the current occupants, will you? She'll want to clean up and dry out, and Nick and I can catch up on some lost years before she joins us again, I'm certain."

"Miss Smith is much too tired to join us," Nick said, smiling lazily at her, his eyes daring her to disagree. "I'm sure she'd prefer a meal in her room, where it's quiet."

Casey looked momentarily startled, but recovered quickly, his words and voice smooth. "Forgive me for being so inconsiderate. A beautiful woman is always such a treat that

I'm afraid I'm being selfish. Tomorrow will be soon enough to acquaint myself with Miss Smith.''

Before Tory could reply, Nick was saying that they would probably leave early, as he was on his way to Coloma in the morning. ''After I see Miss Smith to her destination, I'll be riding out. But we've got tonight to catch up on old news. I don't suppose you have any whiskey behind that bar, do you?''

Laughing, Casey said that he certainly did, and as Sally arrived, telling Tory to come with her, she heard Nick ask what had ever happened to Juanita Morales before they were out of earshot.

Seething inside that she had been so summarily dismissed, without even a chance to say what *she* wanted to do, she followed Sally to the small room behind the saloon. It was quieter there, though by no means quiet, but at least distanced from the smoke and noise.

''I can have one of the boys bring you a tub if you like,'' Sally offered once they were in the room. ''No bath house yet, so we have to make do with a wooden job, but it'll get you clean.''

''I'd like that very much.''

Shivering, she stood in the middle of a small room that held an iron bed, a dresser, a table, two chairs, and a lamp. A mirror hung on one wall, and the window had actual curtains, the fanciest accommodations she'd encountered since leaving Monterey behind. Sally was stripping sheets from the bed, talking matter-of-factly about the weather and how so many people were coming in every day that Sutter's Fort would soon be grown all the way to Sacramento City.

Loosening the damp braid of her hair, Tory raked her fingers through it, shaking rain from the long, curling strands. Wet weather always made her hair curl into ringlets almost impossible to get a comb through, and she sighed, regretting the loss of her silver brush. Soon she would be back in civilization, and these annoyances would be only dim memories.

''Do many steamers dock in Sacramento City, Sally?''

''Oh my yes, every day. Ships, too, coming up from the

bay and down the river.'' Sally straightened, the load of sheets in her arms, and looked at Tory. ''We've got a regular shipping route now, what with all the men coming in to work the gold fields.''

Good. That meant she should be able buy passage easily enough. Or rather, Nick could make the purchase. It was small compensation for the money he'd taken from her. Had he already sent someone to claim it? She hadn't asked. Why give him the satisfaction of knowing how it rankled that he had been so devious? She hadn't even asked him what he intended to do with it once he retrieved it from the bank. And really, what did it matter now? It would only be spent on weapons or some other immoral pursuit.

At that moment, Nick was sitting down at a table in the smoky corner of the saloon, while Casey dealt a hand of poker. Also at the table was the man they called General, who had first founded the New Helvetia called Sutter's Fort and Sutter's Mill. Slender, with a receding hairline, thick mustache, and small goatee, Sutter regarded the table with glum intensity.

''Are you in the game, General?'' Casey asked when Sutter just sat there, and he looked up, grimacing as he tossed in a coin.

He spoke with an accent that betrayed his German-Swiss heritage. ''This time, perhaps. If you don't try to cheat me, like last time I played cards with you.''

Casey grinned. ''You've just got bad luck, General. I couldn't lose that night.''

One of the men at the table laughed. ''Bad luck? The General? When he owns the richest find in California?''

Sutter looked grave. ''I own land, my friend, a tannery, mill, and shops. But how long will I keep them? Already I cannot keep trespassers away. They come in droves, by the dozens, overrunning my land so fast I cannot keep count. And they do not go away, even if I tell them they are on private land, that I have grants for the streams they are working, the gold dust they are panning—bah! I knew, when John Marshall found that gold nugget, that it might come to this. I tried to keep it quiet, but that Mormon merchant, Sam Brannan, he saw profit, and there was no keeping him silent. Through the streets of San Francisco he rode, shouting 'Gold!' at the top of his lungs, and who profits now? He does. His stores sell flour, coffee, and supplies at ten times their value, while I am left watching my workers leave me to go dig for gold.''

Shaking his head, Sutter lapsed into gloomy silence.

''Ah,'' Casey said consolingly, ''you will make money, General. I heard that Mason Granger, up on the American where the river forks, found a nugget worth five hundred dollars last week. Many more finds like that, and you can charge whatever you like for your land.''

''You are missing the point, my friend. No one pays for what they can take. I cannot find men enough to protect my claim. They think it easier and more profitable to look for gold instead.''

Nick leaned back in his chair, watching Sutter over the rim of his whiskey glass. The General was more than likely right, though it was a damn shame. He hadn't the manpower to protect his interests. With gold-crazed men coming in every day, it would take an army to keep them off his land. Like other immigrants to California, Sutter had come when it was still owned by Mexico, and had even become a Mexican citizen. Now he stood to lose everything.

''You in the game, Nick?''

He looked up, nodded at Casey, and for a while they concentrated on poker. Later, when he'd won a few dollars and some gold dust, he quit, joining Casey at the long table that served as a bar against the back wall.

''Too bad about Sutter.''

Casey nodded. ''Yes. He's right, I fear. Squatters are all over his land, and I don't think the government will do anything about it. But he's got several shops, the tannery and the grist mill, and if he can keep enough workers and ride this out, he may come out of it with some money in his pocket.'' He smiled faintly and scratched his chin beneath the dark, bushy beard. ''It's all fate, my boy, all capricious fate.''

''Sometimes one can arrange fate to his advantage.''

Casey gave him a keen look. "I have the feeling you're talking about something in particular, Nick. What is it?"

"I'm looking for someone."

Nodding, Casey lifted a brow, one pudgy hand smoothing the immaculate crease of his coat lapel. "There are a lot of people who come through these doors lately. If I don't know whoever it is you seek, someone here will."

"Name's Pickering. Kiah Pickering. Tall, blond, lanky. Talks with a Southern drawl. A Tennessee boy."

Casey considered a moment, then shook his head. "Offhand, I can't say I've met him."

"He works for a man with interests up here—Don Sebastian Montoya."

Casey's eyes hardened slightly, the congenial glint usually present fading. "Ah. *That* name I know. He was up here in June, arrogant and as proud as any Spaniard can be—outright stole a claim from a friend of mine—had his men come in with drawn weapons and there wasn't a thing could be done. Once he'd been run off, it was up for the taking—and it was taken by Montoya and his band of cutthroats."

"See what else you can find out for me, Casey. I'd appreciate it. I've been following Pickering for a while now."

A faint smile curved Casey's mouth under the curling beard. "You saved my life that time down in San Antonio. Don't think I've forgotten it. I'll do my best, you can count on it, Nick."

It was late when Nick went to the room where Tory had been placed, and he was bone-tired and slightly drunk. He shouldn't have kept drinking, but Casey wasn't a man who liked to take no for an answer; he hadn't been when Nick had known him in San Antonio, either, back when Mexican general Rafael Vasquez had captured the city for two entire days. Nick had been riding with Captain Hays, along with about one hundred men up from Gonzales. They'd followed the Mexican general and his troops back to the Rio Grande, but had not had enough men to successfully attack. From March to September, he'd worked for Captain Jack, as he was known then, running spy missions between San Antonio and the Rio Grande during a time when the government couldn't afford to pay him. If it hadn't been for Casey keeping him full of frijoles, there were plenty of nights he would have gone hungry.

Repayment had come when they'd taken back San Antonio the second time it was occupied, and he'd come upon Casey wounded and fighting desperately with a Mexican infantryman. The short, portly merchant was no match for a honed *soldado*, and Nick had barely arrived in time. That had been six years ago. Things had changed a lot since then. He'd changed a lot.

But some things hadn't changed, he thought wryly when Tory refused to open the door for him. He leaned against it, his head throbbing, and considered leaving the damn room to her. But that would be too easy, and why should he let the little bitch dictate to him like that? It was his money paying for it, for all that she thought it was hers, and though he didn't give a damn about that, he was getting weary of having her act as if he were a thief and worse. She didn't mind wrapping her legs around him at night, but in the light of day, it was a very different matter. Then she was the ice queen, all haughty and moralistic, treating him as if he were only a hireling.

Maybe it was time he reminded her of a few things.

"Open the door, Tory," he said again without raising his voice. "Now."

"Go away!" There was the sound of something scraping over wood, and then the creak of a bed.

It occurred to him suddenly that she might have someone in there with her, a thought that brought him upright and coldly furious. Stepping back in the narrow hallway, he lifted a foot and slammed his boot against the door just above the knob. It gave instantly, the flimsy wood splintering and swinging into the room with a shattering crack.

Alone on her knees in the middle of the bed, Tory faced him defiantly, her loose hair tumbling around her shoulders in curling ringlets that looked soft and sun-kissed, her eyes blazing like twin stones. He leaned against the doorjamb, raking her with a mocking gaze guaranteed to make her mad.

"What the hell is the matter with you now?"

"You've ruined the door—"

"I'll pay for it." He turned when he heard a voice in the hallway to calmly reassure the wide-eyed young boy who had been sent to discover the source of the trouble, then stepped into the room, shut the door, and dragged the table in front of it to hold it closed.

Tory was silent, though still on her knees in the bed, wearing a lace-trimmed chemise that had seen better days, and her knee-length cotton drawers. She said nothing when he went to the window and opened it, but dragged a blanket up and around her. The curtains fluttered at the cool wet breeze sweeping inside.

"Just whose money will you use to pay for the door?" she asked tartly when he turned back around. "The money you stole from my father?"

"Since when did you get so concerned about it? I seem to remember that you had your sticky little hands on it for a while. Still would, if I hadn't done you a favor and relieved you of it."

"Done me—you *bastard!* You have no right to talk to me that way, without even knowing the facts . . . Did you stop to think it might be my only inheritance? You *used* me! And you don't even care . . . What you did wasn't right at all!"

He studied her furious face for a moment, angry himself. His head was throbbing evilly. Damn that rotgut whiskey Casey served. You'd think a man of his intelligence would keep something decent around.

"Before you get too moral, Tory, maybe I should remind you that I know where the money came from. I know a hell of a lot more about it than you obviously realize, and so if you intend to get too damn outraged, you might keep in mind that men like Patrick Ryan who sell weapons by the case lot to mercenaries and Indians are responsible for a lot of deaths. It's men like your father, uncle, and brother who subsidize private little wars, and sometimes wholescale slaughter."

"How noble you are, when I've seen you kill men without

a qualm. Tackett. The Indians. Does it make any difference if it's an individual or en masse? I hardly think so, not to them, anyway. They're just as dead—''

''For your information,'' he ground out, ''the Indians I killed that day happened to have brand-new rifles, and whether you want to hear it or not, they were shooting new Colt revolver rifles—the same kind that were found by the hundreds in your father's wine cellar. It can't be an accident that the Shoshone were miles from their own territory, and started shooting when we came upon them unexpectedly.''

She was silent, and some of the angry color bleached from her face. He almost felt sorry for her, but dammit, he was getting weary of her accusing glances.

''That doesn't excuse your taking my father's money.''

''Is that all you care about—the money?''

She flashed him a strange glance, then shook her head. ''No. Oh, why must you always put me in a position of defending myself? You're wrong, yet you twist things around so that I'm wrong.''

''Look, I don't feel like arguing. I feel like sleeping. If you want to argue, I suggest you go to the saloon. You'll find plenty of men there who might oblige you. Of course, they'll probably want to oblige you with something else, too, but then you wouldn't mind that, I don't think. Not until morning, anyway, when you take your morals back out of your drawers, dust 'em off, and put 'em in place again.''

He wasn't prepared for the way she lunged at him, all fight and fury, nails raking at his face and her body a determined weight that took him back a step or two before he caught his balance. Angry now, he grabbed her arms and bent them back cruelly, shoving her back on the bed with a harsh thrust. He held her squirming body down, his hands pressing her arms into the thin mattress.

''You little hellcat, simmer down! *Quien llama el toro aguanta la cornada*—He who calls the bull must endure the horn wound. Remember that the next time you feel like making accusations. The truth is a two-edged sword.''

''Spare me your trite cliches!''

"Fine. When you spare me your moralistic distortions."

Panting, her rage amazing him, Tory struggled and twisted, trying to kick him, and after a few minutes of waiting her out, he swore under his breath. What had gotten into her? He'd expected to find her asleep, not this raging shrew. And irritating enough, the feel of her barely clad struggles under him had summoned an unwilling physical response.

She must have felt it because she suddenly grew still, looking up at him with wide, shadowed eyes.

"Let me up, Nick."

Prompted by a devil he didn't really understand but had no inclination to ignore at this moment, he lowered his head, capturing her mouth before she could jerk away. Christ, but she was so sweet, so soft, and damn her for rousing this unwilling reaction.

"Oh why must you do this?" she half-sobbed when he moved to kiss the tiny throbbing pulse in the hollow of her throat, but already her body was arching upward, meeting his caresses with an eagerness she couldn't hide. "I swear I hate you, I swear I do . . ."

Perhaps she hated him at times, but she could not deny that she wanted him, wanted this, the way he could make her feel, shivering at his touch. And it was justice of a sorts, he thought, retribution for the reluctant need he had for her.

He smiled down into her face. "Hate me then, Venus, as long as you hate me this well . . ."

Still voicing her hatred, she put her arms around his neck and offered her lips to his, and he muffled the words with his mouth, forgetting everything but the sweet release she promised with her body. And afterward, he buried his face in the fragrant cup of her neck and shoulder, his breath stirring damp tendrils of her hair, until he felt her move again.

"Let me up, please."

After a moment, he released her and watched silently as she flung herself from the bed and struggled into her undergarments, then the skirt and blouse he'd bought her at Santa Clara. Her movements were quick, a bit clumsy as she braided her hair and put on her shoes and stockings, grimacing a little at the still-wet cotton.

Silent, he stretched out on the bed and crossed his arms behind his head, watching with more amusement now as she struggled to move the heavy table from in front of the door. He didn't offer to help, and could tell that she would choke before she'd ask, and after a moment of exertion, she managed to pull it out far enough to wedge open the door. With a final, scathing glance at him, she flounced out into the hallway, slamming the door behind her. It immediately swung back open with a rusty little creak. He eyed it, and wondered if he should bother to go after her.

The men in Casey's saloon were not exactly civilized, and some of them hadn't seen a pretty woman in a while, except for Sally, who was young but haggard-looking from the life she led. A woman like Tory, all fire and shimmering beauty, would attract some unwanted attention.

But Casey was still there, and he had sense enough not to let anything happen to her, knowing she was with his friend. Maybe it would be good for her to test the waters a little bit, find out that keeping her safely away from a camp full of lusty miners wasn't such a bad idea after all. A few encounters with some of the men he'd seen out there, and she'd be back quickly enough.

Twisting up from the bed, he shut the door.

Twenty-four

Still frustrated and resentful of how easily he could corrupt even her firmest intentions, Tory stormed down the narrow hallway that was barely lit with oil lamps that sputtered, hissed, and filled the air with noxious fumes. Damn Nick Kincade, *damn him!* She always made it so easy for him.

An image of him, naked, his left arm bent under his dark head and his eyes slightly narrowed and knowing, sprawled on the bed like a golden flame, tormented her. He knew, of course, that her resistance could not hold out against his sensual assault. He knew and used it, as he had from the first, that day on the beach, when he had gazed at her with the same knowing light in his eyes, and she had put herself in his hands without a qualm or hesitation.

God, she really was a blind fool. All this time, she had thought he was a mercenary, spurred by a motive at least noble to himself, some cause he felt important, when he was really no more than a common thief. She had ascribed a much more heroic incentive to him than he possessed. But if he hadn't been one of her father's clients, why hadn't he told her this before? Because of the money, perhaps? Oh, she didn't even care about the money, not anymore. Except for enough to buy her passage to Boston and pay her expenses, she'd intended to give it all to Uncle Seamus and let him deal with it. He would have known what to do.

She reached the doorway to the saloon and paused uncertainly, feeling the avid gazes turned toward her, glimpsing the lust in men's eyes as they stared at her. Nervously, she lifted her chin, setting her jaw in defiance. Let them look. It would do them no good, and she dared them—yes, *dared them* to say anything to her about coming alone into a room full of men. She had a right to be here, for all that she wished she were anywhere else.

"Miss Smith. You're up late tonight." When Tory whirled around, startled, Casey smiled, his eyes sharp behind the air of congeniality. "I trust you found the room to your liking?"

"The room is the nicest I've been in since I left Monterey, but it is, at the moment, a little crowded. I came out for some fresh air."

Sweeping a glance over the crowded saloon filled with the fumes of tobacco, whiskey, and unwashed miners, Casey was kind enough not to point out the obvious. "Then by all means, let me escort you to our best table. Did you enjoy your meal, or should I see if Sally can tempt you with something else?"

The food had been adequate but not plentiful, but as hungry as she was, it was the last thing she wanted. She shook her head. "I'm quite full, though I wonder if you have any wine, perhaps?"

"Wine? Ah, I'm afraid not. My usual clientele prefers stronger fare, and for the sake of profit, I oblige them."

He smiled and put a light hand on her arm, leading her through a throng of men to a small table near the rear of the room. A lantern hung overhead, and swung light across the table and walls. Sawdust took the place of carpet underfoot, and the walls were raw, unpainted wood. Primitive furnishings for primitive men, from the looks of them. It didn't make her feel better to discover that Nick was right. These men looked rough, and more than one or two kept sliding glances her way, some of them quite bold. She began to feel uneasy, and was glad that Casey was there and seemed such a gentleman, bowing slightly and saying he would bring her some coffee. At least *he* seemed to have some sort of propriety, and was tactful enough not to ask about the broken door, or why she was really out there instead of in the room with Nick.

She didn't think she could have borne another night with him—not knowing that she was leaving, probably tomorrow, and would never see him again. She wished she didn't feel this way, all lost and abandoned, everything she'd known all her life suddenly gone in a matter of weeks. All she had to cling to now was Boston. And Peter, of course. His ring still circled her finger, tiny diamonds and amethyst, a promise she had made. Would he still want her when she told him? Told him about Nick? She'd have to. It wasn't fair not to. What would he say? Would he show shock? Disappointment? Raging fury?

It was hard to imagine Peter raging furiously, hard to imagine him displaying any sort of violence. Not like Nick Kincade, who made violence a way of life. He was so comfortable with weapons, wearing two pistols in his belt, along with knives; reckless and dangerous and indifferent.

He cared about nothing, not even his own life, so why had she thought, ever, that he would care about her? Would want her to stay with him? Or say that he would go with her?

When Casey returned with her coffee she managed a smile, and took a cautious sip of the strong, scalding brew. He sat down in a chair next to her, studying her for a moment, his fingers toying idly with a metal spoon left on the table by a previous patron.

"What do you think of our gold fields, Miss Smith?"

"I've not seen much of them, but what I have seen is rather primitive. Men standing knee-deep in ice-cold water, bending over and dipping that flat little pan over and over, and for what? Not even a dollar a day at times." She shook her head. "I don't understand the attraction."

"Do you not? It's the lure of great wealth, the promise of a future that draws most." He spread an expansive hand to indicate the crowded room. "See these men? Most of them came from nothing, had nothing. If they still don't, it will not be a tremendous change. For now, they have hope. Dreams of a bright, golden future. There are men who go through life with no dreams, Miss Smith. At least these man have that.''

''Yes, and will lose them quickly enough, I think. It will be like everywhere else that common men come to seek a livelihood—someone with real money will come along, buy it all out from under them, and leave them with nothing but broken dreams and broken backs. There are too many dishonest men in the world for the honest men to have much opportunity.''

She knew she sounded bitter, saw the surprise in Casey's eyes, and knew he wondered, too, but she couldn't help it. If not for her father's greed, for his dishonesty, she might still be in Boston, not taking refuge in a crude room behind a saloon with a man who'd made it very obvious he cared about no one but himself.

''It's not often we see a lovely woman such as yourself up here, Miss Smith. Forgive me, for I have been told I am much too curious for my own good, but do you mind if I ask how you met Kincade?''

''Not at all.'' She set down the hot coffee and looked up at him. ''He knew my father. They met several years ago when Papa was in Texas.''

''Ah. I wondered. I knew Kincade years ago, as I'm certain you have surmised by now. It's been some time since I have seen him. He seems much the same.''

''No doubt,'' she muttered, looking down at her coffee with a frown. ''I can't imagine that he's the kind of man to change.''

''Hopefully not.'' Apparently, she looked surprised, for he smiled at her and shrugged. ''There is much about him to admire. I admit he's a bit reckless, but then these are reckless times for men who want more than to sit at home on the porch and hope for the best. It is men like Nick Kincade who go out and make things safe for those men on the porch.''

''Safe?'' She knew she sounded incredulous now, and

shook her head. "Trouble follows him. And if it's too slow, he goes out to find it. I don't think *safe* is quite the world I'd use in connection with Nick Kincade."

"Nevertheless," Casey said, his smile widening a little, "in a fight, I would want no other man more than Kincade with me. I'm certain you've heard the familiar motto 'One riot—one Ranger.' Appropriate, I think."

"I don't understand why everything must be reduced to combat, why men must operate on such elemental levels! Is there no longer room in the world for simple discussion, for calm debates on principles and ideals? Why must it all be so . . . so brutal! Men must be superior, must be able to dominate the weaker, and God help anyone who gets in a man's way when he has decided on a certain course of action . . ."

Her hand had clenched into a fist atop the table, and her breath was short, anger making her voice shake slightly. What was the matter with her? She felt so restless, furious, and uncertain—and scared.

Casey's brow lifted, the little smile still on his mouth. "Do I detect a proponent of women's rights, Miss Smith? Not that I disapprove, necessarily, but I'd just like to know where I stand. In a debate, it is always wise to know one's opponent."

"Forgive me if I've been rude, Mr. Casey. It must be the long journey. And I need fresh air—this smoke is so thick. Will you excuse me, please?"

As she rose, he did also, his eyes concerned. "You will allow me to escort you, of course."

"No. No, I'd rather be alone for a few minutes. The rain has stopped, and I only want to stand outside."

"In normal circumstances, I would agree. But this is a rather crowded camp, with men of uncertain morals abounding. I would feel much better if you would—"

"Mr. Casey, I have grown quite accustomed to men of *uncertain morals* lately, and am very comfortable with my ability to take care of myself. I appreciate your concern, but I am only going to be outside for a few minutes, and I cannot imagine anything too dreadful will happen right outside this establishment. Now, if you will please excuse me?"

With the last few words her voice had risen, and Casey stepped back to let her push past him. The smoke made her throat ache and stung her eyes, and the noise and smells of whiskey and unwashed men were making her dizzy. She had to get outside before she was sick.

A cool blast of air swept in the door when she opened it. She shivered. She should have thought to bring the oilskin, or at least the serape that smelled of wet wool and woodsmoke but was warm. But I'm *not* going back inside, she thought, especially since I made such a fuss about going outside.

She shut the door behind her and stepped carefully over a large rock being used as a porch floor, making her way along the slick surface to the side of the saloon. Yellow light from the windows made small squares across the porch. Other buildings staggered along the street at intervals, few of them as elaborate as Casey's, but all of them seeming to be saloons, or perhaps mercantile establishments.

Despite the dampness, the air was crisp and clean and refreshing, and she stood for a few moments in the shadows of the overhang jutting out from the saloon and breathed deeply. It was calm, the cool air seeming to clear her head of cobwebs. Laughter came from down the street, and snatches of music. The drip of rain from the eaves was constant, and though she stood beneath the overhang, dripped on her hair and shoulders.

After several moments, she felt better. She turned, and a shadow fell across one of the squares of yellow light on the porch. Startled, she gasped, and a man laughed softly.

"Ain't no need to be scared, ma'am. I don't mean no harm. Kincade sent me to fetch you to him, but I was waitin' till you was ready."

"Kincade?" She scowled, rubbing her hands up her arms where the flesh was damp and cold-prickled. "He can just wait. I'm perfectly fine out here."

"Yes, ma'am, I'm sure you are. But jes' the same, I reckon

you'd best come along with me. You got any problem, you can take it up with him.''

Infuriated, she peered at the man in the shadows. He was just beyond the square of light, but she had the impression of height, and a lanky frame and pale hair. How autocratic. It was just like Nick Kincade to send someone after her, some rustic who smelled to high heaven of whiskey and worse. She should flatly refuse, but the thought of another scene so hard on the heels of the spectacle she had provided in the saloon was rather daunting at this moment. Besides, as the fog cleared from her brain, she'd realized a numbing weariness, and even if she had to share the room with Kincade, she wanted to go to bed.

"Very well," she said, shivering at the cool air, "escort me to him. Not that I need an escort, you understand."

"Oh, I don't know, ma'am. Bad things have been known to happen to pretty ladies when they ain't careful." He held out a hand, and when she hesitated, leaned forward to put it on her arm, firmly, his fingers a little too hard on her wrist. "Come on along with me, now."

It wasn't what he said, it was his tone—gloating, satisfied—that made her draw back. "On second thought, I think I'll—"

"Ah no—you're goin' with me, and I ain't listenin' to no shit about it," he said, roughly jerking her from the rock porch to the muddy street.

She opened her mouth to scream, but before she could, the cold, hard edge of a knife pressed against her throat. "I wouldn't do that, ma'am. It might be the last sound you make."

Terrified, Tory had no choice but to be dragged along, slipping in the mud, gasping with pain when his hand dug into her arm. She had a blurred view of shacks and new buildings, thinner now as he pulled her with him down the street, until he ducked between some buildings and up a low slope, cursing her when she fell, yanking hard on her until she thought her arm was going to be torn from the socket. And always, the knife against her, a vivid reminder of mortal danger.

And this time she knew fear—a soul-sick, gut-wrenching fear that she had never felt before.

Time passed in a blur of hard riding, rain, and cold nights, punctuated by a day or two of warm, sunny weather that revived her a little, enough anyway to contemplate ways to murder her captor. If she'd had any sleep, she was certain she would dream of it, of different methods to kill the cruel man who was driving her so relentlessly.

He'd not told her his name, other than "Corporal," and any attempt she made to question him was met with brutal retaliation. Tory had learned quickly not to ask any questions, or even comment. Already, she had bruises on her face and arms, and on her hip where he had kicked her.

He'd not bothered her in any other way yet, though she suspected with rising dread that when he felt safe from pursuit, he would do what his eyes told her he wanted to do, and what he taunted her with when they were riding, sometimes holding her in front of him on his large, raw-boned horse, his arm tight under her breasts and occasionally reaching up to stroke or pinch her nipple through the blouse, hard, enjoying her cry of pain. She'd already learned to hide reaction to his rough handling, and even the things he said about Nick Kincade.

It was Kincade he really wanted, Kincade he wanted to kill, but not until he was ready, and then he would make him watch while he took his woman before he killed him.

All this Tory heard in a kind of daze, a numb haze that protected her from the worst, the shock of finding herself in so much danger. But as the haze wore off, the hazard of her position came sharply into focus.

"Hurry up, bitch! I ain't got time to mess around with no fancy woman, so you jes' do what you're told and it'll go a lot easier."

Crouched in the bushes, Tory briefly closed her eyes. He'd allowed her only a few moments to take care of her needs, always on the run, keeping up a fast pace that threatened to kill both their horses.

As she stood, straightening her skirts, he came through a stand of yucca plants, eyeing her with a wolfish grin, his pale eyes like pinpoint blue flames. She met his gaze without flinching, retreating into as much dignity as she could muster under the circumstances.

"I'm through now," she said coldly as she pushed through the low bush and into the small clearing where they had paused.

He caught her arm and twisted it behind her back in a motion too fast for her to avoid, his breath hot against her cheek as he pulled her hard up against him. "Don't be puttin' on no airs with me, bitch. I know how to make you lose 'em fast enough. When we get to my camp, I'll show you jes' how quick you can jump for me." His hand tangled in her loose hair, winding it around his fist, pulling painfully until her head was bent back in an unnatural arch, her throat bared and her body left vulnerable to him. He took advantage, laughing softly when she made a sound of revulsion, his hard, callused hand jerking down the neck of her blouse, cupping her breasts in his palm, pinching her when she tried to jerk away.

White-hot pain flared, and she couldn't stop the reflexive twist of her body, so that he grabbed her even harder, squeezing her sore nipple between his thumb and finger until she went still, panting with the agony, but knowing not to move or it would only grow worse.

"That's right. You learn quick enough. Too bad I ain't got time to show you more, but I will soon enough. Soon as we get to camp, I'll show you more'n that bastard Kincade ever thought of doin'. Make you hot for it, squirmin' and yellin' . . . ain't never had no woman yet that didn't like it hard and rough . . ."

Forcing herself to remain still, Tory thought despairingly that she would kill him first. He would never have her *that* way. Not like Kincade had done, the sweet aching desire he'd been able to summon, and the thrilling ecstasy of release. Oh God, Nick . . . where are you? Why does this man hate you so? And dear God, do you know or care that I'm not there, that I left, or do you think I just left on my own?

No. He would come after her. She *knew* he would. He had to, had to know that no matter how angry she'd been with him, she could not have left alone like that, in the middle of the night, with no money, no plans. Nick would come after her, he would . . . he would.

She held to thoughts of Kincade while the corporal put his hands on her, jerked up her skirt and touched her between the legs, his hand rough and hurting. He laughed when she flinched, his breath sour across her face, making the bile rise in her throat until she thought she would truly retch. She would not let this man violate her, not let him do the things he said he was going to do . . . and oh God, she couldn't stop him!

In a moment, the corporal pushed her away from him, his hand still tangled in her hair, using it like a tether as he forced her back to the horses, steering her toward his horse to throw her atop and mount behind her. The little dun Kincade had given her trotted behind, led by a rope tied to the corporal's saddle as they moved down the wooded slope that smelled of pine needles.

She squirmed helplessly in the saddle in front of him, pinned between the high pommel and his groin, and he laughed.

"We'll ride this way awhile, baby doll. I like to feel you rubbin' up against me. My camp ain't far now. We'll git there pretty soon, and I can teach you a few things before Kincade shows up to die."

Chuckling, he pulled her blouse down so that her breasts were bared, nipples hard in the cool air washing over them. When she made an involuntary move to cover herself, he knocked her hand away. "Naw, you ride like this, so's I can touch you when I want, think about what I got waitin' for me in a little while. I like waitin', thinkin' about it, thinkin' up ways to do it so that when it happens, I'm so hard I hurt.

Yeah, I like it when you fight a little, makes it all that much more fun tamin' you . . . makin' you beg for it . . . Jesus! Makes me hard jes' thinkin' about it, and I don't know what'll be better, fuckin' you or killin' Nick Kincade . . .''

Tory closed her eyes, feeling dizzy and weak from lack of food and rest, but she held tight to the hope—and fear—that Nick would come after her.

Twenty-five

Incredible, that he should even care or put himself out enough to look, but Nick Kincade thoroughly searched the clutches of dingy tents and ramshackle huts that comprised Sutter's Fort, cursing Victoria Ryan under his breath with every step, every empty corner. And worse, he felt like a fool, thinking bitterly how he must look chasing after a woman who'd left him in the middle of the night. He had considered doing nothing, just allowing her to leave, but the creeping worry that perhaps something had happened to her had prompted him to speak to Casey.

"She is gone? I thought she returned to your room," Casey told him, frowning with concern.

Now, along with the anger at her, apprehension motivated Nick to make an effort to find her. It didn't lessen when he discovered that Tory's dun mare was gone from the livery, and that the stable boy didn't know when it had been taken, protesting his ignorance with eyes wide in his freckled face.

"She must have come late in the night, for when I woke this morning, it was gone, I swear!"

To ease the boy's fright, Nick tossed him a coin, though something in his face must have been unnerving, for the boy caught it deftly and backed away with swift apprehension.

Nick's mouth curled sardonically. Now he was frightening children. What the hell was the matter with him? He should be glad she was gone, freeing him to his own business without worry of coping with her, her rebellion and her changing moods, her accusations that were as irritating as they were wrong. Most of them, anyway. Maybe he *had* used her as she'd accused him, but even though he had his reasons, he doubted she would understand them or care. Not that he could blame her in a way. But what had she expected? That she would be able to walk blithely away with a dishonest fortune? No one could be that naive. Even if her uncle and brother had failed, it would be extremely difficult for a young woman like Victoria Ryan to manage without help the sundry details that attended getting so much money surreptitiously out of California.

Not even Dave Brock had the experience needed to be much help, and though Roy Martin had dismissed any suggestion that the lieutenant was involved, Nick wasn't quite so certain. It would be easy for Tory to persuade Brock to any scheme she concocted, and he seemed resourceful enough to at least try. That was evidenced by his agreement to get her out of Monterey, wasn't it?

He thought about the way Brock had looked at Tory at her father's funeral, and then so eagerly escorted her back to the hacienda, solicitous and attentive, glancing smugly at Nick as they passed him where he stood aside with Gil, too respectful of her grief to intrude at such a moment—like a damn fool. Yes, it was certain Dave Brock would do anything she asked.

As would many men. Tory would know how to get what she wanted, and how to leave him behind without a qualm. He should have trusted her more to take care of herself. It would have saved him a lot of time and irritation. At this moment, she was probably already ensconced in a neat, comfortable little cabin aboard a steamer headed for San Francisco and then Boston, no doubt laughing to herself how she had so easily managed to elude him.

But even as he thought that, he was saddling his big black

and nudging it into a trot out of Sutter's Fort, riding in the direction of Sacramento City.

Situated on the east bank of the Sacramento River just below the mouth of the American, the city was a lot larger than when he'd last seen it. Some things were the same, like the strip of timber nearly a mile wide that shaded the streets, huge oak trunks far apart, with ancient old branches interlocking overhead in a kind of natural arbor. Houses, tents, and rough sheds had sprouted along the streets under the oaks in a surprisingly thick tangle.

The harbor resembled a forest, with masts and spars rising as high as the timber on shore, swaying along the wharves in the bay. Barks, brigs, schooners, and steamers clamored for space in a harbor bristling with activity. Gold generated a lot of excitement, and a lot of eager seekers, all crowding the burgeoning city in impatient droves.

By the time he'd convinced himself that no woman fitting Tory's description had secured passage aboard a vessel bound for San Francisco or anywhere else for that matter, it was almost dark. Black shadows crept along the wharves and crouched between hastily erected wooden buildings housing the pursers and shipping offices as he walked through a short alley to reach his horse.

Because he had his mind on Tory, uneasy now with the evidence that she was not aboard a ship, he did not hear the stealthy steps behind him until they were too close. He turned swiftly, a pistol in his hand, and saw the telltale gleam of a gun barrel in the dense light. Orange flame spurted from his pistol muzzle in a shattering explosion, and someone yelped loudly with pain. Still half-crouched, all his senses attuned to danger, he knew that there were several men in the alley even before he saw the faint sheen of their eyes in the deep shadows, and braced himself for their next move.

"Don't shoot! Don't—Granville put down the *damn* gun, you idiot!"

This didn't sound like an ambush, and Nick straightened slowly, still wary, but recognizing the fury and frustration in the voice.

"Stand in the light." His eyes were better adjusted now and he saw the vague shadows shift, then move to a patch of light in the center of the alley. "Throw down your weapons."

A metallic clatter followed a resentful mutter, then one of the men stepped forward. "Kincade, we were sent here by Roy Martin."

Nick relaxed slightly, but watched warily as the man came a bit closer; he looked familiar. "Do I know you?"

"We haven't been formerly introduced, no," was the rather dry reply, "but I did see you once, in a saloon in Bear Creek. I was there when a man commended you on your excellent work with a knife in Monterey."

"I remember. You were at the end of the bar. What does Martin want?"

"He thought you might want to know that Kiah Pickering has been staying in Sutter's Fort. I saw him there myself day before yesterday."

Holstering his pistol, Nick approached the man, who said his name was Campbell.

"Chris Campbell. And this is Joe Cooper to my left, and the trigger-happy Granville Alpha behind me. We all work for Martin."

Tall, with sandy hair and an open, honest face, Campbell shook his head slightly. "You're fast with that weapon, Kincade, just like Martin said you were. Sorry about Granville. He was just being a little too cautious."

"Are you hurt?"

"Naw, a little scratch, that's all." Campbell grinned, his blue eyes glistening in the murky light. "I've had worse."

"Tell me about Pickering."

"Nothing much to tell, except that he rode out of Sutter's Fort last night with some girl. I would have warned you earlier, but—ah—you were busy, I was told."

The premonition that so frequently saved Nick warned him now that he wasn't going to like the answer to the next question, but he had to ask it anyway.

"Can you describe the girl?"

Campbell nodded. "Pretty thing, much too pretty for a man

like Pickering, I thought. Slender, with long dark hair that shines almost red in the light. Rides a little dun mare—hey! You leaving? Got anything you want to tell Martin?''

''Tell him what you told me,'' Nick said grimly, his strides swift as he moved toward his horse. ''He'll know what to do.''

Tory huddled under a thin blanket thrown over her, an afterthought only when her lips had turned blue and her teeth were chattering loud enough to annoy the two men by the fire.

''Shit,'' a burly man her captor had called Glanton said in disgust, ''get the whore a blanket or she won't be worth a damn to us.''

Grumbling, the corporal lurched to his feet a bit unsteadily from all the whiskey he'd been drinking since they'd arrived in this rough camp, and found a blanket that smelled of things she'd rather not think about, but was at least some protection against the cold. He'd thrown it over her carelessly, reaching down to grab her chin in his palm, squeezing until tears of pain started in her eyes, then laughed at her.

''Bet you can't wait to see what we got planned for you, baby doll. You're gonna like it, I can tell.''

The man named Glanton looked over at them, firelight illuminating a face pocked with scars, his bushy brows almost hiding small eyes that reflected the flames in red lights. He rubbed at his crotch idly, watching her. ''Don't see why we can't go ahead and have her, Pickering. Won't matter none later.''

Pickering straightened, looking over his shoulder at Glanton. ''I done told you. I got it all planned out. Planned it two weeks ago, back when I seen this little whore dancin' at the mission with her tits flashin'—and then I seen the way Kincade acted when she let some hombre rub up against her. Yeah, I knew then I could end this before he got to me, so I followed 'em. Almost got her in Sutter's Mill, but Kincade came back too quick, so I waited for the right time, and next thing I know, she made it real easy. Came right outside for me, didn't ya, baby doll?''

The look he gave Tory was triumphant, and she shuddered. So it *had* been danger in the shadows, not just someone looking for the latrine. Pickering. The name was so familiar, a vague memory at the back of her mind . . . of course. In the plaza of the presidio that day, when she had seen Nick Kincade kill Tackett, he'd asked about Pickering. She felt sick. They had killed a girl, she remembered, a girl important to Nick. She'd always wanted to ask him about her, but never dared.

Pickering went back to the fire, only a few feet from her, close enough to keep an eye on her, as he said. She wanted to close her eyes, wanted to sleep, and when she awakened, be back in her bed in Boston, back in the warm security of the sprawling Ryan household, where Uncle Seamus and Aunt Katherine kept them all safe, and plump little Marie would be coming up the stairs with a tray of hot chocolate and cinnamon buns . . . God, it seemed a lifetime ago, not six months since she had last felt that secure.

It was only a matter of time before Pickering and Glanton did whatever it was they were waiting to do, only a matter of time before she would be forced to endure unspeakable horror and degradation.

Her cheeks flamed at the memory of Pickering forcing her to ride in front of him with her breasts naked, even when they rode past a camp of men near a bridge. It had been the most humiliating moment of her life, and she'd had no choice but to keep her chin lifted and her eyes averted, staring straight ahead as if they were not there. They had gawked up at her, shocked and disgusted, not knowing that the sharp tip of a knife nudged her back beneath Pickering's wool serape.

He had remained warm and covered, his hand idly caressing her while the men watched, and he'd seemed to get some kind of perverse pleasure out of the men's reaction as he walked the horses slowly past their camp. Indeed, she had heard the harsh tempo of his breathing increase, and his muttered groan as he whispered filthy words in her ear, promises of what he would do to her, things that she'd never heard of, not even with Nick.

Nick. Would he come for her? Or did he even care that she was gone? Worst of all, she shuddered to think that he would assume she had left for Boston, as she had threatened. If he did, then she was doomed. She would not survive these men and what they wanted to do to her. Oh God, if only she had listened to Nick, to Casey, instead of being so stubborn and angry.

Glanton got up from the fire, moving toward her, and she shrank back against the tree as far as she could, watching him warily. He crouched in front of her, licking his lips.

"Ain't seen what you got yet, girl. Show me. I want to see what I'm riskin' my hide for."

"Aw shit, Johnny, you ain't riskin' nothin'. Think Kincade can take five of us? He can't." Pickering got up and came toward them. "You got three of your boys with us, and hell, me and you alone could take him on with no trouble, long as we got his woman."

Still crouched in front of her, Glanton shifted a little on the balls of his feet, looking up at Pickering. "I don't know Kincade, so I don't know that for sure. All I know is what you tole me."

"Yeah, well I ain't got no reason to lie. He's been after me for almost a year now, after his little *chileña* done gone and got herself kilt by bein' stupid. You remember Tackett, don't you?"

Glanton nodded, his small eyes darting back to Tory, glittering. "Yeah. I remember Tackett. A Georgia boy."

"Right. After we left Tennessee, we went down to Texas and fought in that Mexican War. That's where I first run into Kincade, when the bastard tried to cut me when I was doin' sentry duty. I made up my mind then to get him back, so when we saw him in Matamoros a few years later, right after the war ended, me and Tackett decided we'd see how he liked sharin' his little whore. Hell, she weren't nothing but one of them greaser bitches, but she fought like she was a general's wife." He leaned over, spat on the ground near Tory's feet, smiling a little at the memory. "Makes me hard thinkin' about it, the way she screamed and clawed and bit—"

"You mean he's chased you damn near a year over some Mex bitch he didn't want to share?" Glanton's eyes raked over Tory. "How's he gonna feel about sharin' this one?"

"Pretty selfish, I'm hopin'." Pickering grinned, and in the dim light of the fire, Tory saw in his eyes what he intended. She was bait, bait to draw Nick Kincade into a trap.

She looked around and saw that though no other men were in sight, there were extra horses, and supplies. In her numbed state, she had not paid attention to details when they'd reached this camp, had only dimly realized they'd stopped for the day, and been grateful to be on the ground instead of atop a horse.

Cold revulsion filled her when Glanton reached out to pull away the blanket, his fingers grazing her skin. "Still want to see what I'm gittin'. Come on, girl. Stand up. Ain't seen nothin' of you but hair and blanket since you rode in. Git up and dance for me, like you done for them other men."

Where had he seen her dance? No, it was Pickering who had seen her, at the mission where she had gone with Nick. God, her head ached, and she was hungry, having eaten only a couple of cold biscuits earlier in the day. This was such a nightmare, and she couldn't quite focus on anything but the terror that seeped through her veins, rendering her immobile. She couldn't move, had the feeble hope that Pickering would interfere, but he didn't.

Pickering moved to the fire and threw on another log, while Glanton grabbed her by the wrists and yanked her up from the ground, pulling her with him. He swung her around so that the light fell across her, warm and glowing red-orange in the night shadows. She stood there trembling by the fire, feeling its heat on her but still frozen inside, staring helplessly at her tormentors.

Impatient, Glanton snarled at her to dance, to show him something before he backhanded her, and oddly enough, Pickering finally intervened.

"Give her a minute, Johnny. She's cold, I reckon. I want

you to see her like I seen her, dancin' like she was fuckin' a man standin' up—but don't git no ideas. We're savin' her. I figure Kincade will git here by this time tomorrow night, and I aim for us to be ready for him.'' He looked at Tory, grinned a little. ''All right, bitch. You had enough time to get warm. Show Johnny how you can move. Do it, or I'll make you do it, and you know I can, don't you?''

She drew in a deep breath and closed her eyes, willing her mind to oblivion, to block out the two men leering at her, to block out everything but the remembered sound of guitars and the driving beat that could remove her from everything but the movements of the dance.

Snapping her fingers at her sides, she threw her head back, feeling her long hair brush against her waist, the thin cotton skirts sway against her bare legs as she twisted her hips, slowly at first, then, as she sought desperately that imaginary place far away, faster, until she was moving as if there really was music, as if she danced for a lover, for Nick, for the man she loved.

And she did love him, though she might never get the chance to tell him now; she knew she had loved him for weeks. Months. There was no good reason for it, save that he had burst into her life and shattered all her plans, stealing her heart and mind and soul with his amber-gold eyes and lopsided smile, and she would give anything at this moment to hear his voice again, soft and husky against her ear as his hands moved over her, calling her Venus, telling her she was beautiful.

She danced until she was exhausted, until her skin beaded with sweat that made her blouse stick to her skin, and then stopped, panting, looking up through the hair in her face.

Glanton and Pickering were staring at her, lust in their eyes, and for a moment she thought they wouldn't wait, that they would rape her right there. Glanton started for her, reaching out, breathing hard, but Pickering stopped him.

''Naw, wait. Wait. I want him to *know* we waited on him, so he can watch it.'' He grinned at Tory, wolfish and cunning. ''We want to wait, don't we, baby doll? You'll dance again.

If you do it good enough, maybe we won't kill Kincade right off, but let him watch you have your fun first.''

Pickering was making no attempt to hide his tracks. Nick knelt on the ground in a stand of yucca plants, examining the hoofprints and scuff marks. Horse droppings indicated they'd passed this way within the last twenty-four hours. He stood up, studying the terrain. He was about fifty miles from Sutter's Mill. Beyond, the peaks of the Sierra Nevada ran in a high ridge that already bore dustings of snow on the lower slopes. He'd passed a steep bluff pocked with caverns, where a mound of rocks formed a tomb, approaching the recent inscription carved into a tree with dread until he made out the names: "To the memory of Daniel Brouett, Ezra H. Allen, and Henderson Cox, who are supposed to have been murdered and buried by the Indians on the night of the 27th of June 1848." Over four months ago.

He left there and watered his horse at a small lake, then pushed on. It had grown cold, winter winds whistling down through rocky canyons and mountain passes, and when he came to Red Lake, he stopped to let his horse graze in the thick, high grass that fringed the margins. Then he moved on again, filled with urgency as he maneuvered the steep, rocky trail, wondering how Tory had endured it. She was pretty tough, he'd found, despite her pampered life, a fact that had surprised him. He hadn't expected it. But he hadn't pushed her hard, either, and Pickering wouldn't give a damn about how she survived, just so she did long enough to satisfy him.

Carefully, he navigated the rough trail through Pass Creek Canyon, over the Carson River. Two new bridges had been built over the roaring torrent, and he stopped to ask about Pickering at a camp of Mormons.

Disapproving glances came his way, and finally one of the bearded men replied that they'd seen such a couple, the brazen woman lewdly baring her breasts and riding the same horse though another horse was led riderless behind them, tempting the man with her to touch her nakedness.

"It was not a sight to look upon," the man added sternly,

"and it is hoped that she will see the error of her ways soon. We have prayed for her soul."

They stared up at him, looking shamefaced when he said softly, "I hope you God-fearing men prayed that she'd survive the cold while you were at it," then he nudged his horse into a trot up the steep slope.

Riding up the narrow, rutted track that ribboned between scarred rocks and brush, he thought about what she must be enduring, cursed himself for letting it happen. He should have sent her on to Sacramento City with Gil, not kept her with him, but he had, and for his own selfish reasons, though he hadn't faced them until now. She'd become an obsession with him, a pressing need he felt when he looked at her, touched her satin-soft skin and held her—good God, was it possible? Had he, who had never before allowed himself to get too close to a woman, who had reveled in his ability to be detached and above emotional entanglements, allowed her to get to him?

It didn't seem possible, but he had.

Near dark, he reached a spot where the river cut a path through a canyon and the trail crooked through a gap leading to a wide valley. High grass was stitched with clear rushing mountain streams that wound from the slopes through the plains. Some of the rills were boggy in places, with clumps of willow trees scattered thickly at intervals across the meadow. Near the foot of the mountain, hot springs had formed a small sulfur lake.

With the sun setting at his back, dying rays spread across the flat plain to the east, glinting on something metal, a flash so brief for a moment he wasn't sure he saw it. He reined in beneath a feather of willow branches nearly denuded of leaves, his horse's hooves sinking into the soggy ground, and waited. In a few minutes, he saw it again, a quicksilver glitter of light on metal.

Up ahead, near one of the hot springs, was a camp. And he would bet a gold dollar it was Kiah Pickering.

Twenty-six

Dusk was falling, shrouding mountain peaks and valleys with a soft haze. Up higher, it was snowing. Tory could see it from where she sat, feet tucked under her, enveloped in the smelly wool blanket she'd been given. The camp was tucked in a rocky ledge, with a high bluff behind that protected it from the worst of the wind, and tall trees on two sides as a wind barrier. Rough lean-tos had been erected, and the horses were tied in a remuda up against the rock wall of the bluff.

All day, she had sat under a tall pine against the rock wall, trying to make herself small, watching Pickering and Glanton make plans, talking in low tones to the two men who had come down from a mountain pass. Another man was out there somewhere, she thought, for she'd heard them mention it, but she had not seen him.

She didn't like the way any of the men looked at her, smirking, with eyes that undressed her and promised things she didn't want to contemplate. Last night, after her dance, she had thought that Glanton would ignore Pickering and take her anyway. His eyes had been hot and narrowed, and his mouth twisted in an ugly grimace as he'd argued that it wouldn't matter. Thank God Pickering was adamant, for whatever demented reason he had.

Glanton had finally been content with making her hike up her skirt and pull down her drawers so that he could look at her, rubbing himself as she stood shivering in the cold wind with her skirt up around her waist and exposing herself, her eyes closed as she pretended that she was far away. But other than that, they had both left her alone, and she had fallen into a fitful sleep rolled up in the blanket near the fire.

All day, she had waited hopefully for an opportunity to escape. She wasn't tied, as if they knew she could not outrun them. Indeed, she was so sore from riding, from Pickering's hands on her so rough, that she could barely walk to the bushes for a moment of privacy. And even that was watched carefully by one of them, so she kept her needs at a minimum if she could, so as not to be humiliated any more.

She knew by the increased activity, Pickering's mounting excitement, that he expected Nick Kincade soon. "Hell, I left a trail a blind man could follow," he boasted to Glanton when he asked how he was so sure he'd come. "He'll be here. And I'll get rid of him finally, and not have to keep lookin' over my shoulder all the time, wonderin' if he's gonna show up and spill my guts into the dirt like he did Tackett's."

Fiercely, feeling savage pleasure rise up in her at the thought, Tory prayed that Pickering would meet the same fate. He deserved it. He deserved it for what he'd done to the first girl, and no telling how many more since her, how many other women he'd enjoyed torturing with his perverted brand of inflicting pain and instilling fear.

When the shadows grew long, a coyote began to bark, short yips that broke off suddenly. Glanton moved to stoke up the fire, building it high so that the area was well-lit. Almost casually, he stretched, grinning a little. Tory's throat tightened. They knew something, something was about to happen.

Then Pickering came toward her, and hunkered down on his heels, his grin yellow and excited. "Just a warnin', baby doll—if you try to signal Kincade, I'll kill him first. Then you—slow, so you'll have plenty of time to feel it comin'. And it won't make no difference in the end, anyway, so keep that in mind."

"Is he out there?" Sudden hope must have sprung into her eyes, for he laughed cruelly.

"He's out there. I heard the signal. He's watchin'. Waitin' for dark. Jes' do what I tell you, and maybe it won't turn out so bad."

"What do you mean—so bad?" She pushed at the hair in her eyes, staring at him warily.

He shrugged. "I got to kill him. If I don't, he'll kill me first chance he gets. But Johnny there, he's of a different mind. He wants to play a little first, like the 'Paches do with a man, you know, see how much they can take before they start screamin'—"

"Oh God!"

"But I ain't quite that way. And if you mind what I tell you, I'll see that he dies clean and quick. Won't be no long, drawn-out thing with knives and a lot of blood . . . Johnny used to hunt scalps after being mustered outa the army. Made some good money doin' that. A hunnerd dollars for a man's scalp, fifty for a woman, and twenty-five for a child. But then the Mexican government figured out that not all them scalps was Apache, see, and so he had to hightail it outa Mexico. But he still likes keepin' a hand in the business, so to speak."

Her face must have shown her horror, for he laughed and reached out to pull the blanket off her shoulders, lifting her to her feet almost gently. "That's right, baby doll. I see you know what I mean. A head of hair like yours would bring a good bit of money somewhere, if you was to lose it. All black and soft, with them red streaks in it that make it look all coppery-like in the sunlight. Purty. Real purty. Now come on, and do what I tell you. You're goin' to dance for us again, until I tell you to stop." His pale eyes took on color from the fire, glittering as he pulled her close to him, running a hand down over her back to squeeze her buttocks and bring her hard against him. "And then later, I'm gonna show you what I been promisin', and you'll like it . . . 'cause if you let on that you don't like it, Johnny is gonna get to make Kincade pay."

Half-sobbing, she stumbled numbly after him, and didn't

protest even when he pulled the shoulders of her blouse down, pulled it down to bare her breasts again, so that the cotton rested just beneath them. When he pinched her nipples to make them erect, she closed her eyes, biting her lower lip until she could taste blood, not making a sound when he took one of her nipples into his mouth with a loud sucking sound, drawing on it painfully until she wanted to scream.

In the distance a wolf howled, the sound wild and lonely, a wail that climbed high and then faded. The fire popped, a tree limb snapping in two and sending up a shower of crackling sparks.

Glanton made a rough sound in the back of his throat, and Pickering released her, turned her around so that her back was to him, running his hands up her sides, fingers digging into the material of her blouse and pulling it up, out of the waistband of her skirt. The fire was hot against her skin, Pickering behind her, and her front exposed to Glanton. Both men rubbed on her a few minutes, and she stood passively, willing her mind elsewhere while they poked and prodded, lifting her skirt to her knees, sliding their hands over her, laughing.

Hot shame clogged her throat, and for a moment she thought she would be sick. With a supreme effort, she forced her mind back to the moment, forced herself to focus on what was happening around her. She could not relax her guard, could not retreat no matter what they did, for if there was the slimmest hope for escape, she had to be alert.

"All right, baby doll," Pickering said in a rasping voice, "it's time for you to dance. I want you to dance like you did at the mission, only this time, I want you to take your clothes off while you do."

She stared at him stupidly. "I . . . I can't."

His eyes narrowed slightly. "I think you can. Jes' think about it a minute. Think about how Kincade's gonna die a piece at a time if you don't. Start with the blouse first, then the skirt, then the rest."

"This ain't the first time you taken your clothes off," Glanton said in a growl. "Do it the way I seen it done in New Orleans oncet. Do it slow, that way it makes a man all knotted up inside, just watchin'. We want Kincade to watch, to get careless. Now do it.''

This was much worse than anything she could have imagined, and for a moment she thought she could not do it, that they would have to kill her. Not even for Nick . . . ''Please,'' she said in a whisper, knowing it was futile but unable to stop the words, ''please don't make me do this.''

''The blouse first,'' Pickering said, his eyes and tone cold. ''Or you know what'll happen.''

Slowly, fighting the numbing haze that threatened to overwhelm her, she began to dance, feet moving in the dirt by the campfire, feeling the heat from the flames and the cool wind wash over her, hearing a silent rhythm as she pulled off the blouse and let if fall to the ground in a pale puddle. She turned, twisted, hair brushing against her back and over her breasts, turning around to feel the warmth of the fire on her front while the cool wind chilled her back, untying the laces that held the skirt around her waist, letting it drop to her ankles and stepping out of it. She danced then in her dingy white chemise, the laces gone, her cotton drawers ripped in places, with the once-pretty lace trim sagging from the hem.

Glanton and Pickering watched, seeming relaxed and entertained, but she was well-aware of the loaded pistols in their belts, the rifles near at hand, and the knives each of them wore dangling from belts at their waists. This night, they drank no whiskey. And there was a coiled, tense expectation in them, more than just the obvious lust as they watched her.

She swung her head, her hair whipping across her face, lightly stinging her bare breasts, and she saw Pickering sit forward a little, licking his lips. Glanton, too, had a glazed look in his eyes, though he looked around him frequently, gaze darting around the perimeters of the camp. If Nick came—*when* he came for her—he could approach from only one direction. And she knew, sickeningly, that three men had been positioned along the trail he would have to take, to block any possible retreat, closing the trap behind him. He was out there, watching right now, perhaps, but definitely out there.

And she had no way of warning him, no way to save herself . . .

But as she danced—the lure to draw Nick in, to make him forget caution in his rage—she saw the raw lust in Glanton and Pickering, and wondered if she could somehow make them less cautious as well. If she could, if she could somehow get her hands on a weapon . . . Knives hung from their belts, and guns as well. If nothing else, she could turn a weapon on herself rather than let them do what they intended. It was a choice, of sorts, *her* choice for a change. She had been told to dance well or suffer the consequences. So she would. She would dance as they wanted and could not expect. Once, a lifetime ago, when she had been someone else, she had wanted to be an actress. Now she would have to play the role of her life, have to distract these men. It was her only hope.

Boldly now, caught up with the fierce promise of hope and determination, she toyed with the straps of her chemise, sliding one back up, then down, her hips swaying and undulating, mimicking the sex act, until she had Pickering and Glanton staring at her narrowly. She slid the straps free, her bare breasts uptilted, watching them, watching their eyes, then caressed herself, palms skimming over her breasts, cupping them, coyly smiling. Glanton gave a strangled moan, and Pickering muttered a hoarse curse. The chemise followed the blouse, and her hands went to the waist of her drawers, the last defense, fingers curling into the laces and slowly pulling them loose. She turned toward the fire, bent slightly, pushing the drawers down over her hips, closing her eyes at the utter shame of what she was doing, feeling sick inside but determined to beat them at their own game. They wanted a distraction, and they would get one.

When the cotton drawers were in a heap on the ground, she turned back around in a lithe whirl of her body, wearing only the thin slippers on her feet, her body naked and gleaming in the light of the fire. Glanton and Pickering were on their feet now, no longer looking relaxed, but filled with lust. She smiled slowly and lifted her arms, pushing the heavy mane of her hair atop her head, spread her feet wide apart,

her body still moving, hips swaying provocatively, seduc-
tively, inviting them to her, to forget what they were doing,
why they were there, to come . . . come and touch, taste, tease,
take . . .

And they did, both at once, hands everywhere on her, fingers digging into her flesh, between her thighs, their breath
harsh and rasping, and then Pickering muttering that it didn't
matter, the sentries would warn them . . . Kincade was out
there watching, and could see them both fuck her at once, by
God . . . just hold her . . . little bitch . . . whore . . . asking for
it like that, by God . . . knew all along that she wanted it this
way, hard and rough like all women did . . .

One of them had her wrists, the other her legs, throwing
her down on the ground, turning her over on her stomach,
and in a haze of fear and horror and desperation, she saw that
it was Pickering in front of her, fumbling with his pants,
yanking her to her knees by her hair so that tears came to her
eyes, while Glanton was behind her, jerking apart her thighs
and kneeling between them, pulling her up, his fingers
roughly digging into her tender skin as he felt between her
legs, then began to unbutton his pants.

Nick, where are you? she wanted to scream, but bit her lip
to keep from crying out. It was up to her to save herself, for
if Nick was there, there were five men waiting to kill him.
No, she had to keep her wits about her.

They were both so intent on what they were doing, panting
and swearing, that neither noticed when she put up a hand as
if to brace herself against Pickering's waist, fingers grazing
the knife on his belt. Glanton moved his hands to her breasts,
kneading them painfully, then pinched her hard so that she
cried out, making Pickering laugh.

"Yeah, beg for it, bitch . . . You like it . . . knew you would
. . . Hold your head up and open your mouth for me, baby . . .
Look up at me so I can watch you take it all . . ."

She felt Glanton behind her, the smooth, hard heat of him
searching against the backs of her thighs, and knew she had
to do something quickly before he was inside her. She looked
up at Pickering as he got his pants open, smiled into his

glazed eyes as her hand found his knife and pulled it from the sheath in a swift motion neither lust-filled man could predict, and then she was bringing it down in a horizontal slash that caught Pickering's exposed member. Blood spurted, and he howled a piercing shriek that sounded loud and shrill like a woman, then fell backward, legs kicking.

Still kneeling behind her, Glanton was slow to react, and she turned in a swift, lithe motion, the knife slicing wickedly upward. It missed its intended target but caught him on his fat, hairy, white belly, laying open a deep red gash that caught him totally unprepared.

And then she was on her feet, running toward the horses, while behind her both men writhed on the ground in agony. Ignoring the cold, and the fact that she wore only shoes, Tory managed to untie one of the ropes holding the horses to the remuda, and they began to scatter, hooves pounding across soft ground. Half-sobbing, she grabbed at one and caught the trailing end of a halter rope, digging her feet in to halt the horse, then somehow managing to climb atop and turn it, heels drumming into the sides as she raced across the camp toward the dark meadow beyond.

She didn't even glance at Pickering and Glanton as she passed, but leaned over the horse's neck to urge it faster. Bullets spanged behind her, coming so close she felt the heat. She slipped a little on the bare back, her naked thighs rubbing painfully against the hide and her most tender part against the backbone, but did not release her hold on the animal's thick mane. Hair whipped across her face, and she couldn't tell if it was hers or the horse's, and with the sun down behind the far mountain ridges, only a faint, faint glow remained in the sky.

The beat of her heart and the drumming of hooves against soft earth was loud, so loud that it seemed to fill the air like thunder. And then she felt someone just behind her, a horse stretching out beside her, neck and neck, and she began to sob, desperate and afraid and despairing, but not yet ready to surrender. She leaned to the side, tried to turn her mount, but a hand reached out to grab the halter. Desperate, she beat at the hand, trying to dislodge it, and then she heard someone swearing harshly, the curse frightening and familiar.

"*Mierda!* Dammit, Lady Godiva, will you slow down for me?"

As her horse came to a jolting stop, slamming her painfully against the sharp backbone, she was vaguely aware of Nick reaching out for her, of the clean, wood-smoke smell of him and his arm safe and protective around her, and then the world began to spin in a slow circle, round and round, while an odd whirring sound filled her ears until it drowned out everything else.

And as if from far away, she heard him saying her name before it was drowned out, too, and then she was falling into velvet oblivion, soft and welcoming and safe, where nothing could hurt her.

Twenty-seven

Tall pines formed a natural shelter next to a towering rock wall, and only a few feet away bubbled a hot spring that smelled of sulfur, but not as strongly as some of the springs did. Nick wrapped Tory tenderly in blankets, rubbing her arms and legs to restore circulation, gut-sick at what she'd been through.

It had taken all his self-control not to start shooting when he'd seen what they were doing to her; it was a trap and it would do neither of them any good if he let them goad him into reaction. The guards stationed at intervals along the rocky trail into the *barranca* were the first to die, with quick, silent slashes of a knife across their throats. They'd never heard him coming, compliments of the old Comanche warrior who had trained him in his youth. But now Glanton and Pickering were left, and he had to go back and finish it.

"Tory, listen to me," he said when she roused a little and opened her eyes, staring up at him with the numb apathy he'd seen in abused animals. "I've got to go back. I can't let him get away. You'll be all right here for a while. It's warm on these rocks, with the steam coming up through the ground, and there's food in my saddlebag. Are you listening to me?"

The wide violet eyes were glazed, remote, and her face so

pale she looked like a ghost, but she nodded after a moment, almost imperceptibly, the slightest movement of her chin. Dammit, he couldn't help it. He had to leave her here for now.

"Here's my revolver. It's loaded and ready. Just point and pull the trigger if you need to." He rested a pistol in her lap, next to the small hand that was trembling violently as if with the ague. But he couldn't wait any longer.

She made no protest when he rode away.

It didn't take him long to return to Pickering's camp. The fire still blazed, but it was deathly quiet in the camp. He heard soft groans, whimpers, and curses, and moved from the shadows into the ring of firelight. Pickering knelt on the ground, sobbing, holding himself with both hands, a high, keening note of desperation in his voice.

"Glanton . . . Johnny, come back here, you bastard . . . Help me, oh God, help me afore I bleed to death . . . She cut me, th' bitch, th' bitch . . ."

Nick stepped closer, and this time Pickering saw him, his head jerking up, eyes dilating with fear. Blood smeared his hands, pooled on the ground between his spread thighs, his pants still halfway down as he clutched at his groin.

"What'sa matter, Pickering? Having a bad day?"

"Kincade . . ." He licked his lips, fear emanating in waves, and his eyes darted around the camp as if searching for help, then returned to Nick, one hand shifting slightly toward his hip.

"No, I don't think I'd reach for that gun, Pickering. It's too late anyway. You're all alone out here. Glanton's gone. Funny thing—those men you set to watch for me weren't paying close enough attention. I got right past them with no trouble . . ."

"Are they—did you—"

"Kill them? They're food for the buzzards right now, just like you're going to be."

"Kincade, listen—I didn't kill your woman. It was Tackett. She was fightin', see, and somehow when he tried to stop her, he hit her a little too hard—"

"Her neck was broken. I'd say that's pretty damn hard."
Nick gazed at him for a minute, then saw something glint
around Pickering's neck, a metallic flash. He leaned forward,
shoved aside the half-open edges of the shirt, and saw a small
cross dangling from a gold chain. It rose and fell with the
harsh breaths Pickering took, the half-sobs. A surge of cold
fury went through him then as he recognized Gisela's necklace, the one he had given her that day to keep her safe,
around Pickering's neck. Nick intended for Pickering to die
with it around his neck.

He sat back and held up his hand, and the blade of his
knife glittered in the reflected firelight, riveting Pickering's
eyes on it. "Thought about it a lot since then, how you did
her. She didn't deserve that, didn't deserve to die. No man
does that, not a real man. But you aren't a real man, are
you?" His eyes shifted meaningfully to Pickering's crotch.
"Justice of a sort, that a woman did that to you . . . that *my*
woman did it."

"Kincade . . . please . . ." It came out in a groan, as if he
knew what was intended, what Nick would do.

"Pedazo de mierda!" Nick rose to his feet, filled with
contempt and disgust while Kiah Pickering groveled on the
ground, pleading, words coming out in choking sobs that
meant nothing to him. Nothing.

He'd seen enough to know what they'd intended for him,
to know what they intended for Tory. He'd watched her dancing by the fire, her pale body gleaming in the rosy light, naked
and glistening, the body that only he had seen, only he had
touched, and he'd fought a killing rage that made him want
to start shooting with reckless fury. He might have forgotten
caution, forgotten everything but the need to kill the men who
touched her and take her away from them. But then they'd
rushed her, both of them on her at once, touching her, spreading her on the ground to rape her, and before he could get a
clear shot, she'd taken matters into her own hands, the swift
glitter of the knife in the light, and Pickering's scream . . . By
the time he got down from the rocks, she was on a horse and
racing past him, and, cursing, he'd found his horse and gone

after her, afraid she would flounder into the bog or one of the hot sulfur pots.

Stepping past Pickering, he knelt at the fire to heat the blade of his knife, smiling through the flames at the wounded man. "I used to come across men the Apache had killed. Very imaginative, those Apache. Did things to a man that would turn your stomach. Ever see that?"

"Kincade . . . oh God . . . you can't . . ."

And then Pickering went for his gun, desperate and swift, but not fast enough. Nick's bullet caught him between the eyes and pitched him backward, where he lay sprawled obscenely on the ground with his pants down and the blood still seeping from where Tory had cut him.

Nick left him that way, not bothering to bury him, taking only a few supplies from the packs back up under the brush shelter against the rock wall. It had started to snow, fat flakes that promised the start of a blizzard that would soon cover the ground and make the mountain passes treacherous. He had to get back to Tory.

White stretched everywhere, as far as she could see, a thick blanket that was beautiful, blinding with the sun shining down on it. In the distance, a huge serrated monster of a mountain cast a long shadow over slopes that stretched for miles, where nothing moved, only occasional shadows of hawks circling overhead.

Tory tucked her feet up under her, warmed by the fire Nick had built, her stomach full from the meal they had just eaten. It was surprisingly warm in the little brush shelter against the mountain face, cozy and dry, with the horses nearby in their own brushy refuge.

"Had enough?"

She glanced at Kincade, where he sat by the fire with the iron skillet. Elk steaks, he'd said, coming back from a hunt with his eyebrows frosted with ice and his lashes snow-clogged, but triumphant and grinning, showing her his prize. After skinning and butchering it and taking the remains they wouldn't use a distance from camp to prevent predators coming too close, he'd cooked for her, the smell of sizzling meat filling the small enclosure with tantalizing aroma.

"Enough, thank you," she said.

After a moment he shrugged and went back to cleaning up, his movements swift and efficient. She looked away, out the wedge of doorway that could be sealed off with a blanket, staring across the pristine white surface of snow, wondering if she would ever feel clean again. She'd washed, bathed in one of the shallow depressions where steam rose from the water, scrubbing herself until Kincade had said her skin was coming off, and then he'd handed her a blanket to cover herself. He'd brought her clothes, the skirt and blouse and undergarments from where she'd left them, and even washed them for her in the hot water, but she could barely bring herself to look at them.

Every time she closed her eyes, she saw Pickering and Glanton, staring at her with hot lust, watching her dance for them, laughing hoarsely and then touching her in the most intimate places, making her feel dirty and used and degraded. Oh God, if only she could wipe it from her mind, the humiliation and sordid acts, the feel of their hands on her, hurting her and enjoying it . . . as she had enjoyed the feel of the knife in her hands, the brief exultation when she'd heard Pickering's scream of horror and pain as the blade sliced into him. Yes, that had been enjoyable.

It was hard to think that once she had declared herself revolted by such violent acts, and she could almost hear the sanctimonious arrogance in her tone as she'd said there was a great deal of difference between vengeance and justice. She wasn't so certain now. Not anymore. The two were intertwined so closely in her mind, it was hard to separate them. But Kiah Pickering had deserved his fate, and she wondered bitterly if she had become as depraved as they were, because she relished the fleeting act of vengeance.

She was glad—*fiercely glad*—that he was dead, and said so, suddenly, the first time she'd mentioned it since Nick had returned that first night almost a week ago.

In the leaping firelight, Kincade's eyes were opaque, regarding her unemotionally, and he nodded. "He deserved it."

"Yes." Her mouth twisted and nausea rose up, almost choking her. "I wish I had killed him myself!"

"You did worse. Justice would have been letting him live like that, but I couldn't do it. I'd made someone a promise a long time ago."

"Gisela." She looked up at him again, away from the blinding white snow outside, and saw the brief explosion of light in his eyes. Regret? Pain for a lost love?

"Yes. Gisela."

"I heard . . . what they did. What Pickering did. He bragged . . . to Glanton how they had killed her. It was horrible." Silence fell, and Nick leaned back against the rough brush wall of the shelter, lighting a thin brown cigar from a burning twig in the fire, then staring up at the low roof as the silence stretched out.

"It shouldn't have happened," he said softly, bitter, his eyes narrowed and hard against the curl of tobacco smoke, "wouldn't have happened if I'd done what I should. They used her as vengeance against me. I knew better than to get involved with a woman for more than a night or two."

Her throat tightened, and it seemed suddenly very stuffy in the shelter, much too close. "We don't always have control over falling in love, Nick."

"Right." His laugh was short and harsh, jarring. "That we don't, Venus. For damn sure. But I was never in love with Gisela. That's the worst part. She was only another woman. I wanted her, would never have hurt her, but I didn't love her. She was just *there*." He looked up at her, a brief glance, then turned to stare out the narrow opening. "We'll start out in a few days, go back to Sacramento City if the weather holds. The passes should be open enough by then."

Numbly, she nodded. Was that how he felt about women? As conveniences? Oh God, was that how he felt about *her*? That cold, emotionless detachment? Despite everything, she had begun to think he felt more for her than just a sense of . . . of *obligation*! There had been hints, signs that he truly cared for her in the gentleness he'd shown her lately, and the things he said, small things but oh so important, though she had been so dazed, so shaken by her experience that she'd not been able to respond as she might have . . . but he'd not tried to touch her in the past week, indeed, had gone out of his way to avoid it, even a slight brushing of his hand against her had made him recoil as if burned, and then look at her with inscrutable eyes, usually a quick glance . . . She wanted to ask how much he'd seen, if he was disgusted by what she'd done, by what *they* had done to her. She wanted to ask . . . but couldn't bring herself to hear the answer.

Another blizzard blew down from the mountains that night, trapping them in the shelter, almost burying the poor horses so that Nick had to wade through waist-deep snow to their brush shelter against the rock, take them melted ice to drink, dig down under trees to find forage.

"If we have to stay here much longer, they'll die of starvation," he told Tory when he came back into the shelter, shivering from the cold. He blew warmth on his fingers and knelt down by the low fire. "Think you can make it if we ride out of here when this storm stops?"

"I can make it. I've survived worse."

His impassivity flickered, and he looked up at her over the fire, yellow light reflected in his eyes like twin flames.

"Yeah. Guess you have at that."

Something in her snapped—maybe it was his flat tone, the neutral indifference that was worse than accusations, worse than the times she caught him staring at her when he thought she was asleep, with a look in his eyes that she couldn't interpret—and she surged to her feet, shaking all over, voice rising, all the hurt and despair tumbling out of her.

"Yes, I've survived worse! How do you think I felt with their hands on me, touching me in places only you had touched me, while he told me what he was going to do to me when you got there, so you could watch—it was humiliating, degrading, but by God it wasn't my choice! I had nothing to do with it, do you hear? I did what I could to survive, to stay alive until you came for me, and if you want to blame me for that, go ahead. I can't stop you. But I won't apologize for

it, do you hear me? I won't apologize for any of it! Damn
you, Nick Kincade, *damn you* for not even *looking* at me
anymore—"

He was on his feet too, expression finally in his face even
if it was anger, white lines on each side of his mouth deepening with tension as he glared at her.

"Yes, damn me! I deserve it. It wasn't your fault, not any
of it. He was after me and you got in the way. I should never
have brought you with me. You should have stayed in San
Francisco with your brother."

His bitter words could not have been more effective if he'd
slapped her in the face. She recoiled. Did he mean that? No,
he couldn't, not after everything that had happened.

"You don't mean that you—"

"Hell yes, I mean it. Do you think I don't know I'm responsible, for Chrissake? I know. *Christ!*" He raked a hand
through his hair, frustration evident in his face and the set of
his mouth. "I've always been too damn hardheaded to listen
to anybody. Too independent to let somebody tell me what
to do. My father was right. He said one day I'd come to grief
for it—but I didn't think it would hurt anyone else. Not this
way. Not like you and Gisela." He drew in a deep breath,
eyes meeting hers at last, a bleak look. "It won't happen
again. I'll leave you alone."

"No . . . no, Nick . . ." It came out a moan that sounded
too much like despair, and she curled her fingers into fists so
tight her nails cut into her palms, digging painfully. Pride
closed her throat for a moment before she swallowed hard,
and as if it was someone else speaking, she heard herself say,
"But I love you."

"Love? No, what you feel isn't love, Tory, but you're too
inexperienced to know that. Christ, I should know, shouldn't
I? If not for me, you'd still be tucked safely in your bed,
dreaming safe, little virgin dreams, not up here in the mountains like this . . . It doesn't matter. I'll get you back to Sacramento City, and you won't ever see me again. I swear it."

"Is that what you want?"

"Yes. It's what I want."

Without looking at her again, he grabbed his buckskin jacket from the floor and ducked out the shelter's low opening and into the snow beyond, leaving a dark trail furrowed in the glistening white.

She was shivering, feeling the world crash in around her, feeling the icy grip of despair take firm hold, and bring it all down around her until she felt nothing at all. Nothing. No pain, no despair, no hope. Nothing.

Icy blasts of wind careened through tight crevices in howling gusts, and Nick wondered how much longer Tory would be able to hold on. They were almost there, almost out of the Sierras, but the snow had descended on them again, clogging the passes and making them treacherous. A false step, a single mistake, could cost their lives, or leave them stranded in this pass just like the Donner party only two years before.

A ledge sheltered by long, bare roots of a tree was just ahead of them on the trail, almost obscured by the blinding whirl of loose snow being blown at them from towering drifts, and he motioned for Tory to stop. She wouldn't have heard him if he'd even attempted speech, for the screaming of the wind. He eyed her critically when they were huddled under the protection of the ledge, noting her snow-frosted lashes and blue lips.

"We have to go on, Tory. We can't stop."

"I know." She met his gaze. "I'll make it."

A smile tugged at his mouth. "I'd wager money on it, Venus.

And she did make it, exhausted and ragged, with a slight case of frostbite on her toes, but otherwise fine, the Sacramento City physician said, shaking his head in amazement.

"A strong woman, Mr. Kincade. Your ordeal would have killed most men."

"Will she be all right?"

"I see no problems ahead for her, other than the usual residual effects from exposure to the cold. You know, weariness, numbness in her extremities, that sort of thing."

Nick looked behind the physician, toward the closed door

of the little room where Tory lay in a fat feather bed, swathed in blankets and with a bright fire burning in the grate. He'd made a promise to himself, and he meant to keep it.

"Sir, I would appreciate it if you would see that she gets this." He held out a small leather sack, meeting the physician's startled gaze with a lifted brow. "I am afraid that I have other obligations, and so must leave before she fully recovers. You'll see that she has this?"

"Why, uh—young man, you're hardly recovered yourself. If you will only be patient she will soon awake and you can give her this yourself. I don't think—"

"Give it to her." Nick took the doctor's hand and pressed the sack firmly into his palm. His eyes narrowed slightly. "Be certain she gets all of it."

"I am not a thief, sir," the old man replied stiffly. "Whatever is in this pouch now, will be in it when I give it to her."

"I'm sure it will."

"Wait," the doctor said when Nick turned to the door, "what shall I tell her?"

"Nothing. She'll know."

He closed the door softly behind him, long strides taking him to the end of the hall, and then out the front door of the hotel. She'd know why he left. There would be no need for explanations.

Part
Five

Twenty-eight

With spring had come balmy days and chilly nights, when after the sun went down warm wraps and cloaks were required. But now, standing at the window of her hotel room and looking out into the street, Tory thought of another time she'd come to San Francisco. Then it had been autumn, and the weather had been as cool, but the streets just as crowded.

Even more ships clogged the harbor now, bringing Easterners filled with a desire to find gold. Along with the influx of gold-seekers came Chinese laborers, some wearing the odd pointed straw hats, and some frequently seen balancing baskets of laundry atop their heads as they scurried down the dirt streets. On the beach below, laundry was still done in huge pots slung over fires at Washerwoman Lagoon, but there were so many needing clean garments that some citizens had begun to send their clothes by ship to the Sandwich Islands where it could be accomplished more swiftly.

A short walk down the street was rife with a vast array of languages being spoken, and more immigrants arriving every day. It would be, Tory thought, a cosmopolitan city in the near future.

"Another cup of hot tea, Victoria?"

Tory turned away from the window, smiling at the dark-haired woman gazing at her.

"I think I've had enough tea to reenact the Boston Tea Party, Jessie. Besides, we should be getting ready for the dinner and reception by now."

Jessie Benton Fremont laughed softly. "Politics is something I was born to, and I think I've become very blasé about these things. It's so boring at times, repeating the same comments to the same people, over and over—but you would know all about that, I suppose."

Tory shrugged lightly and looked away, back out the window overlooking the San Francisco Bay. It was hard to see it now for the numerous buildings that had sprung up almost overnight. New wharves had been built, with ships still thick in the harbor like a forest of mountain pines.

"Not really. My father was never involved in politics like yours. I hadn't seen him since I was a child, and when I returned—well, he died so soon after."

"Oh yes, I'm so sorry. I'd forgotten." Jessie's dark eyes were sympathetic and filled with pain, and Tory remembered that she had only recently suffered the loss of an infant son. Now Jessie leaned forward, her high, smooth brow creasing slightly. "Do forgive me, Victoria. I didn't mean to remind you of such sad times."

"You didn't." It was true; it wasn't Papa's death that made her sad, but all that had followed. How could she explain something like that to Jessie Fremont, wife of the famous John Charles Fremont, daughter of Thomas Hart Benton, the leading advocate of expansionism and a U.S. senator? She couldn't, of course. It would be too sordid, too scandalous, even for a woman who had endured scandal concerning her husband's business dealings.

Smiling, Jessie said, "Good. I suppose I was thinking of your brother. For a young man, he has become very involved in politics, I understand."

Tory returned the smile. Since Don Sebastian's untimely—and unexplained—death, Diego had become involved in several energetic enterprises, not the least of which was playing gallant to the ladies. Apparently, Diego had managed to charm yet another woman, though Jessie Benton Fremont was not easily charmed. She was an extremely intelligent, gracious woman, loyal to her husband and strong-willed. In the short time she had been in San Francisco, Mrs. Fremont had already managed to gather a devoted following of admirers.

It had been Mrs. Fremont who had sought her out, saying she had been told that Victoria was the perfect woman to help her learn more about the city, since Tory had been there almost since the gold rush had begun. Tory had tried to tell her that she been a resident only for the past six months, but Jessie Fremont was not a woman to take no easily, and before she knew it, Tory was involved. It was easier than resistance, and really, what else did she have to do? The money her brother gave her—part of her inheritance he'd said, smiling a little—more than satisfied her few needs. Though she was grateful to Diego for his generosity and for not asking too many questions she did not want to answer—"Do not ask me how our uncle died," he'd said, "and I will not ask you what happened with Kincade"—she realized that she was only waiting.

In the midst of a city crammed with people all exuding a sense of urgency, she felt only tedium, a sense of suspension, as if she were waiting for something to happen. At any time she could have bought passage back to Boston, despite Diego's urging her to remain, to come back to Monterey where he would see that she was cared for. But still, she waited, demurring to any efforts to coax her from San Francisco, repeating over and over again that she was only waiting for decent traveling weather to return to Boston.

It took her several months to realize that she was waiting for Nick Kincade instead of decent traveling weather, and that realization had shocked her to her very soul. *Nick* . . . How could she keep from thinking of him? He invaded even her dreams; sometimes at night she would wake suddenly, sitting up in bed in a cold sweat despite the chill breeze from the bay coming through her open window, and think she had heard his voice whispering her name. Only foolish dreams, of course.

But how could she keep from thinking of him? It had been such a shock to wake and find him gone, and the doctor had looked embarrassed, stumbling over clumsy explanations that men often had strange reactions after such a harrowing experience, as he put into her hand a heavy leather pouch filled with gold coins. For a week after, she had lain in the bed with her face turned toward the wall, until she heard the whispers that she was grieving herself to death and decided that, after all, life was preferable to being gossiped about while she lay dying. Even now, there were times she thought of him, wondered if he missed her, if he ever thought of those nights they'd spent together.

Jessie Fremont was looking at her very strangely, and she flushed, knowing that she had once more gone into what Jessie laughingly called "a trance," as she so frequently did of late.

Tory plucked at the expensive braid edging the cuff of her gown and smiled.

"Diego has become an ardent admirer of Don Mariano Vallejo. He hangs on his every word. I'm not at all certain it is to either man's advantage."

"Don Mariano still has friends in high places, though since California became a territory, his influence has waned." Jessie hesitated, then set down her teacup on the small table between then. "I am still rather dazzled by our recent good fortune, and am so grateful that you have been kind enough to educate me about California. It's beautiful, and since Charles has had such good fortune with his investment, I'm certain we will be staying."

"Your husband's investment has caused quite a local commotion. To think that he bought land by mistake, only to have gold discovered on it. I'm certain he travels under a lucky star."

"So it would seem." Jessie smiled, her brown eyes sparkling with delicious glee. "Charles had instructed his agent to purchase a small plot near San Francisco, but for some reason—trouble with the title, I think—the man bought seventy square miles of wilderness in the Sierra foothills. Charles was furious—do you know he was considering legal action to recover his three thousand dollars when the gold was found?'' Shaking her head with a bemused smile, Jessie poured more tea, then looked up at Tory. Over the rim of her teacup, she said, ''It was fortunate for your former guide that he had also purchased land under the same lucky star.''

''So I understand.''

The subject of Nick Kincade always made her uneasy, and she wished Jessie had not mentioned him. There was always an awkwardness when she did, as if Jessie expected Tory to validate or deny the rumors that rippled through the city like wildfire. Tales of their survival in the Sierras had drifted down from Sacramento City, along with speculative rumors about the connection between Nick Kincade and the daughter of a prominent Californio. Tory had heard them, of course, but shrugged them off and let people think what they would. Why should she explain? It wasn't as if she saw Nick anymore. Indeed, she knew of him only through gossip and what she read in the papers, all about his recent good fortune.

Kincade's investment had been small—the thousand acres in the Sierra foothills he'd bought through her father worth a small fortune now that a wandering prospector had discovered gold in several of the streams, and even a rich vein imbedded in a hill. Nick had left San Francisco almost immediately on hearing the news, taking Gil Garcia and going into the hills to protect his property.

Jessie was saying, ''This dinner tonight promises to be quite an affair, with all of San Francisco and half of California in attendance, all to celebrate Charles's bungling the purchase of some property. Your brother promised he would attend, and bring Don Mariano as well if he can coax him into coming. I hope he keeps his promise, because I have invited some very lovely young ladies to attend tonight, and there will be music and dancing.''

''Diego loves a festive evening,'' Tory said dryly. ''He'll

be here if it's at all possible. Especially since he wants so badly to meet your husband.''

"*If* Charles remembers to come. Or can find the ballroom." Jessie laughed with fond resignation. "For a man known as the Pathfinder, who crosses the Rocky Mountains as if they are no bigger than Montgomery Street, he seems to have a great deal of difficulty arriving at any function I wish him to attend. It boggles the mind."

"A purely male peculiarity," Tory agreed with amusement. It was known that John Charles Fremont had endured more than his share of pitfalls, but always seemed to escape unscathed. Only this past December, he and a party of men set out on an expedition across the midwinter Rockies to test the practicality of a transcontinental railroad route, and had been stranded in the San Juan Mountains above the headwaters of the Rio Grande when the temperature dropped to twenty degrees below zero. Ten of the expedition had died of cold and hunger in the mountains, and Fremont himself barely made it back to Taos by the end of January.

The Fremont expedition had elicited inevitable comparisons with the survival of only two people in the same blizzard, but few mentioned it to those involved, preferring anonymous speculation that, of course, was common gossip.

Nick had come back to town, but not to see Tory. Instead, he kept company with the Fremonts and, as was faithfully reported in the Alta newspaper, with a very beautiful woman who was a cousin of the territorial governor. They had been seen together at political functions, and Tory supposed ironically that with his newfound wealth, Kincade was now accepted into society. But she remembered him as a gun-hung bandit, using a knife with swift efficiency on a man in the Monterey presidio, and dressed in buckskins and wearing a leather headband like an Indian, crouched in front of a campfire up in the mountains.

Now it was May, and she had delayed long enough. Her waiting was at an end, for she had already made the arrangements to return home within the week, to return to Boston.

So why did she feel as if her world had fallen apart? As if she had lost everything?

"Well, your brother is very handsome, you know," Jessie was saying with a light twinkle in her eye. "He has captured the attention of quite a few young ladies, I understand."

"Diego has his charms, I suppose. He is in no hurry to wed, however, as he so recently informed me."

"And you?" Jessie asked after a moment, one brow lifting and her dark eyes studying Tory intently. "Do you still intend to leave for Boston?"

"Yes. Of course. Why do you ask?"

After a tiny hesitation, Jessie shook her head. "Only that I wondered. You seem so . . . unhappy . . . for a woman going home to her betrothed."

Tory's hands tightened in her lap, and she surged up from her chair to walk to the windows and look out across the bay, nervously pleating folds of her striped cotton skirt between her fingers.

"I'm not unhappy. I'm uncertain. There's a vast difference."

"As well I know." Jessie got up from her chair. She smelled of verbena scent as she joined Tory at the window. "Did I ever tell you about my father's objection to my husband?"

"No." Where was this leading? Why did Jessie feel it necessary to speak of her husband, when Tory's situation was not at all the same? But, of course, Jessie did not know that, only knew that Tory was going home to her betrothed and was uncertain about it. She should tell her the truth, tell her that it wasn't anyone *else* who disapproved of the match, only her own heart.

But Jessie was continuing, leaning back against the window to look at her, sunlight coming through the glass gleaming in the dark hair she wore parted in the middle and tucked into a soft knot on her neck.

"The senator objected strongly to the alliance. Father said his daughter was not going to be married to a penniless man with more ambition than sense." Jessie's mouth curved into a wry smile. "We married in secret, then waited a month to tell my father. He has a reputation for being . . . gruff . . . as well as stubborn, and tried to throw my husband out of the house. I had to stand bodily between them and pronounce my vow to stay with the man I love. Father was silenced, and this past October marked seven years that Charles and I have been married."

When Tory lifted a brow, not knowing what to say, Jessie Fremont laughed. "I suppose you wonder why I'm telling you. Only this: when there is something you want very badly, you must seize it, or lose all hope of happiness."

There was no point in telling Jessie that it was not her choice.

Diego had brought her the ball gown Señora Valdez had begun over ten months before, the unfinished dress now completed and beautiful, a creation of shot-silver and amethyst, flashing in the reflected light from lamps and mirrors around the hotel room.

"I thought you'd like it," he said with triumph, and stretched his long legs out in front of him, a picture of male satisfaction. "Had a seamstress finish it after Tía Benita said you had specifically requested the style."

"Yes . . . Diego, I don't know what to say except thank you. You've been too good to me."

"I just want to see you smile again. No, I mean *really* smile, like you used to. Now your lips just curl up a little, as if you had stomach pains."

She laughed. She couldn't help it; sometimes, he was as amusing as he was irritating. "You are incorrigible. How did you ever get so insufferable?"

He grinned. "Practice. Lots of practice. I had my older sister as a model." He got up in a smooth motion and came toward her, the grin fading. "Are you certain this is what you want to do? Go back to Boston?"

"Yes, of course. There is nothing for me here. I'll never be really comfortable at Buena Vista, and you're doing so many wonderful things with it, the vineyards and wine that all the merchants want to buy—I believe you're going to be an excellent businessman, Diego.''

"Perhaps. I learned a lot from our father, though some of the lessons must now be ignored.'' He lapsed into silence for a moment, then said suddenly, "I knew that he had been cheating people, but it was a long time before I knew that he was selling guns to mercenaries and foreign powers. I thought of it as a business like any other, and never explored below the surface. Bah, I was so young and foolish then, thinking how smart he was to do this and that, and if people were stupid enough to allow him, they deserved it. After seeing Tío Sebastian as he really was, I realized how I must look as well. I did not want to be that person, Tory. I did not like seeing fear in men's eyes when they looked at me, and see the women hold tight to their children when I passed by, as if I would take them away or harm them. It made me sick.''

Pacing, with his hands behind his back, he moved across the floor with long strides, until Tory began to think he had forgotten she was there. Then he looked up, his eyes a dark, fierce blue.

"I killed him, you know. Sebastian did not die of a fever, as it was said, unless you want to think of it as the kind of fever one gets from a sword.''

"Diego, you don't have to tell me this—''

"I know. But you should know, after all that you have been through—you should hear that he paid for what he did, for what he wanted to do. He thought I was so young and stupid—inept, I think he said.'' Diego laughed, a harsh sound in the quiet of the hotel room. "But I think he soon learned how he had misjudged me, and how much I learned in the fencing lessons Papa paid for all those years. I surprised him on the beach, down by the wine cellars, and I think the vaqueros knew, for they just disappeared, leaving him there with me. He laughed at me, Tory—*laughed*!—when I challenged him to a duel. It wasn't long before he stopped laughing . . . before surf washed over the rocks and foam scoured the sand clean of his blood. Then I was free. You were free. And our mother was free, though I think she no longer cares.

She has gone to a convent, where she says she should have gone so many years ago, and when I visit her, she seems content. Serene.''

Diego stood in the middle of the room, panting slightly as if the effort of confession had drained him, and Tory went to him, drawing him to her and holding him as she had not held him since he was seven years old and too proud to allow his sister to hug him. This time, he did not resist, but put his arms around her, too, patting her clumsily and murmuring affectionate words in a slightly embarrassed tone.

To ease his embarrassment, she finally pushed him away, teasing, ''You will make me late, and then I will have to watch while you must explain to your friends about your poor homely spinster sister standing in the corner . . . Go. I have to get ready for the ball.''

Diego grinned. ''You could never be homely. I don't know what it is, but you are more beautiful than ever. I thought at first you were too thin, that your cheekbones looked too sharp, but I think they only make your eyes look larger now. You will not lack for dancing partners tonight, Tory, so wear your most comfortable slippers.''

''I will not dance,'' she said, stiffening, trying to ward away the memories of a mountain camp and lustful eyes.

Surprised, Diego said, ''Even with me? I was hoping we would dance as you used to when we were children. You remember, how on the patio you could hear the music—''

''I remember. I don't want to dance, Diego. Please. I can't explain, but I just could not—''

Something in her face must have revealed the sudden panic she felt, the revulsion at the thought of dancing, for he nodded quickly and said of course, he understood.

''And anyway, there will be so many men admiring your beauty and fetching you champagne punch that you will not have time to dance, eh?'' He moved to the door and looked back to smile at her reassuringly. ''Be your most beautiful tonight, for I have a surprise for you.''

''Not another prospect you think would be much more suitable as a husband than Peter Gideon, I hope!'' She smiled at his sudden scowl. "Really, Diego, you are not very subtle."

"But when you leave San Francisco, you will leave behind a trail of broken hearts if I do not convince you to stay. I have several lined up for you to choose from, *hermana*. Take care with your appearance tonight." Grinning, he ducked out the door, saying as he closed it behind him, "Wear the new necklace I bought you!"

Tory shook her head in exasperation. He refused to accept the fact that she was leaving. But he must, for she could not stay. There were too many memories here, too many things to remind her of all that had happened.

Oh, it was all too much, and she had told Dave Brock only yesterday when he had pleaded with her to stay, to marry him, that she must leave it all behind.

"You know I cannot, Dave, so please do not ask me again."

"It's *him*, isn't it? Nick Kincade. He's the reason you're leaving." Angry and despairing, he took her hands in his, ignoring her efforts to pull away. "Tory, you're so beautiful, and you need a man who truly loves you! I can be that man if you'll only let me, if you'll only forget that damn rogue. He's nothing but an adventurer, and he may have stumbled into some luck now, but it won't last. It never does with a man like him. He's trouble. He'll get tired of mining and ranching and take off one day, wearing his guns and looking for another war, can't you see that?"

Gently withdrawing her hands, Tory sighed. "Yes, of course I see that, Dave. And Kincade is not the reason I'm leaving. It's . . . everything."

"But the charges against your brother have been dropped—as if they would ever amount to anything anyway since he's such good friends with the governor, and since he was not involved, it's not a crime to keep information to yourself. If it was, there would be a lot of men in jail out here."

Frustrated, Dave's blue eyes were dark with pain as he gazed at her, and she was faintly surprised when he said with vehemence, "I should have killed Kincade! I wish I'd done it when I had the chance!"

She must have looked shocked, for Brock added darkly, "I saw him on the beach that day with you. It was obvious what you'd been doing, and then you ran away, and I waited for a minute, intending to go down and confront him. But I was worried . . . You seemed so upset, so I followed you instead to be certain you got back home all right." He took a deep breath, his face darkening even more. "That night at dinner, I wanted you to see him for what he was, but when I mentioned the duel, you practically called him a murderer, and I hoped that you had already seen the light, that there would be a chance for me. I was wrong, it seems."

"Oh Dave. I'm . . . sorry. You're a good friend and a good man, but I don't love you. Not that way. Please forgive me."

He'd left finally, but not until he'd vowed that he would do everything he could to change her mind.

"I have land of my own now, you know," he added, "and my sister and her husband are helping me make a success of it. I'll prosper one day, I swear I will."

"I know you will, Dave. I don't doubt it for a minute. Perhaps when I return to Boston, you'll come for a visit."

After he'd gone, she'd twisted the ring on her finger, the diamond and amethyst promise she had made to Peter Gideon, and tried to envision him. Try as she might, she could not summon up his image. When she tried, Peter's blond hair was much too dark, and long, like an Indian's, and his green eyes were somehow much too yellow, wolf eyes, gleaming like old Spanish coins.

Oh God, I have to get away, she thought despairingly, before I drive myself mad . . .

Twenty-nine

The lobby of the Astor House was crowded with elegantly dressed men and women. Fresh coats of paint still glistened on walls and wainscoting, and wallpaper brought from France was almost hidden by tall, potted palms. The most elegant chandeliers yet seen in San Francisco hung from the lobby ceiling and in the ballroom, where musicians played on a dais discreetly tucked into an alcove. Uniformed waiters scurried back and forth with trays of food, though after the sumptuous dinner in the main dining hall, few guests were interested in food.

"Your hands are so cold," Diego said to Tory, looking down at her with a slight frown. "Are you all right?"

"Why wouldn't I be?" She smiled, but it was one of the bright, brittle smiles that he'd grown so used to seeing, and he sighed. *Dios*, but he would like to know what had happened to her in those weeks she'd been gone with Nick Kincade, but knew instinctively that he should not ask. There was always such a distant look in her eyes now, where once there had been laughter and teasing. Even when she laughed, it was something of a shock, unexpected, and sounding false. What had that *cabron* done to her to put this look on her face? He'd seen him once since coming to San Francisco, and they had eyed each other like two male dogs, wary and bristling with animosity, until Don Mariano had intervened, coming between them to suggest they part company.

Maybe he'd never know, but Diego was certain Kincade was the cause of Tory's misery, though she had said he was not, that she had been foolish enough to fall in with the wrong company and Kincade had rescued her. That had been all she would say, and he didn't press her for the details, but he was still convinced that Kincade had somehow caused the trouble. He had never forgotten the day Tory had run to Kincade, and he had taken her up on his huge black gelding and ridden away with her. There had been something in his cold eyes then, possessive and demanding, that had left a lingering impression.

But he would not think of *los diablo Tejanos* tonight, would allow nothing to interfere in his plans. Tory looked beautiful, wearing the dress that caught light from lanterns and mirrors, and caught the attention of every man there. Did she not know how beautiful she was? With her dark hair gleaming with russet lights, and her peach-tinted skin, and those huge, thick-lashed violet eyes that caught at a man's soul? And her body—she was so slender, with her womanly curves displayed to perfection in the daringly cut gown that only Tory could have worn so well. The dress fit her snugly, the neckline plunging in a vee to a tight-fitting waist, the tiny, puffed sleeves mere straps just off her shoulders, leaving them bare and gleaming like polished bronze. Her hair was worn in a cluster of curls on her neck, with a knot of flowers tucked into the center, spilling down in long fronds to mingle with the gleaming mahogany coils.

Dios mío! His sister was definitely a woman to be seen, not tucked away in the house of some Boston preacher.

As they entered the ballroom and the musicians played a waltz, Tory looked up at him; her fingers tightened slightly on his arm.

"Diego, I have something to tell you."

"Then tell me. You know I hate waiting."

Her mouth curved into a slight smile that looked remote

and sad, and he cursed silently when she nodded.

"Yes, I know. I have booked passage on a ship that leaves tomorrow afternoon for Boston. I've waited too long and it is past time for me to go."

"Tomorrow!" Dismayed, Diego glanced from her around the room. Where was he? Always late, that one, with no sense of time at all, no matter that he thought himself such a businessman now. What if he didn't arrive in time? If he was a day late? It would be inexcusable . . . "No, Tory, you cannot go so soon. Why do you rush?"

"I want to go back to Boston. I've wanted to since I arrived in California, as you must know, Diego."

"Yes, yes, but it is too soon. Always this time of year the storms are bad, and you know that." Almost desperately, he dragged his gaze from Tory's frowning face, glancing again at the doors at the far end of the room, swearing under his breath. It would be too late . . . but no.

Across the room, pushing his way toward them, came his tardy surprise, and relief mingled with satisfaction. Just in time, he thought, for Tory looked as if she was ready to go down to the docks this minute.

He squeezed her arm and pulled her close to say against her ear, "But Boston has come to you, *hermanita.*"

Looking perplexed, Tory slowly turned her head in the direction he indicated; then her face changed, and she flung herself from him toward the tall, blond man approaching with a grin on his face that was so huge it looked as if it must hurt.

"Sean!" she cried, and reached her cousin in three steps, laughing and crying at the same time, her elegant coiffure tumbling loose as she threw herself at him, not caring if people stared or whispered as she hugged Sean Ryan joyfully. "Is it you? Is it really you?"

"It's me, Tory. Do I not look the same? Hey, don't tell me you're glad to see me!"

"Oh, I can't tell you—but how? When did you get here?" She whirled to look accusingly over her shoulder at Diego. "And why didn't you tell me he was here?"

"Because he is always late, and I wanted to surprise you. I did warn you of a surprise, didn't I?"

Turning back to Sean, with her hands still holding on to his arms, smiling, she said, "Why are you here?"

"To see you, of course. Did you think you could leave Boston and forget about me? Oh no. Besides, Father has made some investments in the railroad, and since they are considering building a transcontinental route once Fremont finds the right path, he wanted me to check things out—and see our little Victoria."

Laughing, with tears making thin paths through the faint dusting of rice powder on her cheeks, Tory looked truly happy, and Diego knew that he had done the right thing. Yes. This may keep her here, now that she had her childhood friend with her. And Sean Ryan cared no more for the idea of Tory marrying that radical Boston minister than he did, so between the two of them, perhaps they could convince her to change her mind. It wouldn't be easy, but with Tory, nothing was ever easy. She was not a woman to be easily swayed once she made up her mind.

As Nick Kincade well knew.

Leaning against a wall beside a tall, potted palm, he only half-listened to the woman at his elbow, focusing instead on Tory Ryan's joyful reunion with the tall, blond young man that must be Peter Gideon. Of course. She would want a man like that, though Gideon didn't look quite how he'd remembered him, not as delicate or intense. He had an impression of a hearty young man, cheerful and pleasant, but his gaze kept straying to Tory instead of her betrothed.

When had he ever seen her laugh like this? With such abandon? Not often, though there were times, in the mountains below San Francisco, when she had teased him and then laughed at his inevitable reaction. But that was before she had been taken by Pickering, before things had happened that should never have occurred.

Apparently, her ordeal had not left permanent damage. If anything, she was more beautiful than ever. She was thinner than he'd remembered, but it suited her, accentuating her high cheekbones and the sultry curve of her mouth, the slight slant of her eyes, like cat eyes, he'd once told her, shining in the night. A necklace circled her throat, amethyst jewels set in gold that dipped into the shadow between her breasts, ripe globes that made him remember things he should probably forget . . .

"Lieutenant Kincade," a soft female voice said, and he jerked his eyes away from Tory to see Jessie Fremont approaching. "How delightful to see you again. And of course, Miss Gibson. It is a pleasure seeing you again, as well."

Nick's companion, Susan Gibson, a tall, redheaded young woman of many accomplishments—not the least of which was being related by marriage to the territorial governor—replied that it was nice to see Mrs. Fremont again.

"Though it was very difficult getting Lieutenant Kincade to escort me tonight," she added with a little laugh. "He seems to consider receptions deadly sins instead of diversions, as I do. Perhaps that is why we get along so well, as he makes me feel as if I have truly triumphed when I am able to get him to attend something other than a business meeting."

Nick's brow lifted. Susan really was getting to be a bore. He was only with her because he needed an escort for the evening. What had been an idle diversion at first had become an annoyance, and the only reason he was at this damn reception tonight was because Roy Martin had wanted him to check out a man who was involved with Diego Montoya in some way. A relative, Martin had said, and perhaps he should be closely watched to see exactly how honest his dealings with the proposed railroad route would be.

So he was here, and Gil was late meeting him as usual, and he didn't even have a decent description of the man he was supposed to investigate, who had only arrived late that afternoon by steamer. It was like being told to find something in a haystack, but not told what it was.

Jessie Fremont laughed, shaking her head. "Business meetings, Lieutenant Kincade? How droll. I never considered you a man of such limited interests. Especially not after some of the things my husband has told me about you, how you have lived such an exciting life. Did you know he wants you to join him on his next expedition? He needs a guide to map out the thirty-eighth parallel that they were unable to complete after that unfortunate experience this past winter. But I suppose now that you're such a wealthy magnate, you wouldn't be interested.''

Behind the light, teasing words was something else, a questioning note that made him look at her a little more closely. Not a woman to be easily fooled, he thought, and smiled crookedly.

"As long as we both seem to be on fact-finding missions, Mrs. Fremont, perhaps you'll tell me why your husband is interested in another expedition. It was my understanding that he intended to stay here in California a while now that the Mariposa has produced gold. He's a wealthy man.''

"All the more reason for him to want to find a reliable guide, then, isn't it? After hearing how you managed to stay warm and dry and well-fed in the same blizzard that almost killed my husband, I wanted to be certain that the best man was available should he attempt it again.''

"I don't know how accurate your information was,'' he said, and looked past Mrs. Fremont to see Tory affectionately hugging her betrothed. Faintly surprised at the rush of vicious hostility he felt, he concentrated on the thread of conversation. "It wasn't that cozy. At one point, I thought we were going to have to eat the horses.''

"Ah, but that is precisely my meaning, Lieutenant. You didn't have to eat the horses, and they survived your ordeal as well. I imagine it was your experience as a Texas Ranger that prepared you so efficiently for such a misfortune.''

Tearing his gaze from Tory—looking wickedly beautiful in a dress that shimmered with the light of a thousand candles, her face radiant, her eyes like gemstones as she laughed up at her companion—he managed to say calmly, "It didn't hurt.''

"Really,'' Susan interrupted, sounding bored, "can't we discuss something else? I'm weary of discussing railroads and guides. The musicians are playing a melody that sounds very interesting, very Spanish. Let us go watch the dancers.''

Mrs. Fremont didn't seem at all shocked by Susan's rudeness, but merely smiled. "You must excuse those of us who grew up in the political world, Miss Gibson. Discussions of railroads and guides *are* diversions when one usually discusses legislative bills and expansionism."

When Susan just looked puzzled, Nick grinned slightly and explained, "Mrs. Fremont's father is Thomas Hart Benton—the U.S. senator who promoted the annexation of Texas, and who is considered the prophet of manifest destiny."

"Oh. I didn't realize . . ." Susan paused, looking bewildered. It was apparent she still didn't realize, and after exchanging a brief glance with Mrs. Fremont, Nick shrugged.

"I appreciate your faith in me, Mrs. Fremont, but I'm afraid that word of my deeds is exaggerated."

"Oh no. Miss Ryan told me it was very true, that if you had not been so capable, both of you would have died in the Sierras and not been discovered until the spring thaw."

His smile tightened. "You know Miss Ryan well?"

"Very well. Delightful young lady. And very intelligent, with an excellent grasp of current events, and vitally interested in promoting women's rights upon her return to Boston. I rather hate to see her leave San Francisco. A new country like this needs young women of her intelligence."

Looking past him, she said suddenly, "Oh, there is Charles, and I must go speak to him before he embarks upon another one of those interminable discussions of guides and routes and rivers that you men so love and we women endure. If you will excuse me—oh, and Lieutenant, if you have any influence over Miss Ryan, I beg that you ask her to stay in California a while longer."

Beside him, Susan Gibson cleared her throat. "Well, what a very talkative woman she is."

"She isn't just a talkative woman, for Chrissake. She's intelligent enough to write a report of over two hundred pages about her husband's adventures as a topographer, and write it so well that Congress ordered ten thousand copies to be printed and distributed. If not for that report, the West would not have attracted so many settlers.''

''Well, my goodness, Nick,'' Susan said crossly, ''you needn't be so mean about it.''

Susan was right. It wasn't her fault she depended more upon her looks than her brains to be attractive. But not every woman was Victoria Ryan—Venus, with a quick wit and more courage than most men. He thought of her sometimes as she had looked in the Salinas River, determinedly tamping down her terror as she crossed the swift currents; and sometimes he remembered how stubbornly resilient she was, riding for days on end with little complaint for her comfort, only for the man who tormented her—and God, would he ever be able to forget her in that mountain camp, the grit and raw courage it had taken to survive Glanton and Pickering? No, he could never put that sight out of his mind, as he was sure she hadn't forgotten it.

Not even the harsh struggle through mountain passes filled with snow had beaten her, and if he hadn't already begun to admire her, he certainly would have then, his beautiful, passionate little Venus with the heart of a lioness.

It was odd that Jessie Fremont would come to ask him to keep Tory here, when he had never mentioned her, nor visited her since she had arrived back in San Francisco in January. He'd assiduously stayed away, careful not to interfere, not to meddle in her life again. He'd done enough.

At least Tory had survived it, and looked happy now, smiling up at her betrothed and drinking punch, laughing with her brother.

Roy Martin seemed to think Diego Montoya was covering up a new illegal enterprise, but it was his job to distrust everyone. Gil was more inclined to believe Diego was making an honest effort to amend his father's former activities. At any rate, the money Patrick Ryan had tucked away in accounts across the country was in government hands now, and a large cache of new weapons had mysteriously appeared in San Diego one night, abandoned in the middle of the presidio to the astonishment of the current commandant. No one knew how they'd gotten there, but Gil said he had a pretty good idea of who'd left them, and Nick agreed.

Susan nudged him, and he escorted her to the far end of the ballroom, where the musicians in the alcove had begun to play another stately waltz.

"Dance with me, Nick," she murmured, smiling at him lazily, and, shrugging, he swept her onto the area of the floor cleared for dancing.

Anything to pass the time until Gil got there, anything to keep his mind off Victoria Ryan. He couldn't help another glance at the man she was to marry, and frowned slightly. For some reason, he'd thought of the temperance preacher being tall but very lean, and certainly not so relaxed. While the man with Tory looked familiar, he kept seeing another face intrude, thinner, with burning eyes and a pale, fervent expression.

"Nick, what *are* you thinking about?" Susan began to pout, nudging close to him, pressing her breasts against his chest a little too close as she tried to snare his attention. "You've been this way all night. Are you all right?"

He gave her a quick glance and eased himself away. "I'm fine. A lot is on my mind tonight. Shall I take you home?"

"No. No, I want to stay. I just want—"

As she launched into a litany of wants, her soft voice droning on in the way women did who had begun to cling and whine, he detached himself mentally. Her words flowed over him in a ceaseless tide, and he found that he was looking in Tory's direction more often than he should, noting everything about her. This was the reason he had stayed away, had remained aloof. He couldn't trust himself not to want her when he saw her.

He danced with Susan until he saw Gil pushing his way across the crowded ballroom, looking trim and uncomfortable in a suit, vest, and cravat, his mustache neatly trimmed and his black hair slicked back from his forehead so that his brown eyes looked rather startled. Nick grinned when he reached them.

"Don't you look fancy—"

"I don't want to hear it, Nick." Gil blew out an exasperated breath, glancing around them. "Is there someplace private we can talk?"

He left Susan with a stout, middle-aged woman sitting in a chair against the wall, and joined Gil in a small niche formed by soaring beams that swept all the way from floor to high ceiling. He stopped beside him, eyes narrowing at the look on Gil's face.

"Tell me what you found out. And make it quick. I don't want to spend much longer in this damn crowd."

"Ryan's nephew is a big, blond hombre, kinda good-looking. It took me an hour to track him down after his ship docked, and by the time I found his hotel, he was leaving."

Nick studied him for a moment, then turned, scanning the crowd until he found Tory and her fiancé. He pointed. "Tell me, Gil—is that him?"

Gil turned, eyes widening with surprise. "Yeah. Guess you already met him, then. Hey, Miss Ryan sure does look beautiful in that dress, don't she, amigo? *Caramba!* Looks like she's wearing silver fire. I don't think I've ever seen her all dressed up. She's a real beauty, all right."

When Nick didn't reply, Gil turned to look at him, then nodded with something like awareness in his eyes before turning away.

"She's leaving tomorrow, amigo. I was at the ticket agent when the purchaser bought the ticket for her. Guess she's going back to Boston to be with her future husband."

Nick stared hard at the tall, blond man, and the memory suddenly returned. He remembered him now, a youthfully defiant face glaring up at him from a tavern floor, ready to defend his pretty young cousin. Of course. It was her cousin, not her betrothed. Not that it made any difference. She was leaving tomorrow. There was no good reason for him to stop her. Not after all that had happened. And hadn't happened. He'd never admitted it, never told her that he loved her, not even when she said it to him, up there in the mountains when she was still so confused, so shattered by all that had happened.

And, to be honest, he hadn't really accepted how he felt about her then, hadn't wanted to admit that he loved her. It was still too new a discovery, still too raw and uncertain to chance being wrong.

In the long months after he'd left her in Sacramento City, he'd thought of telling her, but hadn't. It seemed so difficult, so pointless. There was too much between them. Now she was going back to the man she loved, the *civilized* man, she'd once told him angrily, who wasn't anything like he was. Civilized—would she dance for her husband as he had seen her dance? With wild abandon, with the fire and grace of a Spanish gypsy? No, if she did dance, it would be a sedate waltz, or perhaps a country dance such as the ones the musicians had been playing for the past half-hour, not a wild, passionate dance to the kind of music that had just begun to soar into the room . . .

"Nick?"

Gil's question was drowned out by the rising thrum of guitars and violins as the musicians began to play a lively tune, not one of the more proper Spanish dances, but the music of old California, of the people, the peasants who worked and loved the land. And Nick remembered how Tory had danced that night at the mission, with her heart and soul, with everything inside her shimmering in her eyes, and she'd looked once at him, eyes wide and filled with an emotion he hadn't wanted to see then, gone so quickly when he'd shoved away her partner to take her from the courtyard.

He realized that he'd crossed the room to her when he was standing in front of her, holding out a hand, seeing the surprise in her eyes, hearing Diego's quick, "*Dios!*" before she put her hand in his, the fingers trembling slightly.

"May I have this dance, Miss Ryan?"

"My sister is not going anywhere with you, *cabron!*"

"Mind your manners, Don Diego," Nick said without looking at him, keeping his gaze on Tory, on the wide amethyst eyes like rich jewels, and the way her lips were slightly parted and moist.

"I think it's you who needs a lesson in manners," Diego

began furiously, and put a hand on the hilt of the dress sword at his side as he took a threatening step forward.

Nick turned slightly, flicking him a glance. "I will not fight you, Don Diego. This is between me and your sister. If she tells me to leave, I will, but not until then."

Tory looked up at Diego, tearing her eyes away from Nick, her voice a soft, hesitant murmur.

"Please . . . do not make a scene, Diego."

"But you do not want to dance with him, do you, Tory? You said you didn't want to dance at all."

"Miss Ryan dances beautifully." Nick willed her to look back at him, and when she did, kept his voice soft and reassuring. "And the musicians are playing a familiar melody that we can both dance to, if she will agree."

He saw the hesitation in her eyes, the indecision and fear and something else, and then she was nodding, ignoring her brother's soft curse and her cousin's perplexed glance, moving with him to the dance floor, her wide skirts flashing silver fire in the lamplight.

"Dance for me alone," he whispered to her as he swept her onto the floor. "Give me something to remember you by, something to dream about at night."

Guitars and violins sobbed and soared, tempo rising, and after standing stock-still for a moment, as if frozen, she began to shuffle her feet, the hem of her skirts only slightly swaying.

"You can do better than that, *querida*. I've seen you. You're magnificent, a song, an enchantment. Don't disappoint me. Dance as you dance for a lover, Venus. Dance for me."

Her chin came up, eyes flashing violet fire, and then she gave him a strange, long look, holding his gaze, her hands moving to lift the hem of her skirts, feet catching the rhythm of the music.

Damn her, she took him at his word . . . moving sinuously, her hips swaying and feet skimming over the floor, chin tilted, and eyes flashing like jewels as she danced. There was something primitive, earthy, provocative about the way she danced, and the sidelong glances she flung him were seductive, an invitation he accepted. He knew this dance as well, had learned it in Texas and Mexico, at fandangos and fiestas.

Tory smiled slowly, her lips curving and wet, her tongue sliding between them in a flicker meant to entice. She was woman to his man, Eve to Adam, and he smiled back, keeping his eyes on hers, not releasing her gaze. She teased, taunted, whirling around and leaning forward, until her breasts brushed against the white of his shirt, eyes still on his face, daring him.

She swayed toward him, inviting with her body, challenging with her eyes, and the next time she started to whirl away, he grabbed her, an arm around her waist, to whirl her back toward him, where she draped over his arm, bent backward so that her breasts were thrust upward and her hair hung down. Instinctively, she'd lifted one leg for balance and it nudged against his thigh. He slid his palm under her knee, holding her leg through the bunched material of her skirts, looking down at her as she bent backward, his hand spread under the small of her back to hold her.

Her breath was coming in rapid pants, lips wet and inviting, and he bent slowly, his mouth very lightly grazing the arch of her throat in a feathery kiss before he released her, swung her away to arm's length, then back again, spinning her toward him. People were staring at them with scandalized gazes, and whispering, and he could see to one side Gil Garcia, grinning, holding Susan Gibson's arm when she would have come angrily onto the dance floor.

And the next time Tory whirled away from him and he brought her back with a firm tug, he swept her with him past the musicians and staring faces, and through French doors out onto the wide verandah.

Tory was panting, eyes wide in the lantern light streaming through the doors. The knot of hair at her nape had loosened, flowers dangling, and he reached up to pull one free, handing it to her.

It was a rose, deep red and velvety, a tight bud on a slender stem, and, slowly, she reached up to take it from him, her fingers brushing against his. He dragged the back of his hand over her damp cheek in a caress, and when she did not protest or move away, he slid his thumb over the trembling outline of her lips.

"I've missed you, Tory."

"Have you?" The words were slightly breathless, a little shaky. "I didn't get your messages."

"I didn't send any." His hand fell away, and he watched her closely, the way she looked up at him, a detached expression in her eyes. A strange compulsion prompted him, and it was irrelevant but he said it anyway.

"I didn't keep the money, Tory. It wasn't for me. I just want you to know that."

She blinked, bit her lip, and looked down at the rose, brushing it against her chin, against the tiny cleft that deepened when she was being stubborn. "Then what—?"

"I can't tell you that. It's not my secret to tell. But I will tell you this—I never meant to hurt you. I never meant for all those things to happen."

"Yes, so you told me." She drew in a deep breath, brushed the rose against her mouth, then looked up at him again, eyes direct and intense. "I've booked passage on a steamer. It leaves tomorrow."

"Gil told me."

"So you just came to say goodbye, then. This time."

He flinched inside at the slightly accusing words, but there was nothing in her face or eyes to accuse him, only his own stinging conscience. He took a deep breath.

"No. I came to take you with me."

Grimly, he realized it was the truth, that the minute he'd seen her again, standing next to her brother like a silver flame, he'd known he was not going to let her get away from him. Not if he had to abduct her from under Diego's nose, throw her on his horse, and take her up into the hills again until she agreed to stay with him.

"Nick, what are you saying?"

"Dammit, it seems clear enough to me. I want you with me."

His arms were around her, holding her hard against him, fingers tangling in the wealth of her hair, pulling it loose to cape her shoulders, the flowers dropping to the verandah stones while he began to kiss her, ignoring her first struggles until she began to kiss him back, her arms lifting to curl around his neck. She moaned softly, and he could taste the salt of her tears when he lifted his head finally, looking down at her critically. He dragged his thumb across her cheek, smearing the silvery track over the light film of face powder.

"Tears, Venus?"

"Those aren't tears."

His mouth twisted. "Right. It must be raining."

"Nick—" She grabbed his hand and held it to her cheek, staring up at him. "Why do you want me to go with you?"

"You know why."

"No, I don't. There must be a good reason for it—can't you tell me?"

"I suppose you have to hear the words?"

"Yes." Her mouth quivered. "I have to hear them—say them for me, Nick."

"All right, damn you—I love you. I think I've loved you since you almost drowned in the Salinas River, and stood there all wet and shivering with your blouse hiding nothing underneath—*Christ!* Is there somewhere we can go?"

"I have a room at the Victor Hotel . . ."

Ignoring Diego's angry sputters and the stares as they passed through the ballroom, Tory's hair hanging loosely around her shoulders and the tear tracks still on her cheeks, they left the Astor House and went to her hotel. Once inside her room, Nick swept her into his arms and to the bed, tugging impatiently at the laces and hooks of her dress until she had to stop him, saying she would do it.

"After waiting six months, I'm not in the mood to be patient," he said with an irritable grunt that made her laugh. "Here—let me do it. I'll buy you another damn dress . . ."

And then the dress was gone, and he was naked and sliding up and across her, while the open window let in the salt-sea breeze and the sound of surf, and she was holding him in her arms, feeling his kisses all over her face, her throat, lower, and her body arched upward for him, hands clutching at him, and she was telling him she loved him, had always loved him, and would never leave.

She knew, as he slid inside her that first time, easing the aching need that had not gone away, she would always want him; that she would never have been happy with anyone else. And all the fear and worries, the months of uncertainty and anguish began to fade as he held her, rocking his body inside hers and whispering that he loved her, *te adora,* telling her she was beautiful, and God, how he'd missed her . . .

Epilogue

It seemed a shame that everything had to end, Tory thought, wistful and sighing, leaning her wet cheek against the slope of her hand. It had been so short, over too soon, and now Sean was gone, his ship sailing that morning from the San Francisco harbor. She could still see him, grinning at her as he boarded the ship, irrepressible as always.

His last whispered words to her still rang in her ears: "A much better choice, Tory. You need a challenge . . ."

She hadn't had to ask what he meant. He was right, she supposed. Peter Gideon would have driven her mad eventually, being constantly involved in social reforms; while she was certainly interested in women's rights and temperance, other things were more important to her, she'd found.

"Did your cousin's ship sail, *querida*?"

Tory looked up, smiling a little through her tears. "Yes. Sean has gone back to Boston. I can't believe the time flew by so fast, Nick. He was here for three months, and it seems like only a few days."

"Do you wish you'd gone back to Boston with him?" He came to take her into his arms, tilting her face up to his with a bent finger under her chin so that sunlight through the window made her blink. They were in the parlor of the small

405

house Nick had built on his land up the Sierras, nestled beneath an ancient stand of pines and cedars, where the wind through the branches provided beautiful melodies.

She smiled, shaking her head. "No. I don't want to be anywhere you're not."

It was true. Her life was Nick Kincade, her handsome husband with the amber-gold eyes and a dangerous smile that could make her knees weak with just a glance. She loved the touch of him, taste of him, sight of him. Nothing could change what she felt for him, for the way he made her feel. She lifted to her toes and kissed him on his mouth, relishing the way he held her so tightly against him, as if he would never let her go.

"Te llevo en el alma . . . eres toda mi vida . . ."

As her husky whisper faded, he released her, still smiling down at her, his eyes sliding over her face. "What about the good Reverend Gideon? Did you tell him he was your life as well?"

"Not in those words—you! Of course, I never said that to him. I don't know what I was thinking. Why I ever thought I would love him. I'm sure he won't be surprised—or disappointed—when Sean gives him back the ring he bought me. I gave it to Sean, you know, and asked him to return it to Peter and tell him I've met someone. Of course, he was glad I've changed my mind, as I'm sure you know."

Nick's raking glance was amused. "He did mention it once or twice, though I got the definite impression that he's not quite sure of me yet, not even after getting drunk at our wedding and passing out at the reception. It was a distinct novelty to have the bride's cousin sleeping on our sitting room sofa on the wedding night."

"Jessie organized a lovely wedding for us, even if Diego glowered the entire time. I suppose Sean felt he had to make up for it. Do you think my brother will ever forgive you?"

Shrugging, Nick tucked one corner of his mouth into a brief smile. "Eventually. It was his suggestion, remember, to testify for me."

"Yes, I haven't forgotten that. I was so relieved, because

I thought that at any moment you would take matters into your own hands and just shoot those foolish claim jumpers. Imagine, trying to steal your land like that, and falsifying those documents. But of course, since Diego had the quit-claims that proved Papa had sold you the land, the judge had no choice but to find in your favor. We can stay here forever."

This time when he looked at her, there was something different in his eyes, a restlessness, and her throat tightened.

"Nick, what is it? Is there something wrong?"

"No, not wrong. Christ, Tory, things are better than they've ever been, with the mines producing good-quality ore and investors beating down the door to talk to me, it's just that—" He halted, frustration creasing his face, and she tried to smother the sudden disquiet. "Dammit, it's just that this isn't what I want."

She must have made some sound, because he pulled her to him roughly, cursing softly before he kissed her again, his mouth demanding and harsh, almost violent. Then he held her against his chest, his fingers spread into her hair as he pulled her head back to look down into her face.

"It's just that I've never been much of a businessman, never cared anything about paperwork and figures—what would you say to going into partnership with your brother? Diego is good at that sort of thing, and it would give me some free time to do what I really want to do."

"Which is?" Oh God, what if he wanted to scout for Fremont? She knew it had been suggested to him, but always he'd refused. Did he want to go back to Texas and be a Ranger again? He'd mentioned it a few times, always with a kind of longing, and lately he'd been so restless. She'd thought being married would give him roots, a sense of stability, but maybe she'd been wrong.

He looked at her with eyes narrowed against the light coming through the window, then sighed. "A long time ago, my father sent me to Europe. He wanted me to get a sense of the world, I guess, and then come back and settle down. I was too young to appreciate it then. Now I think I might like to give it another try. What do you say, Venus? You could spread a message of women's rights all over Europe. It should be most entertaining. Ever been to Italy? France? You could improve your atrocious French accent—''

Laughing with relief and growing excitement, she began whispering some of the French phrases she'd heard Colette use, until he began laughing, too, his hands moving over her in that sweet, familiar way she loved and needed.

''Do you have any idea what you just asked me, Venus?''

She didn't, but wasn't about to let him know that, and lifted her brow casually. ''Of course.''

He grinned wickedly.

''Good. Then come along, my sweet, and we'll put it to the test.''

It wasn't until they were in bed, naked and panting, that he reminded her of her words, and then she realized her mistake, remembered where she had heard those French phrases, and the day Colette confronted Nick in the woods before reaching San Francisco, when she'd bent to take him into her mouth . . .

Grinning, his eyes alight with that familiar gleam, he whispered huskily, ''Now, *bébé,* do for me what I just did for you . . . slowly, with your tongue first . . .''

Face flaming, she stared at him, but as he began to rub her and stroke her, making her shiver with aching need, she reached out for him, sliding her hand over him until his eyes closed and he groaned. And as his hands tangled in her hair, holding her, she heard him say huskily, ''I love you, Tory, *avec tout de mon coeur, mon amour, pour éternité . . .*

And even with her rusty schoolroom French, she knew that he'd said he loved her with all his heart, his love, for eternity.